MW01349501

Books by This Author

The Spurred Trilogy

Spurred to Justice

Spurred to Jump

Spurred to Jealousy

The Silver Cowgirls

The Silver Cowgirls

The Silver Cowgirls Ride Again

Private Mom

The SILVER COWGIRLS

ALICIA STEPHENS MARTIN

Year of the Book
135 Glen Avenue
Glen Rock, PA 17327

ISBN: 978-1-64649-385-2 (paperback)
ISBN: 978-1-64649-386-9 (ebook)

Cover design: Pixelstudio

Photo credit: Bailey Grundowski Photography

Dedication

Carol, Connie, Carla, and Peg!
Thank you for one of the most memorable years in my life!

Part One

The Women

Chapter 1

Presley

Presley had not ridden bareback in years, let alone in a pair of cut-off shorts. Yet here she was, in celebration of her fiftieth birthday, mounted on her mare Cleo, basking in the afternoon sun. The surf surged onto the shore and practically touched the mare's front hooves. Cleo pricked her ears forward with a snort as if rendering a warning in the event the approaching line of watery foam presented any danger. The two watched the wave retreat and get consumed under the next breaker that trundled toward them. Someone had once commented that riding on the beach was awesome. As Presley savored this wish come true, she had to disagree. This moment was beyond awesome, for Presley—it was nothing short of spectacular.

Cleo, her old and faithful friend, remained stationary as another wave approached.

"Good girl," Presley whispered in praise and centered herself atop the mare.

She freed the scrunchies which secured her pig tails then shook her head. The woman's thick russet locks, a blessing inherited from her father, spread out like angel's wings as if inflating with air and fluttered down her back to tickle her bare shoulders. Presley closed her eyes, lifting her chin to let the sun's energy coat warmth across her entire face. Her cheeks flushed, sparking a dose of much needed color to her ashen skin.

Heat radiated between her and the mare. Presley inhaled the hope that this glorious moment would be the prescription to release the tensions and burdens of her past year. She seized a weft of Cleo's coarse mane in her left hand while her right massaged the horse's shoulder below the withers in soothing circles.

It had been years since Presley had been brave enough to mount a horse wearing anything but jeans. Despite her illness and losing weight in the past months, her long legs had maintained some strength from decades of exercise required to raise a family of four while tirelessly spanning the country at a moment's notice. But this year had been an exhausting game changer after a cocktail of an alarming diagnosis and a monumental half-century birthday. She wanted to relish and exploit every sense God had given her. No more taking life for granted.

Presley inhaled a symphony of summer scents: the salty sea that dampened the white sand to a slurpy grey and ripe grasses swaying in the breeze. Floating shells clattered in the foam like her favorite silver bracelet heavy with charms from every state in which she had lived.

Her exposed calves pressed against Cleo's barreled sides as the waves cascaded to shore, diminishing in frothy curls that seemed to vanish into the sand. They ebbed over the mare's hooves, then retreated to the sea, sinking Cleo's weight slightly deeper each time.

Cleo appeared as spry as a filly, except for a slight sway in her back, greying muzzle and some bonier bumps on her joints. A sparkle reignited in her rich chocolate eyes which almost appeared etched in black liner like an Egyptian princess. She was clearly excited. Her quick heartbeats aroused Presley's anticipation. As Cleo's ears twitched, the two shared the enchantment of the novel environment. Riding in the ocean had been an aspiration, for so long.

Presley leaned into Cleo's arched neck and whispered, "Here we are, girl. Finally. Only took us eighteen years to fulfill this promise."

Presley refused to let the events of the past year trickle down her cheeks as tears. She had sulked enough, and her meditation psychologist adamantly prescribed she guard against negative thoughts. She repeated her chosen mantra, "Good feelings only. Love and life. Breathe."

The ocean was mesmerizing. The encroaching waves roared, then unfolded and melded to soft hums along the shore. Gulls and terns hovered in flocks, taking random dives seemingly to peck at the water's surface, then squawked for attention.

Cleo could no longer resist the urge to paw. As waves curled in, she shifted her weight to fight the suction that imprisoned her, then raised a knee and hooked her hoof to splash.

It was time.

Presley nudged her forward and the two waded into the surf as the sea crested Cleo's underbelly, making slight smacking sounds. Presley's toes touched the surf and she cued the mare to continue until her calves were engulfed. The water released a flurry of chills that prickled up her thighs, to her backbone, all the way to her head.

Cleo whinnied and skimmed the waves with her muzzle, then raised her neck, rotating her head, reaching to the sky. The mare's lips flapped, and her nostrils flared so wide they might flip inside out. Then she released rapid snorts of air.

"It's salty, girl. That's the sea." Presley gave her another pat. "Okay. Let's do this."

Although Presley did not have the security of a bridle or saddle, she guided Cleo steadily with her seat and complete trust. She prompted the faithful mare to move a quarter circle on her haunches and stand parallel to the shore.

Cleo swished and side-passed through the water as Presley asked her to angle back to the coastline. Once her fetlock and cannon bone were the only part remaining submerged, Presley's legs fused to the mare, igniting momentum. Cleo rocketed forward as if anticipating the starting gun at a race. The mare reeled in a canter after only two strides, seemingly undaunted by the surging whitecaps.

The ocean waves cascaded onto the sandy beach, but they did not prevent Cleo's stride. The sun rays that had heated Presley's body were now cooled by droplets showered upon them. Her white tank top was soaked. The mare too was saturated; her roan color shimmered with flecks of grey.

Cleo rounded in playful leaps, her neck bowed and her head shaking as if giggling inside. Presley's insides tumbled too. The movement tickled and she laughed out loud for the first time in months.

The two continued in a joyous dance. Presley's tresses bounced and swung like a pendulum across her shoulder blades. She and Cleo were finally loping along the white sandy beach under the cerulean sky, the inviting sun and the rush of waves roaring in a constant rhythm.

The smooth intensity with which Cleo was loping unexpectedly stopped. Presley was jarred off center as if bouncing to steady a Pogo stick. The mare lost her cadence, perhaps imprisoned in the thick sand, or caught by the uneven shoreline. To make matters worse, the two had apparently annoyed a flock of feeding gulls. Several masses of grey and white feathers dive-bombed them in a territorial ambush.

The army of aggravated fowl assaulted them with stabbing beaks and scratching talons. This forced Presley to defensively shoo their barraging with her free hand. But when she tried to lift her arm, she whacked something hard with her wrist. The strike forced her off balance. Cleo responded, in a sharp pivot which vaulted Presley forward, striking the mare's neck.

More gulls swooped in a frenzy, their squawking deafening to her ears. Presley's hair was being pulled, slapping her back like a whip.

The thunder of the ocean gained intensity, losing its own soothing sound to a monotone rumble. Ominous grey clouds suddenly engulfed the opalescent blue sky. The sun disappeared and the wetness of Cleo's hide and her own clothes nipped her to the marrow.

Cleo was fading under her as darkness descended. The birds' squawking had escalated to high-pitched cackles. Someone was calling her name? She blinked, then again. Had she been sleeping?

Presley realized she was entombed in a cold metal shaft, almost suffocating. Her back and spine were rigid and restrained against a hard surface. All was dark, except for an opening of light beyond her head. Cleo was gone, the ocean dissipated. Then she remembered the tunnel, her nose plastered against the enclosure, her body barely moveable. The only sounds were a grumbling machine motor and a discordant beeping. The reverberating clamor brought Presley to reality like a tornado that quakes as it nears. Presley remembered storm threats when her husband and family were stationed in the mid-west. The rigid slab that held her body jolted, then inched backwards. Light streaming from above was closing in. She was moving now, out of the tunnel.

"Mrs. Petrone. Presley Petrone? Are you okay?" A voice resonated over an intercom from beyond the light, becoming clearer as Presley regained her senses. "The test is over. You did great. A technician will be entering the room in just a minute, and you can dress."

Presley was alone, flat on her back, arms by her side on a stiff unyielding surface. She was clothed in a lightweight gown which was three sizes too big and similar to her great aunt's house dress. Presley delicately fingered the pencil thin bowtie that held the fabric together as she gathered her thoughts.

A slight glow from the rear of her head intensified, until Presley was blinded by painfully bright florescent lights inserted in a white tile dropped ceiling. She fluttered her eyelids consecutively then squinted in pain. Her body, damp from nerves, chilled as if she'd stepped out of a cold shower.

Presley shivered and scanned the room's circumference. The floor was as cold as the winter temperature outside: a vinyl composite tile in marbleized white and steel shades which were most likely waxed, probably every night, as hospitals do with oversized commercial buffers. The walls followed suit. Their dreary grey emitted a sanitized odor of cleaning chemicals. The surroundings were bare, vacant of any decorative objects that could diffuse the lifeless tedium or provide a subtle bit of ambiance.

Presley sighed, then held her breath. Cleo had disappeared. The sea, the gulls, the aqua ocean capped in foamed waves, the white sand, and the endless azure sky—all vanished. All a product of her imagination, motivated by her hopes and dreams of riding her aged soulmate, Cleo, on the beach. The dream that never managed to materialize as life had stepped in the way.

Presley's head was lying against metal. Her neck ached but not from a bulging mass of russet hair. Once clear of the tunnel rim, her arms were free. She reached her hand up and patted her scalp, scraping the sharp tips of nubby bristles emerging from her hair follicles. Presley reminded herself that she was bald, having lost her hair during months of treatments. Although, the chemo was now complete and her mane would eventually return, the process of healing was painstaking and unhurried. The return of Presley's golden auburn highlights and waves, a feature people complimented her on, was highly anticipated. She just wanted to be normal again.

Presley lowered her hands back to her sides, tucking the see-through gown under her body to try and stay warm. She remained motionless. The roaring machine was spinning in deceleration, the sound drifting to a hum. She waited for the technician, Darby, whom she had met earlier. The adorable blonde-haired blue-eyed girl with a gleaming smile was young enough to be her child.

Finally, after what felt like an hour, the heavy steel bar that opened the door clicked, and a cheery young technician entered the room.

"Well, Mrs. Petrone, you did awesome," Darby cheered.

Awesome? Presley loathed that word as she tilted her head away from the light.

Darby was organizing and shifting the blanket as Presley sat up and dangled her legs over the side. *Bubbly and cute and half my age. An age that loves the word awesome.* Presley had heard it repeatedly this year, after treatments, after results, or anytime anyone couldn't think of another vocabulary choice to brighten her day, *'Wow that wig looks awesome,'* or *'Awesome, just like your hair.'* How about *'The scarf looks awesome,'* or *'You're doing awesome'*?

Awesome, my a— Presley's thoughts were interrupted.

"Just awesome, Mrs. Petrone! You are good to go!"

Darby handed her a clipboard to review paperwork.

"You maintained even breathing, pulse and heart rate." Her pen was tapping the clipboard. "Your blood pressure was awesome too! You must have been dreaming about something very soothing!"

Presley captured the crystal blue spark in Darby's eye. "I was." *And why did you wake me? I was in a beautiful place. Cleo and I on the beach, in the surf.*

Darby drifted almost too close, almost like a child sparking Presley to surge with a pang of envy. The tech's wheat-colored tresses were styled in that seamless silky wave that everyone was sporting—separated tendrils that drop to the shoulders with a rhythmic swing like a 1950's poodle skirt. Darby appeared to be millennium born and barely graduated from nursing or tech school. The twenty-something could hardly understand what Presley was experiencing.

The young girl leaned in closer to capture Presley's focus which was in a hypnotic stare, admiring the girl's milky white skin. The technician lacked one wrinkle except for the concern cracked across her forehead.

"Mrs. Petrone?" Darby was awaiting a response. "Were you meditating?"

"Honestly, I was in the ocean with Cleo." Presley's voice sounded distant. She hesitated before she continued. "Cleopatra." How she had loved that horse. Her heart horse, even though the mare was practically a pasture ornament at age eighteen.

The girl kept speaking, "Cleopatra? Awesome name. Is this your daughter? She must be your happy peaceful place. Your vitals were..."

"Don't say it..." Presley did not need to hear the awesome word again, so she clutched the gown around her. "I was riding Cleo... as if we were both young."

Darby smiled, her teeth glimmering white as the fluorescents above. "Riding?"

Probably just had her braces off, Presley thought.

"King Roan's Cleopatra, Cleo for short. She's my mare."

"Oh, you were riding a horse. I like horses, but I'm afraid of them. They're behemoth creatures. Is that one of those official names that breeders use? Who was King Roan?"

"His Majesty the King, he was her sire. His progeny were quite successful. Roan is a color type." Presley attempted to educate Darby, but the technician shrugged and flashed a half-interested smile.

"I love the ocean. My girlfriends and I just booked a summer weekend in Ocean City, Maryland. Winter has us all down in the dumps." Darby was shuffling with the clipboard papers. "Good news, you can dress and skedaddle. The doctor would like to see you tomorrow at 12:15 with your results."

"Come back tomorrow?" Presley snapped. *Skedaddle?*

"Tomorrow. Yes. Says right here." Darby tapped the bottom of the clipboard.

"But I thought Dr. Offelson could tell me if the treatment worked today? It's my... I thought for my..."

"For your birthday? I see it is your birthday." Darby's smile was ear to ear, puffing out her flawless rosy cheeks. "Go enjoy your birthday. Here are your clothes."

Darby handed her a plastic bag drawn tight with a white string. "Your chariot awaits." The technician tilted her head toward the reception area beyond the steel door and giggled in an attempt to lighten the air. She whispered, "There really is no horse and wagon. I was only kidding because you like horses. It's your hubby. He's been pacing for an hour in the waiting area."

The girl was blathering. Presley's scowl must have scared the young woman because she fidgeted like a cement block had fallen between them. "Uh, what color is Cleo?"

Presley gradually rose and stumbled to respond. "Cleo? She was a roan, what they call a Blue Roan with different flecks of colors, kind of like a brindle."

"Was?" Darby breathed in with exaggeration. "I am sorry. When did she pass?"

Presley snatched the bag in frustration. Darby was not understanding a word of what she was saying. "My Cleo is quite alive. She's more silver and white now. Guess she's aged and is achromatic... like me." She stroked her head.

Another lull of silence stuck between them like the bag the technician gripped. Presley tugged on the string. Darby released it and headed for the door.

"Well, Mrs. Petrone, you dress and enjoy your 'big' birthday. Room 58C tomorrow. The doc will see you at 12:15 on the nose. And don't look for results in your health portal. Experimental treatment results are not visible on the site." Darby heaved the steel exit door open and slanted back. "You sure look awesome for your age." Then the door clamped shut with an inhospitable suction.

Could she be anymore insincere? Lordy, that twenty-something knows as little about horses as she does about a bald fifty-year-old. Presley felt anything but *awesome*.

Chapter 2

Brad was leaning in the corner, away from the others who were patiently waiting for loved ones. Presley's husband, pretending to page through a *What's New in Springfield Magazine* insert, perked up upon seeing her. He instantly dropped the flier on a side table. Brad was a dedicated Lieutenant Colonel of the United States Army. He was an expert at maintaining control in critical situations. However, when it involved Presley, especially since her recent health scare, she knew Brad was falling apart.

Presley half-hearted a smile as he rushed between the waiting chairs.

"Pres, what's wrong?" Brad gripped her forearms, bringing her close. Presley was tall but Brad was over six foot.

As soon as she lifted her eyes to his soft and concerned gaze, her caged tears were set free. "I have to wait for results. Tomorrow 12:15. How can they do this?"

Brad's eagerness to see her faded as he witnessed her discouragement. The last year had taken a toll on them both. The creases at the corner of his eyes had deepened, added wires of grey that glistened throughout his fresh haircut, yet even so, he was quite handsome. Brad was always clean shaven and in outstanding physical condition. His skin was kissed by the sun for so many summers that he seemed to maintain a constant tan even in the dead of winter.

Again, a melancholy feeling choked her; she was glossy white, bald and old.

As to his character as a doting husband, it was as if Brad read her mind. He tapped the brim of her ball cap that replaced her once crowning glory. "Come on, baby. You're beautiful." He wrapped his solid arms around her waist. "I have birthday plans for you."

Presley drooped as he coaxed her with some pressure from his body. She hoped a nurse would rush to stop them, surprise her with the news that the doctor could review her test results today instead of tomorrow. *Nada.*

The people in the waiting area peered up as Brad persuaded her toward the exit. Presley knew behind their uncomfortable stares and quirky smiles were thoughts preoccupied with the elephant in the room. The bald woman. She lowered her ball cap to her brow as if to mask her face. The gawkers couldn't hide their uneasiness as the two passed, perhaps worried about their own health, or wondering what kind of cancer cursed her, or whether she was going to survive.

Brad squeezed her side. "Hold your head high. You're made of steel and courage."

He wrapped her scarf tighter and held the door open. The chill of January actually refreshed her after the awkward rubbernecking created a hot flash of irritation.

She leaned her head into his shoulder just under his chin as they reached the car. "Me? Steel and courage? That's funny, coming from the man who spent years willing to sacrifice his life for his country and others. Several tours overseas all while being a dedicated husband and father of three wild and crazy boys."

"Who are you kidding?" He opened the door. "You single-handedly raised our boys. And now it's time for you. That's why we're back here in Springfield."

"We're back here to help my mother get settled in assisted living, to visit and wait for your next orders." Presley confirmed this, although she dreamed of settling right here in Springfield for many reasons.

Strange though, Brad opened the car door and slid her an obscure grin. Something was up. "Brad?"

"Speaking of your mother, let's make a visit to her new residence." Brad shut the passenger door before Presley had a chance to answer.

Again, an odd feeling surged through her. *Brad wants to see my mother?*

Presley removed the ballcap, then lowered the visor mirror as her husband cranked up the heat and drove their SUV from the parking lot. Since she had lost weight, Presley thought she looked like her mother. A thin woman who barely ate, seemingly fueling her body with daily martinis and excessive amounts of olives, her mother had recently moved to Plum Haven Senior Community, and was anything but frail.

Although the facility had many levels of assistant living, her mother was in the independent division, at eighty-three years old. She was the same bossy-overseer-go-getter-grossly-protective-inhumanely-nosey, not to mention opinionated, woman. A Judge Judy in her own right since Presley's birth.

Presley had always been the opposite of her mother. Like her father she was compliant, sweet, the yes parent, the good partner fulfilling a duty and never creating friction. She followed direction at whatever job she performed, her own life desires never as much a priority as Brad or the boys. As for her own mother, it was easier to oblige than create a confrontation. That's why Presley agreed to see her mother on her birthday; it's what Brad suggested.

Presley traced the circles under her eyes. She was tired. Tonight she would have preferred to spend time in the barn, then curl up with Brad in the comfort of her childhood home. The last month moving her mother, organizing the new apartment, and settling her in had been exhausting. But as usual, Presley conformed.

Presley slapped the ball cap on with pent-up frustration and stared in the mirror. The pink hat was accented with a rhinestone horseshoe and the mantra "Let's Ride." Brad gifted it to her that very morning when she awoke. A note read, *Happy Birthday, my love. More to come.*

Presley loved horses, but riding was a past dream, let alone riding in the ocean. Life was certainly not about her dreams. When the technician told Presley to imagine something relaxing during the MRI, she utilized the skill her meditation therapist taught her. The technique surprisingly worked as her vitals were *awesome.*

Guess I learned something. At least how to meditate.

Brad pulled the car into the Plum Haven facility. "I hope your mom is happy here. Looks more like a fancy resort."

"I wouldn't expect anything less of my mother. She does life in thoroughbred style," Presley whispered.

She ogled the property grounds. The earth was crispy, frozen, months from thawing. Bare plum trees had been perfectly placed, the empty flower boxes awaiting care, the pond skimmed with thin ice and the geese all missing until spring. The setting was picturesque with the green of flowing White Pines, birdfeeders hanging on every porch and window, benches still decorated with leftover withered red Christmas ribbon positioned along gravel pathways. The colors and lights of the past holiday lingered in silver and gold decorations.

Normally the double front glass doors were visible. However, today the colossal porch with six massive columns—which in spring would be lined with white wicker rockers and settees—was hidden by an enormous coach tour bus. The bus was blocking the entrance as residents prepared to board. All were bundled in winter coats, most trimmed in fur with hand-knitted scarves and woolen hats. Men and women. Bags draping from one arm, canes in their other, some with walkers and still others in wheelchairs, impatient to board and determined to live.

"Nothing stops them, does it?" Brad was smiling. The creases indented at his eyes. "Look, there's Marge, your mom's friend, sporting her mink."

Presley nodded. "Nothing stops Marge... or Tilly." Tilly was the nickname her mother preferred instead of her real name Phyllis. She insisted everyone, including Presley, call her that.

"They must be off to the casino. Hell, they have to spend their Christmas cash." Brad swung into a parking space.

Presley sighed and leaned forward. "Oh Lordy, there she is."

A skinny woman in a black leather coat was standing at the back corner of the coach frantically waving their car into the carport. The bus driver, busy loading suitcases, was obligated to stop on her mother's commands. The woman's coat, like her sunglasses, appeared three sizes too big as she was such a petite figure. But size did not matter; Tilly was a force to be reckoned with.

"She's waving me forward. The sign says 'please do not enter the carport today. For the bus only,'" Brad stammered. "God darn it, Tilly."

Presley shook her head. Only her mother could infiltrate Brad's years of hard-core training and convince him to disobey orders.

Whipping off her sunglasses, her mother's pointer finger, which was hidden in matching leather gloves, definitively directed them to the space behind the coach. The bus driver was moving an orange cone although clearly annoyed.

"She's going on an overnight casino trip—on my birthday? I thought she was going to wait to see me. Maybe have a little lunch. Hear about my... results." Presley looked to Brad who parked as directed.

Brad jumped out of the car as soon as he stopped and rushed to Presley's door.

Her mother was burrowing through an oversized Calvin Klein purse, and barely raised her head. "You're late. The bus pulls out in ten minutes, Brad." Then she darted him an evil look.

"I apologize, Tilly, but the test your daughter had was running late. We thought you might want to hear how..."

She was ignoring him, finally discovering a white envelope. Tilly waved it high in the winter air. "Again, you're late, and I don't have time. I'm sure Presley has passed her test with flying colors."

That was Tilly. Her positive attitude on everything was always fine, even when her father had passed. *"It's life,"* she had said.

Presley was slow to approach, apologizing to the bus driver. Brad started to help him load bags.

"Mom, I mean Tilly, I don't have any results. I'm—"

"Honey, no news is good news."

Presley squinted. "Could you console me a little? I am fifty today."

"Fifty?" Tilly fluttered the envelope in front of her. "You are a baby. Now here, here is my gift. But Brad," her mother flicked Brad another glare, "knows the rules. No looking until tonight."

Presley reluctantly took the envelope, although she wished to tell her mother the truth. How her callous flare for life hurt.

A man with a cane gently interrupted the momentary silence between Presley and her mom, "Hey, Tilly. The bus is loaded, waiting for you."

"Oh, let it wait. Does Marge have the olives?"

"Tilly, I don't—" the fellow resident tried to object.

"Go ask, please. I can tell you that no one is leaving without olives for the martinis."

The older gentleman did as he was told.

Tilly faced Brad. "I knew you would be late. Bad enough you dragged her across the country. I thought I would miss another birthday." Then she pivoted back to Presley. "Honey, you look ragged. Where's your wig? You would be warmer with more than a ballcap."

"What? We all came back to help *you* move. You could celebrate my birthday," Presley exclaimed meekly.

"Is that what your husband told you?"

Presley hated when her mother called Brad "her husband." She wanted to say, *"He has a name, mother."* And if she wanted to go wig-less, it was her business. But she zipped her lips shut.

"So, he told you that you were just here to help me move?" This time Tilly slithered her eyes then released a laugh that reminded Presley of Cruella de Vil. Red lips spread wide as if she were going to bellow an opera tune. "Presley, I am not going to stop living because your father died years ago, or because you are sick. It's life. You are holding a grudge; didn't the therapist teach you anything?"

Presley's insides were in turmoil, but she remained complacent, as Tilly continued.

"We only have so much time on this earth. I thought you would realize this, especially now. You will understand more when you open the envelope."

"Can't you come over for cake as my mom? I need you."

"Cake? I can drink martinis and eat olives galore and pull a honey stick at the casino all weekend. No thank you, dear. I love you, but *you* need to start living. You are fifty." She glared at Brad.

The coach driver locked the compartment and shared an understanding sentiment with Brad regarding the woman.

"Tilly, I loved my life." Presley knew her mother blamed Brad for keeping her away from Springfield. Tilly was angry at the constant travel for the Army and his career.

"Sure, you did," Tilly exaggerated with pretend empathy. "You are like your father was, a soft-hearted conformist. You even shared that horsey thing I didn't understand. I remember the birthday he bought you Cleopatra, the roan foal that he fell in love with and bought for his princess. A shame your father had to see you practically give up your passion; at least you had something of your own." Tilly slapped a brief smile and another pathetic eye at Brad.

Presley shivered.

"Your three grandsons were my passion," Presley reminded her mother.

Brad neared then wrapped his arms around Presley, trying to give support.

"Yes. I have a blessing in them, thanks to you." She eyed the bus driver. "Mr. Ferring, this is my daughter, Presley. She had my first grandson in Alaska, the second in Colorado and the third in Texas. Imagine if there was no birth control what she could have accomplished in the eleven other states where they lived. Good thing my daughter was smart."

Mr. Ferring chuckled to appease Tilly.

"Tilly!" Presley gasped, but efforts to control her would be futile. Better to let Tilly seethe.

"By child number three, she couldn't afford to keep Cleo with her on the road, constantly changing residences." Tilly was holding her own conversation with the driver. "Her father had to take care of the horse before he passed away. Where is Cleo today, a pasture ornament? I've looked after that horse all these years on the farmette he bought for Presley—not me. At least her father had the horse in the back yard. I guess that was a gift for him, Cleo at our home." Tilly turned to Presley. The cold air was permeating in clouds from her as she spoke. "Someday, he always hoped you would return."

"I've ridden Cleo every time I came home," Presley defended, but was captivated by the white envelope. Her eyes were ponding with tears of embarrassment and loss.

"Honey," Tilly softened. "Look over to the left. That's the other side of Plum Haven, the dark side, where the old become decrepit."

All three followed her pointer finger to the north wing of the facility.

"They wait for Father Time to come and snatch them up." Tilly clawed her hand in a quick unexpected motion like a cat, causing Mr. Ferring to jump and grip his chest. "Scary, right? Go over there once. The ambulance doesn't miss a day. They listen to elevator music, sleep the day away, and their happy hour consists of watered-down morphine."

"Is there such a thing, Tilly?"

"Brad, I am speaking," she scolded. "I refuse to be a pasture ornament."

Brad held on to Presley. Their eyes rolled upward when the slide of a tinted bus window above them caught their attention.

Marge was hanging out the window. "Come on, Tilly." The elderly woman held a jar of olives. "Damn, it's cold out here." Then she slid the window shut with a slap.

"This bus has got to go," the driver announced and headed to the front. "You have one minute!"

"Five minutes, Mr. Ferring," Tilly ranted. "Or I won't tip you. I am your elder!"

"Not a minute more," the man ordered as he boarded the bus.

Tilly faced Presley and pressed the sides of her grey French twist which was teased to perfection. She slipped on her sunglasses. "I love you, honey. You gave me three beautiful grandsons, but all that cross-country traveling made *your* life stand still. This illness, yes, is a scare, so live, baby. The horse waited. Now, go ride."

"Mom, she is too old." A tear streamed down Presley's cheek. "We're moving again..." she sniffed. "Cleo's too old for the commotion. When you put the farm on the market this month, I can find a nice family for Cleo."

"You know, Presley, people say that about me and the others on this bus. Too old for happy hour, too old for tattoos, too old for sex."

Presley's eyes widened; her tears halted at the thought of her mother having sex. Brad shook his head, clearly unamused.

"See you Monday, after you've opened your envelope. That contains something worth more than gold, especially to your father. Then you can tell me how you're going to live the next fifty years of *your* life. Right, Brad?"

Brad and Tilly locked eyes in an odd almost affable stare. Then Presley's mother turned on a dime like a military general, although she sashayed to the front at her own pace... heeding her time, not Mr. Ferring's request.

Presley studied Brad. He shrugged as if repentant. Something was up; she sensed it.

Chapter 3

Presley and Brad were left encased in fumes as the Live Casino tour bus pulled away from the Plum Haven facility. The roar of the bus was deafening.

Brad embraced her tighter. "Come on, you're freezing. Let's go home. I have a surprise for you."

Presley contained her feelings as usual. *Home?* It wasn't *their* home. Presently, they were home-less. Brad was awaiting orders, and they were residing at Tilly's to help her move. Had he forgotten? Yes, the sound of home, in one place for a change, would be a dream come true: maybe a babbling brook, a barn, green pastures and Cleo.

"Baby, listen to me. Our boys are grown." Brad hesitated as he turned on the car.

Presley waited for him to continue, but he kept focusing on the road ahead.

She gave a confused glance. "Jamie is far from grown. When he turns eighteen, the real problems begin."

Brad grinned. "Come on, our third son has the same awesome foundation as the older two because of you. That's why he's been offered two semesters studying abroad. Tilly's right; it's time for you." He slid a hand across to touch her thigh.

"Please refrain from using the word *awesome*," Presley swiftly remarked.

"Okay?" Brad seemed bewildered.

"Never mind." She didn't have the energy to explain the technician's limited vocabulary. "Jamie needs a lot of attention right now. He leaves in a month. Forget the manicure, pedicure and get your hair done bit. I don't have hair anyway."

Brad retracted his hand to the steering wheel.

Presley realized she was being insensitive. Perhaps she harbored more resentment than her therapist could help heal.

"I'm sorry. I'm... it's just... I'm only pitying myself. I apologize."

"Absolutely no apology. You've been through so much. And supportive in everything the boys and I ever did." Brad's hand found her again.

"It's just... I'm fifty. Life passes in the blink of an eye. One day I'm fine, and the next day, I'm going through this illness. And there was so much I wanted to do." Presley tipped off her ball cap.

"And you still will. Plus, you're gorgeous."

Presley curled her lips. *At least he didn't say awesome.*

The lane to her childhood home was tucked on the outskirts of Springfield. Many called the farm a hidden gem amidst fields and orchards with two ponds, one waterfalling into the other. Although the trees were barren from winter's vestige, the apple and peach trees that lined the lane would be littered in pink and white blossoms by spring. As a child, she had the fondest of memories picking wildflowers, climbing fruit trees and riding her pony home from school on the dirt lane.

They traveled down the private drive in silence while Presley reminisced. She had shared a love of the outdoors, animals, and especially horses with her father from the moment she was born. Her mother was probably right; her dad purchased the farm for Presley. Tilly was busy playing bridge, exercising at the YWCA, shopping, luncheons, and socializing. Horse showing was not in her agenda, nor her blood. Without Dad, it wouldn't have been in Presley's either.

Presley was so entwined in her recollection that suddenly she exclaimed to Brad, "I think I told you my dad surprised me with a pony not long after he bought the farm. I was eight, and every day after school he was waiting at the mailbox with the chunky, painted colored pony named Pistol. I'd hop on, book bag slung over my shoulder, and he would lead us down the lane bareback. Eventually, Dad let go of the reins, and I trotted myself. Finally, he met me with Pistol, but Dad was riding the tractor. He handed the pony off to me. I would hop on with the reins in one hand, my book bag banging my back while we'd race to a pretend finish back at the stable. Dad always let me win. Then Pistol and I would do a victory lap around the house and jump the bridge between the two ponds. I could see Tilly on the porch cupping her mouth in fear."

Presley pointed to the field.

"The worst habit you could ever teach your horse is to race back to the stables. But Pistol, he was a good boy, as ponies go. He was a bugger at times when I started to grow more confident, but he taught me to keep my seat." She giggled. Presley didn't realize how her smile discharged warmth until she looked at Brad. He was beaming as if sitting in front of a warm fire.

"You loved that time, didn't you?"

She nodded as a wedge of sadness lodged in her throat.

"Dad said I was a natural. I grew out of the pony, of course, with these long legs. So he bought me a quarter horse of the same age when I was ten—a gelding named Bruno. Kindest horse. Signed me up for 4-H. Now those were the best times. Had that horse until he passed." She shook her head and sank into the passenger seat as if melting.

"Bruno died the year we were married."

"Yes. My father, his heart was so broken that year. We got married and moved away, then Bruno passed." Presley lowered her head.

Brad squeezed her arm. "Ahh, baby."

They parked in front of the red brick farmhouse. A cement keystone was inlaid in the bricks dead center between the two attic windows and marked 1855. Her father shared her love for old farmhouses, too. After teaching all day he'd toiled at restoring this one. Tilly desperately tried to convince him to sell and buy a condo with a crew that manicures the lawns and weeds the flowerbeds.

"That man went to every 4-H meeting and event with me. Tilly prayed my interest would change from tomboy to debutante."

"Not a chance, huh?" Brad added.

"I was in love with horses. A feeling that cannot be explained if the arrow of addiction pierces your heart. Even the smells—hay, straw, oats, mane and—"

"Manure," Brad interjected with a chuckle. "I'm sure Tilly hated that!"

Presley couldn't stop, as if a fire had ignited the memories. Her thin body perched forward. She scanned the pasture glazed with a film of snow, the kind that crunches when you walk on it.

"I was hooked. Dad helped me with everything, including projects like *How a Horse's Teeth Tell Their Age.*" Her fingers were touching the tips of each other as if counting. "I won an award in the Animal Husbandry division for my senior year science project and went on to states with *How a Saddle Aids a Rider to be One with Her Horse.* Sounds stupid, but we did so much research. You know the wrong saddle can really cause complications?" Presley's hazel eyes widened as she turned to Brad.

The car was parked, still in idle. However, because of the chill, steam from her breath lingered between them as she appeared as excited as a child at a playground for the first time in months.

"Did you know about General George Brinton McClellan of the United States Army?" she asked. "During the Civil War, 1861, he designed and developed a saddle specifically for the cavalry and their equipment. It's called the McClellan and is still used today. Bet you didn't know that?" Presley gloated.

"You are something. I am elated to see your smile." Brad leaned toward her. "Come on, let's get you inside to warm up. I have something very special planned for your birthday. And you heard Tilly; we have the envelope."

"Look at the time. Let me go feed Cleo. Time to tuck her in."

"I can do it. You need to stay warm..." He stopped. "I'm doing it again, keeping you from your dream. I'm so sorry about that..."

"Brad, stop this. I was a grown woman in love with her boys and her husband. But right now, I only have a short time with Cleo before your orders come, so, yes, let me savor every minute."

Brad took a breath as if to prevent another word on the subject. "Okay. But put your earmuffs on under your ballcap." He was searching the center console.

"This is the best part of the day. All good." Presley leaped out of the car, forgetting that her bones ached terribly from the treatment, forgetting she had been nauseous most of the last year and devoid of the thought that she had no hair. It was Cleo time.

Presley entered the stables, instantly inhaled, and held her breath for a few seconds. Hay, oats and Cleo.

Cleo started neighing promptly as the barn door slid open, circling in her stall.

"I'm coming, girl. I know you're hungry."

Presley unlatched the stall. Cleo stepped back, letting her enter, but she pawed the bedding with her front hoof and snorted.

"Patience is a virtue, girl. That's what they tell me, anyway. I must wait for my test results until tomorrow. How about that?"

Presley let the oats rain from her scoop into the feed bucket. Cleo stepped forward as soon as the last morsel dropped. Presley massaged the horse's neck under the thick black and grey mane notorious to a blue roan.

Cleo was small and stocky, a registered quarter horse. She maintained a fit physique even at pushing eighteen, although she was slightly overweight. Her full rump, generous shoulder, and agile abilities made Cleo the epitome of compact and quick.

Presley tossed the fresh green alfalfa hay, two large slices, in the corner. "That will keep you warm. You and I were going to be superstars. Life took a different path, didn't it, girl? You managed to top the charts with the lady that ended up leasing you. Dad sure was right about your pedigree; it was impeccable. And the training he provided, the best. What was that trainer's name? I know it will come to me. Between the treatments and my age, I'm forever in a fog."

Cleo maintained a rhythmic chewing, oblivious to Presley who pressed into the horse's neck with her cheek.

After a few quiet minutes of meditation, she left the stall and stood in the aisleway. Although it was cold, the stable was cozy, and she studied the surroundings. Her father had built the structure—three stalls, a tack area, and feed room with hay storage above. He was proud of the pristine conditions. Every visit home, the barn was the same, even after his death. Presley wondered how Tilly had managed. She had never inquired. Every 4-H ribbon was strung on lines across the wall, her multiple trophies, the plaques with her name engraved in gold plating all free of dust. And the belt buckles lined on a rack, clean, spotless. Was it a neighbor, maybe a kid from the local school that Tilly paid?

Presley shivered. A familiar voice brought her to reality.

"Mom, are you okay?"

"Jamie." A lanky boy all but eighteen was sliding the barn door shut.

"Taking it in?" he asked. "You sure get caught up out here."

"Ah, my soccer star." Presley tilted her head in admiration of the curly-haired boy. He inherited the curls from her and her father. At least the ones which once adorned her head.

"I know you miss this." His pointer finger moved in a circular motion. "Sure would be nice to stay put, huh? You loved this barn Pap built."

"Ahhh, Jamie." Presley neared him. Jamie was her gentle soul. The homebody, the most like her father, in both spirit and looks. "I know it's hard to understand. Horses, that is."

"You probably wished you had a girl instead of three boys."

"Not at all, my dear." She watched him as he moved toward the ribbons.

"Your wall of fame, eh? Maybe my big brothers will have a baby soon. A little girl for Cleo? Or a boy that likes horses."

"Jamie." She tilted her head. "Matt might be in a serious relationship, but Derek, well, he's having fun traveling the world."

"So, then you should ride Cleo."

"Alright, you are joining forces with your father and grandmother? Enough. We'll find a nice family for Cleo."

"Pap bought *you* Cleo to ride, didn't he?" Jamie was scrutinizing each award and item.

Her youngest son was like her, the one who loved home, being in one spot.

"He did. But things don't always work out the way we want."

Jamie ignored her. "I guess he was trying to lure us home. He bought Cleo the year before I was born." Jamie tapped a picture. Cleo neighed as if in agreement from behind. "Guess, I messed up his plans." He touched the last picture on the wall. "You sure were smiling."

Jamie was at the end of the *wall of fame* as her dad called it, where pictures hung—photos of her dad, Pistol, Bruno, Cleo, and of course Presley. Jamie stopped at the final picture before the feed room—a 4x6 photo from almost thirty years prior.

"Talk about big hair. Who are these ladies? You sure were pretty. How old were you? There's that horse Bruno in the background, right?"

"First, young man, don't you ever forget that you fulfilled my heart. And yes, before we put our hats on in those days, our big hair was all the rage. Come on, I can tell you the story inside, about those ladies. Before your father has a coronary wondering where we are."

Jamie snatched the picture off the wall. "That's a deal because you cheer up when you talk about this horsey stuff. Wish we could stay here forever, don't you, Mom?"

He faced her, the picture in his hand. Presley caught an odd twinkle in the center of his eyes.

She experienced a peculiar intuition again. "Somebody is up to something around here. I feel it."

Jamie slinked his arm inside her elbow, and they made a brisk pace to the farmhouse.

Once inside, she immediately caught a whiff, a delicious aroma teasing her from the kitchen. Jamie helped her remove her coat, then coaxed her to follow. "Come on, Mom. It's your favorite!"

The farmhouse floor creaked as she inched along the oak plank boards. She followed the center stairwell that split the four original rooms. Her father had reconstructed the back two, creating an open kitchen and sunroom that overlooked the pasture, two ponds and the stream she'd jumped over with Pistol as a youth.

She passed the living room with the stone hearth that heated the entire house, shimmering blue and golden embers behind the glass insert.

Jamie put the picture from the barn in front of her place setting at the lengthy wooden table. He offered her a chair with an arched arm, pretending to be shocked when he discovered a rather large square box resting on the seat, wrapped in floral paper.

"Oh boy, what's this?" he questioned in an exaggerated tone. "Guess you'll have to open it before you eat. After, you can open the envelope Grandma gave you, followed by the finale, which is going to floor you, Mom." Jamie was bursting with anticipation. "Dad has a surprise that I agreed to."

Presley appeared puzzled and tried to question, but Brad interjected, "Okay, young man. One gift at a time. Why don't you go connect to your brothers on Zoom?" Brad added a dash of sternness with his order to Jamie.

That stare was typically the only gesture he had to execute to control the boys. They called it his Army grimace.

"The doc told me you can enjoy red wine again." Brad placed a glass in front of Presley.

"You talked to my doctor?" Presley practically leaped from the chair. But Jamie positioned the wrapped box on her lap pressing her down.

"Maybe."

"Do you know the results of my MRI?"

Jamie interrupted them from the counter where he was fiddling with the computer. "I have them. Matt and Derek are on Zoom."

"No, little miss. You must wait until tomorrow for the results, but for right now you need to open this." Brad bestowed the grimace to her and fingered the box. "Happy fiftieth, baby. You are gorgeous."

CHAPTER 4

Presley read the card for the third time.

'Happy fiftieth, baby. You are beautiful and an incredibly strong lady. Now it's your time. Time to enjoy your passion and live your dream.'

She glanced at Brad as Jamie was leaning over her. The other boys were frozen on the computer screen in two small squares at different locations across the United States. Hard to believe they were both a live image resting on the kitchen counter. Eyes that mirrored their father's, all plastered on her.

"My passion?"

"Mom, come on," Jamie coaxed, his auburn hair corkscrewing in disarrayed curls.

"Yeah, Mom, come on. Do the honors."

"Obviously, none of you is telling me what the heck is happening." Presley examined the large square box on her lap.

She shrugged in surrender, and with some trepidation began to split the taped seam. The box was branded with the name *Wrangler*. She flashed an inquisitive glimpse toward her husband before continuing. As soon as she cracked the lid, the odor of leather, cowhide, and everything a horse lover would immerse in, seeped out of the box. The contents were undeniably purchased at a tack shop.

Presley peeked inside.

"What is this?" She unfolded the tissue paper, revealing a bone-colored cowgirl hat. "Another hat?"

Jamie lifted the felt hat from the box. Presley was enthralled. Her fingers streamlined the edge as if memories were released like magic from her touch.

Derek whistled from the computer on the counter. "Mom, you are going to be the classiest cowgirl in the show!"

"Put it on," Jamie insisted.

Brad smiled at the eighteen-year-old's enthusiasm. "She said it may fit a little big, baby," he hesitated slightly, "having no… em… hair but, she said if you showed horses in the past, you would know how to secure it with foam tucked right here on the inside." Brad reached across and motioned to the inside lip of the brim that sits on the forehead.

Presley confirmed what Brad was trying to explain with an adamant nod. She drew back the material. "Yes, I do know about securing a cowgirl hat, but we were a little more creative than foam for the insert," she added, yet not about to explain further. She fiddled with the space.

Presley forgot about her birthday and submerged in a long-lost memory, stuffing Kotex inside the inner rim right before entering the show ring. That ensured the hat was in position and unable to move even if the mount pirouetted in the air in angst. *Desperate times take desperate measures.* Presley's lips arched upward at the memory. The hat might have been secure but it had branded the forehead with an indent the rest of the day.

"Mom?" Jamie refocused her attention. "Please try it on."

Jamie was considerate, kind and a straight-A student. He followed directions, tried his best and wore his heart on his sleeve. She could never hurt his feelings by objecting, even though her days of wearing a cowgirl hat were water under the bridge.

She appeased him, removed her ball cap, bent her head forward and placed the hat on from front to back.

"Howdy, gentlemen. What do y'all think?" Presley raised her head sporting the hat and spoke with a twang. She ended with a wink.

The boys cheered *hooplas* and *yeehaws.*

Another hat, a cowgirl hat.

"You'll look like you were born in the saddle when you enter the ring with that hat. The lady at the tack shop was nice and helpful. She said if it wasn't the right one, you could exchange for another that fits your needs."

Exchange? Fits my needs? "Well, I am positive I won't be showing a horse, but it is beautiful. Thank you, all."

"Never say never, Mom! That's what you told me when I said I would never fall in love," Matt echoed from the computer screen. "Look at me now."

"Yeah, Mom, all the years of meticulously folding our uniforms, preparing perfect lunches, keeping a spotless house..."

"Agreed, you ran a tight ship. And picking up after Derek and his room littered with laundry, candy wrappers and dirty dishes," Matt joked. "How did you take him, Mom? Remember the time he had a moldy peanut butter and jelly sandwich under his bed?"

"Hey, I was doing an experiment. And look, now I'm a biologist," Derek defended.

"How about the critters she tolerated and cleaned up after for you? Your garter snake went MIA in the house! You even had baby bunnies she fed with droppers while you were at practice!"

"Well, I am a veterinarian! But I must say, I'm sorry about the snake, Mom." Derek winked.

"Seriously," Jamie ended the ribbing. "All the times you waited at practices, helped with homework, and stepped up to the plate when we needed you. Thank you," said Jamie with his customary sincerity.

"Not to mention, packing our belongings and our children all by yourself while I was already relocated to our next Army living arrangements," Brad added. "You are incredible."

"Alright, I understand," Presley announced as if she discovered the answer to a riddle. "Me time. But horses are work. What if I were injured? Not a good thing right now after a year of treatments." Presley had an edge to her tone as if lecturing the four. "I won't be showing horses. I believe a facial and pedicure will count as pampering."

"Mom, open Grandma Tilly's envelope. The presents will align together like dominoes."

Presley's hazel eyes widened. She scrutinized the envelope which Brad had placed against her wine glass. Tilly had said "not the normal monetary gift" and claimed it was "better than gold."

The envelope was elongated, more ivory than white, not a typical Hallmark card. More like an official document style. The contents felt thick as she pinched it, more than merely a card. Her long delicate fingers inched it open while Jamie almost ruptured with suspense and clapped his hands.

The new cowgirl hat was slightly big and slid over her brow. Presley pushed the brim back, engrossed in the contents of the envelope.

"Mom… what is it?"

"This looks like a deed… to here… the farm?" Presley scanned the paper, hesitated, then dropped the pages in front of her wineglass. She rested her elbows on the table placing her cheeks in her palms. "Brad, the farm?"

"Tilly wants you to have it. No strings attached," he replied. "She said your father would have wanted this, and she doesn't need a dime." He placed a hand on Presley's shoulder. "You can keep Cleo, right here."

"She discussed this with you? Without me?"

He nodded in apprehension, perhaps fearing her response.

"I guess we could rent the property out. The tenants would have to take care of Cleo? Right?" Presley wanted to verify that Brad was on board since they would be moving soon when his orders arrived. "If you're okay with managing the farm and renters?"

"Mom, don't you get it?" Jamie intercepted.

Brad raised his hand, clearly stopping their son. The room fell silent. Derek and Matt waited from the counter.

Brad reached over Presley, then raised her Blue Fiesta dinner plate to reveal a tri-folded paper.

"What's this? Another present?"

"You could say this gift is from the United States Army." She watched Brad's Adam's apple bounce after a hard swallow. "My orders."

Presley's cheeks flushed, not from the hearth which was filling the farmhouse with a sudden explosion of heat, nor another one of her personal summers which had bombarded her since her illness.

Her rise in temperature resulted from anticipation regarding their future.

One of the boys on the screen cleared his throat.

"Maybe you better have a swig of the wine, Mom," Matt attempted to lighten the heaviness in the room.

Presley held the paper to her heart. *Where in the world would they be headed?*

"I already cleared this with Jamie. He agreed. So, if you're not elated, take it up with him." Brad's voice was as dry as her wine. "The acceptance had to be made at midnight, last night."

Simultaneously the oven timer sent a piercing ring throughout the room.

Brad immediately turned away toward the stove reaching for two hot pads. "Chicken Parm is calling."

He'd blindsided her. He had never moved them to a new location without confiding in her. Presley was overcome with a sense of betrayal but held her tongue. Jamie was all that mattered, and although he would be studying abroad in a few weeks, right now for some reason he was smiling.

Presley didn't realize how severely she had crumpled the paper in her hand.

"Mom!" Jamie touched the document. "I can read this for you," he whispered.

Presley loosened her grip, letting the paper slip away. To her angst, Brad didn't stop dishing parmigiana onto the platter.

Jamie stood at attention and began to chuckle, barely able to read. He cleared his throat. "The United States Army requests your presence in a new and permanent position... at... Fort Meade."

Presley arched her head while dabbing a tear with her napkin. "In Maryland? Permanent position?"

"That's what it says, Mom. The Army needs Dad right here. It's a matter of national security."

The other two on the computer screen united in a celebratory laugh with Jamie.

Brad placed the platter in the center of the table with a display of no emotion.

"Brad? Would you please tell me what's going on?"

"Mom, don't you understand?" Jaime shouted. "We have a home! Here! With Cleo!"

"Brad?" Presley elevated her voice.

Her tears seemed to soften him.

"If you're okay with this, of course," he said. "We'd be living in this house, your childhood homestead on the Mason Dixon line. My commute to Fort Meade is a piece of cake." Brad circled the table to reach her side. He didn't wait for her to respond. He simply bent on one knee and cupped her hand in his. "Yes, baby, living here indefinitely. A permanent position."

Presley could barely focus on eating, drinking or engaging in conversation the rest of the meal. Derek and Matt had signed off with their typical "I love you," but swore they would be home soon to visit and maybe witness her "show." She was crying with joy and could hardly speak, let alone object on the horse issue again.

That evening Presley placed the picture Jamie had brought from the barn on her vanity next to her new cowgirl hat. She examined her appearance in the mirror, comparing it to herself almost three decades prior. Her bald head itched from the new stubbles piercing the glowing white-as-snow scalp under the lights. In the picture, her abundant hair that was coifed in massive curls had been her crowning glory.

Brad entered their bedroom, softly clicking the door closed. He was carrying the glass of red wine which she'd barely sipped at supper.

Presley immediately spoke. "I can't believe I have to wait until tomorrow. What the heck! What am I going to do? It seems like a lifetime."

"You'll be okay. Look how far you've come, and what you've faced. Besides, I have one more gift for you." He held out a long thin wooden box about the length of a ruler and an inch in depth.

"Brad, you've given enough—a permanent home, Jamie's smile, and Cleo can stay with me."

"It's not from me." He eyed her as he reluctantly inched the box toward her. "This may not be easy. Tilly kept it since his passing. It's from your father."

"My father? What?"

"Tilly shared this with me. I must say it's a tearjerker. The story goes, he had some sort of agreement with a certain horse trainer regarding a student rider who was in a lease. The trainer named Gert..." He hesitated in thought. "Gertrude somebody. Anyway, the student ran out of money to pay. But Gertrude was desperate herself and didn't want the girl to quit. The trainer knew your father well and conveyed to him if he paid for the student, she would return the favor. Your father, the good man and horse lover he was, paid. In exchange, the trainer vowed her time in return to repay him, among other promises. Evidently, your father never used the I.O.U. Instead, he saved it for you."

Presley gasped, snatching the box. "Gertrude Steele!"

"Obviously, you know the name," Brad mumbled staring at his empty hand.

"Shh, don't say it again. That name makes me want to hide in fear. Of course, I remember her. How could I ever forget?"

She edged the wooden lid open to reveal a letter, addressed to Presley and underneath signed by her father. She unfolded a message for the second time that day, this one written in her father's hand. She fought back tears and read.

My dearest Presley,

Horses are in your blood. Besides, you are a natural. Someday the urge will resurface. You will realize a piece of your heart has been missing—the shared beat of being one with the most breathtaking beast on this earth, a horse.

Follow your heart.

You know I watch every penny, and God knows, it's been a job with your mother. Ms. Gertrude Steele owes me. Be certain, this debt is to be repaid to you. All parts of it! And Ms. Steele knows this. Cleo benefited from the lease when you couldn't return home. She is a splendid mare. Someday you may need to recondition Cleo, or you will need to break another foal. I have a feeling I won't live to see this as I've been very ill. Perhaps, I will be watching from heaven. I love you, squirt.

"He always called me squirt." Presley mumbled between sniffles.

"I researched this person, this trainer. Pays to be a specialist in national security."

Presley barely heard his attempted joke.

"She's still living. Presley, are you listening?"

"What?"

"The year of free training in exchange for the lease of King Roan's Cleopatra, your Cleo. Read the agreement. This Gert Steele—"

"Please do not say her name!" Those words tazed Presley with a zap of fear. She tucked the memory of the trainer away before reading the certificate.

Brad waited until Presley placed the paper on the vanity. "You look like you've seen a ghost."

"Let me briefly explain. You watched Harry Potter, right?"

Brad nodded. "How could I not? Jamie was addicted."

"Well, in a *Harry Potter* way, in the horse trainer world, Gertrude Steele is *she who must not be named.*" Presley took a gulp of the cabernet "She was the best at one time. Bred Cleo. But let's say, this trainer lost her way and instead became the most feared name on the show circuit. Finally, the industry lost all respect for her. She even managed to be barred from showing."

Brad sat on the bed and steepled his hands.

"I have never stopped thinking about horses. My father's right, but really, this is a silly dream."

"No dream, little lady. Your mother has been holding this one over my head for years. Now, you'll have a place for the grandkids when they come, maybe in ten years." He smiled. "Listen, I'll be completely busy with this new job, and I won't have a lot of free time. You will, though, with Jamie leaving to study abroad."

Presley tried to interrupt, but she was flagged by the Army grimace.

"You and Jamie are like two peas in a pod. He's gifted, but if he thinks you won't be okay, he'll opt out of this amazing opportunity. The way I see it, you need to appear content and busy, that way he feels secure about the study."

Presley pondered her husband's words while taking another sip, feeling a warm rush, as she had not had any alcohol for quite some time.

"At least think about calling this woman. Cleo certainly needs a tune-up before you hop on, and so will you."

"What if I was to be hurt? You make it sound like a done deal."

Brad rose and walked to the vanity. He placed the cowgirl hat on her head, then directed her to look in the mirror.

"We don't even have a trailer, Brad. And really, there are days I feel weak and tired, and..."

He eyed the certificate of debt. "Seems like this Gert—" He held up a hand. "I mean, this *trainer* owes a lot more than training alone. You'll figure it out. Now, if you don't mind, birthday girl, I'm going to get a shower. Then hold the woman I love."

"Brad, I'm fifty years old..."

"You have nothing to lose except your passion. Live, honey, live. In Tilly's words: you should've done this a long time ago. None of us knows if we have tomorrow."

"Let's wait until we get the test results. I'm sure the doctor will say no."

Brad bent down and kissed her cheek.

When Presley heard the shower running in the master bath, she touched the picture of four ladies in their early twenties at a horseshow. Bruno, in the background with another horse. The time of her life.

Then she remembered Gertrude Steele and shivered, the trainer holding the Kodak and snapping a picture that Presley would hold in her heart forever.

Chapter 5

Rachel

Rachel Snow kissed the opening of a paper bag with her lips then pressed it tight. Sucking in air, she blew in quick puffs, but she continued hyperventilating from her pathetic crying. This evening over fifty guests were mingling in her home, and she was the hostess in hiding. She was breathing into a paper bag as she spun in a styling chair, eyeing pictures that depicted the story of her life. Many photos were of the man Rachel never stopped loving, now gone, and the daughter she couldn't live without, soon to be three thousand miles on the other side of the country.

Rachel had made a career of instilling happiness and beauty in others even when her own heart was suffering. However tonight, her life was in shambles, she barely could go on. Jemma, her daughter, was leaving for an elite internship in San Francisco to fulfill her dream as an architect, *of all professions.* Not the career Rachel planned for her daughter, living so far away! The thought frightened her. She inhaled between tears, the bag scrunching flat. Instead, she caught the lingering fumes of hair color and perm odors from the past week. She reached up and removed a smaller picture from the end of her workstation wall.

Rachel lowered the paper bag and evaluated herself in a mirror. The chair she was resting in had been the first at this location, where her success was hatched when she opened *Waves and Shades Salon.* She added fifteen more styling stations over the last two decades. Clients were not only from Springfield, but from surrounding locales including Chester, Bennington, and Warfield. She had been voted the most successful salon owner in *What's New in Springfield* magazine three years in a row. She recalled the day she and Heath bought the dilapidated farm property on five acres. "Someday you'll have that horse," he'd promised. They hadn't had a nickel to rub between them, simply love and hope. Someday never happened.

Heath became ill before they barely hammered in a nail to remodel the house. Instead, he coaxed her to open a salon in the barn, since she needed a way to support herself. Maybe he saw into the future. Heath passed away a few years after their daughter Jemma was born. And not from the illness he was diagnosed with. For that she would never forgive either of them.

Rachel buried her life into her career to support them. For the last two-plus decades, she focused solely on working and raising Jemma. She couldn't imagine anything else.

Rachel nestled back and examined the wall of photos hanging like patchwork by her styling station: Heath and Jemma, Jemma and her horses, Jemma and Rachel, Rachel, Roxie and her staff, her volunteer work certificates for the kindergarten Sunday school and the Cinderella classes she taught. At the end there was a tiny 4x6 picture of life before Heath and Jemma—a photo of four young women in their twenties.

Rachel removed the picture, reflecting on the moment. Practically three decades had passed since Gertrude Steele, a horse trainer, offered to snap the photo at a mid-summer horseshow. Rachel recalled it was during the lunch break between English and Western classes as if it were yesterday.

Thoughts of Gert, the woman who never cracked a sliver of emotion, made Rachel shudder. Good thing Gert wasn't in the pic; she was a disturbing memory, perhaps an added reason Rachel was afraid to ride. Rachel remembered how Gert scolded, *"We aren't going to be taking anymore silly photos! You're here to win." That woman cracked the whip, and we paid for it.* Of course. Rachel was afraid of everything other than what she knew for most of her life. She was afraid of the highway, snowstorms and even the pet gerbil Jemma had when she was seven.

Funny, that was one of the best years of Rachel's life. Certainly, the best before she married Heath and before Jemma was born. But no one can retrace time, no matter how hard one prayed. And Rachel could pray; she was Catholic.

A familiar voice from the back entrance restored her to the present.

"Mom, we finally found you! Why would you leave the house during a party where you're the hostess?" Jemma entered through the rear entrance of the salon. "It's freezing out there."

"Blessed Mary Mother of God, Jemma. You act like you had to brave twenty miles in the cold to find me, when I was simply twenty feet away," Rachel murmured between sniffles.

"Mom, you have to stop." Jemma sat in the adjacent styling chair and spun to face her.

Jemma was a beautiful girl. Her looks mirrored Rachel's, but her personality was undeniably her father's—poised, calm and discreet. Rachel was all the opposite. She was, at heart, a talented hairstylist and excellent business manager, but pure chaos when dealing with most everything else, like domestic or organizational skills.

"I agree," said Roxie, Rachel's longtime assistant. She nabbed the paper bag and replaced it with a box of Kleenex from a supply cabinet. "Hyperventilating again, I see."

"I'm scheduled to teach a Cinderella class tomorrow at the Peach Tree Women and Imaging Center to women who are experiencing the effects of cancer treatments or other illnesses. We educate them on skills like makeup and how to wear scarves, which helps them feel a little better. This certainly aids in coping. I forgot to pack something in the bag."

"I know what a Cinderella class is, Rachel. I've helped you with them for years. Where's the Cinderella bag?" Roxie snapped and spun around searching the area. The woman slapped her plum cheeks in mockery. "Oh, look. Over there by the door, right where I placed it... after I packed it. What could possibly be missing?" Her highlights of pink sparkled in the light along with the sequins across the shoulders of her top. Roxie loved bling.

Rachel ignored her, even though she would be lost without Roxie and her skills—packing bags, washing hair, organizing the stock, cleaning tools, reordering, simply sweeping… the list went on and on.

"You cannot continue like this," Jemma stated. "Mom, there are dozens of friends, family, and clients who watched me grow up, mingling in our house without the party hostess."

"That's you, Rachel," Roxie added.

Rachel rolled her eyes. "I know who the hostess is, just like I know to pray every day. The party is for you, Jemma, before you leave. Please, you go enjoy."

Roxie flagged her hand, attempting to transform the mood. "Yada, yada…"

"Why in God's name are you hiding out in the salon?" Jemma asked.

"I opened this place before your father died. You were only two at the time. Do you remember?"

"Mother, I was two," Jemma reiterated in a soft tone. "How could I possibly remember? But I've been told…" Her voice drifted away.

Rachel blew her nose into a rolled-up, flaking, and over-used tissue, then sucked in air. "Your father encouraged me to live my passion even though we didn't have a dime between us. He left me nothing but you and the courage to run a business."

Roxie handed a fresh tissue to Rachel with a mumbled, "Here we go. Next comes the guilt, then confession and fifty Hail Marys."

Jemma sighed. "Mom, I know the story. Please, listen..."

Rachel soldiered into defense mode. When it came to her life journey, she needed others to know the sacrifices and hardships she'd endured. "Here at our home location, this is where it all began."

Rachel rotated the chair in a room that once stalled beef cattle, remodeled as a modern styling area with refurbished wood flooring, open second story and 8x8 beams.

"I went through hell to put two styling chairs in an old stable. Damn township. Remember that, Roxie? You've been with me since the beginning." Rachel careened her arms like an eagle, not allowing her long-time employee and friend to retaliate. "Then *Waves and Shades* grew to fifteen chairs, followed by more shops. I was a single mother. I continued working behind the chair right out our backdoor to be home every night with you." Rachel pointed to Jemma. "This salon provided us with a lifestyle. You've had a horse ever since you were eight years old. And..." Rachel blew her nose again.

Jemma and Roxie were volleying eye rolls and simultaneously recited Rachel's last sentence in unison with her. "That took a lot, Jemma."

"Oh, you two!" Rachel flicked the tissue in disgust and snatched another out of the box. "I pray for you both every day!"

"Please, Mom. We all know how hard you've struggled to pay our bills, build a lucrative career, provide me with the best you could afford, you worked 24/7 and prayed—"

Roxie slipped in a barely audible stab, "Until your fingers and toes bled. Woe is you."

Rachel shot her a glare as Jemma continued. "I am thankful. Honestly, Mom, all so I could show horses and go to college. You were amazing. But you gave me wings and now I am going to fly."

"Rach, that's what you worked for, right? Your daughter to succeed?" Roxie added.

Rachel sniffled. "Jemma, it's just... Sweet Mary Mother above knows I am so going to miss you. And all the fun we had with you showing horses, and Hannibal, well I will miss that horse."

"Mom, you're going to have to compose yourself. You need to take up a hobby. Focus on you." Jemma pointed to the picture in her hands—the photo among a lifetime of those hung next to her workstation from the very moment she opened this salon.

"Jemma, I can't ride without you," Rachel explained. "I will join the Rosary Society. Or something."

Jemma frowned. "I'm not following you on that, Mom."

"Oh, sure it's safe there. No chance of hyperventilating." Roxie confirmed. "Geez, Rachel, you make no sense."

"I'm too old."

"Forty-nine? Didn't you recently rant about that legendary Brazilian in the horsey magazine? Isn't he in his late fifties? What was his name?" Roxie snapped her fingers. "Glick something."

Rachel squinted evil eyes as she responded in a dry tone, "Wyndham."

"That's it, Wyndham Glick, the handsome world-renowned horse whisperer."

"Mom, maybe you could find one of your old friends from the pic." Jemma noted the photo in her hand again. "And search out this Wyndham Glick. You did have a crush on him."

"Oh, hell, she's afraid of meeting a man, too," Roxie nipped. "God knows, that's dangerous." She had a method of restoring Rachel from a dark abyss. The two women had cut and styled next to each other for over twenty-two years. She knew Rachel's darkest secrets, things Jemma wasn't even privy to, like why Rachel was petrified to ride without Jemma, and the truth about Heath's death.

Rachel's tears dried up. "Alright, back to the party. Both of you. I will be over after I refresh my makeup." Rachel stood, wiped her eyes, then escorted them both to the door. "See, the rosary I was saying worked."

Roxie raised her eyebrow as if Rachel was hopeless and headed out. Jemma pivoted around before leaving, softly sealing the door to keep the winter cold out.

"Mom, it really is your turn," Jemma spoke in a low somber tone.

"I thought when you first attended college you would take the scholarship for equestrian studies, major in business management, then return home, obtain your cosmetology license, and take over the business. We would have a wonderful life. Work, ride and go to church on Sundays. We could expand, open more salons, you could still compete..." Rachel tilted her head like a needy puppy.

"Horses were your dream, Mom. I hate to break this to you if you haven't realized the truth. And please don't take this out of context. My riding was fun. The horse taught me so much, and I was close to you. But honestly, you were the one smiling." Jemma exhaled as if she finally was about to release a confession that had burdened her for years. "I want to be an architect. Maybe play tennis and travel. Architecture is what I majored in, top of my class, no less. There will be no changing my mind. And church, well..."

"Sweet Mary, don't say it. I will have to go to confession."

There was a silence between them that rose to the open cavities of the two-story stable, all the way to the cupola in the center of the vaulted ceiling. The moment of quiet seemed like eternity.

"Mom, are you listening to me? Yes, you are successful. Yes, you are amazing. Yes, you gave your time, but now I need to fly."

The words stung harder than the slash of a riding crop.

Jemma clearly read the sadness that permeated Rachel's face. "I did the horse thing all for you. You smiled when you led the horse around. I wanted you to smile. You have drowned yourself in work since Dad died. I never even knew him. You, Roxie, and your clients raised me. Please stop hiding. Heath left this earth long ago, and we know you worked very hard. Look at your accomplishments."

Jemma closed the door behind her, leaving Rachel alone, her rosary beads clenched in her hand, staring at the picture wall, and the album of her life. This stirred a pressure rising in her chest, her lungs constricting. *Oh, God.*

Rachel was left feeling discounted. She re-evaluated her appearance in the mirror. She most certainly didn't look forty-nine, or at least that's what others told her. Fortunately, her skin had been spared of too many wrinkles because she rarely spent time in the sun, didn't smoke and moisturized every night before she prayed. Her silver hair was highlighted to a pale blonde and toned with a pearl hue that shimmered in the light. Rachel's sharp, angular inverted bob received compliments daily. *Imagine this hairdo under a cowgirl hat?*

Rachel rendered a halfhearted smile. Tonight, her heart had been severed by Jemma's remarks. She couldn't imagine a world without her daughter or a world without horses. This wasn't what she planned for her life. But life never seemed to go as planned.

Rosary beads were not enough. Rachel opened the drawer of her hairstyling station in search of another paper bag.

Chapter 6

Rachel slipped into the kitchen of her log home, a paper bag in one hand—in the event she hyperventilated again—and a picture in the other. She was hoping to enter unnoticed. However, Roxie was scraping extra taco dip into a Tupperware container. Rachel paused, prepared to be confronted. Frozen, she watched Roxie work in swift movements to remove every morsel until the plate was spotless, then placed it in the dishwasher. What would Rachel have done without this woman? Roxie had no children, and she was like a second mother to Jemma.

On the outer surface, Rachel was nothing short of a force of nature, appearing to have her life all together, committed to her customers, her daughter and her faith. Truth be told, she was successful, but the power of a good support system, like Roxie and her clients, made things possible. Beneath her secure shell, Rachel was a colossal mess, always in a hurry, usually afraid, and on the constant brink of hyperventilation.

Rachel was "shushly," as her family tagged her, always leaving a trail wherever she went. Her grandmother once said she wasn't born to cook or clean. Rachel agreed and assumed that's why God made washers, rags, Clorox, swifter-jetters, rosary beads and assistants.

Roxie had been her first employee, which transformed into a friendship. She kept her on her feet and tidied up the pieces Rachel left behind, whether they were crumbs, hair or her heart.

"A bit nippy out there, isn't it?" Roxie didn't stop working. "You need to get control of these panic attacks. Maybe some medication? They have little white pills. These episodes have spoiled your life's joy for years... and Jemma's."

"Always to the point, aren't you?" Rachel snipped. "I don't need medicine. I have the Blessed Mother."

"How is that going for you?" Roxie paused. "Truth hurts sometimes. You can't change the fact that Jemma is leaving."

Rachel ignored her, reflecting instead on the statement. Rachel's panic attacks were indeed raging more frequently. The initial bouts had loomed soon after Heath's death. Her therapist advised that horseback riding might help relieve stress. *"The electromagnetic field of a horse is five times bigger than that of humans. A horse can influence our own heart rate when we are in their presence. I took the liberty of finding you a local place that is giving lessons. Why don't you give it a try?"*

So one day she missed Sunday church to take a riding lesson.

Rachel was only a novice equestrian even though she'd showed one year with the other ladies in the photo. Unfortunately, not every Christian is Christian, and not every instructor is good. As an amateur horseman, Rachel should never have mounted a horse named Bullet. After the riding disaster, and the panic attack that ensued from that tragic episode, Rachel quit riding, and the therapist to boot. She never missed a Sunday after.

"How you ever ran this salon and fifteen stylists, I will never know. Good thing you have a stock of paper bags."

Rachel placed the thirty-year-old picture of her riding friends on the table. She studied it and wondered why she'd been motivated to carry it with her to the house from the salon.

Roxie approached, wringing a dish rag. She leaned into Rachel's ear. "You're doing it again."

"What?" Rachel's brow pinched.

"Wishing you could go back in time. Like maybe when Jemma was young, Heath was living, or the year you rode with these three lovely ladies in your photo." Roxie pointed. "Rachel, you have to get yourself together, for Jemma's sake."

Rachel didn't respond. Instead, she peered into the great room where Jemma was hugging clients and friends as they exited the congratulations–farewell party. Mrs. Anderson was giving Jemma a pep talk. "We all watched you grow up in the salon. Your father would be proud."

"Listen to them," Roxie whispered to Rachel. "You don't want to jeopardize her leaving because she pitied her almost fifty-year-old mother, who is a sappy mess and simply needs rejuvenating."

"Rejuvenating? My hair needs rejuvenating!" Marion Walton entered the kitchen carrying a dirty plate and glass. The eighty-something had been one of Rachel's first clients. "My appointment is on Friday, so pull yourself together, Rachel."

"Exactly. I second that motion." Roxie raised the dish rag in the air, and the thirty silver bracelets on her tattooed arm jingled.

"Great party," Marion said. "And listen, Miss Rachel Snow. You did a fine job raising that young lady. You better get out in the world before it's too late. Look at me. I'm moving into Plum Haven. So live, dear."

Rachel sighed. "Not another lecture." She pressed her palms into her temples.

"I motion again to live today," Roxie chanted.

Then a mob of seven remaining guests barged into the kitchen.

"What do you suppose I do?" Rachel dropped her hands.

"Hey, get a tattoo like Roxie," one of the women suggested as she set her dishes on the counter.

"How about a date? Go on that eHarmony site," another added.

"They don't use eHarmony anymore," Marion remarked as if she were a computer whiz.

"Hell, she has trouble with the salon computer," Roxie spoke as if Rachel were absent from the room. "Let alone a dating site. If she takes up the horse-riding hobby again, maybe she could meet the infamous Brazilian horse-whisperer, Wyndham Glick. That's her best bet!"

"Wyndham Glick?" Marion questioned.

"Would you all please!" Rachel voiced, louder than she realized. "I will be praying for all your souls."

The room momentarily hushed, watching her catch her breath.

With that, Roxie careened her arms, herding the ladies away from her counter space. "Thank you all for coming but look at the time." She returned to the counter mumbling, "Always this way at a party. Everyone ends up in the kitchen."

"Oh, Roxie," Marion relinquished. After she kissed Jemma, the others began to follow.

Mrs. Anderson was the last one. "Young lady, don't you worry a stitch about your mother. Ignore her panic attacks. It's time for her to face reality. We are going to watch over her." Then she cupped her hand at Jemma's ear as if to dull her voice, however, the final remark was loud and clear. "Won't hurt her to have a Xanax."

Roxie tossed Rachel a discerning glance.

"Or a man," one of the others added from the living room.

A serenade of laughter from the group filled the room, except for Rachel.

Jemma giggled as discreetly as possible. "I know you'll take care of her, thank you."

Roxie continued stacking the dishwasher and placing leftovers in the refrigerator.

Rachel plopped on a wooden kitchen chair, disgusted. She propped her elbows on the table, her chin on her fist, and sulked because the ladies had grilled her faults, each one like a needle prick. She'd managed to raise her daughter, alone, run a business and find time to volunteer. Didn't they see how hard she worked? She fingered the paper bag as she chanted her attempt to ward off an attack. *You are okay. Breathe deep. Ignore them.*

Roxie eyed her. "If you keep being dependent on that paper bag, you will never stop the panic attacks."

Jemma had escorted the guests out the front door, but she heard Roxie. Lips turned down, she re-entered the kitchen. "Mom?"

In a mood of sympathizing, Jemma took the chair next to Rachel. The photo of the four girls stared back at her. "You said this picture was from one of the most memorable times of your life. Why?"

Rachel released the bag and scrunched her pearly blonde and grey waves. She probably looked frazzled, her makeup smeared from a river of tears. She sighed. "Before you and your dad, I never stepped out of my comfort zone. I was timid and lacked confidence. I loved horses, but they seemed so big."

"I mean, if you were afraid of horses, how did you end up showing? You look in your early twenties in the photo."

"It was a few years before she fell head over heels for your dad, I've been told," Roxie added.

Rachel nodded. "I was born loving horses. Read about them all the time. Just afraid to ride. By dumb luck—or miracle, should I say—I ended up at Gertrude Steele's Holly Hill Farm, for lessons and a few shows."

"Well, who are these other girls?"

Rachel grinned for the first time that evening. Jemma appeared interested in her story. She straightened her shoulders and lifted the collar of her white blouse. "We all ended up at the same stable. Long story short, we spent the year riding together. Turns out we really clicked. Not at first, mind you."

Roxie flipped the towel over her shoulder, then seated herself directly across. "Well, I'm interested, too. I always wondered who they were and where they are." Her fuchsia sequin top sparkled under the dinette light.

"You were beautiful, Mom, but who is this tall one? Her hair!" Jemma tapped the girl with the auburn hair. "It's like a helmet of curls."

"Oh, that was so in then—*big hair, don't care*," Roxie snickered.

Rachel arched her lips. "Presley. Everything about her was beautiful. Long legs, long hair, even her name. And oh, could she ride. She was always elegant even if her horse was rearing or bucking. She made it look easy. I believe we could have been friends for life."

"What happened?" Jemma listened intently.

Always a serious child, Jemma's dark hair and hazel eyes were a gift from her father. It was like Rachel could still see into his soul everyday.

"Mom?"

Roxie banged the table dead center on the brown bag. "Rachel? Don't touch the bag. Stay with us."

Rachel jumped, shooting Roxie a despairing glare. "Life happened. We both fell madly in love, and Presley married a man in the Army. We lost touch. I read about her in the *Horse Chronicle* for the first few years. You would have loved her, Roxie. She was a real rhinestone cowgirl, never a pin out of place." Rachel was staring at Jemma again.

Roxie intercepted, pointing to another person in the photo. "And this lady?"

"Louisa Mae, better known as Wheezy. From over in center city Bennington. Never so much as owned a pet bird but loved horses. Unfortunately, as she used to say, Black girls from the city had limited access to equestrian centers. Especially thirty years ago. She was part of a diversity program. The owner of the farm permitted her to work in exchange for riding lessons. Wheezy had to find her own transportation, though. She was perhaps the most strongminded person I've ever met. Next to maybe you, Jemma." Rachel touched her daughter's arm. "Wasn't afraid of anything. She swore one day, she would learn to drive the horse trailer and haul us to rodeos. I always wondered what happened to her. If she ever made a rodeo."

Roxie and Jemma waited as Rachel hesitated. Roxie pushed the picture closer. "Geez, Rachel, come on. Keep on it."

Rachel's voice dimmed. She looked at the fourth girl in the picture. "Gigi Tetless. Or Gigi *Titless*, as the cowboys tagged her. Wouldn't get away with talking like that today."

"Do I denote a sound of annoyance?"

"Look closely."

The two leaned in further. Gigi was dressed in a stark white outfit, not a spot of dirt on her.

"Looks as if she was freshly dipped in Clorox," Roxie noted.

"Spoiled piece of work was what she was. Gigi came from money. We were beneath her. I heard she married money, like she wanted. Mrs. Anderson told me one time that Gigi's husband owns an elaborate estate and breeds thoroughbreds across the river. She's lathered in jewelry and equines. And probably owns and rides as many horses as one could dream. Ditched us like hotcakes."

"How the heck did she wind up at the stables where you all were?" Roxie asked.

"Another story, but she was Wheezy's driver—part of the diversity program. Gigi despised the job. And she wasn't always congenial, let me tell you."

"Mom," Jemma said, "You're smiling."

Roxie laughed. "Why yes, Rachel, you are."

"The most I ever laughed in one year," Rachel agreed. "Except for the time Roxie's wax paper got stuck fast in Marilyn Munchel's bikini wax. Remember that?"

"How could I forget." Roxie stood. "Well, I have work to do."

"Sure was the time of my life, for a shy girl." Rachel continued to grin at the photo. "I thank the Blessed Mary for that year."

"Mom, I have an idea. You can lease my horse, Hannibal, from the lady if she hasn't set up another rider yet. Why don't you take lessons and show the gelding? He's broke and ready to go. Or at least take the lessons."

"That's a great idea," Roxie chimed in.

"I can't," Rachel replied. "I have clients, commitments, a business."

"You're scared," Roxie blurted.

"Maybe I am, but this conversation stops here." Rachel rose and headed toward the stairs. "First off, I can't ride. I also can't drive a trailer… and your horse is named Hannibal for a reason."

"Mom, it's the perfect opportunity for Roxie to take more responsibility in the salon. You're exhausted. You also *hate* the computer… and some of the clients. What did Marion say? You need *rejuvenated* with an adventure. Find these girls in the photo."

Rachel pivoted to face them again. "Jemma, *you* were my best adventure. You and your father."

"Mom…"

"Enough, I'm turning in. I have an early client before heading to the Peach Tree Center tomorrow. I want to be well rested to teach that Cinderella class."

Rachel reached back for the paper bag. She was certainly going to need it as her breathing was quickening.

Roxie intercepted in a flash, her hand preventing Rachel from snatching it.

Rachel huffed. She grasped the picture instead, stamped from the kitchen, and promenaded up the staircase while the two whispered. She dodged into her bedroom and leaned against the door, as if they would try to break in.

Rachel laid one hand on her chest, wishing she had the paper bag to regulate her inhales and exhales instead of her rosary. Then she eyed the picture in her other.

Me, ride a horse again? Meet Wyndham Glick? With a body like this? I haven't worked out in years.

Chapter 7

Rachel rose early although she hadn't slept well. But for the first time in months the thought Jemma's leaving was not the culprit of her tossing and turning. Nor was her pillow which had been smashed to smithereens from clutching it every night these last months. She had not blubbered, prayed, or hyperventilated at all. Instead, Rachel had reminisced about the picture resting on her nightstand. Four women in their early twenties, smiling, with a horse named Bruno in the background.

Several times throughout the night she had even giggled out loud remembering incidents with the women on horseback. Like the time Rachel forgot the barrel pattern. First problem, she had no business entering a barrel class as a novice. But their trainer, Gert Steele, insisted and wanted nothing short of winning the overall versatility award representing her farm, Holly Hill. The four would often joke behind Gert's back, *"Are we spending money for this kind of treatment?"*

That had been Rachel's first year to learn riding skills, patterns and different equestrian disciplines. Gert entered them in the Silver Spur finals in versatility, meaning highest point standings overall in every event. Rachel assumed it was a perfect way to introduce her to everything equestrian. But the one thing she feared almost as much as Gert Steele herself was the Barrel Race.

Gert insisted she enter, *"For the barn."* Presley had also encouraged her, without Gert's knowledge. *"Even if you walk or trot the pattern, it still counts toward points. You'll be fine. You just go around the three barrels set in a triangle, then home. Ta da!"*

Wheezy had touched her shoulder. *"Remember, go to the right first. The judges are sitting awfully close to the left barrel. You don't need a catastrophe."* Then she'd laughed but probably read concern on Rachel's face. *"I'm kidding, Rachel. You can do this."*

"But I haven't mastered a canter yet, let alone a gallop."

"Just walk or trot," Presley encouraged again.

This was the end of the year, the final show. Rachel, riding Marco, was the last entry after a twelve-hour day in the saddle. Every competitor and equine was starved, crusted in layers of dust and exhausted, ready to go home. She and her horse had managed a position in the top five. Her mount was a child-safe quiet horse giving no reason to doubt that he could trot a triangle pattern of three barrels quietly.

Rachel recalled standing at the entry gate of the arena, watching the horses curve tight around the barrels, without touching, at lightning speed. Some leaned with such agility that the rider appeared to almost touch the dirt. The entire course was completed in less than twenty seconds. Dust clouds oscillated in the air. Spectators hollered and whistled, anything but a serene environment.

The excitement seemed to exhilarate Marco, who was quite a sizable bay. He normally stood with his head down and a dopey stare into the distance. Not a care in the world. However, that day he raised his head to the yelling and galloping mates. His sides swelled in increments until Rachel's legs felt shorter, pointing east and west instead of north and south. Marco's middle puffed out like the cylinder of a beer barrel. His quick snorts shocked her as he'd never so much as kicked out in objection. Perhaps this moment of panic was really her first anxiety attack and when she said her first prayer.

She'd shot a plea back at trainer Gert. Rachel wanted nothing more than to dismount, the words, *'I can't'* mouthing from her lips. Gert adamantly shook her head, an index finger stiffly pointed toward the opening gate, like a wicked witch sending Rachel to the dungeon of fire.

Rachel had eyed the judges; two men and one lady were sitting slouched in aluminum lawn chairs by the left barrel. Their Stetson hats rested above stern brows. Their lips flatlined as all three tapped their clipboards, impatiently waiting to call time out on Rachel and go home.

As the clock ticked down, Rachel recalled searching the crowd for support as the gatekeeper called her number for the third and final time. She hesitated until she eyed Presley, Gigi and Wheezy hanging on the wooden rail, smiling, cheering her on in the distance. She didn't want to let them down.

By the time Marco and Rachel stood at the half open gate, the horse was like a cannon ready to fire. Suddenly the gatekeeper whipped it wide open with a "Let's go, lady! My dinner's waiting!"

The crowd rose to rapture, hungry as hell with hollers of hallelujahs. Rachel's mind went blank. She froze, her last year of endless lessons and preparations vanished. Marco's mind, on the other hand, shot into overdrive. His once cumbersome walk was now a high thundering prance. Rachel squeezed the reins tighter, pulling them like a winch to her lap.

Perhaps Marco confused her thumping heart as a squeeze, or perhaps Gert should have informed her the little girl who owned Marco loved to barrel race. Or maybe it was the agitated gatekeeper's swat on Marco's rump that rocketed him off at the speed of light, leaving Rachel stirrup-less and hanging on like a ragdoll. He skipped *walk*, leaped past *trot*, and ejected over the *canter* into fourth gear... the dreaded *gallop*.

Rachel remembered nothing after that point. She'd been in complete panic. Her body went stiff like a pogo stick, hitting the cantle hard, most certainly ticking Marco off. There was almost no way she could maintain her seat other than to squeeze him harder, a cue for the horse to proceed forward. Yes, the pattern was simple, but not when the rider's brain was bouncing at a hundred miles an hour. It was nothing more than a blur as Marco took it upon himself to conquer the course. He veered left instead of right.

Headed straight for the judges, Rachel could not maneuver a muscle to cue Marco to spin around the first barrel. She remembered the fear that smeared the faces of the two male judges previously plastered with boredom. The female judge's mouth was wide open in a scream, waving her to pivot Marco in the correct direction. With less than seconds to disaster, they had no choice but to scatter like ants.

Luckily no one was hurt, but the metal lawn chairs clattered as if blown by a tornado, bent at multiple angles. After Marco rammed through the chairs, he cut the right barrel out of the pattern and scored the third in a quick circle. The horse had one intention. It had been a long day for him too. He eyed the gate, and in a final thrusting buck he headed home.

Once over the finish line, his neck stretched and arched downward all the way back to the barn, where Marco, in a magical transformation, returned to his mopey self with a snort and a shoulder twitch.

She was still reflecting the next day. Rachel didn't realize she was laughing out loud at the memory until a client cleared her throat, the one she had squeezed in on her day off.

"Rachel, please hurry. I must get to the wedding."

The entire salon of customers was gazing her way with confused expressions. The other girls had ceased blowing and talking in the styling area. The rushing water at the shampoo bowls throttled back just like Marco.

"You seem to be having a terrible time with that credit card machine," the client later snipped. "And look here." She rammed a finger in her front bang area. "This is out of place. Rachel, you have to fix this."

Rachel flushed with embarrassment.

Suddenly a stylist called from the back, "Don't forget. There's a leak on the third shampoo bowl. Please call the plumber!"

The phone interrupted with consecutive rings. Rachel closed her eyes and inhaled. Twenty-plus years of this and she was going to be late to teach her Cinderella class.

A familiar hand touched hers. "Rachel." Roxie slipped the credit card into her own palm. "I got this. Go teach. Don't forget your bag."

Rachel gave in and seized the Cinderella bag.

Roxie stuck the credit card in the machine. "Oh and FYI, check your emails today. I took the liberty of looking up Wyndham Glick." Roxie cleared her throat. "And your old trainer Gertrude Steele. I provided you the information. If you have a free moment later today, you could look them up."

Rachel snapped her coat shut and squinted at her assistant. She searched for the words to protest, yet something detained her. She merely whispered a thank you and left.

Rachel arrived at the Peach Tree Women and Imaging Center right on the nose. The director, Fran, was in the office next to the classroom where Rachel would oversee the Cinderella program. She was setting up the wigs, makeup kits and scarf displays at each of the six women's assigned places when Fran peeked around the corner.

"Morning, Rachel. I have a favor."

"Hello. Of course." Rachel could never say no even before she heard the question. "Sure."

"Listen, I have a lady who missed the first round of the Cinderella classes." Fran was scanning the paperwork through her pince-nez. "And we owe her a complimentary makeup kit. She is one of Dr. Offelson's patients. The nurse called me to let us know she has a follow-up appointment today in his office at 12:15. I wondered if you could drop the kit off and give her the information. Introduce yourself and let her know if she needs anything, we are here."

"Of course," Rachel answered.

"I have a lunch meeting, and it would be so helpful. As usual, I am only permitted to give you the last name until you sign the HIPAA notice." Fran laid the papers down, still sifting through them. "You could give her this bag on your way out. The patient's name is Petrone."

"Sure, Fran." Rachel took the paper. "I don't mind. My daughter's leaving for an internship. I have nothing else to do but join the Rosary Society."

"Ahh, honey." Fran appeared sympathetic. "Come on. You've been so involved with people, so giving to others. Maybe it's time to start a hobby?"

"I'm having trouble thinking of life without Jemma. Here I am a little under accomplished."

"Are you kidding?" Fran hugged her. "You give to your clients, your daughter, and you made quite a difference here. Maybe you're due for a little rejuvenation."

"Rejuvenation?" Rachel whispered. "That's funny."

"You look as though I said something wrong."

Rachel smiled. "Oh, I've been hearing that word a lot." She took the extra makeup bag and placed it to the side next to her purse. "That's what others have been telling me." Rachel studied the tag stapled to the gift bag. "Petrone?" The name sounded familiar.

"She was on the schedule months ago but had to cancel. I found the gift bag in the back closet. Could you see that she receives it? Evidently, she's been through a critical series of treatments."

"At your service, and hers."

For the next hour and a half, Rachel concentrated on the six women gathered at the u-shaped table surrounding her. Three were suffering with the effects of cancer, two with severe anxiety and one with Alopecia. Their somber expressions transformed to beaming smiles as she demonstrated makeup application, wigs and scarf options. It warmed Rachel's heart. Who was she to pity herself because of age and an empty nest?

"Well, ladies, look at you all." She spread her arms. "You are rockin' it! God bless you all." Rachel began cleaning up as attendees exchanged numbers with their new support system of comrades.

Rachel caught herself in one of the mirrors as she placed it in her tote. She scrunched her pearly highlights to refresh, mixing the grey with her blonde streaks. "An inverted bob of grey hair under a cowgirl hat? How would that work?" She eyed her watch. "Oh no, I've got to get moving! 12:10." She had to deliver the makeup kit. The paper Fran had handed her read Petrone, Room 32B at 12:15.

Rachel gathered the wigs, assorted scarves, brushes, extra makeup, mirrors, placemats and other contents, recklessly stuffing them in the containers. Some of the ladies attempted to help, but Rachel urged them to mingle and share stories. She missed her wing-woman Roxie, always neatly organizing, setting the stage, greeting the patients, and packing Rachel's bag. Perhaps it was Roxie's time to take the lead.

With that thought, Rachel dashed toward the door. The paper with the office number was peeking out of the tote so she could see it, the makeup kit for Ms. Petrone cradled in her bent elbow. Rachel forgot she had no free hand to say farewell so when she tried to wave, a tote dropped to the floor. A handsome male physician walked past, smiled and reached down, retrieving the bag with its contents haphazardly bursting from the unzippered top. He placed the bag back in her hand and attempted to speak, but she bulldozed past him with a thank you. As usual, no time for a flirtatious encounter.

Unfortunately, the paper with the office number was flipped backward on top of the tote. She couldn't read the number. As she sped down the Peach Tree corridor, Rachel read every doctor's name out loud until someone finally offered assistance. Room 32B was on the second floor. Upon discovery, Rachel burst in the door, and a room of startled patients looked up as if a train had railroaded through the building.

The receptionist quickly rose, then shook her head. She returned to her seat with a disgusted stare.

"I'm sorry." Rachel eyed the clock on the wall—12:14. Catching her breath, she said, "I'm looking for a Ms. Petrone. I have a gift bag from the Cinderella Program... that she was due to receive and..."

The woman on the other side of the desk was not amused.

"You do know Fran, don't you? Well, she pilots the program..." Rachel was rambling and carelessly trying to organize her hands in order to set the bag on the desk.

The woman was making her nervous. Again, another tote dropped to the floor, and a man in his fifties stood to help her. He towered above her, then bent down. Rachel thought momentarily, *Two handsome men in one day, wow.*

As he rose to help her, his face looked older, but familiar.

"Did you say Petrone?" he asked, reaching to help free her hands.

Rachel was shifting her gear to take the bag, or hand him another, she wasn't sure.

"She did." The receptionist shook her head, annoyed.

"I'm a Mister Petrone, if that counts."

Rachel froze as another tote dropped to the floor. "Well, I don't think this kit was for a Mister." Rachel attempted a joke as she sifted to find the paper from Fran.

Simultaneously, a slender woman in a pink baseball cap rose and stepped toward them. The hat caught Rachel's attention because of the rhinestone horseshoe. It read, *Let's ride.*

Rachel assumed the woman was the patient, as befit the Cinderella classes. Her heart ached for this lady. However, she sensed something familiar, too. Rachel recognized her eyes.

"Well, I'm Mrs. Petrone." The woman came to stand next to the man.

He smiled, wrapping an arm around her. Rachel hesitated to respond.

"The one and only," he announced, clearly proud of her.

"Presley?" Rachel couldn't help but question. "And Brad Petrone, right?"

The taller woman tilted her head. She slightly raised the brim of her hat, revealing a scrunch in her forehead.

"It's me." Rachel grinned from ear to ear. "Rachel Snow. Well, it wasn't Snow when you knew me. But you two were dating when we knew each other before." Rachel was babbling. "Let me—"

"From riding over thirty years ago," Presley interrupted. "You rode Marco, right?"

"Well, look at that smile," her husband remarked. "On both you ladies. Must be contagious."

"This is Rachel, the woman in the picture." Presley appeared to ebb an aura of disbelief.

"Oh my gosh, not the picture of the four of us?" Rachel's eyes widened.

"Yes, yes, I was just looking at it. Do you still have it too? It's been hanging in the barn all these years. I never expected to see you again."

"Sweet Mary. You're kidding. I've looked at that photo every day at work for the last several decades!" Rachel sighed. "I dream about that year all the time."

"How did you even recognize me? If you haven't noticed, I don't have hair and I look..."

"You look fabulous. I could never forget your face. Especially under a hat. Though usually a *cowgirl* hat!" Rachel exaggerated the word cowgirl. "I was envious of the way you dressed and rode with style."

"Girls." Brad tried to gain their attention in a soft request.

"Are you still riding?" Presley reached toward her.

"Saint Agnes, no! Look at me. I'm a few pounds overweight." Rachel leaned closer, and she whispered her age. "But you were a born equestrian."

"I haven't had much energy the last few months. And the years before that... well, we were traveling. I have three boys."

Brad's voice heightened. "Ladies."

"How ironic! I was staring at the same picture in the barn last evening."

"I was telling my daughter how put together you are. She wanted to know who the woman was with all the beautiful hair."

"I miss my hair."

Rachel filled with guilt. She reached a free hand to touch Presley. "You have an unforgettable glow. The hair will grow back. I wish you would've come to the Cinderella class. I would've loved to help you."

"You still have that same caring concern." Presley's grin returned.

"I am a mess, that's what I am. And I still leave a trail like horse's manure." Rachel squeezed Presley's hand. They both chuckled.

"Ahem."

They both looked at Brad.

"I don't know about that," Presley said, "but we sure had fun, didn't we?"

"Memories that lasted a lifetime." Rachel's voice almost hummed.

The receptionist leaned over her desk, her pen aimed at the clock. "The doctor will see you now, Mrs. Petrone. He does have a schedule to keep."

Presley's smile disappeared instantly. She stepped back, and Rachel let her hand slip away.

"I have to..." Presley pointed to the door leading to the doctor's office. "I am finding out if... well, it doesn't matter. I'm so happy to see you. If I hadn't come here today for this diagnosis, we would not have seen each other."

"God works in mysterious ways." Rachel remembered the gift bag pressed under her arm. "Oh, wait. This is for you. A gift from the Cinderella program and Peach Tree Center. Hopefully this will help you feel better." She tried to hand Presley the bag, but Brad stopped her.

The two women faced him with almost identical obscure stares.

"Presley, Rachel, I have an idea. I want to see that colossal smile on both your faces again. Let me give you our number." He pointed to Rachel. "You can help Presley with the makeup since she missed the original class. Then maybe reminisce about the horsey stuff. I can arrange it all. Agreed?"

Neither Presley nor Rachel had to look up to confirm. Instead both answered in unison, "Agreed."

Chapter 8

Presley was leaning forward on her childhood vanity in the bedroom that was once again hers. A muted-gold folder containing her diagnosis sat next to the riding picture from thirty years earlier. She tapped on the envelope as Brad entered carrying a glass of red wine.

"Here you go, cowgirl. Bet you never thought you'd be having wine in this bedroom." He set the glass on the vanity.

"You are making me a wino, but thank you." She rested her cheek on her fist. Presley studied Brad as he sat on the edge of the bed.

"A wino and a cowgirl." He noted she was wearing the hat from her birthday.

"Brad, Doc Offelson said I have to wait an entire year to officially be declared in remission!"

"What's one year? Look how fast the decades have gone by, in the blink of an eye. Plus, the doctor didn't say to hibernate, now did he?" He neared to kiss the top of her prickly head.

"All those years I couldn't wait for you to retire so we could settle somewhere in the country. Well, here I am, sick. The golden years?" Presley frowned. "Why didn't I enjoy that moment in time?" She fingered the picture.

"First, little lady, we are far from our golden years. You skipped a decade or something?" He grinned. "Second, the doctor said all your results appear to be exceptional. You need to continue the experimental drug for twelve months. Then officially they can document that you are in remission."

"I've been through chemo and losing my hair, now another year!"

"Today may be the best day you get, baby. Don't dwell on the future." Brad knelt to the floor, then encircled her hands in his. "Honey, I took this job so you could fulfill that dream. I've been captivated with my career and seemed to forget your hopes. I remember when you were in that competition with those girls. I fell in love with that contagious smile you had when you rode. You ended second in the nation in versatility. Missed by only a few points because your horse suffered an injury. You are a natural."

"Cleo's too old. Besides, I didn't miss by a few points." Presley's voice elevated. "The title was stolen from me. It should have been mine. All the hard work, the teamwork..." A fervor rushed through Presley.

Brad obviously noticed and stepped back. "Whoa, there's my baby girl! I am behind you one hundred percent. If you want to find another horse, if you think Cleo is too old, well, we have a gift from your father. This trainer Gertrude Steele... maybe she can help."

"You have an answer for everything." Presley sipped her wine, as if to clamp down her excitement, because inside, her heart was thumping from the real possibility of riding again.

Both Presley and Brad turned to the door when Jamie gently peeked his head in the bedroom. "Mom, I think I should reschedule the study abroad trip. I could spend time with you."

Brad didn't say a word.

Presley set the glass down. "Are you kidding? What would you do here? First, I have a lot of remodeling to do. I need to update this old farmhouse. Secondly, young man, I am going to be busy riding."

"Mom?"

"You're not going to believe this, but I ran into someone today from the photo. Did I ever tell you about the Versatility title that was stolen from us thirty years ago?" Presley rose, picture in hand.

She snuggled an arm around Jamie who towered over.

"Let's go light a fire and have some hot chocolate. I can tell you a story you are not going to believe about your old mom and a woman with nerves as cold as steel."

She heard Brad whisper as she led Jamie back to the farmhouse kitchen. "God sure does work in mysterious ways."

Rachel could barely corral her anticipation as she drove into Presley's farm lane outside of Springfield. Brad had arranged a private lunch since Presley had some lingering bouts of nausea and light-headedness. This would allow Rachel to comfortably demonstrate scarves and makeup with Presley, and talk "horsey stuff," as he'd termed it.

One thing for sure, Rachel's insides were bubbling with so much warmth that she ignored the frigid weather as she walked the bricked sidewalk to the front door of the matching brick farmhouse. Stepping onto the large porch with spindle railings that wrapped the entire length, she shifted her wool sweater. Her knee-high, leather boots were crusted from the thin layer of snow, and she stamped them on the welcome mat.

Rachel stole a moment to tuck her hair behind her ears and breathe deep, then she raised her fist to knock.

Presley must have been standing directly on the other side, waiting, because she opened the door instantly.

Once escorted inside, the friendship rekindled as if the fire was never extinguished. Logs crackled behind the orangish blue tint of tempered glass, and the room was furnished with a carnival of antiques and modern touches.

Rachel sat Presley on an antique oak chair where the chandelier from above best lit her work area. The makeup kit rested on a marble-topped table with thick spindled legs, curled on the bottom into lion paws. With each brush of blush and stroke of lip gloss, the two stopped and shared a memory about the year that forever stained their hearts.

"Remember how poor we were? Trying to pay training fees and horse boarding at our age." Rachel stepped back, the facial sponge moistened in hand. "I was so determined, I worked three jobs."

Presley opened her eyes. "Mere twenty-year-olds. We were up against those spoiled children whose parents bought them the best horses and clothes—the more glitter and fringe the better.

Remember the blingy belts with buckles the size of our once tiny waists!" Presley squeezed her sides.

"Well, your middle is still skinny. Besides you probably lost some weight this past year. What's my excuse!" Rachel raised her arms in the air. "I love sweets, not to mention wine. Of course, I'm not doing an ounce of exercise."

Rachel rambled on until Presley interrupted. "You look great." Presley's almond eyes widened. They appeared more striking with the added liner Rachel had applied.

"And your eyes are brilliant," Rachel replied. "Wait until you see them. I understand you lost a lot of your eyelashes. Most patients do, but liner can help give those babies a pop."

Rachel dabbed on some *Pink Paradise* eyeshadow, then handed Presley a small mirror.

"We made our own show jackets, remember?" Rachel continued. "We would go to the fabric store and have Gertrude Steele's partner sew for us. I know mine are in a trunk or closet somewhere. I never had the nerve to throw them out."

"Me neither," Presley agreed.

"Always thought I would return to riding." Rachel touched Presley's cheek with a stroke of blush for added color.

Presley gripped Rachel's wrist, preventing her sponge from moving. "Even if it was with Gertrude Steele?"

"The mention of her name gives me the creeps. But it *was* one of the best years in my life. I followed my heart for once." Rachel continued. "If Gertrude Steele hadn't failed us, you would have most likely been number one in your division. I thought I would read about you some day."

Presley dropped her hand from Rachel's wrist. "Remember Wyndham Glick? The tall, dark sensation! He was the one that signed our shirts in black Scripto marker. He wrote *Follow your heart* and his signature. I saved that shirt... somewhere."

"The handsome horse whisperer. How could one forget?" Rachel whispered. "He was one sexy Brazilian."

"Quite honestly, someone stole the Versatility award. I never believed Gert was capable of what others later accused her. Even though she was cold as steel. Excuse the pun." Presley's tone turned serious. "Another trainer made the initial claim. Gert may have been harsh on her students, but never the horses."

"There was something strange about that trainer. Remember when we needed an extra tail bag after bathing Marco? That guy lent it to us. Unfortunately, it was vibrant red. The next morning when I slid it off Marco's tail, it swished a lovely hue of red. All because I secured it when his tail was soaking wet after his rinse down." Rachel was holding back a chuckle. "I bathed him, I swear, five times to no avail. He became the gelding everyone called Big Red. You think they set me up?"

The two laughed in unison. "Well, one thing it taught us—always wash new blankets and tail bags before use, eh?"

"Gigi was appalled," Presley said. "Everything embarrassed her!"

Rachel bent over the makeup table laughing. "That girl, everything had to be perfect... without her doing the dirty work."

"Her parents made her perform community service with the diversity project. They probably thought it would help her attitude, but she acted like Wheezy was her assistant instead of a comrade on the team." Presley's eyes were sparkling from the makeup and perhaps the conversation.

"Wheezy was so determined. I wonder what happened to her?" Presley settled back, cradling the small mirror on her lap.

Neither heard Brad clear his throat from the doorway.

"I was laughing in bed last night. Do you remember when we ran the barrel pattern, and I scared the judges right off their chairs?"

"Ladies," Brad interjected. "I hate to interrupt the smiles, but dinner is served."

When Rachel turned toward him, Presley was in full view.

"Honey, you are absolutely gorgeous."

Presley and Rachel both giggled. "Thanks to Rachel."

The two continued chattering at the table. Brad could barely sneak in a word, but he clearly didn't mind.

"Hey, I have a great idea!" Presley said. "How about you and your husband come out to dinner with Brad and me? I bet the four of us would have a good time." Presley was about to indulge another sip of wine when she noticed Rachel's sudden dismal expression.

"I mean, I have so few friends around since we just moved back, being an Army wife…" She hesitated. "Have I said something wrong?"

Rachel twirled the wedding ring on her finger. "I haven't taken this off in fifteen years. I'm no longer married."

Presley slipped Brad a glance. "I saw your ring and assumed. Divorced?"

"Widow. My daughter and I have been alone since she was four."

Both Brad and Presley appeared stunned. "We're so very sorry. How did he…?" Presley stopped, obviously concerned she might be prying. "You must have had to work very hard?"

A silence lingered except for Brad collecting the silverware from the table.

Rachel changed the subject. She didn't want to talk about Heath's death, not now while her dreams seemed within reach. "Did I tell you my daughter was an accomplished equestrian? We still have a horse leased until the end of this month. Too bad the gelding isn't being ridden."

"Well girls, I have a proposal for both of you." Brad continued to clear the table as he spoke. "Better than dinner. Since I'm going to be quite busy with my new position, and it seems you both have a horse that needs ridden…"

"Hannibal?" Rachel meekly responded. "Oh, no. I can't ride my daughter's horse."

Presley muttered, "The horse's name is Hannibal?"

Brad ignored them. "Yes, you both need to revive your old hobby. Think of it as helping one another. Presley needs to keep her mind off her diagnosis, and you need to enjoy life, it seems."

Rachel shook her head. "Not you too? Have you been chatting with my daughter and friend Roxie?"

Presley was staring at Rachel. "I see smoke."

"What?" Rachel studied her, confused.

"You know when we rode, how we read each other's minds?" Presley explained. "I'm reading yours. We would be following our hearts, like Wyndham Glick wrote on our shirts that we never washed. Maybe we could even look him up."

"I have the perfect way to start," Brad called from the kitchen as he loaded the dishwasher. "There's a rodeo right at Camry Center in Bennington."

"Are you kidding? That's downtown center city. I wonder how they stall the horses."

"Probably underground, don't you think?" Presley perked up.

"Well, you can both find out, tomorrow," Brad said. "I have errands to run in Bennington before I report to Fort Meade on Monday, so I can drop you both off. Then later I'll take you and Presley to dinner where arrangements can be discussed to schedule riding lessons… perhaps with this Gertrude Steele?"

They eyeballed Brad in unison. "You have this all planned, don't you?" Presley sipped her wine.

He winked at her.

"Well?" Presley looked to Rachel. "Wouldn't it be something if we ran into the other girls from the picture? I always wondered what happened to Gigi and Wheezy. I'm a go if you are."

Rachel didn't have to respond. Presley read her mind.

Presley watched as Rachel's lights faded down the driveway. Brad stoked the fire, then came to her at the window.

"Well, Mr. Petrone, you are a remarkable husband. What would I do without you? I can't imagine what Rachel went through."

"I don't think the two of you finding each other was mere coincidence. She sure made you smile and look pretty." He wrapped his arms around her from behind and kissed her neck. "But of course, you were already pretty. Now you glow."

"It's one thing to attend the rodeo, another to ride. How would I even trailer the horse? You won't have time." She noticed a bright silver belt buckle sitting on the table where Rachel's makeup case had been. Her prize for reserve, second place. "You brought my buckle in from the barn."

"Yes. You'll need it for your belt. And we'll figure everything else out."

Presley pressed back into his body as he cocooned her. Tomorrow seemed like light years away, but so had age fifty when she was twenty. She touched the belt buckle, *reserve,* which was one step away from champion, then the picture of the four women. Suddenly, she forgot about her age, about Jamie leaving, that she was bald as a cue stick, and about her diagnosis. All those negative thoughts were replaced by a dream of capturing the champion title in a Silver Spur versatility competition.

Once home, Rachel raced upstairs and opened the massive trunk at the foot of the bed, not a thought about Jemma, Roxie or clients in her head. She was on a mission and knew exactly where the old show clothes were hidden. In the chest. She pushed the lid up, shocked when it fell back with a slam, almost smashing her hand.

Slow down.

She reopened the chest cautiously then secured the latch. With a deep breath, Rachel peered in.

She'd been prepared for the smell of old musty barn and putrid worn clothes. Yet, a potent aroma of leather and horse burst into the room as if freed from a lifetime of imprisonment.

Rachel rummaged through the contents, her hands working frantically. The square-toed boots still fit. But the Wrangler jeans zipper only went halfway up. Fifteen pounds over? Try twenty.

Rachel slumped forward. She held up a blue blazer of glitter which had lost many series of rhinestones. She had worn the jacket at practically every show.

Finally wrestling her arms and shoulders into its sleeves, Rachel stared in the mirror with a frown of disgust. Her broader shoulders would not allow her arms to bend. And when she tried to heave them together, the back seam released a retching tear.

"Mom, what are you doing?"

Rachel was shocked. "Jemma. You surprised me." She fought the imprisoning material to remove her arms. "Why would I even think to wear any of this again?" She pulled the hat down on her head. "And look at this pearly grey inverted bob. What cowgirl looks like this?"

"Mom, you can buy new clothes. Tuck your hair behind your ear." Jemma fiddled with the hair under Rachel's hat, but she kept up the resistance.

"Look at me. The wrinkles. The out of shape body. Why would I think I could mount a horse? Let alone devote the time and money. How many clients would have to move their appointments? And really, this middle-aged woman on Hannibal. Ridiculous! People my age attend church events and pray because we are in the last phase of life."

Jemma continued to assist in her usual calm manner. "Like Roxie says, things happen if you open your heart. God miraculously put something in your lap. Stop making excuses. There's a horse waiting for you. You have money and time."

Rachel ignored her, continuing to wrestle with the jacket. "And what about a trailer? I can't drive a trailer even if I had one. Hell, I crashed the lawn tractor the first day I bought it. That's why I have a yard service..."

"Mom, stop." Jemma pressed her arms down, freezing her position. They both stared at the reflection in the mirror.

"Honey, I can't cancel my clients. They would be so angry. And I don't have your abilities to ride Hannibal."

Jemma let her mother rant while she handed her a tissue. "Roxie can take care of it. Stop being afraid. You know who will be angry one day? Rachel Snow, for not following her dream." Her daughter spun her to the mirror. "So, buckle up, buttercup."

That night, alone in bed, Rachel had a feeling... ESP again. She touched the image of Presley in the picture, excited to go to the rodeo. She found herself lying in bed dreaming about winning a barrel run even at age forty-nine, racing for the finish gate on a behemoth bay horse named Hannibal.

Chapter 9

Wheezy

Wheezy straightened her uniform name tag as if using a level. Louisa Mae Valspar examined her reflection in a full-length mirror behind her office door. She hung it the moment she had been promoted. As a Black woman, she wanted to emerge impressive, especially in this work environment. This position was her last stop before reaching her goal, the aspiration she'd worked twenty-plus years to achieve.

Wheezy surveyed herself one more time then caught the reflection of a picture on the desk behind her. The photo of four women, decades ago. She'd had another dream, once. Unfortunately, that dream never came to fruition, and for good reason.

She adjusted the collar of her coffee shaded uniform for F.G. Transport, a renowned trucking company. Brown wasn't the best shade to highlight her nearly flawless skin. She was proud of her heritage, a conviction her grandmother instilled in her. The valiant woman raised Wheezy and implanted the motto that she could accomplish anything.

Today and every day, Wheezy tucked a scarf impeccably in her collar. Usually gifted from her grandmother, sometimes from her children, all were made of material and colors like burnt orange and yellow that enhanced her appearance. Today more than ever, Wheezy burst with brilliance from her lucky scarf, a blue and white hydrangea pattern, her grandmother's favorite flower.

Wheezy stroked the sides of her slicked back hair leading into a manageable ponytail. The ebony strands appeared iced over, making the white strands glisten, every one of which she'd earned.

Wheezy returned to her desk weighted with thoughts of how she had labored for twenty years. She had left an abusive man in her early twenties, raised two children solo, and returned to school while caring for her grandmother until the woman's very last breath. She observed the time on her phone—five minutes until Frank Galzone would be parading through her office door to promote her as the next CEO.

Frank treated Wheezy as an equal. She had made it her mission not to be considered as a woman of color, but instead as a valuable team member. The entire company of mostly men, at present, regarded Wheezy as a highly effective leader. The only obstruction was the smooth-talking Asher Devine, a thirty-five-year-old cocky thorn in her side.

Asher tried to sabotage any project Wheezy touched. He'd vied to steal clients like Randall Emerson and block any possibility of her becoming CEO. Wheezy was also aware that Frank Galzone's stance regarding her had not wavered, despite Asher's failed attempts.

She organized her desktop as she had the previous one hundred times that morning—two pens, the land line phone, her computer, and an oversized date calendar which helped her never to miss a detail. She repositioned the three pictures in a perfect overlapping arc on the left corner... her grandmother, who ironically was wearing the exact hydrangea scarf she wore today, her two devoted and successful children, and the photo of herself as one of four women from the past. She touched the gold frame of the latter and fixated on the other three ladies.

Wheezy still remembered their names. She flicked the face of Gigi Tetless. *Miss Priss, if you could see me today! I'm not driving a horse trailer, but I am about to manage one of the largest trucking firms on the East Coast. We each made a promise that day. I certainly fulfilled mine.*

Gigi had essentially ubered her every day to the farm of Gertrude Steele where Wheezy cleaned stalls, groomed horses and dreamt of driving the trailer. Wheezy's grandmother had enrolled her in a diversity program at the local YWCA to immerse her namesake in circles other girls from her community never thought possible.

That summer, Wheezy fell in love with every aspect of horses. Handling an animal she was grossly afraid of—that willingly responded to her touch—impacted her. Especially, the day Gertrude Steele offered her a chance behind the wheel, steering the one-ton pickup truck towing a ten-thousand-pound trailer. When she'd felt powerless in the rest of her life, those opportunities transformed her soul.

Unfortunately, after that year her grandmother fell ill. Wheezy had no assistance until she met a man she'd like to forget. Wheezy's friendships disappeared, and she became pregnant with twins, broke and caring for a lot more than she alone could handle. Horses would never be a part of her world; the sport was too expensive, and she had no time. All that remained were the memories and a picture.

Wheezy's confidence was marred by the toxic relationship. With her grandmother's coaxing she'd returned home. Wheezy could help tend to the older woman's failing health while her grandmother helped with the only gift the abusive man left—her two children, Thurston and Adele. Wheezy bravely ditched her deadbeat husband and applied for a job at F.G. Transport. Her grandmother insisted she had enough energy to watch the toddlers with help from neighbors. The small firm transported commodities like vehicles and horses. She remembered observing the rigs as they rolled into horseshow venues for those fortunate equestrians who didn't have to worry about their mounts. They simply needed to show up, dressed and ready to ride. It had been a way for Wheezy to stay close to horses and at the same time fulfill her dream of driving a rig.

The local vocational school offered a five-month course for her CDL license. Wheezy signed on. However, driving forward versus in reverse were two different skills. She almost quit. Then one of the instructors suggested she take a side job mowing his lawn. "If you can back up a lawn tractor with a cart, you can back up that rig."

That advice launched her mission. On weekends, she mowed for anybody who owned a cart and tractor. For every row she mowed, she would back the cart and tractor then mow the next. The process was painstaking and grueling, endless hours of studying and practice. But almost thirty years later, Wheezy could back up a semi better than any man or woman at the facility.

Another advantage that developed from working with Gertrude Steele, Wheezy could manage a horse that normally refused to load—without tranquilizers. That placed her in the forefront with equestrian owners like Randall Emerson, Sr. He always requested Wheezy. That's when Frank Galzone had noticed her.

The company paid for her continuing education in exchange for a B average. Of course, Wheezy accepted nothing short of an A, finally graduating Magna Cum Laude with a business degree. F.G. even helped her complete a masters degree and advance her twins through college.

As the firm grew to one of the largest on the east coast, Wheezy was promoted. Her current office came with a six-figure salary and her own personal assistant, Stan Bumble. Unfortunately, her grandmother never lived to see that.

Her pondering was abruptly interrupted by the intercom. Stan was speaking as if in a tunnel, excited yet whispering. Wheezy imagined him cupping the device with his hand like a soup ladle.

"Wheezy!" Stan took a breath. "They're coming down the hall now!"

"They?" Wheezy questioned.

"I mean pronto! This is the moment you've been waiting for! The office I have been waiting for..." His voice lowered. "The one on the third floor, with its own elevator that goes everywhere—the breakroom, the loading dock, the lobby, the management division, even warehouse storage."

"Stan, pull yourself together. I got this and so do you. I have my lucky scarf on."

Wheezy was tough as nails. She never let anyone see her sweat. She was one hundred percent confident the position was hers.

"Put your big girl pants on, Stan."

"Okay, but remember, you are taking me with you! I want a new desk in front of the wall of windows. Finally, windows!"

Wheezy smiled at his childlike exhilaration. Stan was a wonderful assistant, sometimes wry, definitely gay, and completely dedicated. He was unsurpassed in his abilities, a master with numbers, and Wheezy had every intention of taking him to the elite third-floor office with her.

"Maybe you can purchase a horse one day… with a trailer!" he joked. "Or… is that a trailer with a horse? Ha."

"Stanley, please. Send them in when they arrive."

She imagined Stan sashaying the owner to her office. As he opened the door, Wheezy set the picture in perfect line with the others and straightened her posture.

"Good morning, Louisa." Frank Galzone strictly used her full name, and she liked that respect from him. A full-bodied, lofty man with a hooked nose and rosy cheeks, he was in his early eighties but didn't appear a day over seventy.

"Come in," Wheezy greeted with a smile.

He scanned the office. There were no windows, and Wheezy had painted the room a soft yellow trimmed in white, with hydrangea wallpaper on the back wall. The room beamed with the same brightness as her scarf.

"You are a gleaming star," he announced.

Wheezy stood taller, preparing for the good news. "Thank you, sir." At that exact second, her phone, on silence, vibrated with a text. She angled her eyes to the desktop. It was Stan.

Frank is not alone.

She didn't comprehend exactly what Stan meant.

Frank proceeded forward with the same strut and confidence she exhibited when inspecting the loading area. Then she understood Stan. Once Frank's oversized six-foot stature stepped into the room, a compact man pressed in behind. He was petitely framed, lucky if he surpassed five feet in height and one-hundred-forty-five in weight, but well maintained and brash as Napoleon in attitude. To Wheezy's dismay it was Asher Devine.

"Wheezy, good day."

"Mr. Galzone, Asher." Best to use formalities at a meeting of this caliber, she thought.

The older man cleared his throat oddly. "I'm here for two reasons. First, to announce the next CEO of my company. As you know, I must step away for health reasons. However, a complication has been brought to my attention."

Asher tossed an arrogant smirk at Wheezy and surged in to slide out the chair for Frank with his free hand. In his other, he clutched a manilla file.

Wheezy squinted, wondering exactly what Asher was scheming.

Then he sat next to Frank, steepled his hands, tapping the tips of his fingers together as if playing the keys of a piano.

Wheezy continued to stand, holding her position as if in battle.

Complication? What exactly was Frank talking about? This could only involve a trick of Asher's.

Stan peeked his head into the doorway.

"Stan," Frank waved him in. "Join us. This involves you, too."

Stan instantly winked at Wheezy and melded against the flowered wallpaper.

"Louisa, please have a seat." Frank waited for her to sit, then snapped his fingers at Asher.

Asher placed the file onto her desk. It read *Louisa Mae Valspar,* in Asher's handwriting.

Wheezy glanced at the folder, narrowed eyes at Asher, then locked on Frank.

"Louisa, I called this meeting with every intention of asking you to fill the position as CEO."

Stan celebrated with a burst. "Yes!"

Frank smiled, but Wheezy maintained eye contact.

"However," Frank continued. "You could say I'm now calling this a... temporary internship."

Wheezy scrunched her forehead. "Internship, sir? Temporary?"

"God willing, my health will improve, and I'll be back as CEO. If what's in the file proves wrong, then the position is yours, Louisa. I will promote you as CEO permanently."

Wheezy leaned forward. "I don't understand."

She could hear Stan's rapid breaths from the corner.

"Asher has brought pertinent information to my attention that has severely affected my decision. I was shocked and devastated."

Wheezy's heart sank with the weight of a cruise ship anchor, however, she remained expressionless. "What exactly are you implying?"

"Louisa, Asher," Frank addressed them. He slid the folder her way, opened to a stack of spreadsheets, with dates, numbers, and names of clients. "These document shipment loads and weight amounts... Asher has pointed out a number of infractions. Shipments have been permitted to be overweight. Right here." Frank tapped the end lines after each entry. "Of course, someone forged the amounts. Is this your signature?"

Frank did not wait for Wheezy to answer. "And this is a USB clip with the correct load weights—data Asher has been tracking under the wire." Frank hesitated. "Louisa, you didn't need to falsify documents. You could have talked to me directly if you thought the company was in trouble rather than attempt to make us look more efficient."

Stan gasped. This time he slapped a hand across his mouth. Wheezy snubbed his emotions.

"Let me get this straight. You are accusing me of allowing too much weight, then forging documents to appear the weight was correct?"

"Louisa, the documents are stating this, not me. Please listen. For this reason, I am selecting Asher to the position of CEO. Clients like Emerson Equine LLC and others in the horse world will be watching. News like this would trickle down to our investors; we will lose business. The Feds will surely show up. So, I must tidy up the matter before they rear their ugly heads to investigate."

Wheezy could no longer hold back. "You know me, Frank. Asher is lying. Clearly, he's attempting to destroy your reputation and mine."

Asher tilted into Frank. "Like I reported, sir, she would say that. No woman in her fifties, especially a bl—"

"What did you say?" Wheezy sprang up.

Frank raised his palm. Asher receded, streaking a hand through his flawless coif.

"I do know you. But rules must be followed. My father and grandfather prided themselves on decades of a family company based on morals and diversity. I was excited for a woman of your caliber to become the next CEO. Set a precedent. However, Asher has threatened to present this information to the authorities if we do not investigate ourselves. My hands are tied."

"And you believe him?"

"He has the proof."

Asher attempted to intercept.

Again, Frank held a hand for silence. "But so help him, if Asher has lied..."

Asher shifted in his seat and pressed two fingers to his eyelids. Probably to avoid Wheezy's stare.

Wheezy focused back to the owner. "Frank, I would never betray the company values. I have followed those standards."

"That I am positive about, but I can't have this over my head or the company. So, for this period of internship, Asher will fill the shoes of CEO. Reality is, Asher has been named in the Top 40 Under 40-year-olds according to *East Coast Business* magazine. Graduated top of his class from an Ivy league school. His record is impeccable, one must admit. I'm left with no other option. I have to give him a chance, for the company."

Wheezy fixated on Frank's lips as he spouted a run-on paragraph. She heard ivy league, up and coming, and impeccable. Things were moving in slow motion like an old movie, his words a garbled mess, as though she was drunk. *Asher CEO.*

"What did you just say?" Stan probably didn't realize he'd spoken out loud.

"We must be vigilant. I promise to clear your name," Frank affirmed.

Asher extended his arm to confiscate the file.

Frank's hand landed on top of the file first with a slap. Stan jumped. "I'm on a time constraint and the file stays with me. I know we will get to the bottom of this before the authorities do an evaluation. That way we can keep Louisa's reputation and the company's clean."

"What does this mean to me?" Wheezy asked.

"I'm giving you a severance retainer. Let's say it's to hold my guarantee that the position is for you. This investigation may take nine months to a year."

Wheezy refused to display one twitch of emotion.

Asher was heaving to stand as if the meeting was complete. A furrow of success ironed between his eyes.

"Louisa, please try to understand," Frank soothed. "You deserve a vacation. Think of this next nine months as some downtime." Frank reached for the pictures that Wheezy once told him about. "Enjoy your children or take up that horsey hobby you told me about in this picture."

"I have been completely loyal to this company, Frank. I'm sure this has to do with my age, skin color or my biology." She shot a glare at Asher. "Not one of our other employees look at any of that. Except for Asher."

Asher shrugged then turned away, examining his recently clear-polished fingernails.

"Plus, the clients, Frank. He has no rapport with them."

"This is not permanent, Louisa," Frank reiterated.

Wheezy was finished. Her one concern was her assistant, who was sucking back tears in the corner.

"What about Stan?"

"Stan," Frank directed. "You will follow Asher to the CEO's office as his personal assistant. You will keep progress reported to me."

Stan appeared ambushed. He froze, his face smeared with contention and disbelief. He gawked at Wheezy for support.

Wheezy absentmindedly stroked the picture from the past.

"You make well over six figures, Louisa," said Frank. "I doubt you can find that anywhere else right now. Trust me, hang tight while we investigate this matter." Frank rose and headed toward the door as Asher puffed his chest and joined in behind the owner.

"Being at F.G. Transport was never about the money, Frank."

Wheezy's remark stopped Frank in his tracks. With head slouched forward, he continued out.

Asher manhandled the door with a slam, leaving Wheezy and Stan hushed in shock. As if that were necessary.

"Stan," Wheezy directed. "Would you please go to the packing department and retrieve me a box?"

Chapter 10

"Wheezy, think about what you are doing, please." Stan was fanning his face with one hand and refusing to release the last item from her desktop—a picture.

Wheezy snatched the riding photo of four women and placed it on top of the packing box.

"There is nothing to think about, Stan." Wheezy scanned the office. She had labored in a 12x12 room for the past three years. "I was so proud of working here," she mumbled as she lifted the container.

"The firm won't survive without you. Let me grab my things. I'm coming with you." Stan whirled around. "I can't work with Asher."

Wheezy stopped at the mirror behind her door. Her heart felt branded by a hot iron, directly under her name tag. Then she trailed Stan carrying her belongings.

He swayed his tight tush like a determined child. His left arm was swinging with a thrust of anger in each step.

"Stan, pull yourself together. Whether I return or not, you need to stay here to discover what Asher's scheming, at least for the company's reputation."

Stan faced her with lemur eyes and blinked back tears.

"Honestly, you are the most efficient personal assistant anyone could ask for. I'm not taking these accusations lightly. Asher's been attempting to sabotage me since he came to this company three years ago. Why would Frank listen to him? Or choose him as CEO?" Wheezy was almost inaudible at the end, thinking aloud.

"But you could stay on," Stan begged. "We could figure this out together. Like *Cagney and Lacey*. Plus, we're scheduled to transport horses for Emerson Equine on Thursday. The Cowtown Auction is in a week. They're one of our largest accounts, and they only talk to you for the arrangements. Don't leave me high and dry, standing in a pile of..."

"Stanley," she interrupted. "As I told Frank, I've taught my children dignity, as my grandmother taught me. Now, open the door, please."

Stan's hand was squeezing his hip so tight, his knee was jerking in a locked and unlocked position like a scolded child. Finally, he relinquished, wiped his tears, then obeyed.

Wheezy passed through to the main office area where over twenty workers nestled behind cubicles. At present most were standing, peering over to adjacent neighbors in conversation. Clearly, the news of her departure had spread. Wheezy inhaled, looked down at the top of her box, and as if drawing strength from the women staring at her, she elevated her chin.

Look at me now, ladies. Life changed as fast as a horse stopping on a dime.

She began a procession down the corridor toward the elevator, sickened to see Asher expecting her with the doors held open.

Whispers silenced as workers ogled her or dipped down into their cubicles pretending not to notice. Most expressed condolences with downturned lips. One lady reached out to touch Wheezy's arm. "We'll miss you so." Another blew in a tissue and nodded agreement.

Upon reaching the elevator, Wheezy lowered her eyes to Asher who wore an edgy hairstyle clippered with precision sides and a coif of waves lifted with a sheen on the top. His perfectly pressed Armani suit already bore a new name tag... Asher Devine, CEO.

Wow. How long had he known?

Wheezy could crush him, but not today. She remained unresponsive as if her heart stopped beating.

Asher stretched his manicured hand with the gold pinky ring to usher her onto the elevator, then whacked the button. "Going down."

He cursed her with a smirk as she pivoted and faced the room of fellow employees, the box containing twenty years of her life's work cradled in her arms. The doors inched closed seemingly so deliberately that the opening remained for what felt like an hour. She scanned the room of puzzled employees. Horror suspended on their faces as if Wheezy was on a descent to the electric chair.

Stan was propped against the wall at her office, mouthing as the door closed, *I will miss you.* Wheezy winked to console him and scanned the room, refusing to tear. That's when she eyed Frank Galzone. He stood in the back, arms folded, eyes locked on her as if his only child had gravely disappointed his trust.

Wheezy concentrated again on the picture. The women stared at her from the top of the files, smiling as if they had no cares in the world. "One more procession, ladies, and we're vanished from F.G. Transport."

The elevator opened to the loading dock where mostly men and a few women, adorned in matching brown uniforms, were all performing typical duties. The hustle halted as one notified another with an elbow or a cough. Over fifty dock employees, clearly in the know, locked attention on Wheezy. Forklifts stopped, garage doors ceased, computerized counting of the bills ended, and all loading of semis stood still. The only sound was the throaty engines and screeching air brakes of trucks backing in or out of bays.

A frigid winter cold motivated Wheezy to move at a brisk pace and avoid conversation as she marched the dock. At the far end, which seemed a football field in length away, was the foreman's booth which was the last point before the parking lot. Every employee entered that gate daily. Wheezy had passed through it at least twice a day for over twenty years. This would be her final time.

One man hollered, "You were a fine boss. Why'd you do it?"

Another affirmed, "No way she did."

The thought of the employees assuming she'd cheated singed her to the core.

Wheezy approached the foreman's booth spurred by resentment. She'd expected this day to be the highlight of her career. Instead, she was relinquishing her lanyard and clearance badge through the open window.

The foreman, Gator, shook his head. "I hope you can clear your name, Wheezy." He rubbernecked into the box she had set on the counter. "Hey, nice photo. Is that you when you were young, with a cowgirl hat? Wow, I never knew you liked horses, Wheezy. Wish I could have known you then."

Wheezy sighed. "That was a long time ago. Indirectly, the reason I love trucks and transporting."

"Wheezy?" He didn't understand her explanation but brushed it off. "What are you going to do now?"

She released the badge and studied the photo of those four women bursting with happiness. Wheezy's image popped, not because she was tall; Presley was the tallest of the four. Wheezy was dark—a rarity in the equestrian world then, and maybe even now.

Somehow her grandmother had managed to find a way for Wheezy to challenge the norm. *"Infiltrate,"* as she'd liked to term it. *"Be a groundbreaker, Wheezy."* Her grandmother taught her well.

She looked to Gator. "Oh, I will think of something, Gator. I always do."

Suddenly a scruffy bearded man, also in brown attire, raced across the loading platform. The human resource manager. "Wheezy. Hey, Wheezy!" He huffed, out of breath. "You can still do the rodeo tomorrow, right? You're the best we have. Our secret weapon."

Wheezy hesitated. "I can't. Besides, it's probably against the company rules."

"Come on, Wheezy, I already checked with Frank. It's an outside event even though it's F.G. Transport's team."

"Get someone else. How about Gator here?" Wheezy pointed to the foreman.

Gator ebbed his head back and pointed to the photo. "No way, not me. Looks like you're the rodeo queen."

Wheezy slouched. "Hardly, Gator."

"Wheezy, it's for the children, with cancer." The man pleaded and blocked her path to the parking lot. "Besides, there's no time to add an entry. Your name is on the rodeo competition card as the sole entry. It's too late. Come on, can't you win the purse for a good cause?"

"Wheezy?" Gator tapped the photo of her in the cowgirl hat.

"We'll see ya on Saturday at 6:00 AM. The Bennington Show Complex." The human resources manager flashed a smile without waiting for Wheezy's confirmation. "Here are the tickets. I gave you plenty. Bring your family. I promise it's for a noble cause."

"Call me tonight," Wheezy snapped, practically bulldozing past him. "I'll think on it."

Wheezy hoisted the box into her maroon F-350 Ford pickup. She remembered the moment she'd purchased every cowgirl's Cadillac dream. The truck was bought with her own funds, just like the two college educations of her children. Well, make that three, including her own. She'd settled on the lovely Tudor house in the suburbs on the edge of Bennington solo, too.

Wheezy wasn't afraid to walk away from the six-figure salary. The severance retainer would enable her to protect her investments. Her main concern was her reputation, which carried more weight than money.

She placed the rodeo entry tickets in the console, turned the key and listened to the Hemi purr. Then she headed home to break the news to the most valuable gifts in her life.

"Mom, what are you going to do? You should hire an attorney. I can't believe Frank Galzone believes any of these accusations."

Adele sipped her last swig of wine. Textbooks were scattered on the coffee table in front of her. Wheezy's daughter was working on a Ph.D. in Women's Studies. Wheezy loved every minute of her company and had insisted she live at home until graduation even if she was inching close to thirty.

"Mom?" The girl's long legs twisted Indian style on the sofa. She was tapping her pen on the inside of a textbook.

Wheezy had managed to find a spot for everything in the bin that she'd brought home. She was fiddling with one more item as she stood in front of an enormous set of cherry bookshelves searching for the right place. She wasn't paying much attention to the conversation. Rather, she was mesmerized by the array of photos on the shelves between the books, snapshots of her life journey.

Wheezy lived in a secluded neighborhood of intricately built 1920's homes not far from where she grew up in center city. The affluent neighborhood of Tudors with nooks and turrets, manicured lawns, magnolias and classic staircases out of *Gone with the Wind* was nestled between the hospital and the university.

"Darren is a well-known Journalism professor at the university. He has numerous connections, Mom. I bet he can refer you to a good lawyer." This lower voice came from a wingback chair across the room. Thurston, Adele's twin brother, had legs so long they practically reached the coffee table where her textbooks were collected. A born brainiac and basketball star, he was studying to become a physician. Presently he was in a so-called gap year. Adele was often envious because he barely had to study for an A.

"Darren, yes! That's a good thought," Adele complimented.

Their chit-chat made Wheezy smile even though she wasn't crazy about gap years, the in thing for his generation. The mention of Wheezy's live-in boyfriend, Darren, came as he entered the room carrying two glasses of Chianti and a plate of cheese. Their routine every Friday night. Wine and cheese right before he bent on one knee and popped the same question.

But the kids were home, so the question had to wait. Darren was the first good man Wheezy had let move into her life, literally. She vowed never to lower standards for herself or her children again.

Wheezy eyed him as he neared. He was worth the wait.

"Doubt if I can help," Darren interjected. "I can't even seem to convince your mother to marry me."

Thurston leaned forward. "Mom. Please accept. I know you won't be sorry."

Darren set the tray down. "If your mother wants an attorney, I'm sure she will find one."

Thurston munched on a cracker with a chuckle. “You’re right about that.” He sank back and disappeared behind the wing.

Darren and Thurston melded to perfection; one was the father the son never had, and vice versa. Wheezy’s heart melted when they interacted. Adele, too. They would one hundred percent support a marriage with Darren. However, Wheezy promised herself that until she reached her goal, going solo was for her. With that thought, her smile retreated. Today her dream had been stolen by a man named Asher Devine. *Men!*

“Mom, did you hear us? Hire an attorney, marry Darren, and throw that dang picture out. You’ve been looking for a place to set it for the last hour.”

“You already have pictures in almost every room,” Thurston remarked.

“This photo was from one of the highlights of my single life,” she defended. “I have photos in every room as inspiration. Right alongside a picture of your Great Grandmother. She was right, you know.” Her voice softened. “She promised that the year I was part of the diversity program would be one to tell my grandkids about. I wish I had a do-over. I’d have heeded her efforts to educate me in so many ways. Instead, I had to learn the hard way.”

“Here it comes,” Adele grumbled under her breath. She returned Thurston’s stare.

Then Adele and Thurston spoke Wheezy’s next sentence in unison. “You both need to heed the lesson.” They had memorized the words by heart like their nighttime prayers, Wheezy’s advice to them from the time they could remember.

“Mom, look at us.” Adele jetted forward. She motioned a pointer finger to herself and Thurston. “I think we followed your plan.”

“Remember, if you hadn’t met our biological father, we wouldn’t be here.” The twins laughed.

Wheezy knew they were right, but she persisted. “Did I tell you how your grandmother paved the way for you two? Making me see how important and worthy I am.”

“Yes, so why don’t you step out of the box, as she said. Infiltrate *new* worlds! Do something your grandkids will talk about!” Adele shut the textbook. "Maybe *you* need to follow the advice and take this moment for a transformation."

"Take a gap year, Mom!"

"Great idea, Thurston!" Adele confirmed.

Wheezy plopped in another wingback chair beside her son. Darren placed the wine on the end table that had belonged to her grandmother. He delivered a sympathetic eye, yet seemingly agreed with Adele.

"Okay, I'll call the school bus company. They're always looking for drivers."

"Mom, really." Thurston set his ice water down.

"Okay, I'll run the school bus company."

"Mom, take the year off if you're not going to pursue legal action. You deserve to enjoy the time. Go rent a horse trailer. Darren said he would buy you a horse for a wedding gift."

Darren stood taller, hovering over Wheezy. "That sounds like a plan."

"Driving a horse trailer and riding horses are two different things, totally. I know very little about riding. I was merely learning the basics that year your grandmother enlisted me in the diversity program." Wheezy touched the picture.

"You know about loading them, so how hard can riding be?" Adele dropped the statement as a kind of gauntlet.

"They're enormous, if you haven't noticed."

All three others zeroed in on Wheezy. "Nothing's ever stopped you. You drive semis. I don't think those beautiful animals would be anything but a delight." As usual Adele was a basket full of opinions.

When Wheezy opened the bedroom door, she smelled roses. Darren had prepared a bubble bath in the connecting master bathroom. She glanced at the four-poster, canopy bed. A diamond ring was placed strategically dead center of the down comforter.

Tonight, the sight of the ring brought her to tears. They both knew her answer to his question. “Darren, I am not ready to get married. I’m fifty years old and not who I want to be yet.”

He hugged her closer and loosened the hydrangea scarf. “Wheezy, I have some suggestions. First, it’s time to get out of this uniform.”

She softened from his touch and dipped her head so her chin touched his hand.

Darren continued to talk as he fiddled with the material. “Second, I need you to believe in the truth. That’s what my journalism career is based on. The truth eventually rises to the surface. Frank gave you two options. Take the severance which should fully last you a year and think of it as a paid vacation. It’s well over your complete salary. Or stay on, but only in the capacity of a truck driver, for which you are quite capable. But why? Frank made one point clear—you’re prohibited from working at a competing trucking or transport service this year. I believe he’s investigating. I have no doubt he will reach the truth.” Darren kissed her forehead. “Now let’s get you a warm bath.”

Wheezy looked at him with disappointment. Darren was not saying words she wanted to hear. *Give Frank a chance after today, after twenty years.* Trust was a hard word to swallow.

Darren led her to the bathroom, retrieved the riding photo and set it on the edge of the claw foot tub. “Why don’t you think about the break? Maybe start by searching for that Gertrude Steele you talk about. She believed in you. Then maybe reach out to one or more of these ladies in the photo.”

A few minutes after he left, Darren peered in the door. “Hey honey, you received a text from the human resources manager at F.G. Transport. Simply said 6:00 AM tomorrow with a question mark. Would you like me to respond?”

Wheezy submerged her body into the warm water, too tired to object.

“Just say… yes,” Wheezy sighed, “for the children.”

Darren asked for no explanation; he never did. He trusted her completely. He agreed and gently closed the door in an exit.

Trust. That had been Gertrude Steele's advice, too. Trust that she could drive the truck. But trust also brought another person to mind that she hadn't thought of in decades—Wyndham Glick, the sexy Brazilian. The infamous horse whisperer had said, *"Trust the horse!"* Wheezy felt her lips curl upward for the first time that day.

As she examined the riding picture, new possibilities sifted into her thoughts. Maybe Darren was right. She closed her eyes and began to devise a plan for the next year. Perhaps she would call Randall Emerson, the client she transported horses for, and ask for help in locating Gertrude Steele. She was the trainer who first sat her in the driver's seat of a truck. The power! City kids didn't drive Ford F-350s.

Soon, Wheezy was drifting in a bath of positive adventures instead of the tragic day's event. But then she thought about Gigi Tetless, and waves of exasperation brought her back to earth.

Chapter 11

Gigi

Gigi peeked into her beaded evening bag pretending to search for lip gloss. She was relieved to discover the parking garage gate key and a riding picture tucked in the side zipper pocket. Her French-tipped nail touched the thirty-year-old moment. The photo, of herself and three other women, was merely a copy, printed on plain loose-leaf paper that she had cut into a small square. Gigi had printed several copies. Good thing because the original had been folded so many times over the years it was now nothing but rivers of white creases and shredded edges. More concerning was that if Randall ever discovered the pic, it would be trash, like her journal and everything else she hid from him.

Her examination of the photo was interrupted by Randall Emerson's name echoing throughout the banquet room. The event emcee had called him to the podium to accept an award as a breeder and horse trainer of excellence in the regional chapter of their racing forum.

Gigi glanced at the man next to her. He was sixty-four, fit from daily visits to the gym, quite handsome, greying with slivers of wrinkles at only the corner of his eyes and charming. Randall Emerson, her husband, was staring over his pince-nez as she rummaged through her purse.

Sensing his gaze, she cast off the picture, located the gloss, then dabbed her lips with the wand in the hopes he believed she was preparing to be her typical belle of the ball. His frown ordered her to snap the purse shut. Gigi obeyed. Then she nervously fingered the five-carat horse diamond pendant and necklace lying on her decolletage. Randall's latest idea of an apology.

The pendant was bursting in twinkles under the chandeliers, catching everyone's eye, until it was shadowed over by him snatching her hand.

She swallowed, wishing to steal her fingers back, but she didn't dare. Her husband pressed on an arrogant grin to acknowledge the room of attendees. Gigi knew it was a mask, like a sticky note he could rip off seconds later. Then Randall placed his glasses in his tuxedo pocket.

"Time to rise, my dear," he said.

The crowd softly cheered as the power couple weaved between tables of eight toward the front. Several ladies reached out. "Gigi, you look stunning. Have you lost weight?" or "Gigi, I can only pray my daughter fairs as well as you," Or "Gigi, you lucky lady."

Gigi's gold dress was splashed with glitter and hugged her figure, veering low between her 34-D breasts. She experienced shooting abdominal pain, mainly because the strangling girdle choked her every breath. Her personal trainer had worked Gigi to the core the previous six weeks to zip up that Versace halter dress. Her brunette locks were perfectly coiffed. Her lips plumped, her latest cosmetic treatment a success to stop her forty-eight-year-old body from aging another day.

Randall demanded that Gigi stay focused on one detail—not her past, nor her writing, nor horses. He stipulated Gigi be forever fresh and the hostess with a smile plastered on her face. Vaseline helped with the latter. Placed strategically inside the lips the slippery goo ensured a constant beam of enjoyment, even if she didn't share the sentiment. That trick was an old horse showing technique. But back then she hadn't needed anything except a horse to make her smile.

Gigi posed in the spotlight next to Randall at the podium. Every word he uttered sounded garbled to her. She was visualizing the picture in her purse, a momentous year in her life. At the time, her mother insisted she volunteer for confirmation credit at church. *"Oh, Gigi, you are eighteen and spoiled, I'm sorry to say. You will feel a reward from such an experience, helping someone else enjoy horses. Otherwise, an inner-city child would have no avenue to participate. Her name is Louisa Mae. The paper says to call her Wheezy."* Gigi could never have imagined the magnitude of her mother's words until years later. However, none of that mattered anymore. Gigi would never see those ladies again, especially not Wheezy.

That same year Gigi had met Randall Emerson, the son of a long succession of Randall Emersons. The man of her dreams followed her around the horse show. He was married at the time. Several years later, when he claimed they were separated, she and Randall had rekindled at an equestrian event. He touted that he'd never been graced by any woman as beautiful as Gigi. A suave businessman, sixteen years her senior, wealthy beyond her dreams. How could she resist? And his hobby was horses.

Initially, Randall tied his "I dos" with a bible of promises, Country Club friends, dinner dances, parties, fundraisers, an estate, and a college building named R. Emerson Study Hall. Gigi could play bridge Tuesdays, drink tea Wednesdays, pickleball on Thursdays, and massages on Fridays, but the principal dowry? Horses every day, as many as she dreamed possible. The whipped cream smothered on top was that Randall promised to be faithful forever.

Suddenly he squeezed her hand to refresh her reality. "Gigi, smile. Are you paying attention?"

A camera flash shocked her eyes shut and brought her to earth. Randall was cradling a massive bronze horse statue, the award. His name was engraved next to the year.

The crowd was standing in a thunderous ovation. Randall constricted her fingers tighter like a starving python. "Could you smile like the woman everyone wants to be?"

They weaved on return to their table through the standing ovation. Again, members of the audience expressed compliments as they passed.

The older lady at their table leaned in. "Oh, dear, you are the perfect wife. You put us all to shame. So much going for you. I hope you'll be able to join us at the fox hunt next year. Randall said your horse had an injury."

An injury? So that was how he was keeping her out of the Sun Tree Fox Hunt Club this year.

Gigi had dreamed of horses in her youth, but rarely ever mounted one anymore. Randall didn't want his wife riding their investments. He forbade it. She realized after a recent turn of events, he was also diverting her presence around the clubhouse and stables since the new head groom was hired. So much for faithful Randall... however his activities were nothing new.

"Your necklace is beautiful. Was this for your anniversary, or birthday?" a woman asked her.

Gigi was scarcely attentive. Her body temperature was rising, perhaps it was the wine, certainly not her age.

Randall interjected when he heard zero response. "No, just because she's my one and only."

"Ahh. Everyone loves him." The lady pointed to Randall, the entire table agreeing. "Don't you worry. The ladies will take good care of him while your horse heals. Was it serious?"

"Serious?" Gigi felt delirious, queasy. "His relationships. They never are."

Everyone fixated on Gigi ... especially Randall. He dabbed his lips with a napkin.

"I think she means the injury," another woman intercepted.

Randall cleared his throat in an effort to speak, but he was interrupted by the emcee announcing the next speaker. "Please welcome our next guest, the new CEO of F.G. Transport, the cutting edge, Asher Devine."

The crowd clapped except for Gigi's table, as they were still distracted by her remark.

"F.G. Transport has a new goal," Asher stated. "To be the leader in equine transport."

The voice at the podium broke Randall's sinister concentration on Gigi, and thankfully he was motivated to look away. Perfect time to excuse herself. The lady's lounge was a good hiding place.

Gigi's life was a façade. Randall had room for three types of women. Gigi was one—the "Front," the good wife. Always on his arm, the hostess, the entertainer, the socialite, the beauty queen and the ostrich. Tight-assed, nice breasts and wrinkle free was a challenge to maintain, no matter how many hours spent at the gym or on starvation diets, but she refused to enter menopause.

The second type of woman was his addiction, his trinkets. The ones bewildered by Randall, falling under his spell—the same haze she'd experienced in the beginning.

Then there was Camilla, the third woman and the only one he worshiped. Randall's spoiled rotten daughter, from the first Front. Gigi was beginning to think she would not be the last Front either. She hastened to the restroom. He was repulsive. Her body weakened, her cheeks flushed, and her stomach went queasy.

As soon as Gigi entered, she was in a panic to hug the throne. She raced through the lounge decorated in ornate gold-trimmed mirrors. Her heels tapped in a rapid beat on the marble floor. The aroma of lilac incense which saturated the room escalated her nausea.

She plowed into the first stall. Gigi could barely click the lock with her shaking hands to barricade herself in. She fervently swallowed, attempting to deter her insides from surfacing.

Her own breathing permeated the hollow bathroom area, until voices bombarded the silence from the adjacent lounge area.

"Did you hear the head groom was fired at the Hunt Club this morning?" a woman asked.

"Hadn't you heard? Gigi herself called me at 3:00 AM. He did it again."

Gigi recognized this voice. *Alverta.*

Horrified, she blocked her mouth to prevent being discovered. Alverta was a friend, she'd thought, a shoulder to cry on when she found Randall in an incriminating position with the head groom. Alverta had pledged silence. Gigi had spilled her guts. *Some friend.*

"God, he screws like a rabbit. Glad I'm not married to him!" The other woman's voice resonated through the lounge.

"Maybe he doesn't with Gigi?" Alverta suggested.

The stranger released a heightened chortle. "Why would she want to? He's disgusting!"

"Because he'll drop another trinket or cash in the shoebox she stores under the bed, that's why."

Gigi almost suffocated herself, guarding her mouth from uttering in defense.

"Did you see the pendant?"

"Lord, the size of that. New?"

Gigi could hear makeup bags unzipped to freshen faces as the women spoke.

"New this morning. Randall has her under his control. What would she do without him? Poor girl's stuck." By her annunciation, Alverta was applying lipstick. "*Wellll, haybe not... tuck. Dapends on how you luk at life.*"

"If she keeps tolerating his playboy ways, she gets the baubles without the effort."

The lipstick application must have completed because Alverta's next utterance came out clear. "That's a thought. What kind of life is one without baubles?"

"Let's go tell Maggie. Come on."

Someone snapped a lid on a lipstick. The makeup bag zippers reverted, luckily for Gigi. She was barely able to prevent the swelling mucus.

"The club is going to run out of employees, what with Randall's third leg running amok." Their laughter rippled in waves back into the bathroom as the door clicked shut. The sound blended with Gigi's gags into the throne.

Minutes later, she perched perfectly still in the stall as if an empty shell. Another wretched person had penetrated her heart and stolen her trust. *Alverta.*

Why didn't Gigi have the strength to leave Randall Emerson? She'd caught him red-handed for the umpteenth time last evening engaging in an interlude with the twenty-something groom. He had ceased restating the empty promises that he would never cheat again. In his latest tactic, Randall threatened to destroy the love of her life if she dared to leave. Kit T Kat, her beloved mare.

She touched the five-carat pendant.

This was the final time the club would have to fire a fox hunting groom or can the head hostess. There had been a trainer three summers ago who had to leave town. Last summer the lifeguard at the country club went extinct like the dodo bird. Randall couldn't keep his peter in his pants, *his third leg.*

Randall was accustomed to controlling people's lives regardless of their line of work. He had archives with names and dates, his files imprisoning a person like a horse restrained in a twitch.

Gigi suddenly felt courageous. She bulldozed out of the lounge to the table. The banquet room lights remained dim. The man from the trucking company had the audience captive with a slideshow. She didn't care if Randall saw her; Gigi was leaving. All she needed was her purse. Without stopping, her delicate hand nabbed her bag from the shoulder of the chair.

Gigi swung her pocketbook strap over her head and across her shoulder while she raced the seemingly endless hall toward the door. She didn't care that the purse was crooked and slapping her mid-back with every step. She didn't care that she was forgetting her beaver fur stole in the cloakroom.

The frosty January air chilled her cheeks, then snatched her breath, but nothing iced her heart like the scene she'd witnessed the night before. Twelve hours later, everyone was gabbing about it.

Gigi could not escape fast enough. Tears blurred her vision, making it difficult to see across the stone patio that wrapped the clubhouse. The heel of her spiked boot caught the beveled step edge. If she had not clasped the arm of another lady proceeding inside, she would have face planted onto the cement.

The woman's husband promptly reached and grasped Gigi with his free hand. He managed to deposit her on an alabaster bench.

The wife leaned in to study her. "Gigi Emerson?" The woman hovered close and Gigi could feel warm breath strike her face. "My goodness, whatsoever happened? You don't look well."

The gentleman shushed the woman. "Clarise. You heard about the incident from Alverta." The two exchanged a hasty glance. Then Clarise cautiously ebbed away as if Gigi had a contagious disease.

Gigi's head snapped upward. *Alverta?*

"Oh." Clarise realized her mistake. "Poor dear. You look wretched."

The man released Gigi, encircled Clarise's arm and heaved his wife in the direction of the entrance. His face was marred with frown lines which embellished the corner of his eyes.

"Randall claims she drinks too much. Says she's a maniac who makes lewd accusations and becomes paranoid." His voice lowered as he opened the door. "She's drunk now. Who else would be out here in this weather, with no coat or gloves? I'll locate the manager. Come on."

Clarise nodded in rapid succession. "Yes. Yes. She's not a proper image for the club."

"Or Randall's reputation," the man barked. "No way would I tolerate this behavior from you."

The two disappeared through the double doors, taking their insults with them.

"Oh, Clarise," Gigi hollered at the closed door. "I have witnessed you drunk. You are *no* angel."

Another couple passed quickly, as if in terror that she might bare her teeth at them next.

"And I am not drunk." Gigi's pointer finger raised like a sword.

They darted inside.

"And you all are late," Gigi continued her rant in between her sniffles, then exhausted, she collapsed on the bench. "Alverta might as well post it on the morning news. Randall Emerson is a cheating, good for nothing bastard with three legs."

Gigi shifted on the stone bench which was strictly for aesthetics. She didn't have an ounce of fat on her rump, and the seat was not meant for rears with no cushion. Everything about the clubhouse was cold, especially in this season, but most of the members iced over all year long.

She shivered and folded her arms, hugging her body. In the spring and summer, the surrounding landscape would be graced by sunshine, the racetrack's perimeter blossoming in pear trees, and the flowerbeds dancing with marigolds, petunias, and geraniums in a burst of color. A fragrance of life and excitement sifting through the air, luncheons on the terrace, while the horses dashed around the track. Wine and brandy, hats and dresses, diamonds and sapphires, laughter and toasts all to cheer on a favorite entry. All for show... and money. Everything Gigi dreamed of. *Right?*

Wrong. A front, just like racing. And just like her life with Randall. She secretly loved someone else, but sadly it was forbidden.

God forbid the beautiful animal didn't win, place or show.

Gigi contemplated a plan. She had to get to her Land Rover in the gated parking lot. She had every intention of leaving this time. Tired of Randall underestimating her, she wasn't only about money, trinkets and horses. She had character. *Didn't she?*

Gigi shuffled through the zippered side pocket of her purse. Where was the key? She'd checked at the table. Dumping the few contents of the evening bag on the bench, she couldn't find the gate key. Or her favorite picture.

"Are you looking for something?" a man's voice asked.

Gigi froze as if sprayed with ice. Randall was hovering over her in his leather coat and Louie Vuitton plaid scarf.

"Now here I am. Evening interrupted. I had to retrieve my coat, gather myself. Leave my own award ceremony and search for my faithful wife. Having a breakdown on the veranda for all to witness in sub-freezing temperatures." Randall sighed. A fog billowed from his mouth. "You are the talk."

"Me? The talk?"

"Whoa, princess. I don't like your tone." He pulled a cigar from his pocket, then, with a horizontal glide under his nose, smelled it. "I have made quite the success in business and horses. You knew from the moment we wed the consequences if you let your anxiety and phobias consume you. I like proper appearances—the Front, as you call it—in exchange for all the valuables that my better half can possess... trinkets, facelifts, clothes, furs and let's not forget that stable of rejects I maintain for you."

"Those horses are not losers simply because they didn't win a race. There is no need to send beautiful animals to slaughter. Guess that's your latest reason to connect with the transport company. Finally convinced them into crossing the border to the slaughter-house. Big money in that, huh?"

Randall's lighter halted mid-air.

She'd touched a nerve. *Not so stupid, am I?*

Gigi grasped the pendant around her neck. "All this in exchange for your own wicked ways?"

Randall finally lit the cigar and blew a smokey ring in the air.

"Princess. You have been getting a little too impetuous. Too much fiction for your pathetic journals."

Gigi shivered from his daunting glare.

Randall produced her key card and riding picture from his pocket. He puffed once more before tossing almost the entire cigar over the rail. He watched the glow flicker in the light covering of snow. Gigi decided to say no more. Instead she waited as if he were about to release the guillotine.

He scrunched her riding picture into a crumpled ball. "If you're going to leave, you'll have to walk out the gate like the regulars. Don't stop at home, either. I'll have the place on lockdown. I remind you of two important points. If you do leave, you can kiss Kit T Kat the mare goodbye. She's no good to me. As for all the others, well, need I say more?"

"And the second point?" Gigi blinked back the encroaching well of tears. *Here it comes, his real weapon.*

"Gigi, the pre-nup? You do remember?" Randall said in a childlike tone. Then he volleyed the wad of paper directly at her, hitting her bare shoulder. "You really are starting to worry me. A little dementia, a little pudge. I might be in the market for a new *Front.*"

Randall pivoted like a general and returned to the clubhouse.

Gigi's teeth were chattering when Alverta sneaked out carrying a woolen shawl and wrapped it around her body. Even if Alverta loved to spread gossip, she was Gigi's only friend.

"Come on, lady. Let's go back in. It's a wonderful party. And you know we love parties. Everyone is wondering if you're okay."

Alverta persuaded her to stand with a squeeze. "You can tell me all about it. You aren't leaving Randall. He's the best husband in the club. This is nothing a little Hot Toddy can't fix."

Chapter 12

Gigi slipped out of the house at 10:00 PM bundled in her white ski jacket trimmed in cocoa-colored fur with matching pants. A hood covered her wet hair which was rolled on pink bendable rollers. Her curls had to be perfect for the rodeo the next day. God knows Randall made it clear they were scheduled to leave at 6:00 AM.

She glanced back at the mansion. Randall's library office light was on. He was probably in search of a location for his latest racing award. That would keep him busy for some time as he was very particular about the placement of trophies and awards in line of sight.

Gigi was later than normal because of the banquet, but she wasn't about to change her typical evening itinerary. Her ballerina shaped legs raced in poignant perfection across the icy grass in fur-lined snow boots. The night sky was a bluish black except for the twinkling winter stars. She had texted Carlos, her ever-devoted stable assistant, and informed him she would be tardy. As suspected, the small-statured man was waiting at the sliding doors of what Randall deemed the "Loser" barn.

Gigi skirted through the opening, then Carlos pinched the doors shut in a flash. His loyalty to her appeared unbreakable.

"So cold, Miss Gigi. You should have skipped tonight," Carlos whispered with a faint accent, as if concerned he might wake the dozen horses stalled there.

Gigi scanned the aisleway while removing her fur-lined gloves. As usual, she still wore a white cotton glove on her right hand. She handed the winter pair to Carlos in exchange for the bag of treats to her left. "Your hair, it is wet. You will be sick."

"I'll be fine, Carlos. You know I worry about these horses. *The losers,* as Randall calls them. I would never miss visiting these beauties."

Gigi checked the zipper on her coat and tightened her alpaca scarf. Although all the warmth from the horses raised the temperature in the barn maybe ten degrees, she didn't want to reveal even a corner of her satin pink nightie. What would Carlos think? She had to be prepared in the event Randall caught her in the house when he expected her in bed.

The first part of her routine was the white glove inspection—floor swept clean with not a flake of hay, pebble of oats nor dropping of dried manure. She surveyed the rafters for one cobweb fluttering from above or one missing bulb high in the ceiling lights, then the stalls for a hinge hanging loose from a missing nail.

"Perfection, Carlos," she complimented and freed her hand from the white glove.

Carlos nodded in affirmation, folding the glove neatly in half and stowing it in his pocket. The way Gigi expected. She detested filth. Especially, in the stables or on her. Her preferred color was white, stark white, trimmed in gold.

This procedure had been her protocol for the last fifteen years. Visit the horses in her care and inspect the stable with Carlos by her side. Each horse would receive a special treat and a kiss.

The strange sense that Randall might possibly harm one of these beauties preyed on her mind. He seemed to continually be searching for ammo against her, to keep her "in her place." Examining the horses put her at ease before each night's rest. *A girl needs her beauty sleep.*

Gigi eyed Carlos. "Are you ready?"

"*Si, si señora*. You know this is also important to me."

Gigi beamed. He honestly gave her an authentic reason to smile. He always had, and she would be lost without him. She certainly couldn't ride or attend a horse show without Carlos. She maintained her white jodhpurs because of him. They had aged together, and although Carlos lacked the funds for filler and Botox, he was quite handsome.

Gigi proceeded to the first stalled horse. Carlos scurried behind.

"Did you know Randall was *doing* the fox hunting groom?" She avoided eye contact. She knew this routine. Carlos would nod, pretending to understand only minimal English even though he was quite fluent. This was unmistakably his scheme when he wanted to avoid difficult discussions. Because she respected him, she never pried further. Gigi feared his answers anyway and hoped he cared so much for her that he didn't want to hurt her with the truth.

Carlos merely shook his head in quick jerks.

Gigi had drifted apart from Randall Emerson in the first ten years of marriage. He'd had his eyes on more than one trinket. But she had the fantasy castle all to herself. The estate was like Disneyland. Camilla, his daughter, fifteen years younger than Gigi, was away at boarding school and college. Gigi had full freedom in the stables. She had everything. But each time Randall was up to his shenanigans, gossip escalated, and Gigi loathed it. Baubles in the shoebox worked for the first fifteen years, but like every Cinderella, she desired a man who would worship her.

Carlos opened the first stall door while Gigi plucked a treat from the bag then tendered the open bag back to him.

"Did you know the groom was fired this morning?" She placed the treat perfectly in the center of her palm.

Again, Carlos vibrated with denial.

The horse neighed, stepped toward her, and stretched his neck. The gelding's warm muzzle flapped across her palm with a tickle and sucked the treat like a vacuum. All that remained was a light film of slobbery residue.

She continued speaking. "They think I live a dream. Owning horses, living in a castle, partying in the clubhouse, rubbing shoulders with the most influential people, drinking, working out, baubles... Right?"

Gigi faced Carlos as he closed the door.

"Carlos, do you like my face, my puffy lips, my perky..." She pointed to her chest without touching her unblemished coat. Gigi watched his expression sprinkle with a slight shock. But he uttered no sound. His jaw flinched as his hand encircled hers, then wiped the drivel gently with the damp rag.

Tonight, her heart hurt. "Carlos, how about my..." She gestured to her tush. "Do you like the lift I had recently on my rump?" Gigi searched for some acknowledgment, some response of appreciation that she was still pretty at forty-eight.

Carlos's ebony eyes bubbled beyond their sockets. He'd witnessed her tantrums in the past, but Gigi had never made uncensored comments or actions for his approval before. She tightened her scarf as if in embarrassment.

Carlos remained vigilant at ignoring her. He merely passed her the bag and proceeded to the next stall as Gigi continued ranting.

"I love riding, but Randall has not permitted me to show this year or fox hunt with my beloved Kit T Kat. All because he was having a rendezvous with the groom," she defended. "I am a good girl, aren't I, Carlos?"

Carlos nudged her toward the next stall. "Miss Gigi, the horses... and you will freeze with the wet hair." He motioned to her head.

Gigi hesitated, then moved forward by the neighing calls and stamping hooves. As they patrolled each stall, the procedure remained consistent. Carlos would hand the bag, she took the treat, he wiped her palm and off to the next horse. All without a smudge. Bag, palm, wipe. A three-step waltz with a handsome man that waited on her hand and foot.

At the eleventh horse she stopped. "Who wouldn't want to be Gigi Tetless Emerson? Or love her? I am not superficial, right? Why does Alverta tell everything? Do you think I spread gossip like that? Is that what friends do? Well, I guess I let the news slip about her husband and the massage therapist at the club." Something warm and moist was drifting down her cheek as she rambled. "Carlos, I am not even tit-less anymore!"

Carlos's hand rose with the rag. Gigi assumed he was about to freshen her palm, but the cloth elevated higher. Carlos unexpectantly wiped a tear from her cheek.

Both paralyzed. She swallowed, afraid to move. He stared at her as she studied his sculpted fingers clenching the cloth. She blinked, and for a moment she flashed back to a larger-than-life horse whisperer named Wyndham Glick. Gigi blinked again, like a genie bringing herself to reality.

"Stall 12, Carlos, the most important one," she announced, in denial of what had just transpired.

The last stall was special. Her very own heart horse. Kit T Kat. Gigi and this mare had spent hours in private jumping instructions and fox hunting after Carlos would do the necessities first. Kit T Kat was sizable. A fifteen and a half hand, white Tobiano with brown markings which were positioned like jewels by God in the right spots—her rump, her face, her ears and a large oval across her lower girth. She glistened like crystal again because of Carlos and Simply Silver shampoo.

Carlos glided the stall door open, and the beautiful Tobiano stopped circling in anticipation, instantly coming to her.

Gigi smiled as wide as her heart grew upon seeing the mare. "I know, baby. It is so hard to wait your turn. But there's a good reason." Gigi's voice was as sweet as if cooing a baby.

"She loves you, Miss Gigi," Carlos whispered.

Gigi's eyes liquified again in response, but she kept a steady focus on Kit T Kat as he placed the treat in her hand. "I hope she loves me, Carlos. She certainly has a funny way of showing it when she gives me the ride of my life sometimes. Thank God for Carlos. Bossy girl, aren't you?" Gigi sniffled. As the mare barely waited for her to open her hand, she snatched the treat like a starving shark.

"Oh my, girl." Gigi scolded with a tap on the muzzle as the mare chomped the apple-flavored biscuit.

Carlos proceeded with the normal routine. He hooked her halter to lead Kit T Kat two steps into the aisleway. Gigi drifted her hand down the mare's neck, fingering the muscles.

Kit T Kat bobbed her head, motioning for another cookie.

"Only one, dear. Now the best part." Gigi kissed her soft fur as Carlos secured the movement with slight tension on the lead. Then Carlos reversed the mare, moving her two steps back into the stall with clomping resistance. He latched the door.

Gigi peered through the iron bars as Carlos wiped her palm. When she faced him, she encountered the rag, this time aiming for her lips.

Gigi raised her hand. "You can leave the kiss. Her soft fur will linger on my lips."

She felt him tug her coat at the elbow and direct her toward the large double doors to exit.

"Carlos, Randall is up to something. We must find homes for some of these horses as I'm afraid Sapphire Silver is not running well at the track. It's her age and I love her. And you know Randall's motto once they can't race."

Carlos stopped her at the door and dressed her hands—one white cotton glove and then the winter pair.

"Carlos, please if ever you know something about Randall, please anything, I could use over his head, so nothing ever happens to these beautiful creatures," Gigi pleaded.

She watched the man work as he seemingly ignored her. When finished, he revealed a piece of paper from his pocket.

"Miss Gigi, I found this in the snow by the car. Must have fallen when you returned."

He had practically ironed all the crinkles out of a familiar 4x6 paper to make it flat again.

"My picture!" Gigi exclaimed. "Carlos."

He released the paper to her. She was going to tell him to trash it, but his rising hands stole her attention. Carlos nabbed her hood by the corners and maneuvered it with some difficulty over her head of pink rollers.

"Now go."

Gigi followed his pointer toward the outside as the cold air rushed at them like an entire football team.

"And Miss Gigi... Camilla is back."

Gigi hesitated at the name. "Back?" Gigi raised a glove to her mouth. "Here at Emerson Estates?"

He nodded in almost a shudder. "Yes. Her husband and her, they fight. Randall asked her to come home and manage the stables."

"Are you kidding? She can't manage anything except trouble."

"Go, Miss Gigi, go!" Carlos feathered a motion to her as he rolled the doors further to the arctic air.

As soon as she had exited the barn, the sense of peace left her. She would reemerge in the side pantry of chaos castle praying not to be noticed.

Gigi's presence forced Carlos's heart to skip a beat. He watched her fade across the path toward the house as the nightly sense of loss overwhelmed him. He closed the barn door and sighed from the duress knowing he would not see her again until tomorrow.

Gigi had been like his knight in shining armor when he first arrived to work at Emerson's. She persisted and battled Randall to allow his mother and sisters to stay safely on the estate in one of the carriage houses. That was when he'd realized her genuine core under the façade of just another spoiled wife. Her care for the so-called worthless racehorses that Randall discarded was proof alone.

Carlos's words could never thank her in full, nor would she ever know the value of her friendship. Unfortunately, Gigi was a forbidden love he could never share.

One thing was for sure. As he passed Kit T Kat's stall, Carlos vowed to always have Gigi's back, no matter the stakes.

Thankfully Randall was still lingering in the library. Gigi saw the light shimmering bright on her return. Good thing she had the nightie hidden under her winter attire.

Once inside, she whipped off the gloves, jacket, boots, and snow pants and scurried past the laundry, kitchen and down the hall to his library. The massive mahogany doors were ajar. She peered inside.

Randall was resting in the small leather office chair which he had moved to face the shelves cluttered with awards. He was idolizing the latest addition. His back to the door, his hands were steepled, his pointers supporting his chin with his legs crossed. He was shirtless, merely dressed in a loose-fitting plaid cotton pant, its string tied at the waist, and Brooks Brothers slippers.

"You're breathing heavy. Spoiling my moment, dear GiGi." Randall spoke without turning in her direction.

Was he that alert or watching a camera?

"You're still up?" she asked, trying to appear surprised.

"I should ask the same," he snipped.

"I needed coffee."

"I didn't like your behavior tonight. Are we on the same page?"

Gigi inched in behind him, simultaneously swallowing her pride. She had made a mistake. She needed to stay on his good side while avoiding Camilla at all costs. She had no choice but to fake an apology.

"Randall, the trophy looks exquisite," she suggested to help diffuse the situation.

He said nothing.

Taking a breath, disheartened, it was time to beg. "Randall, you were right. I made a terrible scene tonight. Please forgive me. I threw out the picture."

He continued facing the opposite way, yet she could see his grin because his cheeks expanded so wide that they ballooned past his ears.

He tapped his right shoulder with a request for a shoulder rub. Gigi's stomach churned.

"Why would you risk everything, princess?"

Gigi creeped her hands forward to touch his bare shoulders, shocked to realize the paper photo was in her hand—the printed picture of four women at a horse show that he had crumpled in a ball earlier.

Randall arched his head back, almost catching her tuck the photo in her cleavage. He tapped his shoulder again. "Are you..."

She cleared her throat and motioned him to face the trophy wall. "I'm right here." She scaled his shoulders, but he jerked.

"Gigi, your hands are like ice. As if you were outside?"

"Randall, really, would I have been outside dressed like this?"

Randall rubbernecked her up then down several times, making her wish she had her winter coat on. Luckily, he receded back to position. He pointed once more to his shoulders.

Her eyes tumbled behind him with relief. The queasy feeling in her stomach—the one she'd experienced in the club bathroom—shot her a wave.

"I know how tired you are at night." Gigi forced her fingers to make contact with his skin again. She was blasted by an internal disgust. She moved the tips in a "scarcely there" circular motion.

"More kneading. My shoulders ache, princess."

She raised her elbows, prepared to dive into his muscles, but not before closing her eyes and dreaming she was riding Kit T Kat instead of touching Randall.

"Oh, you stay in such good shape. I don't deserve you." Gigi dropped a compliment in the hope Randall would fall under her spell for a change. She hesitated until he let out a moan. She lowered with a sensual whisper, "I asked Carlos to find a home for some of my horses, okay? In case you have more… rejects."

"You will have to take that up with the new stable manager, Camilla."

Gigi's nauseous sensation bid hello again. The massaging stopped. She wanted to choke him.

His finger rotated in the air. "Gigi, massage?"

At least Carlos had prepared her.

"Well, please one favor from you? I will be good, I promise. Can I please go back to Sun Tree Hunt Club? That was why I was so angry. I miss it. I understand your reasons, Randall. I promise to wear blinders like a Standardbred."

Unexpectedly, Randall rose. Gigi's hands plummeted off him. She found herself level with his bare chest. Quite the firm bare chest. She stared at the hair in curls over his pecs and gathered strength. "Look at you."

Randall stood taller, billowing out his chest.

"And look at you in that negligee, perky princess. If I didn't know better, I might think you want something more than a goodnight kiss. Long time since you teased me. You must really be sorry."

Gigi searched for words as he gripped her forearms and towed her close. She wanted to resist, thinking of the picture wedged in the crevasse between her breasts.

Randall manipulated his fingers in a dance down her spine. "Tomorrow is the rodeo. If you are a good girl, your shoebox might hold a new trinket. Then we'll see about fox hunting again. Would you like that?"

Her cheek was pressed firmly against his pecs, the hairs tickling her nose. Smashed, Gigi felt the vibration of his heart and prayed she would not feel the pulsation of other body parts. She stared straight ahead and saw the safe door was ajar.

"Look nice tomorrow. Wear something low-cut. I have a participant, and I want her to win."

"You do?" Gigi freed herself. That would be a new venture for his style, a rodeo horse?

"Well, kinda," Randall said, attempting to coax her back against him. "I am soon to be partners with the owner, although the owner doesn't know it yet. Let's say it's a coup d'etat."

"Really?" Gigi's interest was sparked. Wasn't that like unlawful seizure? Was there abuse? Why didn't the owner know? This sounded like information she could use against Randall, plus a way to keep interest off her body at present.

"Shhh." Randall touched her lips with his finger.

She mumbled between them, "Is there a name to cheer on tomorrow?"

He hesitated. "How about... Louisa."

"Louisa, what a pretty name for a horse." Gigi edged away but she was imprisoned. Randall puckered his lips and angled toward hers. She fisted the nightie close against her chest then squinted, bracing for contact.

"Daddy?" A voice beckoning from the doorway saved her.

Camilla.

Gigi cringed at the thought, but she couldn't have been more thankful when Randall's daughter entered the library.

"Camilla?" Randall greeted.

"Daddy, can we talk?" Camilla pouted with plump lips.

When she realized Gigi was the woman in his arms, the girl cursed her with a witchy glare as if casting a spell. "I need a new horse."

"I just bought you one recently," he said, dropping Gigi from his clutches. "And I promised you Silver Sapphire, the grey thoroughbred."

"Daddy, the mare doesn't listen to me."

Make that two of us. Gigi tiptoed backward. "Well, you two talk. Father-daughter time. I'll get some shut eye. It's going to be an early morning." She shifted her nightie, securing the top as she retreated.

Randall sailed a wink her way, igniting her nausea. Then he focused on his daughter.

As soon as Gigi escaped, she raced to her bedroom which seemed miles away. Once inside the door, she clicked the lock and headed for her king-size bed.

She dropped to the floor, lifted the edge of the white faux fur comforter and peered under in a search. Not for the Jimmy Choo shoebox where Randall stashed her newly acquired baubles and trinkets, but for her journal.

Under her bed was probably the most dangerous place to keep her diary, but Randall would never suspect Gigi might hide it so close to the shoebox.

She reached into a plastic storage bag which was completely transparent. Inside was her summer bedspread which she interchanged with the white faux fur winter one. She unzipped the bag, fingered through the folds and smiled on discovery of the book.

GiGi leaped onto her bed, sat Indian style and opened the page to the pen that was clipped inside. She recorded the events of the day religiously every evening. Gigi chronicled Randall's business dealings if she learned anything new or unusual. Perhaps one day, she would have a wedge to shove in his side. Gigi had been stupid that night. She needed to play her cards right to keep her lifestyle in a way she was accustomed. She jotted down the horse's name, Louisa, mentioned Randall's words of a coup d'etat, and noted the safe was open.

Gigi removed the picture shoved between her breasts. Why couldn't Randall be more like Carlos? For the same reason she could never associate with the three ladies in the picture. What a scandal that would be for Alverta's gossip trail.

Good to see you, ladies. We shall never meet again, but thanks for the memory. Gigi pressed the photo in the journal pages and tucked the book into the folds of the comforter again.

Gigi had it all, except a faithful husband. Why would she mess that up?

She applied lotion, slipped her hands into pre-moisturized cotton gloves, pressed in the ear plugs, and covered her eyes with a gel-filled cover. The rodeo was a rougher equestrian environment for her liking, but she could cheer for Louisa. She set her alarm for 5:00 AM.

Part Two

The Reunion

Chapter 13

Presley's husband, Brad, drove the two women toward the Bennington complex in the next county. Although early because of the distance, the SUV was bursting with conversation until he reached the curved drop-off location at the facility's entrance.

"Wow, it sure didn't feel like an hour drive!" Rachel announced.

She and Presley fell silent when they saw the stone structure. The main venue had been built primarily of massive square boulders in the early 1930s. An army of sculptured soldiers, some on horseback, was etched in the marble, seemingly guarding the top edge of the structure. Numerous arenas and buildings had been added and connected in a labyrinth, but this first facility was never matched in its architecture. The impressive structure had been home to some of the grandest events on the east coast for the last century.

"As majestic today as it was thirty years ago, isn't it? I remember when we came to show for the Silver Spur versality competition!" Presley recollected.

The two lurched forward to gawk.

"It's even grander than I recall. I haven't been to Bennington since... well, forever."

Rachel clutched her whimsical cowgirl hat on the backseat. Roxie had let her borrow a straw one she'd purchased at a thrift shop. A large horseshoe in bronze glitter was imprinted on the front.

"I am ready to rock this rodeo." She plopped the cowgirl hat on her head. "I can't thank you enough for bringing us, Brad. And I will take care of little Miss Presley here, no worries on that."

Mesmerized, Presley seemingly ignored Rachel. "I will never forget the day we pulled in. The four of us were a nervous mess, about to enter the year-end all-around competition. Smashed in the pickup truck towing a fifth wheel with Gertrude Steele. She was lecturing us to gather ourselves together with no silly antics."

"Eww, the thought of that woman." Rachel buttoned her coat, preparing to exit. "She sends shivers up my spine worse than the chill outside."

"What's a versatility competition?" Brad asked as he maneuvered past buses unloading attendees.

"Well, you have a team..." Rachel leaned toward the front seat.

Presley continued, "...representing a barn. We represented Gertrude Steele's Holly Hill Farms."

"Right. And you have one entry in English, one in the gaming discipline..." Rachel explained.

"...another in Western, and a fourth in showmanship and halter," Presley completed the answer.

"That last one's usually the newbie," Rachel added. "We talked Wheezy into halter, remember? I wonder if that girl ever rode a horse."

Presley smiled thinking of Wheezy. "Or drove a truck and trailer. That was her dream."

"Wheezy was determined. I thought of her a lot over the years when I wanted to give up," Rachel admitted in her own hypnotized voice.

"Yes, anyway, I've been following the competition for the last few years on Facebook. Recently, they've even added a para-equestrian division. The competitors with the highest total win the title Silver Spur Champions."

Presley and Rachel were volleying the conversation so fast that Brad had difficulty following. "Girls, whoa. Too much in one lesson. What in the world is showmanship or para-equestrian?"

"Para? Come on, Brad, that's an easy one. You're familiar with challenges, especially with soldiers. The equine world is trying to include the underrepresented, those living with a disability," Presley scolded. "Horses have been found to be therapeutic and healing."

"Nothing like the back of a horse to heal one's soul," Rachel agreed, tucking the hair of her inverted bob behind her ears and preparing to plop the straw hat over silver and blonde waves.

Presley continued, "Anyway, the team that racks up the most points wins the title. Each exhibitor on the winning team receives a silver belt buckle embedded with a gem of their choice."

"Just a pipe dream!" Rachel noted.

"Ha, what a dream that would be. To show in this facility again would be an accomplishment. When I was researching, I saw next year's schedule—October 8 is the championship."

"Less than a year away. Maybe we can attend."

They slouched in unison. "Not as competitors. Another decade, perhaps."

"Alright," Brad raised his voice, catching them both off guard. "This is no longer a dream, ladies." He parked the SUV in one flowing move. "Nothing is impossible. That's what I tell my troops. Now I'm telling you two. If you want to be enrolled next fall in this Silver Spur show, then we find out what it takes. You said any level rider and experience, correct?"

"Brad, I love you, but that is near impossible." Presley fingered the brim of her new birthday cowgirl hat. "You don't jump on a horse and expect to win. It would take a miracle to prepare us, not to mention our horses, Cleo and Hannibal. I can't imagine that coming to fruition."

He placed a finger to Presley's lips. Rachel watched from the back seat with admiration. Brad peered under the car visor, blocking the sun as his finger remained. "Nice to see the sun. Why don't you leave your coats in the car? You won't have to lug them around. I know it's cold but you both have bulky sweaters to keep you warm. You won't be coming out until I pick you up right here at this entrance." Then his finger slipped from Presley's lip, and his palm brushed her cheek.

"The sun is uplifting." Presley removed her ballcap and laid it on the dash. The warm morning rays reflected off the rhinestones in twinkles. "That's a good plan."

Rachel envied the couple's interaction.

"Remember you won't be able to reach me at the depot facility. I'll be returning hopefully around lunch. You can text, but I will be in a secure area."

"Thank you again." Rachel added, "And for connecting us."

"I think there was a greater hand in this chance meeting. But you're welcome. Have a great day, ladies."

Rachel watched as Presley thanked Brad with a kiss. The twinkle from her eyes matched the rhinestones on the ballcap.

He winked in response. "Happy to see my wife excited and smiling after months of treatments."

They each placed a cowgirl hat on their heads—Rachel a quirky straw one, and Presley a subdued and authentic tan Wrangler.

Brad tipped her hat lower to touch her brow. Momentarily, Rachel rushed with a sadness in her heart.

Heath, why did you have to die? I was sorry.

Presley interrupted her thoughts. "What do you think? I feel somewhat uncomfortable with a bald head under the hat. I stuffed the lining to fit." She secured it over a pink bandana for warmth and perhaps a crutch. She reached for the car door.

"The hat looks great! Look at this silly one!" Rachel pointed to her head. "Mine from thirty years ago was scarred with a permanent hoof print. I think it was stomped on in the last barrel race. My friend Roxie lent me this one."

They giggled in unison, removed their coats, and exited the car. The girls stiffened—not from the blast of cold, instead in awe. They were standing together once again, thirty years later in the same spot.

"Bennington State T & T Rodeo," Rachel read the banner hanging above the entrance doors.

Crowds were attempting to form lines and file in through several sets of double doors.

"Not a cowboy hat among them?" Presley whispered.

"Well, we're wearing ours," Rachel coached. "But funny, we haven't seen one horse trailer either."

Brad beeped as he sped out the roundabout.

"Well, it doesn't matter. We're stuck now. Don't worry about them. We look like professionals. Let's purchase our tickets and find good, warm seats in the arena."

The girls interlocked arms and blazed a trail to one of the entrances. Once inside, it was clear to Rachel that the event was going to be a sellout. Children and adults were shoving their way to the ticket booths. She thought she would at least catch a faint odor of straw or hay, but nothing. Then she pointed up the escalator to the mezzanine.

"That's where the shopping area used to be, right? Maybe I can buy a new hat," Rachel said as they approached a booth. "And I'm sure they have delicious treats. At least they did when we attended."

Presley glanced at her watch. "No time now. I hope we can still manage a good seat with these crowds. Never heard of this rodeo, but it sure is popular. Wonder if the horses are stalled below the arena? Funny. I haven't heard a neigh or a whinny."

The man in the ticket booth overheard her question and crunched his forehead. "You mean rumble and horsepower, right?"

"Horsepower?" Rachel lifted her straw hat to view him better.

He studied their appearance and shook his head. "Come on, you'll see soon enough. Keep moving." He fluttered his fingers. "Stamp, ladies. I have to stamp your hand."

He impatiently thrust forward, grasping Presley's wrist. Then he reached for Rachel, smacking the back of their hands with a red inked circle that looked like a truck tire.

"Interesting hat." Then he shoved them along with a heavy sigh.

They entered one of the aisleways labeled K leading to the main arena. "Wow, could you even imagine showing here again, but knowing what you know now?"

"You mean, knowing life is short? Certainly, would make me appreciate the moment." The two were ogling the arena below until someone bumped Rachel's side.

"You're holding up traffic. Could you please find a seat?" A woman who was clearly an attendant, by her white shirt and navy pants, pointed toward the judge's area. "There are some great seats over near the judging ledge. The sponsors are in the booth above. See the two right below? Better hurry."

Rachel tugged on Presley. "Okay. Still seeing no boots or buckles. Weird."

As they selected seats, Presley noticed a woman in dark sunglasses, her brown hair in mammoth Farrah Fawcett curls. "Who wears sunglasses indoors?"

Rachel studied the woman. "At least she has jodhpurs on. That's horsey."

"But white? To a winter rodeo. And expensive English riding boots, not to mention that exquisite satin cocoa blouse, buttoned low to see her million-dollar sparkling pendant."

"I guess things never change. Sponsors usually have money and princesses. I think she's drinking a mimosa in that champagne glass."

"Well, she doesn't look happy to me."

Rachel was occupied perusing the crowd. No cowgirl hats. "You know what else is strange? I never knew a rodeo to have an obstacle trail class. Look at the arena."

Presley examined the football size area lined in red, white, and blue cones. Orange cones were arrayed in the middle in different locations, a pattern formation. White PVC fences by cones seemed an extreme width for a typical trail pattern.

"Maybe they jump the fences. Trail must have evolved since our time. And look at the excessive room to ride the serpentine. A herd of elephants could fit through."

The two eyed what they thought were judges and riders walking the course. However, most wore stark white shirts and blue work pants with dangling lanyards. "Why would the attendants walk the course?" Rachel asked.

Presley zoomed in on the woman sitting in the sponsor booth again before an older gentleman sat next to her. His seat blocked her view. There was something about the lady, the manner she toted on the drink, crossed her legs and cocked her head in the dark shades.

Then a man tapped her shoulder from behind. "You ladies mind removing those interesting cowboy hats. My kids here can't see. What do you think this is, a real rodeo?"

Gigi Emerson was accustomed to Randall nabbing a front parking space. He always obtained a crucial position at events like this with valet parking. The gate attendant peered out of a hood squeezed so tight his cheeks bulged. He instantly welcomed Randall as a man of importance.

"Damn cold, sir. Judges and sponsors, go left. You don't want to be tied up in the lane that bears off for participants. And to the right, over here, is for the attendees. The traffic is a mess in those areas. An assistant will be waiting by the large metal garage doors, sir." He handed Randall two badges hooked to lanyards.

Gigi smiled. She secretly wished that she was a competitor. She wiggled forward as they passed the other lane hoping he would accidently veer, mixing with horses and trailers. Maybe she could meet a famous horse whisperer like Wyndham Glick.

Gigi inhaled, wondering if he was still performing. How she went gaga over that man! Unfortunately, she could not capture sight of even a cowboy hat at this point, which for a rodeo was surprising.

That morning, when Randall inspected her outfit, he had a moment of silence. At first, he appeared to object, then shrugged. "Okay, if you want to wear the horsey garb. Go for it."

Gigi had responded, "It's a rodeo, right?" But Randall had disregarded her in his usual manner.

She finished slipping into her English riding boots, opened another button on her satin blouse to reveal her endowment and fluffed her massive brunette tendrils in waves over her shoulders like a barrel racer. That roller set had worked perfectly. Maybe it was a rodeo, but she would be the epitome of equestrian attire and all the rage when presenting awards by Randall's side.

The indoor arena crowds were practically diving for seats as Gigi shadowed behind Randall. He had handed her a clipboard. He said, "Appear professional, Gigi," as he waltzed around with the judges evaluating the course obstacles.

Randall was debonair in his casual brown leather jacket and Ralph Lauren jeans. But she wanted to object to his choice of shoes. *Clarks, to a rodeo?* Gigi kept her opinion that he should wear Wrangler boots to herself. No need for another tiff.

Gigi pretended to write something although she was bored stiff. One judge was measuring the back up to the fence, and she mistakenly blurted, "A stagecoach could fit in these obstacles. Shouldn't they be tighter? More of a challenge for the horse and rider?"

By the scowl on Randall's face, she knew she should have kept her mouth shut.

"Randall, the course at a rodeo consists of three barrels or a line of poles... right?" Her voice drifted softer, hoping for forgiveness, until she was speaking only to herself.

Trail Class at a rodeo, that's a new concept.

The judge and Randall snubbed her by not answering.

"Randall, I would really like to go to the stables now. Maybe I could meet your horse, Louisa." Gigi double stepped to catch him.

"Gigi, please." He pivoted to face her with a slice of his hand.

She sighed and tapped her lip with the pen, pretending to ogle the crowds as they were filling the arena to capacity.

An engine roar caused her to jump, clutching at the judge.

The arena filled with the pungent odor of diesel fuel. Realizing she was gripping his arm, she let go and dusted the man's white shirt with her palm.

"Randall, do you smell that?" Gigi coughed. "Please let me go to the horses. Why are you even measuring for a trail class?" She stamped her boot hard into the dust, making her cough again.

Randall pointed to the sponsor seats. "Gigi, stop your damn whining. This isn't a typical rodeo. This is a truck rodeo. Go sit down."

Gigi pouted. "Trucks? I hate trucks. Or do you mean it's a class for the fifth wheels that haul the horses?"

The fumes and dust were now irritating her eyes. She removed her sunglasses from the top of her head and secured them on her face. Her true intent was to hide.

"Oh, a truck and trailer competition. That's different. I was never very good at backing up the trailer, but that's why I have a groom named Carlos."

The judge didn't seem entertained.

"You know, Randall has a six-horse for me. But Carlos drives it to all our events." She cleared her throat from his uncomfortable glare. "Plenty of room here for the competition, now that I understand."

Randall aimed his focus toward the sponsor ledge. It was his order to her.

"Well, to the sponsor stand for a mimosa." She exited, radiating an outer confidence but exploding with inner embarrassment.

The attendant had delivered a fresh drink on a miniature silver tray when Gigi observed two women in pathetic cowgirl hats. *Well, two typical rodeo fans.* Good they couldn't see the roll of her eyes under those shades.

Simultaneously, Randall entered the box and unfolded the seat next to her with an extended creak.

"When do I get to meet the horse? The one you named Louisa?"

Randall pointed down to the arena. "Right there. That's Louisa. She's the black one. The drivers are walking the course at present, and the rodeo will start soon. So, drink up."

Gigi squinted and searched for a dark horse. Not one anywhere.

"You meant the riders, not drivers, right? And why are they all dressed in white shirts and blue pants? Randall, I don't see one horse." Gigi rambled and sulked. "Oh, Louisa is your *rider*. She's an African American woman?"

"Great deduction, Gigi," he snapped. "Yes, she is the driver."

"I never knew you employed a woman of color as a jockey... or is it a driver. Which is the correct term for the rodeo? I knew a girl once... when my mother thought I needed to be part of an underprivileged program to develop my cultural side, I guess. She was the only Black person on the show grounds thirty years ago.

Every day that summer I drove her to the farm. Can you believe it. Me, inner city!" Randall didn't blink. "I was her Carlos." Gigi let out a fake giggle, trying to humor Randall.

"Gigi, I am not amused."

"How did you come to know Louisa?" Gigi reverted to a serious tone.

"She works for the transport company I was telling you about last night, Gigi. She's a hell of a driver. They sometimes call them jockeys on the trucking docks. They move the freight around for the regular truckers. Now, not another word."

"I'm so confused." Gigi decided to isolate herself in her seat, shut her mouth and act like a lady. She crossed her legs and fluffed her curls.

When the usher confiscated the empty glass, Gigi ordered another mimosa. "With a double shot, please. I hate trucks."

Chapter 14

Gator was pacing by the exhibitor entrance checking his watch when Wheezy arrived. He insisted she was late, and they would have to hurry. "The class begins at 9:00 AM sharp, Wheezy, and hopefully you won't be the first draw!" His cheek was visibly distended where he'd lodged a wad of chew inside his mouth.

She watched him wince when he seemed to bite his lip from the built-up tension. The pinch must have ticked him off because he pressed Wheezy to hurry more.

"We have a lot to do—fill out paperwork, sign release forms, and review the course. I want you to have enough time to feel the horsepower under you. It's our new transport truck! Frank offered the use of the semi free for the competition." He stepped ahead of her as he spoke.

"Gator, don't mention that name today. It makes me want to go back out the door. Technically, he has no connection to this fundraiser."

"I know, Wheezy, it's for..."

"I am fully aware, Gator. This is for the children with cancer."

"You are the best driver I know, but Wheezy, you haven't driven in quite some time."

"I've been trying to explain this to you, Gator."

Gator stopped at the secretary stand to sign papers and retrieve Wheezy's number. "Here you are, and that's what counts. Let's get 'er done. By the way, the entire staff is behind you with this incident. I'm sure your name will be cleared."

"Well, Frank Galzone is responsible for that. I'm not sure I will ever forgive him, even if he does clear my reputation, because he trusted Asher Devine over me."

The secretary at the competitor stand was sailing papers across the desk as fast as Gator could talk. In between each sentence, Gator tapped the next paper and said, "Sign here. Oh, and Wheezy, don't blow your stack... initial here, please it's the release... when you see Asher Devine..." He flipped another paper to the secretary. "...Sign here, please."

The knowledge that Asher was present in the arena paralyzed Wheezy with the pen in midair. "Asher, here?"

Gator tapped the paper. "Sign, Wheezy. We need your number, so we have time to review the course."

She didn't budge. "He's here with Frank?"

Gator munched on the chew and rolled his eyes in submission. "No, not with Frank. Another man, a sponsor. You know him, Randall Emerson. He always requested you to oversee the horse transports for him. And his prissy trinket of a wife is with them. She seems like a real piece of work. Sunglasses and built like a..."

"Gator! Are you for real?"

"I am for real. Sign here," he insisted. "Remember, Wheezy. This event does not have a connection to the company. You said this yourself. You may need Emerson's push to clear your name. He is a powerful man on the inside, and Frank likes him."

"I will clear my own name, Gator. I won't sell my integrity for a man who hangs with Asher Devine. I'll watch my back too. That's what I'm going to do."

"Just saying, maybe keep him in your back pocket."

The secretary was holding a numbered magnetic strip that was for the door of the truck, and a lanyard for Wheezy that read, *Louisa Mae*.

"Beautiful name," the woman complimented but Gator kept talking.

"And you have to sign autographs after the competition, whether you win or not."

"You didn't say a thing about autographs," Wheezy complained.

He handed her a paper with a diagram. "The course. And the autographing, it's for..."

"The children," Wheezy interjected, then snatched the paper.

Gator took a paper bag out of the pocket of his brown Carhartt. He thrust it toward her.

"What's this?" She squeezed the bag. "Gator, you know I don't chew."

"It's not chew! I remember back when you were a driver, going to school, raising your kids. You said this stuff gave you the power. And I see you forgot yours."

Wheezy inched the top open and peeked inside. "You are a good man, Gator." She softened, touching her neck. She rolled the bag closed with a crinkle. "I'll be sure to use them both."

"Now, let's go check out your ride, because you, my dear, are going to be impressed."

Gator led the way down a sloped ramp to the lower level, making two sharp turns. Under normal circumstances their tread would have echoed in the concrete corridor until they reached the bottom where Wheezy recalled thirty years prior the horses were stalled, and the competitors entered the arena. But the wailing brakes and roaring horsepower intensified and deadened their footsteps.

Gator turned back before reaching the bottom. "Here, you're going to need these earplugs."

Wheezy stiffened with surprise when he opened the lower entrance. The stalls had been removed, and thirteen monster rigs lined an open bay area which was the size of a football field. The pungent aroma of diesel and machine saturated the air, thicker than the straw and oats she remembered.

Wheezy paused, entangled in her thoughts. *Well, girls, I am at least at this arena to compete again. Although, not for the Silver Spur title, but for a silver belt buckle with the imprint of a tire. How ironic is life?*

"Wheezy, are you with me?" Gator gripped her shoulders and shook her. "Come on!"

Wheezy nodded, then followed him past the line of powerful machines.

"All thirteen entries lined up right here, and you, Wheezy, are lucky Number 7. You have the most sizable rig, an 18-wheeler, a class 8, with the most horsepower. That makes the course more difficult for you. Of course, you will rack up extra points if you succeed because of the degree of difficulty."

"So, what are my odds, Gator?"

Gator hesitated. "One in thirteen."

Wheezy wavered in her walk like a drunken sailor but Gator clipped her elbow. "You've beat the odds all your life, Wheezy."

As she tailed Gator, Wheezy recognized several drivers. They acknowledged her, some with a wave or nod. Then she eyed the tandem UPS rig and her nemesis, Semi Sam. Tandems received extra points, too, as backing up and maneuvering a double truck was a higher level of difficulty. The beefy man was about to board. Clutching onto the truck handle, he dropped back to the ground, landing on both feet. He scrutinized her up then down.

"Well, Wheezy." He spit the cigarette he had hanging off his lips to the ground, stamped it out and placed his solid hands on his hips.

Sam's biceps bulged, the right one imprinted with a tattoo of a seductive large-bosomed woman. Sam was a bull of a man fit to handle a rig and advanced in skill. Five years ago, Wheezy had stripped him of his championship title by a mere five points. He was out for blood; Wheezy could see it in his eyes.

"Sam," Wheezy acknowledged.

"You better put your big girl panties on, Sam," threatened Gator, "because Wheezy, here, has been practicing extra."

"Gator!" Wheezy grumbled low, her almond-shaped eyes enlarged.

"Don't you worry." Sam reached his pointer finger inside his belted jeans and hooked the edge of what appeared to be a flirty pair of lacey purple panties. "I got 'em on."

Wheezy reached in her bag. "Well, Sam, I have my lucky scarf." Wheezy pulled out the scarf that Gator gifted her from the bag. She criss-crossed the red, white, and blue fabric around her neck in an exaggerated display. "See you at the finish line."

He slammed the truck door, gunned the rig and screeched by in a turn around them toward the practice area. Wheezy locked on Sam until Gator spoke.

"And there she is. Ain't she a beauty? The boys already have her purring for ya!"

Gator arched his arm like a butler at the shimmering monster of steel butted next to Sam's tandem as the other man pulled away. A mammoth eighteen-wheeler was parked with a gathering of drivers staring in admiration.

Gator took the magnetic square sign with her Number 7 and centered it on the door.

Wheezy scanned the course paper. "I've never driven such a beauty through a course like this, Gator. Are you crazy for telling Semi Sam I'd practiced? I'm going to make a fool of myself."

Gator was hypnotized, petting the door. "She's a beauty—72 feet long, 8.5 feet wide and 13.5 feet tall, and unladen she weighs 35,000 pounds. That is one hell of a woman. She needs 600 feet to stop at 65 miles an hour fully loaded."

Gator leaped up on the running board and opened her door. "She's got fourteen gears, three hundred gallons of fuel and a tank on each side." His hand flattened against the steel. "Two thousand and fifty pounds of torque! I could kiss her up."

"Gator, who said she's a girl?" Wheezy squeezed his cheeks as she vaulted in the cab. "I think I'll call her Wyndham... Wyndham Glick, after one sexy Brazilian I once knew."

Gator had a perplexed expression as she settled in the cab.

Wheezy studied the paper and inhaled the fresh scent. "You are like a new car, Wyndham. You even smell handsome."

She reached in the bag and popped the two wads of bubble gum in her mouth, checked her scarf in the rear mirror and flattened her hair.

"You got this. Like riding a bike, Wheezy," she chanted to herself.

"Don't ding her, Wheezy." She narrowed her eyes at Gator's final words, then shifted the truck into gear.

Wheezy was repeating the pattern in her head. She knew how to study and juggle. The years she'd spent struggling through college and life had made her an expert.

The course ran through her head: *Right turn at gate, weave serpentine of orange cones.*

In between her memorizing, she rummaged through her life choices.

This was as close as Wheezy had ever been to something like her past adventure decades ago. And transporting, unfortunately, was most likely the closest she would ever be to a horse. Ironically, here she was competing in an obstacle course similar to an equestrian trail pattern, only she was handling a mega dose of horsepower.

Focus on the course. She drilled the pattern to herself: *Rear tire curl as close to the fire hydrant, right hand turn, then serpentine two barrels.*

Her thoughts drifted once more. Wheezy knew for a woman of color to be an equestrian during her lifetime was nearly impossible and not the norm. Besides she had her hands full with living.

The course, Wheezy. She sobered her thoughts. *Plates are positioned on the ground at all obstacles, alarm sounds if touched, point deduction.*

Minutes later, she was engrossed in another reflection, thinking of her namesake. Her grandmother would say, *"Louisa Mae, that is a cop-out. Get yourself a horse and ride."* Grandma's tiny voice sounded in her ear. *"What was the most memorable thing you ever did in your life? What will you tell your grandkids?"*

Wheezy lassoed her concentration, roping it back on the course. *Pull yourself together, girl.*

Follow the orange cones back up into the chute. The judge will measure how close you are to the white fence and how centered. Beep when complete. Do not knock over any of the red, white or blue cones that line the edges of the course during the pattern, or a five-point deduction for each.

The semi vibrated under her, sending waves of excitement, electrifying her attitude. Wheezy breathed and a determination filled her spirit. She was at home. She'd started her career as a jockey on the docks, moving forklifts around to set the cubs and loads in place for the drivers. Then in the cab of a semi, where she established a reputation as an unsurpassed truck driver at F.G. Transport.

Wheezy rumbled her rig to the double gates of the area, as Number 6, a reflective steel milk tanker was exiting. She let Wyndham purr while she scanned the arena. Her family and

Darren were somewhere in the stands cheering her on. Yet so were Randall Emerson and Asher Devine. That thought, more than her family, ignited a desire to prove her capabilities.

Wheezy snapped her bubble gum. She hated snappers, but in this situation, she was drowning in elevated tension.

The gates opened in a butterfly swing, and she rolled the thundering beast into the arena.

Wheezy fixated on every obstacle, losing thought of anything else. On the final back up, she let out a bellowing honk, and the air brakes screeched to a stop. The crowd was in complete silence as the judge measured the distance.

She watched in her rear side mirrors. Then he thrust his hands into the air as if she made a field goal.

Wheezy could not see the flashing billboard with her score, but when the crowd soared into applause, she knew it was posted in blinking lights.

The audience rose in a thunderous eruption, cementing that Wheezy was the leader.

She sucked in air, almost choking on her gum. She'd done it, but this competition was not over until Number 13, Semi Sam, finished the course.

Wheezy thought about Gertrude Steele as she drove the semi out of the arena. Even though Gert appeared to have a heart as hard as her name implied, if it had not been for her faith, Wheezy would never have been able to perform today. *I think that old trainer could have taught me to ride, too. Oh well, at fifty-one it's a little late.*

Wheezy rubbed the steering wheel as if praising the truck. She breathed and lingered for a moment, appreciating the power, the satisfaction that she conquered and handled the beast. Then she exited the area anticipating Number 13, her major contender, to finish.

"Look, ladies. My kids can't see over your cowgirl hats. These girls have waited since Christmas to come to this truck rodeo. I'm sorry you thought there'd be broncos and bulls, but it is what it is. So could you please lose the hats?"

He wiggled in his seat, gripping black binoculars.

"The winner gets a silver belt buckle?"

"I've told you a thousand times. It's for the kids with cancer from St. Mary's Hospital. Brings tears to my eyes."

The man in the seat behind Presley and Rachel was clearly trying to appeal to their emotions.

"I know the feeling," Presley added, removing her hat and modeling her pink bandana that wrapped her shiny head.

She had to practically close Rachel's mouth who was in shock that they were at a truck rodeo and not the typical horse rodeo.

"Boy, Brad got this wrong," Presley said as she slipped Rachel's hat from her head. "So sorry."

"It's okay," Rachel said. "We could uber somewhere, but Brad might come looking for us. Plus, we don't have coats, and you probably shouldn't be out in the cold. We might as well enjoy it."

The emcee announced a roster. Again, the crowd thundered in applause. Suddenly, the two women broke into laughter. By the time the first truck entered the arena, Rachel and Presley had drifted into their own conversation and future plans. The lone hindrance was the reverberating engines and the crowd's boisterous outburst.

They couldn't stop laughing in between discussing arrangements for their dream. Not until the man behind uttered an announcement to his daughters, were they interrupted.

"It's a woman driver, the only one! Number 7. You girls watch this one!" he instructed.

The emcee heralded the entrance of Number 7 into the arena, "Louisa Mae Valspar, Number 7, driving a mind-blowing piece of machinery."

"Louisa Mae?" Presley repeated as the words resonated in vibration through the arena.

Presley and Rachel simultaneously echoed the name, "Louisa Mae?"

"A woman of color handling a monster truck named Louisa Mae?" Rachel asked.

"It can't be. Can it?" Presley reached back in an unprecedented move and stole the binoculars from the man. She placed them to her eyes and leaned forward in her seat.

For Wheezy, from the moment Semi Sam executed the near impossible feat of backing up a tandem, her mind was suspended in a virtual prayer. She tried to speak to Gator, but her mouth was numb from chewing on the now tasteless gum turned putty. She was not positive that she could have maneuvered two tandem pups; few drivers could, no matter how skilled.

The crowd appeared to hold their breath as the judge measured the distance. When they stood in an ovation, Wheezy was afraid to check the flashing billboard because Sam had completed the task to near perfection.

But suddenly they were chanting her name to enter the winner's circle.

Gator was jumping and pounding on her shoulder. "Wheezy, you did it… by half a point! You scarfed up the win again… from Semi Sam."

Wheezy's body was stationary, aware only of Gator's punches and the tear streaming down her cheek.

"Your odds of 13 to 1 will raise a colossal amount of cash for the children."

Wheezy's happiness was a double-edged sword. Sam had followed her into the middle of the arena, as the crowd applauded ahead of the official declaration. Wheezy experienced both admiration and sadness for him.

"Sam, you were incredible." Wheezy turned into him, unsure of his response.

He stretched his arm and his substantial hand jetted outward for a shake. "No doubt. Wheezy, you deserve this. Next time, you're mine. You are one hell of a trucker and a fine woman." His voice was throaty from years of smoking and perhaps emotion. "Look at those kids. They love you!" He pointed to the audience.

Randall Emerson and his wife entered the circle, taking their place at the podium and prize table. The woman was dressed in perfectly unmarred jodhpurs and a satin top. She was completely masked with shades on her eyes under a massive head of curls.

"Gigi, you will have to take those glasses off for pics!" Wheezy heard Randall grunt a faint order.

The dainty woman reluctantly removed the glasses, merely long enough for the photographer and to dart a glance around the podium.

In the reflection of the arena lights, her eyes appeared to be a striking violet. Then Wheezy heard her whine, "The fumes are atrocious, Randall. I'm feeling faint. This is not my type of event."

A suspicion nagged at Wheezy. Perhaps it was the high-pitched moan, but she had the foreboding they'd met before.

Randall blocked her view when he wrapped Wheezy in an awkward bear squeeze after the photo shoot. His hands rested between her shoulder blades then rubbed horizontally several times. After this movement he unpleasantly scaled down to the top of her belt and vertically fingered two strokes until his palms pressed on her dead center. He initiated a final smash, her body against his chest, which lasted too long for Wheezy's taste.

When he released Wheezy, the tiny brunette had disappeared, probably to avoid one of her husband's sleezy hugs.

Chapter 15

Wheezy was signing autographs for the last two nine-year-old fans. The children were awestruck to see a woman of color seal the championship for the T & T competition. She handed them each a picture of the truck she tagged "Wyndham" plus her name scripted on the bottom edge.

"You can do anything! Don't ever give up!" Wheezy encouraged the two, suddenly realizing she sounded like her grandmother.

She glanced at her watch while gathering the articles spewed across the table. She was starving. Then a whiff of funnel fries delicately covered in fluffy white powdered sugar consumed her. Peering over the edge of her readers, she observed the waistlines of two female adults. The curvy figure placed a paper plate on the table. Wheezy's mouth watered. Funnel fries. *No more autographs, please!*

Wheezy scanned higher as she rose. The women stood motionless as if they had seen a ghost. The thin one wore a cream-colored Wrangler hat and the shorter woman sported a straw cowgirl hat with an over-exaggerated rolled brim.

"You two are a little grown-up for autographs, aren't you? I'm about to head out, but I can sign for your... children or grandkids?" Wheezy hoped they would move on and not want to strike up a lengthy conversation.

"You sure handled that semi! Certainly fulfilled one of your lifetime dreams. Congrats!" The thin woman curled a fist of empowerment.

"I second that!" The woman in the straw hat dabbed the corner of her lip with a napkin. She had powder dusted across her shirt, her hands and now the table. "I'm such a mess. That's why I could never back up a trailer. Remember the day I crashed out the back window of Gertrude Steele's truck, jacking the rig too hard?"

The Wrangler bounced as the other girl giggled and shivered simultaneously. "I will never forget that woman's expression. I thought you wouldn't be allowed to step foot on Holly Hill Farm again!"

"Do you remember it too, Louisa?"

Wheezy squinted, silently marinating in the words Holly Hill Farm. Then her chocolate almost ebony eyes widened.

After an awkward moment of silence, the woman covered in powder spoke. "Want a piece of funnel cake? It's delicious, Wheezy!"

"Thank you?" she stammered, tilting her head. *It can't be.* Then her eyes blinked.

"Don't you recognize us?"

They removed their hats in succession. "Bald and grey." The one pointed at her pink bandana. "But still the same girls. Gertrude Steele would be so proud of you. And your red, white, and blue scarf for a win. You are rocking it, girl!"

Wheezy gasped. "Oh my gosh, Rachel? Presley?" She stretched her arms across the autograph table. "I thought I would never see you again, let alone in this arena. How can I say it? This is so ironic."

"Oh, believe us, this chance meeting is truly a miracle."

"I've thought about you ladies so many times! I still have the picture..."

"This one?" Rachel and Presley both fiddled in their pockets, then pulled out matching tattered photos. "We couldn't believe it either."

"Yes, that one!" Wheezy exclaimed. "I thought you married and traveled the globe, Presley? An Army Lieutenant or something? And you, Rachel, didn't you marry that man, Heath? Did either of you keep riding?"

Wheezy was firing questions like a machine gun. Presley had to intercept.

"Well, that is quite an interesting story. But we googled you. Top tier of a truck and transport company. Wow!"

The discovery was disrupted by a thin figure galloping toward them. He appeared to be a forty-year-old male bellowing exclamations of joy.

"Stan?" Wheezy whispered. "Thank goodness." She hadn't wanted to explain the lost job.

"Wheezy, Wheezy, you did it!" Stan was slowing to a skip, his arms vexing in the air like windmills. "Your family is waiting outside. They want to treat you to lunch. I bet you're hungry!" He nodded at the two visitors and wrapped his arms around Wheezy's neck.

Wheezy smiled with embarrassment. "Stanley, these are the ladies from that picture... from decades ago. The horse ladies. And Stan, here, is my secretary. The best!" Wheezy winked to Stan, hoping he would pipe down.

The girls smiled. Stan was embarrassing Wheezy.

"Well, I was," he confessed. "That's the other thing, Wheezy. See, I have to talk to you about the severance pay." He cleared his throat and uttered a low, "It's frozen. Locked up."

"Locked up?" Wheezy yanked Stan's hand from her body.

"Asher Devine, he suspended the account until you're proven..." He shifted his eyes to the two ladies who couldn't help overhearing the conversation. Then covered his mouth. "Until your name is cleared."

"Frank believes him, and listened?" A heaviness compressed her chest.

"Wheezy, your friends." He shied with a bashful bow.

Wheezy glanced at Rachel and Presley, their smiles sagging, clearly uncomfortable.

Rachel slid the plate further into the center of the metal folding table. "Funnel fries, anyone?" That was the Rachel that Wheezy remembered, food always easing the moment.

The event staff was gathering chairs and tables for clean-up, unnerving the three women. "I would love to hear your story." Presley spoke with haste and touched Wheezy's wrist.

"Sweet Mary! Yes, we would," Rachel uttered. "And we're sure you're very busy. Or maybe you're not?"

Presley poked Rachel and stepped closer. "We'd love to have lunch. The two of us were discussing the possibility of riding again. You see, we each have a horse, Hannibal and Cleo, but..."

"We need a driver, to haul us," Rachel interrupted, then stuffed a fry in her mouth as if to say, *"Get to the point."*

"Oh my God!" Stan grabbed his hips. "Wheezy, they've been sent by God!"

Rachel nodded in consent, "That's it! It's a miracle!"

A worker began to collapse Wheezy's chair. He motioned to the table. "You all need to move this conversation elsewhere... it's closing time."

Stan scrunched his eyes at the man. "She just won the championship title. Maybe a little respect."

"See, we want to enter the Silver Spur!" Rachel divulged, ignoring the staff. "It's been on both our bucket lists."

"Rachel, really." Presley placed her Wrangler over her pink bandana. "As I was saying... we're *discussing* the possibility of riding again. We're not in any kind of shape—us or the horses, but we'll need a driver to haul us to a barn, when we do find somewhere to take lessons. With the goal, maybe, of entering a show or two someday."

Methodical. The Presley Wheezy remembered.

Stan gasped, "Wheezy?" His hand raised as if holding the event worker at bay.

"Maybe you could recommend someone to drive us?" Presley continued to be diplomatic.

"What do you mean recommend? Wheezy needs this."

"Stan!" Wheezy grumbled between clenched teeth.

"She's free as a bird," Stan reiterated.

"Stan!" Wheezy's voice elevated. She yanked on his shirt.

"She can drive your trailer!" he announced as if in church singing Hallelujah.

"Stan!" Wheezy yelled. "Enough!"

The staffer ceased folding the chairs, ebbing away. "I'll give you a few more minutes."

Stan flashed him a triumphant smirk, then stole one of Rachel's fries. He began to brush powdered sugar off her chest. Rachel proceeded to thank him.

"Wheezy," Stan insisted. "I'm helping you live *your* dream. I've been staring at that picture since the Titanic burned to the ground."

"It sank, Stan," Wheezy snapped. "And you know it!"

"Are you looking for work, maybe interested?" Presley asked. "We might have a proposal for you."

Wheezy lifted a brow. "Looking for work? Well, my job... that's a long story too. Let's meet for that lunch. What do I have to lose? Would be nice to laugh about old times."

"How about tomorrow?" Rachel lit up.

Stan leaped with a clap. "Sure, she can!"

Wheezy slapped his fingers as he cleared the table and gathered their belongings.

They walked together toward the exit. Wheezy had a lot of questions. "What kind of rig do you have?"

Rachel peered from under her straw hat. "That's the problem. We don't have one... yet."

"You don't?" Wheezy slowed.

Presley took her arm. "We're searching for a trailer but need help. We could use your assistance. It's a pipe dream. But we'd love for you to dream with us."

"I thought of you girls so often." Unbelievably to her, Wheezy was contemplating the possibility of reliving the past. "Where are you thinking about getting the trailer? And what kind?"

"Trailer World!" Rachel exclaimed.

"In Texas?" Wheezy questioned.

Rachel tamed her excitement down. "No, we can't drive to Texas. We'd need a truck too. Not to mention, they're very expensive."

Wheezy and Presley both halted. They were the same height and their eyes level. They exchanged a glance, and Wheezy rushed with a warm sense that her rekindled friend had ESP. The same ESP aura Presley used to have when they were younger. As if Presley already knew that Wheezy had a F-350 Ford pickup parked right out front.

She clamped down a smile for two reasons—preventing a slipped secret about the powerful machine and keeping another brainstorm to herself. Wheezy already had an idea where to get a trailer.

Brad was waiting at the Bennington Camry Center entrance. He tightened the collar of his coat and opened the car doors as Rachel and Presley rushed in from the cold. The car exploded with the heat of conversation.

"You're never going to believe this, Brad!" Presley leaned over with a quick kiss.

"It wasn't a rodeo at all!" Rachel revealed.

"No?" Brad sounded concerned.

"No worries, honey. It was amazing! Wheezy was there." Presley touched his forearm.

"She won the championship!" Rachel cheered.

"Wheezy? Who's Wheezy?"

"Wheezy from the picture!" they belted in unison like two schoolgirls.

"Simmer down. I can't keep up." He was grinning over their elation.

When they had finished volleying a recount of the day, they had practically reached the farm lane. Brad made a surprise revelation of his own. "I did some research."

"Research?" Presley perked.

"I was thinking about what you said. Each of you has a horse, but you need a trainer to start lessons."

"Well, we were going to google that after we found a trailer and someone to haul us."

"You have that voucher with Gertrude Steele's name. I took the liberty of calling her."

"Gertrude Steele!" Rachel gasped. "I doubt she would allow me on her farm again."

Brad peered in the rearview mirror. "I talked to a woman named Maggie."

He took such a long break while pulling in the lane, the girls were sitting on the edge of their seats.

"Brad? Did she even remember us?"

"Or want to?" Rachel mumbled. "She gave me the willies!"

"Well, after I did some let's say, *negotiating*, she put me on hold and..." he continued almost enjoying the tease, "this Maggie took a long time to get back to me. But you are to bring your horses to the farm. The same location as thirty years ago if you know where that is in the boonies. Last Saturday of this month!"

"Negotiating?" Presley questioned.

"End of the... Saturday?" Rachel gripped the back of his seat so hard her fingers must have cramped.

Brad reached over to massage Presley's shoulder as he drove down the gravel lane.

"Unfortunately, I have business and I won't be much help. Perhaps you can rent a trailer and hire a driver? Maybe Jemma, Rachel's daughter, might have some thoughts. She used to show Hannibal, right?

Rachel was repeating, "end of the month," and almost hyperventilating. Upon hearing her name she spoke, "No go. Hannibal's trainer moved to the west coast. Packed everything up. The horse has to be moved from the property by the end of the month. I was meaning to sell him until I met Presley. I can't even believe this is happening."

"Ladies, this feels right. Look how it's played out. You got this!" Brad's confidence floated across to Presley as if blanketing her with support. "I've seen you handle the last year, fighting for your life... for us. Nothing stops you when you want something."

His words were so loving that Rachel pressed against the passenger door with a swell of envy. She had merely experienced such a tenderness for a moment in her life, barely appreciating that love until it was gone.

Gigi was praying the sunglasses kept her incognito as she left the coliseum. There was something uncomfortable about the Black woman, the one called Louisa, the winner. She had been studying Gigi, and Randall hugged her a little too affectionately.

Feeling faint from the arena's odorous smell and commotion, she quickly slipped from the ring, unnoticed. Rodeos with trucks were not her style.

Once back at the house, after her nightly barn routine and a kiss on Kit T Kat's muzzle, she jotted in her diary. She made a collection of notes regarding Randall's relationship with his latest business acquaintance named Asher Devine. The two appeared to have a deal transpiring which had a malicious air involving a buyout. Gigi had overheard the name of Frank Galzone and the words "taking him down" by Asher.

She slapped the diary shut when she overheard footsteps. Randall must have entered his office for his nightly cigar and brandy.

Gigi stowed the diary under her bed and studied herself in the mirror. Time to utilize the skills she'd mastered best. She gathered her brunette locks, piled them on top of her head then loosened a few messy tendrils around her face. She smeared black liner under her eyes as if she'd been crying. Her delicate fingers spread the lacy nightie wider, revealing her entire chest which she dusted with a spritz of musk.

Gigi tiptoed to Randall's office and pressed her ear against the door. She assumed he was on the phone because he was talking in an elevated and firm tone. Her husband would be irate if she entered without knocking. Gigi tapped, calling his name.

He didn't respond immediately, and she was about to knock harder when she heard Randall cough several times.

After an endless minute, he ordered her in. The room was dim, the corners dark, the bookshelves towering to an eerie height. The only light was at the desk where he was seated, reflecting an evil glow across his face. She hoped her appearance would dissolve his abrasive state.

Gigi rounded the desk in a wiggly, seductive stride. Once again she noticed the safe door open. As she approached the rear of the chair, she summoned strength to rub his shoulders. But before she placed her hands on him, he spun the chair to face her in a flash, nabbed her hips and dragged her body between his legs like a vice grip.

"Now what?"

Gigi tried to restrain the shock that resonated through her body. The odor of cigar was as offensive as the arena today, and she had to pretend not to be bothered.

"Randall," she moaned. She reached to touch his shoulder, hoping he didn't see her tremble from the repugnance. She blinked her violet eyes.

"Yes?" he said, enjoying himself as he toyed with her.

"Please, have you considered the riding? Carlos can take me to the events. I was a pretty wife today..." Gigi was dying inside without Kit T Kat.

"Pretty is as pretty does, baby."

That was his secret remark to her, meaning *we will see*. Yet tonight her *pretty* worked faster than expected. Randall freed his grip and nodded in agreement.

"I will definitely see." He paused. And thankfully he shoved her away. "Off to bed."

Gigi inched backwards, delighted inside. As she passed the desk in a somewhat catatonic state, she noticed two glasses of brandy on his desk. She captured Randall's stare, forcing her to spin and sprint from the room.

After Gigi left the office, Randall rose. He gestured to the man hiding in one of the dark wings behind a movable cabinet.

"Coast is clear."

A figure edged toward the desk, shadowed by the table lamp. He parked in the chair across from Randall, reaching for the second brandy and savored a swig.

"I need that woman out of my hair. Honestly!" Randall sucked the end of his cigar as if stealing the last breath of life.

Asher swallowed. "She is a looker, if you don't mind me saying. Toss her my way."

Randall ignored the slur. "I'm going to have to allow her to ride, but I can't give her Carlos. He's my best barn assistant to help my daughter as she steps into the manager position."

The discussion was interrupted when his cell phone chirped. Randall read the name, releasing an exhale before answering.

"Louisa? Hello. Yes, you did great today... Certainly, you've proven yourself." Randall listened, mouthing the name Louisa to Asher. "What? Are you kidding? Frank what? Asher Devine? Yes, I met him... Hmmm..." He rolled his eyes. "Yes, Asher seems untrustworthy." Randall smirked. "I see, you plan on a gap year, like kids in college... Well, I know you have dedicated decades to Frank... How can I help you?"

Randall listened, repeating her words for Asher to hear. "You need a trailer, hmmm. You want to help some friends. Would I have or know of a spare to rent? Let me see what I can do. I'll be in touch tomorrow."

Randall held the phone in his hand and stared at the device. "Can you believe that? Small world."

Asher crossed his legs and spiked a snarky grin. "That wasn't who I think it was?"

"Seems Louisa needs a trailer. She's taking a break, to reflect, a year for herself while she waits for a decision. Her severance and funds have been frozen. Imagine that."

"You have a plan?" Asher swirled the brandy in the glass.

"We can snare all the birdies in one net." Randall raised his glass. "My wife will be out of our hair. Wheezy's reputation will be destroyed because she caused the company's demise, inevitably taking Frank Galzone right with her. And I will inherit a trucking company too... by, let's say, eminent domain. Who could ask for a better plan?"

Asher raised his brandy. "Cheers!"

Chapter 16

Gigi was sitting on the floor with her back resting on the mahogany frame of the canopy bed she loved, mostly because Randall slept across the hall. The full, winter moon penetrated her room through sheer curtains, illuminating the pages of her journal. Wrapped in her faux fur robe and fuzzy matching slippers, she touched the pen to her bottom lip and reread her journal words in a whisper.

> It isn't called making love, not with Randall. To be blunt, it's called having sex. I swallowed my disgust this morning for good reason, to reciprocate a gift in return. And not merely any gift. Randall informed me he found a driver for one of his extra fifth wheels and a trainer to assist me with showing my beloved mare, Kit T Kat. I will do anything to be with Kit. You probably think that's completely crazy, dear diary, but let me defend my obsession.
>
> The minute I mount my beautiful Tobiano I am mesmerized, focused intently on her. I experience the acceleration of her heartbeats, the bulging as her muscles tense and a serenading tap dance of her hooves. She is a ball of fire, as anxious as I am. But that's why I have Carlos and his methods.
>
> This morning when I had to appease Randall, I transformed my thoughts. Mind over matter, right? I thought of none other than Carlos, a late-night rendezvous in the tack room. Then something extraordinary happened. I was so entranced trying to outfox my brain that a dark and handsome man entered my mind as real as the moonlight dancing on these pages. Wyndham Glick appeared like magic. I was making love with the Brazilian horse whisperer from decades ago! Or was it... Carlos?

Gigi closed her diary and held it to her heart like a teenager. She prayed her husband, Randall, would come through on his promise, the possibility of spending the next year showing her treasured horse. Regrettably, he had refused to provide further explanation. He claimed his plan was merely in the early stages.

"And Gigi," he explained, "you might have to live near Kit T Kat through the week, away from our estate. The new stable might be too far to drive you back and forth on a daily basis."

"Oh, Randall, that would be difficult, but for Kit T Kat I would have to do it!"

Gigi remembered acting pouty, but inside her was a celebration of joy taking place. She nodded her agreement as if Randall was Santa himself and she was five years old sitting on his knee with a request. Then she performed the deed. Gigi had sex with him—not with Santa, but with Wyndham Glick, the mysterious horse trainer posing as Randall.

Wheezy was comfortable in her robe as Darren placed a smoking hot cup of tea next to her on the end table. She watched him stoke the fire. The man was compassionate, attentive to her and an avid listener as he was proving tonight.

She reenacted her recent phone call with Randall Emerson. "Then I said, 'What did you say, Randall?' His answer left me in a daze, and I simply hung up without even a goodbye."

Earlier, while on the phone, Wheezy had swallowed her pride. She had called Randall Emerson and told the truth before asking for his assistance. "I told Randall I was one step away from my dream position." Wheezy grabbed Darren by his hand and pulled him near her. "I knew Emerson respected me, but his response tonight verified he holds me in the highest regard."

Darren settled alongside her, then wrapped his arm around her. She loved him, yet still she fought the urge to reply yes to his weekly proposal. What was the root of her resistance? For gosh sakes, Darren embodied all the traits she desired in a partner.

"You don't need his faith in you, Wheezy. You are an incredible woman. Believe in yourself," Darren coached.

"And guess what? Randall said when he saw my skill at the truck rodeo, there was no doubt that when he needed a favor, I would be the driver. And the heavens opened, because he does need a favor. Plus, I informed him how Frank has frozen my accounts, severance too, so this job as a driver to horse shows would take my mind off things."

Darren's reaction was constrained. "Exactly what is the favor? I thought you were the one asking him for help?"

Wheezy watched a concern wash his smile into a straight line. "You don't like him, do you?"

"It's not that. Just something is off. I like Frank Galzone better."

"How could you?"

"As I said, something *isn't* following suit. The truth is missing. So, I ask, what's this favor?"

Always the journalist, Wheezy thought as she squinted at Darren. She didn't answer. She pretended to be examining the steam coming from her teacup. She didn't dare express that when Randall hugged her in an odd way that morning, she'd had that exact feeling. Something was off.

But Wheezy knew she could handle Randall if necessary.

"Okay, so I see the conversation is going nowhere," Darren affirmed.

Wheezy finally spoke after a sip of her tea. "He said he would call me in the morning."

"Okay." Darren's hand stroked hers as if to apologize. "I'm sorry, I was just expressing how I feel. Let's see what the deal is tomorrow. We should have an answer before you get together with the girls at lunch. Maybe this all will indeed work out."

Wheezy tossed the entire night, awakening every hour from a merry-go-round of dreams; 1:00 AM she was in a heated argument with Frank Galzone, 2:00 AM she was laughing and in a truck with Presley and Rachel, 3:00 AM Randall Emerson was hugging her in a peculiar way, 4:00 AM she was strangling Asher Devine and it was easy, and 5:00 AM Gertrude Steele was teaching her to ride one humongous horse, then she couldn't go back to sleep.

Wheezy never had a chance to ride a horse, but inside she had a secret. She had an affinity for the sport. Or maybe more for the horse. Riders three decades ago were generic—white, and generally affluent. Gertrude Steele had shocked Wheezy by insisting she enter a halter class in the Silver Spur competition with one of the horses she owned.

"Wheezy, our team needs another entry for extra points," Gertrude had commanded. And with Steele there was no such thing as replying *no* or shedding a tear.

Wheezy remembered being paralyzed as Gertrude forced a lead into her hand. On the other end was a beast of a horse, seventeen hands and counting. She remembered Rachel coaxing, *"Wheezy, you don't have to ride! Just lead the horse in the ring, trot to the judge and stand her square. Nothing to it. The horse is judged on her appearance. Think of it as a beauty contest. Oh, and maybe a little of you... so go ahead and look pretty."*

Wheezy's eyes had inflated. *"But she's so big."* Size was all Wheezy could fixate on. The gate had opened and there was no turning back. She trotted the horse in a straight line to the judge. A sensation pulsated inside Wheezy as the animal's hooves hit the earth. The horse stretched her neck until Wheezy eyed the muzzle aligned with her waist. She was doing it! The two were in unison! Not like when she sat in the driver's seat of a truck, but as in the spirit of camaraderie. Wheezy had a silent urge to perform again, never thinking of the possibility.

The last thing Wheezy remembered before entering the class was a spectator's comment, *"It's a Black woman?"*

As soon as the entrance gates closed, she'd forgotten about her world at home, how she would manage college, or her grandmother growing ill. The horse was not aware of any hurdles a Black woman faced with inner-city roadblocks and the racial slurs, nor what brought her to Gertrude Steele's farm and the show arena. Instead, Wheezy had to concentrate on her hand holding the lead, her body positions, and the ease in her voice.

The early morning thoughts forced Wheezy to rise quietly, leaving Darren without stirring him. She picked up the picture on her nightstand and headed to the kitchen for tea. There she waited at the table with her cell phone in her left hand and the photo of four young girls in her right.

When Randall Emerson's name flashed across the top of her cell screen, she swiped it up like a ground ball to second base. She inhaled and reinstalled self-control as if she were entering the halter class decades ago. She answered with a nonchalant hello.

"I have a proposal for you, Louisa."

"I'm listening, Randall."

"I have a four-horse trailer with living quarters that I can spare. No charge. I believe this will fit nicely with that truck you drive. If there must be any alterations to the mount or the fifth wheel, my service man can make the adjustments at no cost. The package comes complete with hay bags, tack, etcetera, to save cost for you and the ladies you were mentioning. Whatever you need, I'm sure my barn staff can supply."

Wheezy hesitated, thinking of Darren's remarks the night before. "That is a lot of no cost, Randall."

"I respect you and…" Randall stopped.

"There's a hitch for this favor, isn't there?"

"I need to send a rider along to this competition. I'm interested in this Silver Spur myself. The one you were telling me about. Your team will need a good English horse and rider team, correct?"

"Whoa, I don't know all the details. I'd have to discuss this with Presley and Rachel." Wheezy had a sudden apprehension that Randall's hand in this adventure may not be wise.

"Well, take it or leave it, Wheezy. It's the best offer I have. I wouldn't trust anyone else with the trailer, and it seems to me you need something to take your mind off your issue at the trucking company."

Wheezy recollected the halter class again. The horse had taken her mind off her anxieties, forcing her to concede. "Who's the rider you want to send along?"

"Let me just say it's a woman, someone I've known for a long time. Very knowledgeable with horses and who isn't afraid to…" he spluttered as if making a joking remark, "get her hands dirty. Definitely a team player. Someone who cares about everyone else first."

Wheezy descended deep in her chair as Darren entered the kitchen. He proceeded to refresh her tea and listen to the conversation with a raised eyebrow.

"I guess I can present this to the girls. If she's everything you say, she sounds like a good team member."

"The best. I'll await your answer this afternoon."

Wheezy glanced at Darren, then brushed her hand over some silvery strands escaping her ponytail. She had no choice but to agree. "OK."

"One more thing, Louisa. You said something about a trainer. Did they provide a name?"

"Gertrude Steele. Crazy, but I knew her a long time ago."

She thought she heard Randall chuckle before questioning, "You're kidding me? No one has seen that hermit for years. There was a time she was all the rage in the equine industry. Then accusations of enhancing and drugging destroyed her career."

"Do you believe those accusations?"

"I do. She accepted far too many horses into her training program. Besides, women are never the best trainers. Too emotional. They tend to be foolishly affectionate. If you know what I mean. And always out to prove something."

Wheezy wanted to correct Randall's statement, but she pinned her lips together.

"When you try and overachieve, you don't make the right decisions. A horse rolled on her. I heard she's a cripple since the accident."

Wheezy did not restrain herself this time. "Randall, your terminology is archaic. So, you were saying, Gertrude Steele is *living with a disability*?"

"I was saying, if you want the use of the trailer to see this crippled trainer then you have to include my rider on your little adventure as part of your team."

Wheezy swallowed. She was surprised at Randall Emerson's attitude, but he was too influential to argue further.

After Wheezy accepted the proposal, Randall placed his cell on the desk and slid a cigar between his fingers. Time for celebration. "One down and one to go."

Asher Devine had advised Randall if he wanted the freedom to forge the weights on loads, or ship products undetected across restricted boundaries for quality control, then Wheezy's presence needed to be eradicated from the trucking firm. Frank Galzone would have no knowledge of this scheme until it was too late. He would not be capable of restoring company ownership or rectifying Louisa's name. What woman, in her fifties, let alone a Black woman, could be CEO of a trucking empire?

Asher confirmed that he'd sequestered Louisa's funds to ensure she had another issue to keep her attention. Randall stared out the window across the frosty pastures. He had searched Gigi's bedroom for her journal to no avail. He didn't want to take the diary. But he did want her to record details of his meetings with Asher and overhear conversations. Let her think she was gaining on him. Besides, all pertinent information was safely locked in his safe.

Now that he had Wheezy contained, it was time to seal the covenant. Gigi would be having her mimosa and muffin in the kitchen. She always had a mimosa when she was stressed.

When he entered, Gigi was at the breakfast bar, her muffin untouched and her mimosa full to the brim. She was arched over the table as if she had a hangover.

Randall proceeded in and poured himself a cup of coffee.

She straightened with vigor and tightened her fuzzy robe over the pink negligee. "Randall?"

He acknowledged her with a nod. "I have a proposition for you. I said last night that if my plan worked, you could show Kit T Kat."

Gigi released the robe and clasped her hands together. "Thank you!"

"There are some guidelines that I had to set to make this all work out."

"Guidelines? Like restrictions?"

"I am expanding my equine business. As you know, Camilla is coming home to manage." Gigi slumped again. "Listen, I'm getting into different disciplines with horses."

Gigi crinkled her perfectly ski-sloped nose. "Beyond racing?"

"Kind of like the rodeo and eventing," he explained.

"Randall, you know I don't like rodeos."

He ignored her. "There is this competition called the Silver Spur. Where horse and rider combinations compete as a team in different..."

Gigi gasped and sat perpendicular in her chair like a soldier. "The Silver Spur! It's still around? You are not going to believe this, but I entered that competition years ago!"

Randall nodded, undaunted by her exhilaration. "You have heard of it *and* entered it? Well, I want you to enter in the English division. I'll be your team sponsor."

"Team?" She twirled at a tendril of loose hair. "I really don't play well with others... as you know."

"Listen, your face will be plastered on the outside of the trailer. Your beautiful face and Kit T Kat, the love of your life. Like a rodeo queen, the entire back door will have an imprint of the two of you. Every car on I-495 will see you!"

"Randall..." Gigi pouted.

"There is no choice. My equine business is sponsoring. I'm writing off everything. This is business, Gigi. Take it or leave it."

"Well, Carlos will drive us, right? I can't go without him. I need a groom and someone to tend to the horses. And I need a trainer. He is always positive I can handle the mare. Who are the other team members? Really, Randall, have you thought this out?" Gigi gulped a sip of her mimosa, now appearing disappointed.

"No Carlos," he flatly responded. "He's needed here with Camilla."

"Randall, Camilla always tops me."

"Calm down. I have another driver for you. She's part of the team."

Gigi stamped her feet as hard as her 110 pounds would permit.

"I need him more," Randall said. "And you will also have a trainer."

"Team members *and* a trainer?" Gigi protested.

"Take it or leave it. I'm done explaining. You can always stay here with me and Camilla. We could use your help anyway." Randall turned to leave with his coffee, setting the trap.

"How much time do I have to prepare?" she snapped at his back.

Randall smirked at the doorway before pivoting around. "I believe I can have this all arranged in a day or two. They'll be coming here to pick up the trailer, and you, on the last Saturday of the month."

"What! You said it would take time. Saturday's only a few days away. I'm not ready to compete! Kit T Kat isn't ready!"

"That's why you'll have a trainer. Unless of course, it's too much for you. I could find another participant." Randall spun around.

Gigi delayed her response, so he was momentarily worried. But when he passed the doorframe, she shouted, "No, Randall. It's fine. Who is the trainer?"

He faced her again. She was quite beautiful, small in stature with unique blue eyes reflecting a violet shade in the kitchen chandelier. Even if she was missing a cookie in that jar of a brain.

"You probably never heard of her. Gertrude Steele."

"Randall! She hates me."

"Gigi," Randall neared her, setting his coffee on the bar.

Gigi seemed to shy away, but that was nothing unusual.

He reached, pulled her close and overcompensated with his words. "Who could hate you? You don't even know her."

"But, Randall..." Her voice was muffled as he pressed her into his chest. He knew Gigi hated this. "Honey, deal or no deal?" He snuggled her closer.

Randall suctioned Gigi to his chest so she could barely nod. He smirked again. "Besides, I want another trophy for my shelf in the library."

Gigi's whiny whisper vibrated against his chest. "But Gertrude Steele hates me."

CHAPTER 17

Wheezy hoisted herself into the driver's seat of her Ford F-350. Although it was January, the next week's forecast for February was to be sunny and above average. A blessing in their favor.

Warming the truck, the afternoon sun streamed in rays that prismed across the windshield in rainbow colors. The morning frost and any dusting of snow outside had melted.

"A good afternoon to go trailer scouting," Wheezy predicted. "Did we ever think we would be together again?"

Presley agreed from the passenger seat. She was bundled in a hunter green Carhartt and a knitted hat with flaps at the ears. "How life can change in a day!" She patted the dash. "Nice truck, by the way. Shouldn't have any problem doing the job, that's for sure. Does she have a name?"

"Thank you. It was a gift to myself for my last promotion. Still smells almost new." Wheezy inhaled. "You could say it's my horse... power. No name." She pressed the starter and fiddled with the thermostat. The truck purred in idle.

"You must name her!" Rachel insisted from the backseat.

"Never thought I'd be towing a horse trailer with it. I had another goal: to be president of a trucking empire."

Presley sympathized with an upward curl of her lips. "I wasn't going to have cancer either." She shifted the hat to cover her bald head.

Then Rachel spread her arms wide over the seat, touching each of their shoulders. "I wasn't going to be fifty, widowed and suffering an empty nest. But here I am. Scared to venture beyond the walls of the beauty salon without my daughter, Jemma, to join the church women's society. Look how our troubles brought us together."

"Something certainly had a hand in reuniting us," Presley said. "That's what Brad says, anyway."

"I should warn you, sometimes I get... nervous." Rachel was seemingly getting organized in the backseat, shifting several bags, then buckling her seat belt. "I brought a couple of goodies and snacks. I know we just ate lunch. A good lunch, by the way, Presley. Thanks for the tour of your property and the barn—especially for introducing us to your horse, Cleo."

Rachel barely took a breath, her excitement elevated as they drifted out the drive of Presley's farm.

"I think we should stop for coffee like the old days," Rachel continued. "Remember every morning before a horse show, like at 4:00 AM or whatever the ungodly hour. We drove our caravan into a convenience store to hydrate and gas up. I always ate one of those white icing buns and sipped coffee with a straw—no spilling while riding. Those healthy nutrients lasted me an entire day of showing because we had no time to dismount and eat. Nor did we want to. I lost fifteen pounds that year. Wish I had that problem now." Rachel laughed, whipping off her scarf. "I'm having a heat flash. Did I tell you I have them too? And how about Venus?"

Wheezy flashed a glance at Rachel, mesmerized by how she rambled all her thoughts into one paragraph. They hadn't even reached the end of the lane yet.

"Venus?" Presley turned back.

"The name for the truck. Sounds fitting, right?

"Group of menopausal women on a midlife crisis journey to search for happiness? Venus might be appropriate," Presley noted.

"How about a midlife adventure to follow a passion?" Rachel announced with a clap as she removed her jacket too.

Wheezy shook her head. "Rachel, you haven't changed. Gotta love ya." She checked both ways at the entrance before pulling out of the drive. "Okay, let's get Venus on the road to Chester County. I always wanted to see the Emerson estate."

Wheezy plugged the address into the GPS and glanced again in the rearview mirror. "And no crumbs on the backseat, Miss Rachel. That is, if you're the same *shushly* girl you were thirty years ago!"

"What crumbs?" Rachel was wedging a cookie between her lips. "Want one?" she innocently offered.

Wheezy peered at her in the mirror. Rachel's silver and blonde hair was perfectly coiffed in waves. She'd stripped her scarf and coat, and was wearing a black winter vest with a matching turtleneck. "I must say, you look the fashion, girl."

"It was my job for thirty years. Make people beautiful and talk at the same time. I'm still a mess though. Nothing has changed in that regard, but I have an assistant now."

A moment of quiet filled the cab. Only the thundering motor hum and a sense of comfort resonated between them.

Presley broke with a cheerful glow. "I like Venus."

That was the last time no one spoke. For the next forty-five minutes, the conversation erupted with reminiscing and laughter.

"Do you remember when she put you in that halter class?" Presley stared at the GPS. "We're a mile from the estate."

"How could I forget! I was scared to death. And no one else looked remotely like me. Well, maybe Wyndham Glick."

"He was mysterious, dark and stood out like a shining star indeed!" Presley acknowledged.

"And sexy. He inspired me to follow my heart. I think I fell in love with horses, but truthfully, I knew my time was limited. I didn't have the availability or money to continue in the sport." Wheezy bent her lip in a quick frown.

"I've been in love with horses since the day my father sat me on one," Presley recalled. "We were on vacation, and he took me for a trail ride. When the ranch director tried to place me on a pony, I was like no. I remember pointing to a mammoth horse that appeared to have been splattered in painted dots over his rump. An Appaloosa!"

"Presley, you were a natural," Wheezy complimented. "The rhinestone cowgirl. I admired you from the rail. You should have won that Silver Spur championship title."

"Do you really think the three of us could get ready for a show like the Silver Spur?" Presley was watching the road. "I never thought anyone would sponsor us. We're novices. I don't think this Emerson understands that his rider may be too advanced for us. We need to be sure he knows that."

"Well, there are novice divisions," Wheezy said. "I was reading how the Silver Spur competition has evolved."

"Yes, but it's a team event. You could even try halter again."

Wheezy gripped the steering wheel at the thought. "Halter, again? Do you remember some of the remarks?"

"Well, now we'll both get remarks," Presley cackled. "*Bald* and *Black*."

They shared a giggle.

"One good thing, I won't have to tolerate that Gigi Tetless. She tried to make me beholden to her for being the driver in the diversity program." As Wheezy sighed in relief, the conversation was halted by a scream from the backseat.

"Holy saints in heaven! That's it! I'll never forget those eyes!" Rachel had been quiet, seemingly busy scrolling her phone. She now leaned forward over the passenger seat, pushing her cell phone at Presley. "It *was* Gigi. Though she's now Gianna Emerson. I am telling you, it's Gigi." Rachel was shaking.

"Let me see! Let's not overreact!" Presley held the phone closer to her face.

Wheezy was stopped at a red light and angled over. "I can't believe I've worked with Randall Emerson for fifteen years and never realized he was married to Gigi Tetless. The same woman who drove me to Gertrude Steele's farm. It can't be. This is all impossible."

The others stayed silent, waiting for Wheezy's reaction. She scrutinized the photo on Facebook: a brunette with eyes that mimicked violet.

Wheezy gasped and straightened. "Oh my. I may be losing my short-term memory with age, but that woman's long-term image is ingrained in my head. I think Rachel's right." Wheezy returned to focus on the light which turned green. "If that's the case, I can't set foot on the property."

"Let's not panic." Presley shifted from one woman to the other. Her voice was calm. "Let's be realistic. Randall Emerson's wife is not going to join us, either to ride or for the Silver Spur competition. She has all the money in the world, the best trainers, impressive horses, and exclusive shows to attend. His wife—if she is Gigi—is certainly not one of his so-called competitors."

"Sweet Mother, we should go incognito, not saying a word regarding the past, Wheezy." Rachel grasped her shoulder. "Do what we need to do and be gone. We need you," she exclaimed.

"Rachel, it will be fine," Presley soothed. "Even if it's her, she isn't going to be involved with us. Quite frankly, this would be impossible. All four of us coming together at once?" Presley zoomed in on the phone screen. "There's no way..." She pressed her face closer. Silent, she appeared to compress an urge to shriek.

"Told ya!" Rachel yelled in an overzealous cry. "I see it in your face."

Presley felt a pinch of defeat. "Definitely a violet hue... in the eyes, but Rachel, the woman was flat as a board."

"Look who she's married to. That could buy a nice visit to a plastic surgeon," Rachel proposed. "And if that's your thing, go for it, right?"

Presley nodded.

Wheezy hit another red light, confiscated the phone and was now scrolling. "Look at this picture from some fox hunting event. Who else wears head to toe white to a fox hunt? I remember my grandmother said she was my angel. And I said to myself, she's the devil."

"I heard through several of my clients that Gigi married a packaging mogul and has an estate of her dreams. Horses out the wazoo! This makes sense!" Rachel professed.

A robotic voice resonated from the truck GPS and seized their attention. *"You have reached your destination."*

"Well, ladies..." Wheezy pointed to an ornate sign reading, *Emerson Elite Stables: Premier Home to Exclusive Equines and Livestock Distributed Around the Globe.*

The three barely twitched as the truck growled on the half-mile lane paralleled by darkly stained four-board fencing on both sides. Horses littered the fields wearing jackets of multiple colors and patterns. The matching halters were most likely etched with each horse's name on a gold label across the strap. Cattle dotted the waves of valleys and hills; in the distance on the far side of the barn was a kennel full of dancing fox hounds, howling and baying to greet their arrival.

The house was built of magnificent stone with different corners and angles jutting from the sides. The women were mesmerized by the extensive property. A glass enclosure covered an Olympic-sized pool, adjacent to a pool house, tennis courts, an outside entertaining area structured in matching stone, and a two-story planetarium. Six enormous columns provided support and a stately appearance across the front porch that reached to the third floor. A widow balcony crowned the rooftop along with four double chimneys. All the outbuildings were a similar style and matching grandeur. Peaked roof lines and cupolas as far as the three could see.

They veered toward a stone barn with a black slate roof cresting like a mountaintop. As the truck hummed and pulsated past a line of trailers, all with the Emerson insignia, Rachel gave a description. "A two-horse trailer, a four-horse, a six-horse, they even have a stock trailer. Take your pick, girls. This is the trailer ice cream shop. Looks like Randall Emerson has one in every shape and size."

"Heaven help us!" Wheezy braked with a sudden screech. She leaned her elbow against the window. The throbbing motor vibrated in her veins, but nothing like the knife that stabbed her chest. "I'm facing my worst nightmare!"

"Oh, mercy me." Rachel pressed her face to her own window as Presley bent into Wheezy's shoulder to capture a view.

"It can't be," Wheezy muttered.

"Oh, that's her. Definitely Gigi Tetless," Rachel responded.

"Must be her personal trailer," Presley summarized in a monotone and stunned voice.

"Still a self-absorbed vile creature," Wheezy confirmed while examining the life-size impression staring at her from the back doors of a four-horse trailer with living quarters. Gigi Tetless

Emerson posed head to toe in English riding attire—white jodhpurs, shining high black boots with a houndstooth black and white checked jacket, and two pointed, sparkling silver spurs. Her chest arched outward to display her endowments. One hand was positioned on her hip, the other pointed a black crop at the names across the top edge.

Wheezy read it in a barely audible grumble. "Gigi Emerson and One Hot Kitty, Three National Championships. Owned by Emerson Elite Stables. Premier Home to Livestock."

"Remember the rodeo queen the year we showed? Her face plastered on her parents' trailer with an oversized pink cowgirl hat and glitter eyelashes. We had to look at it after she won the barrel race event at the Silver Spur. We drove halfway home behind her and that trailer," Presley recalled.

"Are you kidding? That race scarred me for life. I call it 'the bucking event of the century'. Breaks my heart." Rachel stole another chip to seemingly ease the pain.

"I'll tell you what I'm scared of..." Wheezy said. "Gigi. If I so much as run into her, I'm out of here," Wheezy testified. "What kind of woman our age plasters herself on the back of a trailer?"

"It's just a trailer," Presley consoled. "Gigi has no clue we're here. I'm sure her husband didn't mention the Silver Spur to her either. She would have no interest in a team event involving western riding and barrel racing. It's clearly beneath her."

"I must say she looks amazing," Rachel commented. "Not a grey hair on her head."

Wheezy squinted. "She colors it!"

Rachel smirked. "I would know that, Wheezy. Doesn't look her age, for sure."

"The rest is called Botox," Wheezy snapped.

"Still looks good!" Rachel tugged on the skin at her temples. "Maybe I should try it."

"Come on, no need to argue," Presley scolded.

Wheezy parked where a man was waiting for them at the barn door. The sun was bright, giving the three good reason to don sunglasses, so as not to be recognized.

The man introduced himself as Carlos and appeared to be alone, allowing the three to relax. He led them toward the end of the brick aisleway through impressively clean stables. The barred stalls were empty as all the horses had been turned out to pasture for the afternoon.

"Check out the chandeliers," Rachel whispered as she noted the intricately designed lights dangling from the peaked ceiling. "I don't have anything that magnificent in my entire house."

Carlos motioned them into another room labeled "Office" on a gold plate.

A man from behind a desk instantly rose. "Louisa, good to see you again. And these are your friends, the other contestants?"

It bothered Wheezy that Randall reeked with charm.

She watched as Rachel smiled shyly, then shook his hand. "Lovely facility, Mr. Emerson."

"Please, call me Randall. Let's face it, we're going to be working together. We'll have a good chance at the title of Silver Spur championship. That is if the three of you are as dedicated as Louisa has expressed. My rider is… let me say… well… she is exceptional."

"Why are you doing this?" Wheezy unexpectedly inquired, causing both Presley and Rachel to react. She couldn't refrain. This was all too good to be true. His previous overeager hug at the trucking event plagued her with ill-feelings. Besides, she had already been a fool once in the past week.

"Louisa, I think I explained, but again, it is ever crucial to publicize our name, our quality stock. I have an ever-growing interest in this industry." Randall stopped, seemingly defensive. "Don't you trust me?"

Wheezy hesitated, eyeing Presley, who had been through so much. Her ball cap twisted to the side. Wheezy nodded her head.

"Good, now my rider is not here at present, but let me show you the first trailer and get this show on the road. I can supply, as I said, any necessities."

Randall led them back outside and headed to the row of trailers. Wheezy chanted under her breath with every step, *Please not that one, not the first one, please, please, oh why…*

Randall halted at the first trailer, the massive one with the life-size picture of his wife, Gigi.

"This is it. The trailer has living quarters, can easily sleep four, haul four horses and tack, and has a full shower and bath. Can't ask for better or safer accommodations. Carlos, give them a tour inside."

The three women were speechless, not one moving to follow Carlos.

"Louisa, I have seen you drive a semi. You aren't afraid of this?" Randall questioned.

"I wasn't expecting an English show girl on the back. We don't need an overabundance of attention as novices."

Randall huffed. A disappointed scowl swept his face. He peered at Wheezy under thick greying eyebrows. "You didn't seem like someone who would let that affect your dream." He inhaled. "Louisa, take it or leave it. It's *my* wife, *my* stock and *my* farm."

Rachel grumbled from behind, "Told ya."

Presley angled into Wheezy. "We can hide it with a magnetic cover like the number placed on your truck at the competition."

Randall clearly overheard. "Unfortunately, my estate name is on the side for a reason. I want to promote my business, and of course, the woman I love. Again, take it or leave it. You girls aren't going to find any hauling and sleeping capabilities like this one on short notice."

An attractive blonde peered out of the barn door. "Daddy, we have business." She made no other acknowledgment of the visitors, then disappeared.

"One minute, Camilla." Randall scrutinized the three like a high school principal. "Listen, I will give you a few moments to decide. Carlos can wait for your answer. I'm a busy man. If you're interested, you can pick up the trailer, my rider and horse on Saturday and head to this Gertrude Steele's training facility. I assume you've made arrangements?"

Randall left them standing at the rear of the trailer, staring at the life-sized image looking down on them. Their breath fogged in clouds from the chill.

"I can't believe the karma. Gigi Tetless will be riding with us in spirit." Rachel shook her head.

"Wheezy, I know this is all crazy. You don't have to be a part. Brad was just dreaming for me because I was..."

Wheezy stopped Presley with a quick gesture. "I will be driving Gigi around this time, and she will be constantly crawling up my butt, won't she?"

"Oh my gosh," Rachel clapped her hands. "We're going to do this! We're going to ride! The Silver Cowgirls—that's what they'll call us! The Silver Cowgirls ride!"

Chapter 18

Rachel raised her morning coffee between Presley and Wheezy in the front seat for a toast filled with hope. A straw was jetting out of the lid at an angle, almost touching the ceiling light of the cab. The three were parked in front of a *Gas and Go* convenience store where they had purchased morning staples of coffee and icing buns. They were bundled in their winter Carhartts, ready to journey to Emerson Estates for a second visit.

"We have to think of this as a gift," Rachel explained. "A miracle that we found each other. The fact that Mr. Randall Emerson is sponsoring us with a beautiful trailer that we could've never imagined, fitted tack and even hay for the journey today, all this is meant to be."

"That's why I'm suspicious." Wheezy stared at the steaming hot coffee cup. "Too good to be true, I think."

"It's destiny," Rachel tried to convince her. "Fate."

"I agree," Presley chimed in. "This is nothing short of a miracle. I guess we'll have to take the positive with the negative." Presley's tea bag string was dangling from the side of her cup. "Wheezy, neither Rachel nor I want you burdened with driving us if you're unhappy. Once the trailer is hooked up today, and Randall Emerson has indeed come through with his commitment, whoever the rider is, we will have to suck it up and accept the person as a team member. It's not like we'll be sleeping in the living quarters with the princess herself. It's just her face plastered on the back of the trailer."

Both Presley and Rachel stiffened with anticipation waiting for Wheezy's answer.

Presley raised her Styrofoam cup with the *Gas and Go* imprint to join Rachel's. "I would love to have one more year like that one so many years ago. One more year with Cleo. I might not get the chance ever again." Both locked eyes on Wheezy in a plea to raise her cup.

Wheezy inched her coffee upward. "It's a deal. If everything goes as planned, we'll return to your house to load Cleo, then to the farm where Hannibal is stalled. Once all three horses are on the trailer, we're off to meet the infamous recluse, Gertrude Steele."

Rachel handed them each a white icing bun wrapped in plastic. Even though she was weighted with excitement, there was something gnawing in the pit of her stomach. Unfortunately, the sugary delight wasn't the antidote to ease the feeling.

Merely a few hours later, the trailer hook-up could not have been smoother. The sunny weather blessed them, and all the calculations were exact. Wheezy was comfortable on connecting and un-connecting after a few lessons.

The hay bags were mounted, tack was checked, and the living quarter staples, like water and heating systems, were explained in full. Yet, the horse and the unknown rider were still unaccounted for until the ground rumbled.

A shadow reflected in the morning sun on the earth at the entrance of the barn. The Goliath-sized figure commanded everyone's attention. A horse stepped into the opening, dragging the handler at the end of the lead like a worm on a fishing line. The horse was flocked in a white and black houndstooth patterned jacket, her neck and head included, her legs wrapped in thick protective sheaths. Almost the only visible part of the horse was her oversized eyes and swishing multi-colored tail.

The groom tugged the mare back, forcing himself ahead of her broad chest to lead her toward the trailer. She gallantly high stepped in thunderous beats, her head perusing like a submarine scope snorting the air. That was the exact moment the "feel good" morning curdled like unrefrigerated milk in ninety-degree weather.

The groom was cursing and fighting for control. "Whoa, Kit T Kat. Damn horse."

Rachel ogled as they passed. "Blessed Saints in heaven." Kit T Kat was certainly the epitome of beauty. Unfortunately, the mare was also the epitome of wickedness. The three watched from a safe distance while handlers tried to load the magnificent Tobiano.

Without warning, the mare balked in opposition, avoiding the ramp. The horse yanked in reverse with enough momentum to dislocate the man's arm from the shoulder.

Rachel repeated the name, "Kit T Kat? I think that's the mare on Facebook with *you know who*. Yes, I'm sure. Gigi was riding her at a foxhunting event."

"She's a beast," Wheezy mumbled. "I think the rough housing is not a good idea. I hope we can handle this girl."

The groom ordered the mare backward with quick jerks, forcing her to curl her muzzle into her chest. Then he attempted to lead Kit T Kat onto the ramp again.

She objected. Her body buckled onto her hind, dragging the handler almost to the ground.

He was fueled with anger. The other grooms circled the two as if at a boxing match, cheering the man and offering their assistance. The situation escalated with each wrench on the lead or whack on the hind. Kit T Kat's tail was wringing in fury, her houndstooth coat shifting to one side as one man chased her in a circle with the stable broom.

Kit T Kat pivoted left, then side-stepped right as her hooves sparked against the concrete each time she approached the tip of the ramp. Her earth-shattering screams announced her revolts. Her head lifted in powerful jerks that forced the handler off his feet, only fortifying both their disdain.

Another man exited the barn. Rachel recognized him as the groom named Carlos. A discouraged scowl stained his face when he witnessed the situation. He scurried to reprimand the handlers and snatched the lead.

The man was a smaller build than the others but appeared to have a sizable horse sense. He guided Kit T Kat in circles, first large then small, regulating her pace with ease. He whispered and stopped to stroke the moistness on her neck under the winter sheet.

The mare settled, her snorts softening. Then when she quieted, Carlos brought her hooves to the edge of the ramp only to stop her. He waited. The mare's neck arched downward to touch her muzzle to the rubber mat.

Kit T Kat stood steadfast until Carlos stepped on the ramp. She propelled her front legs in a revolution ending in a refusing stomp.

The man did not shift or twitch, nor swat nor whip; instead, he stationed himself like a statue. His voice coaxed her, ignoring Kit T Kat's pawing as she scraped the blacktop. Carlos remained motionless.

Finally, the mare pulsated her left leg several times until touching the rubber surface as if it were a bed of hot coals.

Rachel pressed her hands in a silent prayer, which was answered when Kit T Kat marched on. The mare followed Carlos, her neck and head erect in a stately manner as if the episode were only a figment of everyone's imagination.

"I sure hope this rider can handle Kit T Kat, or we are going to have our hands full," Wheezy remarked. "Because I am no horse whisperer."

The memory of the other horse whisperer flashed in Rachel's mind. When Carlos exited the trailer, Rachel helped to close the slant. "Carlos, you remind me of a man long ago. He was a horse whisperer named Wyndham Glick."

Carlos nodded. Kit T Kat was screaming in between bites of hay, clearly disturbed that her stable friends were not coming on the journey.

"I know him." Carlos latched the metal bar.

"You do?" the three responded in unison.

"I wonder what ever happened to him," Rachel asked.

"After years around the globe, he is to be at the Silver Spur competition."

"The Silver Spur?" Presley lifted her ballcap slightly above her brow.

Rachel gasped. "I'm going to faint. The heavens are showering down on us."

"Oh, you *are* going to faint," Wheezy grumbled. She was staring at the barn.

A woman in white appeared in the doorway like an angel wearing a fur-lined ski coat, spotless white jodhpurs, pristine boots and sunglasses hiding her eyes.

Two men passed her, lugging an oversized trunk that belonged on the Titanic, and headed to the trailer tack room door. The men grunted from the weight, hoisting the case inside.

"Hey," the woman demanded. "Be careful with my stuff." Then she turned to Carlos. "Carlos, I told them to wait for you to load Kit T Kat! They didn't hurt my baby, did they? What will I do without you?"

Wheezy stiffened like a statue. Rachel's mouth was half open in disbelief, and Presley was nodding in confirmation. "It is her. It is Gigi."

Wheezy's fists were clenched, seemingly about to contest, until Randall Emerson appeared from behind. "I see you've met my horse and rider. This is my beautiful wife, Gigi, and of course, the exquisite mare, One Hot Kitty. I believe an asset for your team."

"Oh yes, we've met." Wheezy faced Gigi in a solemn stare.

"You..." Gigi pointed her dainty finger at Wheezy. "You're the woman from the competition. You'll be driving the trailer? Can *you* handle my Kit T Kat?"

Presley's fingers curled onto Wheezy's arm. "Thank you, sir. Wheezy, I'm feeling a little wobbly. Can you excuse us? Rachel, perhaps you'd do the honors?"

Rachel watched as Presley and Wheezy headed to the cab exchanging words. She slipped a quick smile at Randall, then at Gigi, praying again, this time hoping Presley could convince Wheezy they were in this together and reminding her they had made a promise. She was searching for an explanation but could only listen to Gigi bellyache with whines at her husband. Gigi clearly had not made a connection to who they were.

"I can't believe you're sending me without Carlos. Who will ride the mare and bathe and feed her? Does this woman do more than drive?" Her voice dropped to a whisper when Wheezy returned.

"Thank you, Randall," Wheezy said. "We're running late, so these Silver Cowgirls gotta roll." She turned to Rachel. "Truck is pulling out, so if you girls are joining, better hop in."

"Yes!" Rachel commented almost to herself. She wasn't sure if she wanted to hug Wheezy or search in her bag for one of those new little white pills the doctor ordered for her.

Wheezy's face was compressed like a closed accordion. She was clearly doing her best to prevent any objection.

Rachel raced up to join her in the trailer. "Wheezy, Gigi has no clue who we are," she whimpered. "Yet."

Wheezy looked at the woman arguing in Randall's space. "God help us, I'm having one of your heat flashes, Rachel." Wheezy slammed the truck door.

The engine rumbled as all three examined the scene in the oversized side mirrors aimed at the trailer rear. Arms folded with a vibrating cocked leg, Gigi looked intently at Randall. Even as the truck engine purred in the drive, her voice bellowed louder. She was ranting as her husband stepped away. Finally, huffing in surrender, Gigi tiptoed, as not to dirty her boots, in an awkward race to the front cab.

Her backpack bounced off her back, landing in the crevice of her elbow. The weight of the oversized sack set the petite woman off balance, almost in a topple as she struggled to open the truck door. All three intently focused on Gigi as she leaped in the back behind Presley.

"What do you have in that bag? It must weigh a ton," Rachel asked, but Gigi ignored her.

She tossed her Coco Channel initialed sack trimmed in gold across the back seat.

Rachel eyeballed her, appalled when it landed on top her own bag of snacks. She heard the chips crack under the blow of what appeared to be a thirty-pound sack.

Gigi offered no apology and rummaged through her backpack, surely smashing any extra icing buns in Rachel's convenience store purchase. When the woman located a makeup mirror, she snapped it open. Her delicate fingers held it as she studied her face without removing the dark glasses. Finally, she rolled her lips together a few times, then snapped it shut before staring out the window.

At present, Rachel didn't know which was more annoying—Gigi Tetless Emerson sharing the back of Wheezy's Ford F-350 loaded with musk oil, makeup, and attitude, or her likewise spoiled mare.

Gigi and her Kit T Kat had caused them to be an hour late to retrieve the other horses. Rachel knew she should call the farm where Jemma was waiting to load Hannibal on the trailer before she was off to her own new life. Unexpectedly, that's when Rachel realized she hadn't thought about her daughter nor life without her the entire morning.

Presley noted how the trailer rocked from Kit T Kat's hooves that tap-danced in the rear. She was screaming in a last-ditch effort for the herd she had left behind.

"Not a happy soul back there, is she?" Rachel asked.

"Kit T Kat will calm down when the others load. She likes company and hasn't been alone for some time. I've had a little hiatus from riding her," Gigi nipped. Then Presley heard a cushion of softness in Gigi's next remark. "She's feeling alone and scared."

"Do you recognize any of us?" Presley glanced back and twirled her index finger around the truck.

Gigi faced them. "I know the driver, Louisa, from the truck competition." Gigi pressed some hair behind her ear.

"Her name is Wheezy. And she *is* a member of our riding team, not simply the driver," Presley defended.

"Wheezy?" Gigi's face appeared distorted. "Rides horses."

"Not exact—" Wheezy tried to answer.

"Yes, she does," Presley interrupted, then lifted her cap above her brow and pushed back the snug covering underneath that kept her bald head warm. "Pretend I have auburn curls or waves, and perhaps fewer wrinkles."

Gigi studied Presley and crinkled her nose.

"Drop the sunglasses, will you?" Wheezy instructed as she pressed the right side of her lip into her cheek.

"Let me introduce myself. I am Presley. We met a long time ago. And this is Rachel, and of course, Wheezy. We all showed horses together under Gertrude Steele. You drove Wheezy to the facility that year."

Gigi lifted her glasses, rotated her violet eyes like a carousel, halting at each of them, then dropped the glasses back in place without a word.

Rachel rummaged through her pocket. She placed a photo on top of the duffle bag between them. "Here. This is us. Now do you remember?"

Gigi didn't remove her glasses this time either. Her entire body turned away after a brief look.

"Thirty years ago?" Rachel dropped another clue.

Gigi shoved the picture back to Rachel. "I don't remember the photo. Must not have been a highlight in my life. All the volunteering... I was *forced* to do... I was like eighteen, or nineteen... for those who were *less fortunate*... certainly made my life a drudge." Gigi added exaggerated emphasis to certain words as she glanced in Wheezy's direction, but for Presley, it was difficult to tell with the sunglasses.

Wheezy was gripping the wheel as she shared eye contact with Presley. "I don't like the looks of the sky ahead. Today was supposed to be sunny, but there's a chance of a snow squall later. And we're running late." She poked a look at Gigi. "Won't be good, pulling this rig."

Presley was a master at remaining calm. She'd maintained composure her entire life, even during the past year. Restraining herself, she tapped her ball cap and proceeded to plug the next stop coordinates into the GPS. "Hopefully the dark clouds will pass. We'll be okay."

She could hear Rachel whispering a Hail Mary.

"You're praying?" Gigi asked.

"Yes, asking the Blessed Mary to watch over us," Rachel defended.

Gigi made a loud *tsk*, then bent into the door as if to protect herself. "Just take care of my mare," she directed toward the driver seat.

The cab fell to a deadening quiet as the truck pulled onto the main road. Only Kit T Kat's frantic screams broke the silence. The mare's bellows were serenaded with the rattling safety chains connected to the hitch in the bed of the truck.

Venus, as they'd tagged the Ford F-350, thundered toward the ominous skies ahead to load the other horses.

Hannibal and Cleo were both loaded without a hitch, unlike Kit T Kat. Rachel was sitting in the truck, catching her breath between tears that echoed from the back seat. The three waited for Wheezy to finish examining the rig with a final safety check.

Presley passed a tissue back to Rachel.

"Really?" Gigi snipped. "Can't you say a prayer like you did earlier, or something to alleviate your misery?"

Presley smiled sympathetically as Rachel rubbed her nose. "An empty nest is very difficult. I hated the thought of Jamie, my youngest, leaving. Maybe Hannibal will help take your mind off missing Jemma. I know my horse, Cleo, takes all my worries away when I spend time with her." Presley ignored the wickedness melted against the opposite door.

Presley eyed the driver side truck mirror as she waited in the passenger seat with the other two in the back. She observed Wheezy who had remained outside to perform a safety check on tire pressure and lights as every efficient hauler knows to complete before hitting the road at sixty miles an hour. A missing brake light or low tire pressure could spell disaster. Wheezy was holding and examining a bridle in her hand. Presley watched as her preoccupied friend approached, unaware as she grabbed the backseat passenger door handle that Gigi was practically pasted against it.

Presley twisted to look back and warn Gigi. She knew the right thing to do; any good friend would alert the other before the door flung open unexpectantly causing Gigi to tumble to the ground. But,

Presley reconsidered, she was so tired of being virtuous. She sat back, pressured by her change of heart. Gigi was no friend. *Witch has it coming.*

Wheezy yanked open the door, enthralled at the contents she carried in her hands.

Gigi screamed, losing her balance, and instantly collided against Wheezy's abdomen with a grunt. Luckily, Wheezy's body blocked her fall. Gigi's head scrunched forward. Her body was suspended, chin to chest, as her arms flailed in the air, searching for safety.

"Woman, what the heck?" Wheezy hollered and luckily shuffled the bridle to her side. After regaining composure, she gave Gigi a push, cementing her straight up again.

Rachel was momentarily shocked while Presley pretended. Fortunately, no one would ever suspect her guilt.

Wheezy disregarded Gigi with a sigh of disgust. "Here, Rachel. Your daughter wanted you to have this." She passed a bridle clipped with a note across Gigi whose sunglasses were now crooked, hair disheveled and her face plastered in shock.

Presley began to giggle, cupping her mouth and turning away. Unfortunately, she couldn't hide her bobbing shoulders.

"Are you laughing?" Gigi questioned.

Rachel was clutching a bridle engraved with Hannibal's and her own name on a gold plate. She fingered the note:

> *Good Luck, Mom, I Love you, Jemma. Remember, Hannibal doesn't like ponies or cows, but otherwise he's a gem. You will do fine! Now have fun. Time for you!*

Rachel wanted to cry, but rather she burst into laughter when she eyed Presley's quivering body.

"Really, you two think it's so funny?" Gigi contested. "I could have been seriously injured if I hit the cement."

Rachel attempted to gain composure. "It's so hard to let go." But she couldn't help releasing another snicker. "Of children, not the… door, I mean."

Wheezy seemed unfazed as she crawled into the driver's seat.

"She was my whole world. After Heath died, it was Jemma and me." Rachel tried to refocus. "I spent every moment… thinking about a… door." Rachel slapped her mouth. "Why did I say door?"

"Happens to me all the time, midlife brain fog," Presley said with a giggle. They both laughed while Wheezy released a slight smile.

"It was the best year! I was so scared… are you supposed to be scared? I wanted to ride from the time I can remember, but when I finally had the chance, I was so afraid. Is that normal?" Rachel confessed.

"Facing your fear is a good thing. Don't let any *door* stop you," Presley consoled.

"Am I correct in assuming none of you show, let alone on a regular basis?" Gigi sounded like a prosecuting attorney.

The others chuckled.

"This is no joke. I don't see what's so funny here. You're telling me you haven't ridden seriously. I thought you were experienced. My horse is the most important creature on this earth. Don't forget who's plastered on the back of this trailer."

The remark stunned everyone. Then Rachel suggested, "Anyone want a broken chip?" She reached for the smashed bag under Gigi's oversized sack.

Wheezy changed the conversation. "The ominous sky has me concerned."

"I'll give you something to be scared about," Gigi cut in. "Gertrude Steele. She's someone to fear. She has to be a hundred years old, and it's said she's demented." Gigi released an exhausting exhale. "I am not happy at all about having her as the trainer."

Wheezy shifted in the seat, then revved the engine asking for a little more speed.

"Heat flash. I feel a flash. Windows down please," Rachel announced.

Presley sank under her cap. Wheezy concentrated on the road.

"Do you mind? It's freezing out." Gigi hugged her door. "Besides, you're going to have more than a hot flash when you meet Steele. It's rumored she's been a recluse, living in filth since the accident."

Rachel was chewing faster. “Accident?”

“She hates people. God knows the woman detested me,” Gigi continued. “Even though I was a model girl, giving of my time, volunteering to drive…” She stopped abruptly.

“Boy, your amnesia is suddenly disappearing,” Wheezy mumbled.

Rachel let out a snicker.

“This all won’t be so funny when we reach Gertrude. Wait till she realizes that only one of us has honed our riding skills. Then we’ll see who’s laughing.”

Chapter 19

Randall Emerson was idolizing his trophies from the leather swivel chair as a fire crackled and warmed the massive open room.

"Daddy, it is a shame," Camilla said from the chair behind him, her long legs entwined as she swirled a stemless wine glass. "You will not be adding the Silver Spur accolade to your collection. That trophy cup is one of the most unique I have ever seen. It's made of one hundred percent sterling silver."

Asher Devine barked a yelping laugh. "Not with the team your lovely wife is on." He winked at Camilla. It was obvious he had an affinity for her.

"You mean the over-the-hill cowgirls?" Camilla discharged a vile laugh, swooning Asher with a return wink. "I would not call my step-mommy lovely either, but you are ever so right. Plus, add the demented and drunk trainer Gertrude Steele, and the entire team will be a ludicrous display of failure. Nothing more than a joke. Steele can't even walk, let alone ride." Camilla drew in on a sip of Cabernet as if it were a cigarette.

Her father spun to face them. "Fact is, I *will* possess this year's Silver Spur trophy. I have entered a very competitive team under one of my other LLC holding companies. They are unmatchable. Good odds they *will* champion a win."

The two appeared delighted. Randall couldn't help but think Asher Devine would make an impressive choice as his next son-in-law. Had him right where he needed. Under his thumb. He watched Asher's overconfident stroll to one of the windows that extended floor to ceiling. "Storm seems to be heading in the direction of the Steele Estate."

"Oh my, Daddy. Can your driver handle the rig in one of the valley's infamous snow squalls?" Camilla pretended to fret.

"Well, it wouldn't be the saddest event in my life if something like an accident happened. Unfortunately, I wouldn't underestimate any woman who climbed to the position she previously held. Something formidable makes that woman tick."

Randall danced his fingers on his thigh. "And I wouldn't exactly call Steele's place an estate. They'll be quite busy this year trying to stay in the saddle, to say the least." He rolled the chair closer to the ornate desk. "Now, let's work on this takeover. By the time the Silver Spur event announces the winner, it will be too late for all of them. I will have added F.G. Transport to my resume of ownerships, replaced Louisa Mae, crushed Steele's reputation one more time and divorced my precious Gigi because she'll be diagnosed with a psychological illness and need to be committed."

"Or better yet, Daddy, jailed for illegal... say... activities?" Camilla tilted her head, batted her eyelashes and pressed a smile. "She can be deemed unfit to even be your wife, Daddy."

By the size of his smirk, Asher was relishing the idea. "Like father, like daughter." Once again Asher Devine raised his glass to share a toast.

"Your destination is twenty miles ahead on the left," the GPS announced in a robotic rhythm. Fortunately, they had managed to skirt the snow squall. That was until now.

Twenty more miles and we've made it. Wheezy had pretended to be comfortable but she was growing uneasy.

She maintained the wheel with both hands as she weaved through the county outskirts, keeping the steel carriage steady behind her. If they would've stayed on schedule, they could've avoided any flurries. Unfortunately, Gigi Tetless Emerson and her spoiled Kit T Kat ruined that plan.

The four women had only light conversation during the drive to Gertrude Steele's. Perhaps the others also felt Wheezy's mounting apprehension. She was struggling to conceal her concern. The horse trailer was approximately thirty-six feet, connected by a hydraulic system in the eight-foot bed of her double cab truck. This stretched the entire length to over forty-five feet. A massive amount of metal and power. Wheezy had championed the truck competition, however, she hadn't driven a rig this size in nasty weather for over a decade. She didn't have a desire to refresh her skills with this particular load either.

Presley exchanged a brief glance with Wheezy. "I would understand if you thought we should turn around."

Wheezy shook her head, then pressed her lips as if undaunted. "Your husband made it clear that Gertrude Steele stipulated we have to arrive today or the entire training deal was off. So, no turning back. We made a commitment."

Wheezy had made it her motto at F.G. Transport, which employed mostly hard-nosed men, to never let them see her sweat. She sustained a level tone, hoping Presley fell for her facade as a mild tornado of white fluffy flakes suddenly blew in swirls like the dust bunnies in her living room.

It was Rachel who chimed in with alarm. "Is the weather changing?"

The question triggered the slumping Gigi to sit up like a periscope and scan the landscape out her window.

"I am not a fan of driving in snow." Rachel crinkled the plastic bag on her lap open again. "Chip, anyone?"

"All good, Rachel," Presley comforted. "Just a light flurry."

Wheezy slid Presley a petulant squint to encourage her to continue. Wheezy hoped Presley's calm voice would mask the reality that there was a ten-thousand-pound steel carriage goading them from behind.

Presley understood Wheezy, thankfully, and stuttered, "A... Rachel... Hannibal, he walked right on the trailer. What a well-mannered gelding."

"Thanks. And your Cleo is so dear. She doesn't look eighteen years old, and she loaded like a lady," Rachel complimented. "You are going to be impressive on her. Western pleasure is your discipline, right? I remember when we showed thirty years ago, you were a natural."

Presley blushed. "Thank you. Cleo and I did do a bit of traveling and showing together. She knows the ropes. You will shine on Hannibal, I'm sure."

"If I can stay in the saddle. I'm at least fifteen pounds overweight."

"Well, stop eating the chips," Gigi snipped.

Rachel purposely snatched another salted treat. "And if I do ever show, I need to be more like you, Presley. Calm as a cucumber. I'm a terror when nervous. Hannibal only has one minor issue, and that's ponies or cows. His name was Hank when we first bought him, until he eyed his first pony. He took Jemma on a joy ride. That's when we sent in the papers to change his name."

Wheezy flipped on the wipers as the snow began to wet the surface.

"Is anyone else getting extremely hot?" Rachel added.

"He's scared of them?" Wheezy felt a hot flash herself. The snow was changing, gripping the road, and dimming any flicker of sunlight. She studied the gauges; the outside temperature had dropped ten degrees in the last thirty minutes. Below freezing. Not good. *Don't wait for the slide. Slow down, shift to four-wheel.*

Rachel steadied the chip to her lips. "No, Hannibal hates them. Pins his ears, levels out like a shark and aims right for any pony or cow, with flexing jaws."

"No worries, we don't have a cow or pony on the trailer," Presley chimed.

Everyone mildly laughed except Gigi.

Presley obviously had an intuition by the intensity of Wheezy's concentration. "The roads are changing?"

"Rachel, we might need a few more Hail Marys," Wheezy said, blunter than expected. "Any heavier, and this road will be a layer of ice. Not good."

"You're all nuts, aren't you?" Gigi said. "Rachel's going to need more than rosary beads." She clawed the back of Wheezy's seat. "We have a lot more than a snowstorm to endure! Have you forgotten who we're heading to see? Gertrude Steele? And listen to you! Which one of you has even been on a horse in the past thirty years?"

There was a pause as Wheezy gathered control. "I did go for lessons... once." Her eyes adhered to the road.

"You did?" Rachel asked.

All three acted surprised.

Wheezy nodded. "Wasn't exactly a good experience. I tried to go out on a trail ride. The horse's name was Bull, a beast. There is a lot to be said about a name, right?"

Rachel agreed, "That's for sure."

"Looking back, the barn did not have a respectable reputation. Bull looked like a giant to me, and felt like one, too. When he reached the wood's edge, he exploded. The horse wanted nothing to do with the trail ride from that point on. That boy did a one-eighty and rocketed back to the barn. Bucked me off right into the best mud puddle he could find. I was drenched and shaking like a leaf. I screamed like a baby and quit on the spot. Vowed never to be breakable again. Always bothered me, though. My grandmother would have been disappointed."

Wheezy shifted into four-wheel drive. She felt the truck's traction as the trailer jolted into control.

Rachel grasped the door. "Sweet mother of God."

"Wheezy, that is a shame," Presley quickly offered. "Remember Wyndham Glick? He said, 'Horses are noble creatures, and humans are the problem'."

"Mm-hmm." Wheezy's lips flat-lined. "Who doesn't remember that man? How about you, Gigi? Memory coming back?"

Gigi's expression remained blank as Wheezy eyed her in the mirror.

"I don't think Wyndham Glick could help me," Rachel sighed. "Hannibal scared me when he raced off. I pretended to be the brave mom, but I was frightened, masking my fear through Jemma. Always coaching her to be tough. Is that normal? Wheezy, are you scared?"

"Jeez. We *are* in trouble," Gigi mumbled from the corner. She pointed at Presley. "I can already assess that this so-called team is pathetic. You are our only other hope. How much have you ridden? And clearly, we're short a horse. Wheezy, what are you planning to ride?"

The three disregarded Gigi's comments. They were not even worth answering. Wheezy witnessed her fold her arms and slump back like a child having a tantrum.

"I remember thinking that riding was in your blood, Presley," Wheezy interjected as she steadied on the road. "Being involved with horses didn't seem a possibility in my world. My grandmother didn't have the money, and other than the YWCA program, equestrian sports weren't available to inner-city kids."

Wheezy tapped her brakes, checking the surface. The white dusting on the road ahead no longer blew apart to reveal blacktop. Instead, the snow was adhering like sheer vinyl tile.

"And here you are, managing an entire trucking company! Bet you never imagined you'd be CEO of F.G. Transport." Rachel handed the chip bag over the seat to the front.

Gigi shifted, turning her ear forward with a puzzled face. "CEO of F.G. Transport? You?"

Wheezy wasn't about to share further details about the dissolved relationship with Frank Galzone, or that she would never be CEO. Besides, the toxic woman in the backseat raised the hair on Wheezy's neck about as much as Asher Devine, and this drive demanded all her skills. She pumped the brakes again, and the icy road generated a shiver in her heart.

They were dead center of a snow squall. Venus's truck wipers were set on high, hardly able to keep the windshield from being glazed between swipes. Wheezy's stomach churned with angst. The issue was not that she couldn't drive in snow, but this rig was carrying priceless cargo—her reunited friends, and three four-legged creatures. All her sole responsibility.

Wheezy's worries were temporarily alleviated when Presley tried to deflect the tension. "My father would have loved to see me compete in the Silver Spur again. He thought Cleo was the dream horse to enter the competition, one of the most unique shows on the East Coast, open to any breed and to most disciplines. But I was too busy raising three boys and following an Army husband around. I'm sure I disappointed my father, but my goal at that time was to be the best mother and wife I could be. Then he passed..." Presley's voice trailed off.

"I share the guilt," Wheezy lamented. "I never thanked my grandmother for what she taught me. That remorse has driven me. And Rachel, you know when I first jumped behind that truck to drive with Gertrude Steele," Wheezy hesitated, "I was practically having convulsions. It's okay to be afraid, but don't let them see you sweat, eh? As my kids have informed me, when you have a passion, go for it." Regrettably, these were mere words. Wheezy needed to believe them too.

Sounded fearless, and that's all that matters at present.

A sudden swerve of the truck bumped her thoughts of liability.

Presley must have felt Venus slip because she reached for the dash while sucking in air. Unfortunately, the jolt also alarmed the passengers in the back. Simultaneously, Kit T Kat belted one of her earth-shattering screams which heightened the anxiety.

Rachel chomped on another handful of chips. "Oh my gosh, that woman did make me nervous... Remember how early we had to get up because you were afraid of being late to a lesson?"

"Yes, yes..." Presley continued, "if one person was late, the entire team suffered the consequences. We had to muck out Steele's entire barn for a week."

"That was called bonding, wasn't it?" Wheezy chimed while eyeing Gigi hiding under the dark glasses. "We rode in the rain, sleet or subzero weather."

There was an extended lull, until Presley championed again. "Do you remember Rachel's pants ripping right down the center, revealing her multi-colored bikini underwear? Steele still forced her to finish the course. Every time Rachel lifted for a posting trot, her tush was exposed with neon peace signs."

The three giggled, and Wheezy thought she heard a snicker from Gigi.

"No worries on that anymore. I can't fit in bikini underwear. Why does stuff always seem to happen to me?" Rachel sipped on her straw. "I liked to post to the extended trot. I always dreamed I could try Hunter Jumping." She bit into a chip, then wavered. "I think?"

Gigi acted as if she had been shocked by a defibrillator. "I am our exclusive competitor in the English division. One hundred percent!" Her voice squeaked. "We are supposed to be in top-notch shape, practice every day, in order to show every weekend. Kit T Kat, if I didn't mention, is an experienced hunter. We jump every chance we get."

"I thought you said you were on a hiatus from riding? Some injury or something, Randall said," Presley calmly asked. "Isn't that why Kit T Kat missed the herd, you claimed?"

Gigi pretended not to hear. "Are any of you listening? It's no different now. That's why we lost years ago. And it seems to me we are short a horse. Just what are you riding, Wheezy?"

Rachel coughed out her last bite of chip. "You completely remember!"

"Hold that thought, girls. Sit tight. We're really sliding."

"Oh, my sweet Mary." Rachel fidgeted for something in her pocket.

Gigi let out a high-pitched yelp.

Presley angled back as if in a rocket at takeoff. "You got this, Wheezy."

Wheezy clenched both hands on the wheel. The terrain was a major factor. They were on the outer edges of the county, nothing but curves, peaks, valleys, and no road shoulders.

She pressed the gas, climbing the next incline as the conversation quelled. It felt like being in church at a funeral right when the pastor rings the bell to bring the casket up the aisle.

Presley secured her ballcap as if it helped her focus on the road. Rachel was praying the rosary again, and Gigi was clutching the door. For an instant, Wheezy wished that door would magically unlock, and the witch would fall out as she had done before.

She crested the rise and decreased her speed. It was late day as she scanned the valley below, clouded by a white blanket rimmed in a dark haze. This was a treacherous kind of squall known as a white-out. The windshield wipers swiped on high with a screech then a slap, forcing her to think about pulling over to wait for salt trucks. However, there was hardly a secure edge; it was too dangerous. If another vehicle approached from behind, blinded by the conditions, it would certainly hit them. Venus could be thrust over the cliff. Who knew the distance of the drop? Wheezy didn't want to find out.

Wheezy shifted into a lower gear. She caught Gigi in the rearview mirror, now erect in her seat and finally lifting the dark bug-eyed shades.

"I hope you know what you're doing. That is my baby in the back. You will be paying for the entire truck and horse if something happens. You will never haul so much as a guinea pig." There was a flame simmering in those violet pupils.

"You got this, Wheezy!" Presley repeated, dousing the negative remarks. "You didn't win that competition because you lacked experience."

Rachel stopped chanting the Hail Mary. "This was my exact feeling in the barrel race thirty years ago. I was petrified." She struggled to remove her coat while imprisoned under her seatbelt. "Heat flash, heat flash..." She nabbed her purse, then began rummaging through the zippered sections.

"Now what are you looking for?" Gigi bent toward her.

"My little white pill," she muttered as if revealing a secret.

Wheezy concentrated on the downhill slope. The snow on the blacktop was merely a film, but that layer was now complete ice. Too much speed could hydroplane the trailer and jackknife it into a free-for-all spin. That would propel them to the lower valley, whether down the hill or over the cliff. All of them would be seriously injured or killed.

"Your prayers aren't enough?" Gigi quipped.

"Sometimes, I need a little help," Rachel mumbled from the corner of her mouth.

Wheezy eased the speed as slowly as possible without touching the brakes. She was fully aware that would be the most dangerous movement she could attempt.

"You're an addict, to boot," Gigi judged.

"I am not!" Rachel screamed.

"Please, Gigi. Wheezy needs to—" Presley started.

"How can we have an addict on our team? You drink, too?" Gigi snarled.

"You are so mean. More like bitter. To think, I tried to defend you." Rachel's hand motioned a halo around her face. "Tell these two, *ah she looks pretty with all the... all your work*."

Gigi squealed, "My work?"

Presley rubbernecked around and reopened the bag of chips Rachel had shared to the front. "Come on, ladies. Wheezy needs to concentrate."

Wheezy was losing control of the rig. The trailer was pressuring Venus to move out of its path. Wheezy choked the shifter again to avoid the brakes. From this point on, pure skill would be required to handle the rig.

"What are you insinuating? I haven't had any cosmetic surgery." Gigi brushed hair from her cheek.

"You had something on those perfectly puckered lips." Rachel seemed to have snapped. Her outburst of "Aha" upon finding the pill bottle shocked even Wheezy. She grunted as she tried to unscrew the sealed lid. "Damn child-safe caps."

Their voices accelerated with the speed of the metal machine as Presley attempted to restore peace, scrunching open the bag to offer chips.

The low gear gripped with a jolt, fighting for control. The force made Venus rumble, using her power to ebb back the ten-thousand-pound trailer.

Suddenly, car lights sliced the haze and snow, heading straight toward them from the opposite direction. The others silenced momentarily, then screamed in different octaves.

Wheezy veered instinctively. They missed the car, but the momentum catapulted the trailer forward, shoving Venus as if her wheels were skates.

Presley tossed the bag to the seat and stretched her arm across Wheezy to protect her like a child.

Gigi's perfectly injected lips were spread open like a whale inhaling plankton.

Rachel was *Our Fathering* as the cap spun off the pill bottle like a top.

By some miracle, the same fate that brought them together edged Venus to the shoulder, scuffing against something stronger than she was. Stealing control from Wheezy, a power rotated the wheel ninety degrees until the entire monster stopped, bent in an L shape. The trailer was impeded from spinning farther in a merry-go-around carrying the truck with it. They were motionless, the trailer behind Venus blocking the road.

The only sound was breathing, along with the rise and fall of wipers which screeched on an all but dry window. They scratched the window and smacked down in a rhythmic beat. The flurries had disappeared; the haze evaporated. Rays of light now struck the hood, melting the crystals.

Little white pills and broken chips decorated Wheezy's beloved truck interior and their bodies like confetti on New Year's.

The robotic sound of the GPS interrupted, *"You have reached your destination."*

Chapter 20

Presley gathered her senses. She had spent the last year praying to live, and she certainly didn't want to die in a snow squall. The flurries had ceased, and rays of sunlight intensified as if the storm never happened. Intermittent crystals lingered and slid across the truck hood while most returned to merely droplets of water. The brightness was sharply enhancing, almost blinding.

She squinted to confirm what was directly in front of them. Venus was facing a stone structure etched in a thin layer of snow that was dissolving to nothing more than drips and slush.

Was I crazy! This is the dumbest idea. A fifty-year-old, bald has-been, showing with three women I hardly know. Because of a 'year to remember,' decades ago?

Before Presley could ask if everyone was okay, her contemplation was interrupted by a familiar blood curdling scream—Kit T Kat. Then she heard the snap of Rachel's seat belt.

"Holy sweet baby Jesus!" Rachel yelled.

"Put that belt back on, are you crazy?" Wheezy ordered. "We are in the middle of the road. Don't you dare get out."

"Is everyone okay?" Presley examined them.

A unison response of one fine and two yeses replied.

Good, no blood either.

Then she nodded to Wheezy, who was double fisted on the wheel, staring straight through the flapping wipers.

"It's a miracle. A miracle, we stopped," she mumbled. "We should be hanging over the cliff on the other side of the road. Instead, we're here, facing..." Wheezy appeared hypnotized, pointing at a stone house aligned with the edge of the road. A mailbox, with a missing door and bent pole, read 223 Harmony Road.

Presley began to pat her own body in a frisk. “Wheezy, it’s no miracle. You did it. We are all quite fine.” She gazed back at the other two again.

Gigi appeared ashen. Rachel was silently re-buckling her belt with one trembling hand and choking an empty pill bottle with the other. Once she was safely snapped in, Presley watched her pick up one white pill and place it on the tip of her tongue, followed by a second. She met Presley’s gaze.

“This calls for one and a half...” she whispered in a warped voice while trying to swallow the pills. “Anybody else want one, feel free.” She motioned to Gigi. “Looks like you would benefit. Want a half?”

“Rachel, no sharing,” Presley insisted.

She scanned the cab. Salt, chips and little white pills littered the seat, the dash, and themselves. Then she examined Wheezy who touched a broken chip on the seat between them, then another as if in mourning.

“We can sweep it up. I have a great dust-buster that will suck this up in no time. You done good, woman.” She clapped her hands, feeling more invigorated than she had in the past year.

“Done good?” Gigi exclaimed as if Presley was a fool. “I beg to differ. We could have been killed. That is twice today that I have almost been fatally hurt.”

Rachel nervously interrupted. “Well, falling out the door—I would not call that almost fatal. That’s an exaggeration.” She scrunched her nose and lips together at Gigi. “But it was funny.”

“You’re laughing about all this?”

Rachel nodded like a bobber on a fishing pole.

“It’s not funny!” Gigi snapped.

“Like I said, do you want a half?” Rachel fanned her palm open, revealing the other half of a small white pill.

“You are ridiculous, an addict,” Gigi accused.

While the two were quarreling, Presley patted Wheezy’s arm, then scaled up to her shoulder, giving it a hearty squeeze. “Don’t you listen. You did it! I knew you could.”

"Presley, you were positive thirty years ago, and positive after all you have been through."

The bantering in the backseat was elevating. "You better hope my sweet baby horse is fine."

"Try one. I'm telling you it will take the edge off. God knows you need it. Sweet mother of Mary, you are going to make me hyperventilate if you don't take it."

Wheezy rolled her eyes. "Those two. I gotta move the rig off the other lane. We're across the entire road." She shut off the wipers.

The GPS repeated, *"Your destination has been reached,"* followed by a prolonged beep from outside. A driver coming from the opposite direction was annoyed as he could not pass.

"Well, 223 Harmony Road, that's the place!" Presley triumphed in discovery. "It's barely recognizable as the once grand stone house I remember."

Wheezy angled the Ford off the road and into the driveway. Their bodies were jarred by the poor condition of the lane, now deteriorated to nothing more than gravel, muddy potholes and broken pieces of blacktop. The chains rattled, as the horses stomped and neighed, announcing their arrival.

The arguing ceased in the backseat as they together observed their surroundings. "That's the house!" Gigi perked up.

The group converged their attention on her.

"I was here with... with Randall," Gigi stumbled in defense, avoiding any eye contact.

The stone house was stamped with a corner plate dated 1840-something. The fourth number was missing as if eroded by time. The residence was dilapidated. Dead ivy crept up the sides to the eaves, eating the mortar. The spouts were unhinged, dangling at angles. Several roof slates were cracked or missing. Presley was stung with an eerie feeling. The property was exactly as Gigi had suggested.

The sun, which once had disappeared as if covered by a curtain, now flourished and rose to attention. But the glare on the window did not obstruct their view of the property—a deteriorated wooden post, the sign swinging sideways secured from one of two chains.

Rachel tilted her head trying to read the missing letters.

Hol y Hill. H me of S eel Perfo an e Hors s.

Only the words *"Hill"* and *"of"* had complete letters, the others were erased from years of wear and lack of care.

"Holly Hill. Home of Steele Performance Horses," Gigi clarified like a college professor. "I remember this place."

"Sounds like your memory is returning after all," Wheezy mumbled and straightened the scarf about her neck.

"Anything but Holy!" Gigi remarked about the missing "L."

Three horses grazed in the fields off to the passenger side. One was solo in a galvanized piped round pen, the other two at the bottom entrance. They were alerted to the visitors with elevated heads and snorts. The stomping and screams of Kit T Kat and the others stirred the two to gallop toward a provisional electric fence that trailed the lane.

"My, the wood fence is broken. Hope the electric is working and those two stay corralled," Rachel cringed. "One string of wire does not seem sufficient."

The horses were not wearing coats, leg wraps, or constricting neck covers called sleazies. They were living like horses, which Presley's dad seemed to believe was when a horse was most content. *Free in the field,* he would say.

One horse was a palomino, the other dark with glistening silver specks. They were scampering free toward the truck, bucking, rearing, full bellied, splashed with mud, manes in spindles of dreadlocks, bushy winter coats sparkling from wet remnants of the squall.

As they neared, Presley noticed unkempt whiskers on their muzzles and hairy ears like little old men. Loud shrieks responded to the others in the trailer as Wheezy maneuvered Venus over potholes on the lane to the barn and round pen.

The lone horse in the pen was racing in circles. He appeared senior to the others, Presley surmised, by the slight sway in his back, and bulging joints. However, the exuberance in which he abruptly stopped, then popped his hind legs in a turn on the haunches did not give way to his age. The stallion dug into the ruts he had created while circling in a repetitive pattern. He arced in one direction then pivoted the other way.

Presley admired the horse. His placid coffee-colored eyes and the indented curve from his head to his muzzle—the same dish trait of her dear Cleo, almost Arabian in appearance. The horse undoubtedly was related to her mare. Perhaps even Cleo's sire. Her father had purchased Cleo from Gertrude's breeding program.

A rusted tractor was rubbish outside the barn, with flattened, cracked tires, the fences split, wire sliced and unattached. Though it was winter, lifeless grey and brown remnants of weeds that had missed years of trimming were tangled on the fences in vines and snaked the wire and boards, choking the place of life. The only undamaged fencing was a makeshift electric wire wrapped around green metal poles like garden stakes. There was plenty of free-range pasture, probably why the horses didn't try to escape.

The gravel road was potholed and slushy from the squall, quite in need of repair where the stones had been washed away. The four rattled with the trailer as Wheezy drove the rig to the turnaround in front of a three-sided pole barn. A trailer, in as rough condition as the tractor, was parked against the structure as if left for a decade. The barn and pole building appeared to be in better shape than the stone residence, giving the impression that the horses' existence was more important than any human shelter.

"Well, I told you," Gigi reveled. "Everything I suspected... or heard. The farm is in ruin. How can anyone live in this filth? Are you prepared for the most terrifying woman you ever want to meet?"

"You mean... re-meet?" Rachel sounded almost drunk.

"We ought to just go home," Gigi demanded. "This place already gives me the creeps and the thought of Gertrude Steele scares me."

Presley caught the violet burst in Gigi's eyes from the reflection of the sun.

Gigi retreated to safety under the bug-eyed shades while Rachel continued the collecting of pills and chips.

"Look, Gigi. Your husband knows Gertrude," Wheezy interjected. "Presley's father, too. She owes her training, and your husband acted as if he had no issues with her. I'm baffled by your lack of trust."

"My father was a good man, and a skilled horseman," Presley said. "If he thought she was up to any ill activity, he never would have bought a horse from her stock."

"Maybe she was fine at that time. Before the struggle with alcoholism," Gigi stressed. "But in the circles I socialize in, she couldn't compete with the other trainers—especially the men. She always had a nasty chip on her shoulder. She lost clients. Then supposedly a horse rolled over onto one of her students—her own daughter. Then her! The poor animal failed the drug test. That was her demise. She festered, wilted, became a shell of herself."

Gigi's voice was raspy like a sinister old lady. Although callous, she conveyed the drama like a master storyteller. "After that Gertrude became a recluse, a pathetic soul, living alone in darkness. Drunk and dirty." She careened her arms in the air. "We can all see the evidence from the driveway." Then Gigi tucked her arms as if waiting for applause.

"Does she eat small children too? You tell an elaborate story. Ever think about being a writer?" Wheezy raised one of her etched ebony brows.

"There are two sides to every story. Let's give this a shot," Presley encouraged. "It's the only chance we have to ride this year."

"Besides, I don't have any other location to board Hannibal," Rachel added in muffled plea. She was harried, attempting to screw the lid onto the pill bottle.

Gigi snatched it from her, tightened the lid and returned the bottle with a bluster of disdain.

Wheezy turned off the ignition then cracked her door. The loss of rumble made the screaming chatter of the horses resonate across the valley. A concentrated aroma of burning wood permeated the cab.

Presley noticed the smoke that billowed from the chimney—a wood stove most likely warmed the old home on a late winter day. She was mesmerized, scanning the property, trying to jog her memories. She recognized the pole barn where they rode during lessons several times a week. Laughing and conversing, not savoring the moment like she would now. For the past year, Presley had worried about dying but today she wasn't dwelling on the constant reminder when she looked in the mirror or touched her head.

She opened her door next and relished the feeling of walking in a place she had been almost thirty years prior.

"I remember this place," Rachel whispered. "It was beautiful. What the heck happened?" She wobbled slightly to regain her balance upon jumping out. "Are you coming?" Rachel asked Gigi.

"All of a sudden you aren't afraid of Gertrude Steele? Have you heard a word I said?"

Rachel brushed some crumbs off the seat. "It's amazing how the extra half works, huh?" She pointed to the bottle on the seat, winked, then shut the door.

Wheezy, Presley and Rachel tightened their coats and walked to the back end of the trailer for a peek at the horses. Wheezy peered in the door, checked legs and surveyed hay bags. "All good here."

Unnoticed, Gigi had tagged behind. She was standing on the trailer wheel well peering in through a window. "You're lucky."

"Oh, for gosh sakes, would you stop with the bitching?" Rachel waved her hand with an arc in the air.

"Definitely the pill talkin'," Presley whispered to Wheezy.

After the horse check, the four headed toward the house. When they reached a partial brick pathway checkered with missing pieces they stopped. The broken gate leaned to one side and there was a sound of an axe hitting wood in the distance.

Presley led the way. The chopping grew louder. Once on the porch, a seemingly frail woman came into view. She wore plaid earmuffs that flattened her pixie haircut, her hair white but tinged in a yellow stain. Short in stature, she was dressed in bib Carhartts, and a woolen red check plaid shirt with a turtleneck underneath. Her pants were tattered with holes and brushed with stains.

She raised an axe to split wood then loaded a bucket with logs at the side of the porch, unaware of their presence. They watched the rise and fall of her axe.

Presley studied her, the corners of her eyes and lips indented with deep wrinkles. She reverently approached the woman. "Gertrude? Ms. Steele?"

The woman rested the axe on her shoulder. "You're the ladies that called?"

Presley nodded timidly. "Yes, Ms. Steele. Well, it was my husband, Brad. He called you first..."

She ignored Presley. Instead, the older woman hoisted the axe from her shoulder, raised it high then swung her arms in an unstoppable arc toward the log.

The axe cut into the wood. She freed her hands, leaving the axe blade in an unyielding position. The woman analyzed the four who were clearly startled.

Gigi and Rachel were wrapped in a bear hug of fear after one of them murmured, "We're mincemeat!" But the woman did not acknowledge them except for an air of aversion.

"Gertrude Steele, right?" Presley repeated. She was not at all as Presley remembered.

The woman shook her head. "I'm Maggie." Her voice was quiet. "I've lived with Ms. Steele since... at least twenty years. I tried to explain to one of your husbands as to the situation. But he wasn't taking a no. I did inform him to wait on bringing horses. But here you are."

She seemed perplexed as to whether to kick them off the property or allow them in.

"We agreed, Gert and I, to let you come out here today. She wasn't open to the idea in the least bit. But this Brad, he insisted, and of course, I had my own reasons for permitting your visit."

Presley shivered from the chilly air. She pressed the ball cap over her protective knitted cap. "Yes, my husband can be persistent. And we really do appreciate this."

"I think once you talk to Gert," Maggie hesitated, "and actually see her, you'll change your minds. Of course, no one wishes more than myself that this will work out but... when you see the situation..."

She must have seen Presley shiver because her demeanor mellowed. Bald heads tend to call on sympathy sometimes, Presley thought.

"Ladies, let's get you in out of the cold. I can explain in more detail and then... then you can see for yourselves."

The woman bent over to take the metal handle of the five-gallon bucket holding four split logs. When she grunted, Wheezy stepped forward and joined her in gripping the handle. The women made eye contact. Maggie refused to release until Wheezy shifted her colorful scarf with her free hand and insisted. "I can take that for you." Then the older woman relinquished the bucket.

"It's been a long time since anyone helped me." Maggie placed her thumbs under her suspenders. "Thank you."

Wheezy nodded. "No problem. Piece of cake."

The woman pressed a fragile smile of appreciation.

The four tailed her to the porch and entered the small foyer of the house warmed by a burning woodstove. As the door closed, another odor rose. A mild sweet aroma meshed with the crackling fire.

Maggie pointed to the hooks on the wall, gesturing them to hang their coats. She then began to introduce herself properly. "My name is Maggie Desinberg. And if I did not say it before, welcome."

Presley drifted in her own examination of the foyer. A scuffed wooden staircase led to the second floor, its risers chipped and scratched. Some rail spindles were missing and the hallway heading up to another room was shadowy. The walls were papered with a 1970's pattern, peeling and in need of updating.

The space was gloomy once Maggie closed the front door. A Tiffany style lamp generated the only ounce of light and was nestled on the sole piece of furniture—an antique sideboard. It barely illuminated the pictures set across the top but could not completely conceal the thick layer of dust.

As Presley introduced each of them, she recognized a picture of Gertrude Steele with none other than the handsome Wyndham Glick, along with a female teen. She continued to the next picture, which featured Gertrude Steele and Maggie. When she reached the fourth image, Presley blinked in surprise. Was there too much dust? Were her eyes deceiving her?

Our picture! The photo of the four of us!

Presley was about to announce her discovery, but Maggie started to lead them down the hall following the sweet aroma. Presley didn't have the heart to interrupt so she held the secret.

"I've lived with Gert for... as long as I care to remember. I thought you would like a chance to understand. Come." She waved a hand and Presley took note that Maggie's were working hands, once packed with strength and withered by time.

Whiffs of caramelized brown sugar, pecans and molasses warming in an oven greeted them. Maggie shoved open the cracked kitchen door.

It was an outdated kitchen, brown stained cabinets, vintage cutting board countertops, and ebony slate floor, yet warmed by the aroma of fresh-baked pies. The woman gestured them to an aged oak table.

"I was just about to come in and slice a pie. We can talk here." Maggie proceeded to wash her hands and gather dishes. "I have fresh coffee, as Gert still loves her coffee. Please, grab a mug from the rack and make yourselves at home. I'll just pull out my last pies."

Maggie covered her hands with mitts and opened the oven. Gelatinous juices oozed down the sides of the pan.

"Oh, we love coffee, too!" Rachel exclaimed. "I can help. Look, a pie for each of us." Rachel seemed even more relaxed thanks to the pills.

"Just what you need," Gigi muttered. Everyone was seated except her who remained in the door frame, bundled in her white fur-trimmed coat.

Rachel joyously chose a fork, then tried to pass one to Gigi. "How about that? A whole pie for you."

"Do you understand why I stay young looking?" Gigi snubbed the utensil. "Clearly, pie doesn't touch my lips."

"I really cannot believe I even hugged you earlier in fear. Next time you can be axed in terror alone."

Maggie ignored the two and licked her fingers. "I tried to explain to this Brad, but when I told Gert, she figured once you see her, you all won't bother her again. I'm sure that Mr. Emerson's coaxing helped with her response. He doesn't take no for an answer either, and he seems to have motivating ways. There's no other way for you to understand why this is not possible."

She handed Rachel a plate. "Not possible?"

"Rachel, like I said the whole way here," Gigi lectured, "this is not going to work. Gertrude Steele is demented." The sting of the outburst blanketed the kitchen in a silence as dark as the room.

Maggie stopped cutting the pie. "I presume you're Randall Emerson's wife. He warned me about you."

Gigi fluttered her eyelashes, folded her arms and leaned against the door frame in protest.

"Please excuse this place," Maggie went on. "I know the light bulbs are blown, and it needs painted and dusted. Money's tight, and I can't do everything anymore. It is a bit of an overwhelm..." She stopped as if she had said too much then gestured Gigi to sit. "Please join us."

"Could we get on with this?" Gigi snapped. "We have a trailer of uneasy, hungry horses."

"They ate hay for the entire drive," Presley refuted. "We'll tend to them shortly. Sit down."

Although Gigi didn't remove her coat, she slipped to the edge of a chair as if ready to escape at a moment's notice.

Maggie stroked her drooping pixie bangs as the heat from the oven appeared to have melted them across her forehead.

"I am sorry," Wheezy apologized for Gigi. "It's just... we heard rumors."

Rachel set her coffee down. "An accident, drugging... Is it true?" She squinted at Gigi to indicate that she was the source of gossip.

"None of that's true. I promise you. Gertrude Steele is a recluse living in a deteriorating farmhouse. She suffers depression and heartache. It's that simple. God knows I've tried to help find her the medical services she needs, to no avail. Can anyone here understand that?"

"Yes, we certainly can," Presley conceded after experiencing her own dark prison.

"Gert would never in a million years hurt or drug horses. She loves those beasts above people. Except for her daughter who she has absolutely no relationship with at present."

Maggie passed a hearty piece of warm gooey pie to Wheezy. "Nor does she drink. And I am aware of the rumors."

"Was there an accident?" Rachel asked.

A throaty call could be heard in the distance, seemingly from the second story.

"Maggie. Maggie, do you hear me!" The voice was hoarse, demanding, like it could almost slice the pie itself.

Everyone glanced in the direction of the door.

"We better talk fast. Keep eating." Maggie cleared her throat from an obvious nervous tickle. "Let's start with the diagnosis." Maggie poured her own coffee, her hand slightly trembling. "Two decades ago, Gert was diagnosed with a degenerative disease. At times when stressed, she stumbles, shakes and slurs her words."

"That explains people thinking she was drunk, eh?" Rachel said.

"Maggie, answer me," came the throaty voice again. "Are they here? Well, they're late. Who's that speaking?"

Someone was coming down the stairs in a cumbersome thump, one riser at a time.

A soberness enveloped the room. Maggie discounted their concern. "Yes, then there was the accident with a crazy horse that dumped a student and rolled on Gert, who was injured. The student happened to be her daughter. Gert was embarrassed."

Rachel gasped, and Maggie continued as if in a trance. "After, her reputation was pulverized, wrongfully. The horse was tested and was found to be drugged. Not sure how, or by who, but it was not Gert. There was so much competition among the trainers at that time for the Silver Spur competition."

The girls had ceased eating, rotating their heads from Maggie to each other and to the door. The pounding of deliberate steps had reached the first level hallway.

Maggie rambled, while standing and pouring another cup of coffee. She slid out the extra chair. "Her daughter begged her to keep showing, not to give up. Gert refused. Then she was hit with the biggest blow of all. As if she wasn't dead inside already. Sepsis set in, so the doctors had no choice but to remove..."

"I'm telling you, Maggie, you need to answer me." The garbled commands were only feet away, now coming from the doorway where Gigi had been standing.

"Removed what?" Rachel asked.

"I'll take matters into my own hands," came the voice. "I have the means. I'm loaded and ready."

Gigi was now bracing the table. "We're goners. Gertrude Steele hates everyone. She holds it against us that we didn't win the Silver Spur thirty years ago. She's been waiting for this moment. To avenge us."

Rachel shuddered. "Does she carry a—"

Maggie didn't answer. "Reality is, I was praying, hoping your being here would put her mind to work again. Give her something to look forward to. But instead, I'm afraid she wants you—"

"She wants what?" Gigi screamed. "To kill us? Take us hostage?"

Wheezy clutched Gigi's wrist and pinned her to the table so she wouldn't leap from her chair.

"Lost her what?" Rachel asked again.

"Breathe, Rachel. Breathe," Presley coaxed. "Calm down."

"I can't." Rachel was gasping for breaths. "I'm... I'm... hyper... ventilating."

Suddenly a shadowy figure filled the doorway. A hunched over body stepped onto the slate floor, cradling a hooked contraption which she raised into the air with her other hand by the elbow. Her face looked beaten by a storm of defeat, scarred with the creases of pain. Long grey hair, thinned and slicked back flat, only made her bushy eyebrows meld together into a frown.

Rachel was clearly driven to do one thing. The fork wedged more pie into her mouth, and she started to chew like she had not eaten in days.

Gigi belted a scream motivated from fear and covered her eyes. "Get down! She has a weapon!"

CHAPTER 21

The woodstove's tempered glass was swirling in blue and orange waves which cast a glow around the shadow who blocked the doorway. Wheezy didn't twitch a muscle as she cupped her warm mug of coffee. Presley and the other two were washed in horror. From what Wheezy could assess, the figure was a woman, short and stocky. Her shoulders, angled off-center, made her posture hunch to the left. Her hair was steel-colored, abundant, and tied into a wiry bun at the nape.

Wheezy determined she was similar in age to Maggie, perhaps late sixties, with sun-damaged skin, although ashen and paler. However, Wheezy still recognized her. The spark of determination may have faded, but without a doubt it was Gertrude Steele. She had a distinctive trait—one blue eye, and the other brown.

The woman's arm drew their attention. Her left limb, from the elbow down, was missing. In its place was an apparatus with metal pinchers in the shape of a claw, wired somehow for control. The pinchers made a slight squeak, as if they needed to be oiled, every time the woman forced a squeeze. But that was not the alarming part. It was Gertrude as she snapped the pinchers in the air like a weapon to intimidate the women at the table.

"Evidently, you all have forgotten the very first rule—never be *late to the gate.* This could cost you a DQ."

Wheezy remembered the shorthand for *disqualification*.

Gertrude pinched the claw again in Gigi and Rachel's direction. "I'm loaded and ready!"

"Oh, sweet mother Mary," Rachel's voice quivered.

"Ignore her." Maggie sliced another piece of pecan pie and drizzled it with caramelized molasses. "She likes to intimidate with that metal prosthetic. It's about the only time Gert savors any joy in life." Maggie's explanation was dry. "Come and sit down. Your coffee's going to get cold."

Gertrude paced methodically around the table, nipping her claw in the air as she passed each one like a sword fighter.

Rachel shuddered.

Upon realizing the woman was wallowing in the moment, Gigi rolled her eyes in irritation.

Gertrude interpreted the disdain and snapped at her twice, then dropped the arm, limping along with an evil eye glued to Gigi until she reached the empty chair.

Gigi leaned into Presley and grumbled, "*Nutball*."

"I tried to explain to that man named Brad," Gertrude said. "Not only am I living with a defiled reputation, but I'm suffering, as if you have not noticed." Gert rested her left elbow on the table with a thump, then pushed her oyster-colored wool fisherman sweater back, revealing the complete metal prosthesis. "Are you all happy now?"

Wheezy studied Gert's other hand. It revealed a story of a lifetime of arduous work. "Which part do you think bothers us? We've all had a journey getting to this point in our lives. Living with diversity. Isn't that obvious?"

The others inflated their eyes like saucers at the brutal truth. Except for Gigi, who shifted in her seat. "I have a diversity?"

Rachel bent toward her. "You, more than anyone."

"What's mine?" Gigi pouted.

Gertrude took a sip of coffee while resting the metal limb on the table. "The world that once respected me has disowned me, even my own child. Clients fear me. That credit voucher ain't enough for all of you and your horses. Maybe you should take a vacation in Grand Cayman instead of wasting your time and money here."

"Well, she hasn't changed." Gigi's voice was tight. "Cold and cynical. I say we head out."

"I never thought you would be the intelligent one, Gigi," Gertrude retorted.

Gigi scrunched her ski-sloped nose in rejoinder.

Wheezy wasn't simply walking away though, as she had from F.G. Transport. Underneath that steel armor that fortified this once renowned trainer was a passion that couldn't be extinguished.

"We're willing to pay for any extra services and expenses. Also, it looks like you and Miss Maggie," Presley noted the other lady with a bow, "who has been so kind to us, could use some assistance around here."

"I was watching you out on that icy road from the window," Gert snapped. "Best case, you could've hit this house. Your insurance might have paid for repairs."

"I brought Cleo," Presley promptly divulged.

The woman's face singed at the mention of this name.

"King Roan's Cleopatra? Yes, I remember when your father bought her as a foal. Lovely creature with all her sire's best features." Gert pointed out to the horse galivanting in the round pen. "I wondered about her so many times. Your father had this dream that she would be a superstar in the quarter horse sector. He even intended to show her in the Silver Spur." Her unique eyes twinkled.

The dingy kitchen was roasting from the oven, the woodstove, and the woman's excitement. Gertrude's hair sprang frizzy from her ponytail. Rachel fanned herself with a napkin.

"He wanted me to train you and her, Presley. The two of you are born nat—" Gertrude ceased as if she had touched on a secret she couldn't reveal.

Presley volleyed to save the conversation. "I suspected that was her sire outside. He blessed Cleo with his gentle eye and dish-shaped head from forelock to muzzle. The same bold rump and defined shoulder. Would you like to see her?"

Gertrude bent in again. It seemed as if she might take the bait. Then her face transformed to steel. "No."

Maggie spit her coffee back into the mug as the others sank back in their chairs. "No?"

Presley attempted again. "Come out and see our horses, including Cleo. I saw you have a young one in the field with all the same characteristics. Is that the last..."

"This has been a joke. The answer is no. Cleo deserves a better chance. I only have one arm. I can't help. What if the horse had three legs? Would you all be here? Of course not. You'd have put her down."

Gertrude's prosthesis dropped from the table, hiding it on her lap. "Now, enough time is wasted. Go home." She iced them with a glare then darted her eyes away, staring into the pie Maggie had placed before her. She snatched the fork with her hand, stabbed a chunk, then shoved it in her mouth, chewing in calculated rotations from cheek to cheek, never raising her head again.

Their departure to the porch was quick, their thumping steps echoing on the farmhouse floors that needed to be sanded and stained.

Maggie could not apologize enough. She shared their disappointment, but hers was a cement block of hopelessness chained to her waist. "I'm sorry. I was hoping... well, I can tell you, my days here will be numbered, for sure. She's hopeless, I fear." Her facial creases indented deeper with sadness.

Maggie observed the four women as her aching hand and heart shut the door. She stepped to the side and regarded them through the window panel. Darkness was looming but there was still enough daylight that she could see them. Presley and Wheezy conversed as they inched off the porch. Gigi, in front, cautiously altered her gait to avoid any possible speckle of dirt on her white attire. It looked like a tiptoed game of hopscotch: missing a puddle, hitting a brick, missing a gully of mud, landing on a stone. Not far behind was the one named Rachel. She was rummaging in her coat pocket for something. *Maybe a tissue? Is she crying? Damn, Gert!*

Maggie's volcano of anger erupted. She hastily burst into the kitchen and began clearing the mugs and plates from the table, clanging them into the vintage porcelain sink.

"You are a witch. I'm tired of feeling pity for you. Lots of people are living with disabilities. For gosh sakes, the girl with no hair... clearly she's been sick. And Wheezy, I heard she's head of a trucking firm. Do you remember her? How hard she must have worked... And you certainly have no fear of that man, Randall Emerson."

Gertrude slid another bite of pie into her mouth, seemingly untouched by Maggie's rant.

"The last of Tut's progeny and you have the opportunity to train them both. Restore your reputation and return him to stardom."

"It's not about stardom," Gert said. "I've lost the fight. Emerson can't make my life any worse with his threats."

"The best thing you could do is to see those girls' dreams through. At least they're trying to live. Not wither away, like the likes of you. Did you ever wonder who drugged that horse? Or were you too afraid to find out?"

Maggie seized the plate as Gertrude tried to stab the last piece of pie.

"Doesn't it nag at you day and night, who would do such a criminal act and then attempt to destroy your reputation? Don't you think I know you suspected your daughter? Or better yet, me, all these years?"

Gertrude met Maggie's accusation with a wall of silence, but the guilt was swimming in her eyes.

"You actually think it was one of us, don't you? But you never asked. The two people who loved you most? Well, you don't deserve your daughter, or me. Or the pie!" Maggie ferociously scraped the remnants off the plate into the trash.

"I thought you and Sheila were covering for me!" Gert shouted. "You drugged the horse to calm him down, but overdosed with the Ace and it caused him to roll over. I wasn't going to bring the culprit to light if it was either of you," she defended. "I was protecting you."

"Too late! You lost your daughter. And now you've lost me. And the damn pie!"

Maggie dropped the plate in the sink. The dish cracked in pieces just like her heart.

She went to the white-framed window and unhooked the inside shutters to swing them open. "Time for you to get some light in so you can look at those women. Watch your last possible chance pull out of this lane. I'm packing my bags and leaving in the morning."

"Excuse me," a voice sifted in.

Maggie spun, studying the woman in the doorway. Their yelling must've kept them from hearing Wheezy reenter. The Black woman stood encased by a halo from the woodstove, as if an angel. Her sleek black hair splintered with white strands that sparkled in the light. Her dark eyes were lit with a golden flare that reflected from the brightly colored scarf cradling her neck.

Maggie was perspiring. She shifted her bangs in a nervous manner. "Wheezy, I'm sorry. We were discussing..."

"No need. I just wanted to mention one thing to Ms. Steele."

"Our conversation's over. Go home." Gertrude rose and faced the window, avoiding Wheezy.

"This is not about the horses or lessons. I just wanted to thank you before we pull out. I'm not sure you remember, but you sat me behind the wheel of your truck and trailer all those years ago. I never felt such power. You believed in me. Well, you and my grandmother. I grew my courage from that. Worked my way through the ranks and became," Wheezy hesitated, "I should say, almost became, CEO of F.G. Transport. To this day, I can drive a semi better than almost anyone. That is thanks to you."

Gertrude was leaning on the sill, her posture slanted. Maggie detected not a twitch of her body or a snap from her prosthesis.

Wheezy paused, pressed a smile at Maggie and was about to exit.

"I remember your grandmother, Louisa Mae, your namesake. She was a force." Gertrude cleared her throat. "Made good pie, too."

Wheezy froze at the mention of her grandmother. "That she did."

"Look at me, Wheezy. It's too late for me."

"Ms. Steele, if I thought that, I wouldn't be here. And my friend Presley, well she just struggled through the worst year of her life. She wouldn't be here either. I never could have endured it, but not her. Presley is so positive. Even now. I'm here today because of her and my grandmother." Wheezy paused. "And you. We stand on the shoulders of the women before us, like my grandmother who never received the due credit she deserved because of the color of her skin.

"And Rachel," Wheezy continued. "She lost her husband. Seems she doesn't know how to love again. Now don't tell her I know this, but she hasn't been with a partner in decades. Believe that one? We kid her and tell her she needs a Wyndham Glick. I see you have a picture of him in the vestibule. I see our picture, too. That year seems to have meant something to all of us."

Wheezy shook her head. "Not like me to ramble. It's getting dark, so thanks again for the encouragement. I'm forever grateful. No one else believed in the little Black girl from the city the way you did."

Gertrude appeared as a statue except her shoulders rose and fell with each breath, her head down, staring at the window. But she said nothing.

Wheezy didn't remember turning to leave, racing down the hallway of the farmhouse, or passing the pictures in the foyer to the door. She flew onto the porch like the words had spilled from her mouth. She was drenched with a flood of emotions rising in her as if it was high tide; her grandmother's unwavering faith, her delicious pies, her life struggles, the trucking firm, Asher Devine, her own failures, Darren's proposals—*he actually appears to love me*—all slamming her like an avalanche. She had overheard Maggie mention something about discovering the truth as to who was responsible for the accident... forcing Wheezy to examine her own life's recent developments. *Who's really been behind me being fired?*

The cold air encased her like an iceberg. Kit T Kat was belching screams of hunger pangs. The other girls were waiting in a cluster by the truck, grousing about how they were leaving with no chance of entering the Silver Spur championship, let alone even getting a lesson.

All eyes glued on Wheezy, knowing they would now check the horses, refresh the hay bags, and start the journey home. Hearts broken. All for nothing. Perhaps fate had brought about this moment, allowing her to finally thank Gertrude for believing in her.

As Wheezy reached the brick path, the porch light flicked on behind her, forcing her to shade her eyes as she looked back to see Maggie peering out the door.

"Gert said to tell you that when she takes on a job, she's serious. No turning back."

Wheezy whirled to see the other three who were attentive.

Maggie's expression was as flat as a dead man's heart. She spoke in the same preset tone. "I take it you can follow instructions, Wheezy?"

Wheezy scrunched her face, slightly perplexed. She blinked into the overhead brightness.

"Gert instructed me to tell you to unload your horses in the first three stalls. Hang their halters on the stall door in front of each one. Place your tack in the room adjacent to the feed area. Go ahead and give any provisions the horses need. Leave instructions for tomorrow's feeding. Then you all return first thing on Monday for an overview and discussion of your schedule. We'll go from there. She'll have time to examine the horses tomorrow."

Maggie's instructions were loudly overexaggerated, as if rehearsed. Something she'd spoken a hundred times.

Then she cleared her throat unexpectantly, a grin expanding from ear to ear. "And don't be late for the gate, she says. You all know the consequences." Maggie clapped her hands and lipped a silent thank you to Wheezy, placing her index finger over her lips... clearly not wanting the shadow of Gertrude behind her to hear or see these emotions.

Wheezy captured the upward curve of Maggie's eyes as she smiled. Wheezy winked back at her and smiled with her beautiful, aligned teeth. Then she hollered to the others, "Unload the horses, ladies!"

Chapter 22

Two hours later, Venus was cruising without the trailer, which remained parked at Gertrude Steele's, as the four women returned home.

It had taken a little while to empty the trailer of the gear, get the horses stalled, and transfer Gigi's trunk. That thing was especially weighty and took both Rachel and Wheezy to hoist it out and carry it down the walkway to the prospective room in the barn. Unfortunately, Gigi was whining that her hands hurt from trying to lead Kit T Kat, so she could not assist. She also was the only one who registered an objection at leaving Kit T Kat with Hannibal and Cleo at the farm after they had been told to unload.

Gigi's rant should have been Wheezy's first clue that the stalling of horses wasn't going to go smoothly.

"First off, I am not leaving Kit T Kat here without me! Secondly, you don't understand. Kit T Kat cannot be unloaded by anyone other than a professional."

Wheezy ignored her and opened the trailer latches. Rachel dropped the ramp. It was cold and everyone was experiencing pangs of hunger. Thank goodness for the sweet pecan pie to hold them over.

Presley seemed tired. Rachel's nerve pills appeared to be wearing off. So Wheezy refused to hear the spoiled woman. She believed in her own abilities.

"Gigi, it will be okay," Presley tried to soothe. "I can buy you a nice cup of hot chocolate when we stop on the way home. Kit T Kat will be fine."

Wheezy stepped away to help Rachel with Hannibal. He was the first in line to exit.

While Wheezy was not skilled at riding—not that she wouldn't love to be, just the timing never worked out—she was very familiar with leading horses. She had taken a crash lesson many decades ago with Gertrude Steele when she was forced to enter the Halter and Showmanship classes. But it was the trucking business that educated her. Back when she was a driver, her specialty became hauling the horse semis. Her mission on every haul had been to protect the goods and be fully responsible for her cargo. Wheezy had experienced a sense on every trip that someone was resting on her shoulders, protecting her and the animals. An angel—her grandmother was overseeing from above.

So, unloading Hannibal, Cleo, and the renegade Kit T Kat without the help of Carlos or Gertrude would be okay. Although Presley appeared exhausted, she could help if needed. Piece of cake.

Right?

Wrong.

The scene was as dramatic as the trunk transfer. Not because of Hannibal, the well-mannered gelding. He dropped his head, clomped down the ramp effortlessly and followed Rachel into a stall on a loose lead. Even though he was hungry and thirsty, he waited patiently for Rachel to unclip his tether, and then as she walked timidly backward from the stall, she repeated the word *whoa* numerous times, with Presley encouraging her from the door. It was obvious Rachel was a ball of nerves around that horse. But as Jemma had predicted, Hannibal was a perfect gentleman.

Once the stall door edged closed, he stretched his body and branded the new bedding with his scent. Then his barreled body lengthened to the fresh water. After a sip, he dipped his oversized head in the oats one bob at a time. Hannibal chewed as if savoring every morsel. Then he systematically munched on his hay in a slow and gratifying process like a seasoned connoisseur.

Presley next led Cleo out. They clearly had years of practice. The two strolled off the trailer with a gentle confidence. The mare halted when Presley stopped, stepped precisely where a well-trained showmanship horse would, and pivoted on cue. The mare ground tied, barely moving, simply a twitch or two of her shoulder as she waited for Presley to return. Cleo's candy bar shaded eyes were soft and intent on her owner.

Presley clipped her in a heavy blanket for the night and the mare neither trod forward nor backward. Finally, when the latch clicked to her halter again, the pair headed to her stall. Cleo inflated with contained anticipation. She walked in the stall tailing Presley. Her blackened and silver mane waved as she shook her head and snorted, yet she restrained from switching position until Presley turned to exit the stall.

Afterward, Cleo darted like a shark then dove nose-first into the feed bucket. She remained submerged, licking the pail with her tongue for every oat. When the bucket was empty, she attacked the hay with exaggerated slurps of water in between.

Kit T Kat, on the other hand, was like her owner. Gigi could barely clip her to a lead, ranting a moan the entire time. "Kit T Kat cannot stay here without me. She has never been without me or Carlos."

Rachel rolled her eyes and retrieved the last saddle out of the trailer to hang in the tack room. She no longer felt any remorse for the woman, as Rachel had unloaded most of Gigi's belongings. "How much stuff did you bring?" she muttered down the aisle of the barn.

Gigi ignored her, busy gaining any stance with the horse. The mare was intent on exiting without a moment to waste. Kit T Kat bolted past her handler and galivanted onto the ramp as if she was Taylor Swift trumpeting on stage to a hundred thousand admirers belting a scream to announce her presence.

Gigi clung to the rope with both hands, drawing the mare back. Hopelessly, the almost seventeen-hand mare targeted the open barn doors, lights, her munching friends, and the smell of oats. Gigi obviously had issues, and Carlos had her as spoiled as the mare.

Kit T Kat circled as Gigi battled. The mare's buckled coat shifted to the side then unhooked. The blanket dragged, the buckles clanging against her. With each hit, Kit T Kat kicked out resentment. The fight ensued to free herself from Gigi. Finally, at the entrance of the barn where the dirt path switched to cement, right where the ground dented in a 3x5 ditch that had probably ponded with water for years because no one repaired the drain, the mare halted. She wrenched her head up.

Wheezy had entered the feed room for another scoop of grain to prepare Kit T Kat's stall. She peered out at the commotion. There was no stopping the mare or the blisters which would most likely appear on Gigi's hands before that cup of chocolate Presley had promised. Gigi was lifted off her feet, let go with a shrill, and toppled to earth.

Bam!

The woman landed in a mixture of slush and the refreezing skim of ice from the squall. "*Ow!*"

"Gigi!" Presley called from the stalls further back.

Kit T Kat had been behind Gigi as she plopped in the mush. The mare's long legs spread-eagled, her head down, perplexed by Gigi on the ground. But once Kit T Kat realized she was free, she leaped over Gigi, the scent of oats and hay tormenting her to gallop toward the others down the aisleway.

"Kit T Kat! She's headed your way!" Gigi shouted.

Wheezy stood immobile at the feed room entrance holding the scoop of grain. The white beast torpedoed toward her with one intent—food. Her blanket flapped, slapping her like a whip, driving her. What would an experienced horse transporter do to stop a locomotive?

Wheezy did the only thing possible. Kit T Kat was a mere four feet away when Wheezy hoisted her arm in the air like a drill sergeant.

"*Whoa!*"

That tactic didn't stop the charging Kit T Kat.

Wheezy throttled backwards. As she did, oats sprinkled across the cement like glitter in a kindergarten room.

The mare instantly startled. Kit T Kat downshifted, sparks lighting from her metal hooves. She awkwardly high-stepped to a prance then a jog, her neck arching down, nostrils flared like a drug dog mid-sniff.

Grain!

The horse stiffened her neck then practically sat on her rump in a full sliding halt. Her upper lip curled. Her elongated tongue stretched like a child licking snowflakes in the air.

All the grain had dispersed, and the mare became obsessed with each morsel.

"Grab the lead," Presley hollered. She had plastered herself in front of Rachel to protect her.

Like a soldier in battle, Wheezy snatched the rope trailing on the ground. Not until that instant did she realize her body was trembling from panic.

Presley rescued her, retrieved the mare, and led the massive horse to a stall. She quickly released the clip that noosed the blanket, stepped aside, and freed Kit T Kat to rush in by herself.

The three women puffed as the mare tore into the bucket of oats, banging it to the boards, and pawing her front leg in the fresh chips with each bite.

Wheezy was bent over, clutching her knees as she tilted her head like a lineman ready to start the play.

"No blanket for her tonight," Presley announced. "Certainly, not worth one of us getting hurt."

"She'll survive one night," Wheezy confirmed with bitterness.

"Oh my, Gigi?" Rachel remembered.

The three turned their heads in unison to the stable entrance where Gigi was rising from the slop. Her white coat was splattered, her rump was pasty with mud, and her hair was disheveled, coated with sludge.

"Go without a blanket? Now that is impossible." The petite woman brushed a tendril of hair thickened with mud from her face. "Never! Not a white horse!"

"We're leaving." Wheezy straightened and trod toward Gigi as if she was one of those obnoxious truck drivers that didn't think a woman, especially a Black woman, could give directions. "That horse practically took us all down. We're out of here."

Gigi cringed and wavered back.

Presley ventured past. "We're all tired. Including Kit T Kat. I'm sure Gertrude will manage her better than we can. We'll be back in a day. Let her get adjusted."

Gigi folded her arms to her chest. Her eyes narrowed at Wheezy.

Rachel, clearly shaken too, retrieved the saddle from the ground where she had tossed it as Kit T Kat was barreling toward them. "I think your horse could use a white pill, too," she muttered.

"You don't understand. I must give her a kiss and a cookie. I do that every night. My Kitty will be a complete terror."

"She already is," Wheezy snarked, then marched toward her. "Are you kidding? Cookies after this episode?"

Her threatening tirade must have intimidated Gigi because the other woman tripped back against the wall.

"What are you going to do?" Gigi raised a hand to her face as if bracing herself. "Please, don't..."

Wheezy stiffened. "Really? You think I'd hit you? Or anyone?" *Maybe someone had abused her in the past.* Wheezy remembered too well the damage from a slap. Though it was thirty years past, a man's punch left a scar embedded in her soul forever.

She shook her head in disbelief. "You better go clean up. Maybe you have extra clothes in that trunk. You're not sitting in my truck like that." Wheezy pointed to Gigi's coat then headed toward Venus.

"Come on, we all need a hot chocolate." Presley smiled and reached for a broom. "Turn around, Gigi. Let's brush you off."

Gigi had smashed herself in the back corner of the truck against the door, the same spot she had on the way to Steele's farm. Tears streaked down her crusted cheeks, not because of leaving her dear Kit T Kat. God knows, the mare needed a trainer. Nor was it because Wheezy refused to allow her to give a cookie or the kiss on her horse's muzzle.

She'd lied when Presley asked her why she was crying. "I give her a cookie every night when I kiss her on her nose."

Rachel cut in. "Why the heck would you give her a treat after that incident?"

"You like them, don't you? Makes you feel better, right?" Gigi digged.

Rachel, offended, sank in the other corner as if she could not get further away.

"And her blanket," Gigi continued again, masking the real reason for her tears. "You don't understand. She'll be covered in dirt."

Wheezy steered the truck into the arched driveway of Gigi's mansion.

"Look, all will be okay," Presley said. "Get some rest. We'll pick you up at 6:00 AM Monday."

"I'll drive myself to Steele's," Gigi broadcasted as she swung her oversized satchel over her shoulder and swayed up the long stamped cement pathway lined in spotlights to the chestnut double doors with gold knockers.

She never turned to say thank you, goodnight, or any snide remark, although she'd heard Wheezy's backlash, "Suits me fine," right before slamming the truck door. Her concern was how she was going to continue to hide the truth.

As Wheezy entered the bedroom, she noticed the box on the center of her bed, as it was every weekend. She turned and met Darren, entering behind her, carrying a glass of cabernet and a manilla envelope.

"Darren, you know the—"

"Hey love, a guy can dream." He leaned in to kiss her forehead then handed her the glass. "Time for a relaxing massage, looks like?"

But she didn't hear him. Wheezy was whipping the scarf from around her neck and began confessing the events of the day in a blotchy tale.

"...the ironic thing was that Gertrude Steele had the three stalls well prepared... fresh chips, water and buckets... like she was going to accept us... but changed her mind. She only has one arm... doesn't bother me in the least. Felt good to finally thank her... I really like Presley... And that Rachel, she's a card. I hate to tell them I'm not going through with this. Gert will have to drive the trailer..."

"Whoa! What was that? You made a deal with these ladies."

She barely acknowledged Darren and sucked a sip of the wine. "It's her… Gigi. I can't deal with her horse… Well, I'd take the horse over Gigi."

"Honey, please. Slow down."

"She's a monster," Wheezy continued, but Darren pushed the envelope closer.

"Someone came to see you. Now, sit." He touched her shoulders in a gentle caress. "You are not dropping out. You never quit anything. Besides, you're finally engrossed in something other than that career you've been obsessed with."

"You don't understand." She stopped, finally processing his words. "Who? Who came to see me."

"Stan."

"That Gigi is impossible. Stan who?"

"*Stan*. Your former secretary. The one who would follow you to the end of the earth."

Suddenly she realized she had completely forgotten her woes at the trucking firm.

Darren curled his lips in a tease and placed the packet on her lap. "That man is so devoted. He also has a keen eye to figures and details. He's risking his own career for you. He suggested the discrepancies started at the time of Asher Devine's hire—right after you refused to drive any loads across state lines to the slaughterhouses for Emerson, or any others for that matter. Odd, huh? He said this contains figures, dates, times. He highlighted concerning issues."

Wheezy's daughter peered into the room. "Mom, Darren? Sorry, I have to leave in the morning for work-study in Belize." She pointed to the box on the bed. "Please say yes. And don't stop this horsey thing. Someday you *will* have grandkids—not just yet—and they are going to hear all about this brave grandmom of theirs pursuing her dreams!" She blew them a kiss and closed the door.

"I have never known you to quit," Darren added. "Seriously, are you afraid of Gigi?"

Wheezy collapsed onto the bed.

All three of them—Darren, Stan and her daughter—unconditionally loved her. She couldn't fail them. Not to mention the thought of grandkids.

"Are you for real? So in love with me." Her words slurred, almost hypnotically.

"Pinch me. I am for real." Darren bent and kissed her cheek. He retrieved the small box and placed it back in his pocket. "I know your answer. You're not ready. But I will not give up."

Wheezy beamed.

Presley curled up next to Brad. "Thank you for being supportive. To say the least, it was a unique day."

Presley laid her head on his shoulder as he stroked her bald scalp. Deep inside, she wanted to tell him this was stupid and she wanted to quit. That she should continue being a wife and mother, and wait to be the best grandmother she could, if she even lived past the next year's results. Maybe she should go learn to spin wool and knit—safer. However, she couldn't bear to disappoint Brad, the boys, or her mother Tilly.

"That makes me happy," Brad said. "Knowing you're finally with Cleo doing what you love."

Presley wanted to say she was too old, too sick, and that she was better at being a mom. But as always, she suppressed her feelings. She wanted to shout, remind him how she had been living close to death an entire year, that she didn't need to die riding a horse. But she couldn't.

"I'm sure your father is looking down from heaven," he added.

Brad didn't see the tears cresting in her eyes. Yes, her father. She could not disappoint an angel in heaven.

Roxie caught Rachel barreling in the front door. It was well past 10:00 PM. She had been cleaning the hair salon, as she always did at the end of the week, and was about to head out. Instead, she carried a brown paper bag as she entered the kitchen of the house.

"Hey, I was heading out and saw you arrived home. How was the day? Hannibal?"

Rachel was breathing in short pants. She had hot chocolate dribbled over her front and her bags spread across the table. "Jemma's right..." *Breathe.* "...Hannibal is great..." *Breathe.* "I'm not sure I can do it..."

"Do what?" Roxie retrieved a wet rag hanging on the faucet. She wiped the chocolate blotches from her friend's coat. "Be without Jemma?"

"I need to stay here," Rachel continued. "My clients will miss me." *Breathe.* "And I'm too old." *Breathe.* "I can't stop these heat flashes, or my eating... as Gigi says."

Roxie kept wiping. "Who cares what Gigi says?"

Rachel shoved the rag away then struggled to remove her coat. "Personal summer happening here."

"Do you want to lose her?" Roxie took the coat.

"Who?"

"Jemma?"

"It's just..."

Roxie nonchalantly maneuvered the coat to find the stains again, then began to dab at them. "You're looking for every excuse not to enjoy your life. I guess you think it's a sin to live with joy? You blame yourself for Heath's death. That was a sin? You think your daughter is gay, and you, oh my, are Catholic. *Sin?* You hide in that church and the salon with your clients. That's the real sin."

Rachel stopped breathing.

Did I really say all that?

Roxie simply continued cleaning the coat. "I said it, didn't I? The truth. After twelve years of Sunday school for Jemma, Catholic School for you, rosary beads and lies of perfection, you've never faced your truths."

Roxie tossed the rag in the sink. She ingested the sting on Rachel's face and offered her the brown paper bag as a precaution. "I ask you again, do you want to lose your daughter?"

Rachel apparently couldn't decide if she should be irate or breathe. "I love her more than anything in the world."

"Then don't you quit riding Hannibal. Stop judging yourself, and your past. Find out what you're made of, Rachel. It is not in the church or your clients... You raised Jemma right. She's an earthly angel."

Roxie swallowed hard. Rachel had never witnessed her this serious since her dog Pansy passed. "One more thing."

"What?"

As if Rachel wasn't shocked already, Roxie was going for the sting.

"Go find a man."

To her dismay, Gigi could hear Camilla and Randall as she passed the office. They were chatting about the trucking company. As much as she wanted to snoop and press her ear to the door, Gigi had another mission—hurry to her bedroom. She didn't care if Randall discovered her in this filthy condition. That wasn't a concern. Frankly, as she examined herself in the bedroom at her full-length mirror, her appearance made her laugh. *Imagine,* Gigi thought, *laughing at myself,* for a faux pas she had not done in decades.

Gigi's main intention was to reach her journal. She had so much churning inside. Then there was Gertrude Steele like some crazed character from a horror novel. She touched the photo of the four women and placed it in her diary like a bookmark.

She had lied about so much that day, and now she was in a bind. She touched the pen to her lip then began to write:

> Today started as a disaster. But in truth it's been a reflection upon myself and the realization I am facing a serious dilemma. I'm envious of these three women (as much as I pretend to hate them).
>
> Wheezy managed an entire trucking facility, and I've accomplished nothing, it seems. Men respect her for reasons I could only dream possible. I have this longing to be a writer, the pages of my journal constantly nagging at me to return, but at 48, I'm simply a pretty little priss.

That Rachel, she eats sweets, makes messes—and she makes me laugh at myself! I will keep that secret. And Presley, a woman of class, even when she doesn't feel well, has the sheer confidence to walk around with no hair.

Another annoyance—they are all mothers, and I must confess, I envy mothers. That too, I will never be, too worried about making Randall impressed with my flat mid-section.

While I'm confessing, listen to this one. When they talk about Wyndham Glick, I tingle inside. The same sensual inner spark Carlos ignites in me. *There, I said it!* If I could love anyone, it would be him.

But I have a serious dilemma. I can't ride Kit T Kat. Not without the aid of Carlos or injections. I'm not sure how to proceed. God knows I don't want to be here, with Randall, away from my dear mare, but I'm at a loss and don't want to make a complete fool of myself.

I wish I could be like Rachel, but I'm frightened of Kit T Kat. That horse is even more of a priss than me. Perhaps I can convince Randall to have Carlos come lunge her, ride her out early before anyone arrives. Better yet, I can give her the injections. No one must ever know. And if she's tested at the events, easy solution—blame Gertrude Steele! Let's face it, her record is already tarnished, but mine will continue to be spotless, and Randall's as well. I'm sure I can convince Randall. He's obsessed with winning. I will plead with him tomorrow. He'll have no choice if he wants the Silver Spur trophy resting on his shelf.

One more truth. Monday, when we return to Steele's, can't come fast enough.

Good night, Gigi

CHAPTER 23

The return time to Gertrude Steele's did not come fast enough for any of them. But when the morning alarms rang, Monday proved to be glorious, as if the weather had been ordered specifically for them. A far transformation from the wintery dark existence of January, the days were finally growing longer and brighter. The weatherman said 65-plus degrees in February could break records.

"We might be able to take our Carhartts off!" Rachel raised her cheeks to soak in the warmth before entering the barn. She had been soul searching ever since Roxie barked those life-altering perceptions at her. Although she'd kept it to herself, most of the accusations were precise. She was thankful to be at the barn and not have to address her personal issues. *Is that a sin? Mortal or venial?* She was exhausted by sin.

The three entered the barn, and the sweet aroma of hay, oats, and horses permeated their senses, along with that one not so sugary stench... manure. That was the first chore on the four-foot chalkboard in Gertrude Steele's signature style. At least that was the signed name at the bottom of the extensive list. Chores were explicitly written in blue chalk. There was not a soul around—not Gertrude, Maggie, or Gigi. But a note read, *Let payment begin*.

The others walked away as Wheezy insisted, "A deal is a deal!"

Presley checked the horses as she meandered down the aisleway assessing the situation. She was concerned how they would handle the white mare. Shifting her in and out of the stall to clean could be a challenge.

The horses snickered greetings, awaiting morning breakfast, yet she found it unusual that there were no belching screams from Kit T Kat's stall. Odd, but perhaps she was lying down exhausted from the journey.

Presley felt a chill as she inched near the stall, praying the mare was okay. How would they explain to Gigi if the mare had colic, or worse, had died? She peered between the bars.

Empty? No Kit T Kat? Although relieved, Presley felt a pang of sadness in her heart.

Gigi must've quit. Evidently came and picked up her horse.

Rachel slumped. "Oh sweet Mary, I did like her though. She was pretty! And funny sitting in that puddle of slush. Too bad. Now we're short a team member."

"It doesn't change our focus." Wheezy came from behind and shifted an olive and blue scarf around her neck. "Personally, she was spoiled rotten."

They stood staring at the barren stall, in their own sea of contemplations.

"Well, ladies, we can't cry over spilled milk. Let's do this!" Presley encouraged with a positive flare.

Together the three worked, checking off every order—from forking manure, cleaning buckets, leading the horses out of their stalls to the wash rack, brushing them, cleaning hooves, and sweeping cobwebs and spiders until they were a good two hours into singing with the vintage radio they had discovered on the ledge under a collection of old brushes, hoof picks, and bathing products.

"Probably twenty years old." Presley brushed the dust off it, relieved she'd worn her mask. "It's like one of those old boom boxes. Remember them?"

"Plug it in!" Rachel had suggested.

Wheezy performed the honors. If anyone was going to get zapped, she declared it would be her.

"It works!" Rachel leaned on a pitchfork. "Search for '80's music!"

Now they were serenading together to The Pointer Sisters, dancing and never hearing the screams billowing from the back pasture.

When Gigi woke to see the time, she popped forward as snappy as a trap that catches a mouse. She was late. Her journal slid from the pink faux fur comforter to the floor. She gathered her thoughts. Her journal not under her bed, out in plain sight? Yes, she remembered falling asleep after writing until 2:00 AM. She bent over like a diver searching for oysters. Her canopy bed was so elevated, she stretched, her brown locks touched the floor as her hair extensions dropped over her head. She snatched the diary then hoisted herself up.

She fluttered through the pages until it opened to the last entry the night before. She had never approached Randall with her dilemma. "Change of plans," her diary read. Gigi wouldn't have to talk to him unless a dire emergency arose, like drug testing. She curled into the fur and slipped lower after reading the name of the person she did confide in. "Carlos." He was the reason she snuck in late, two hours past midnight, like Cinderella. A warm sensation seared through her limbs. Gigi didn't believe such a feeling would ever be possible again especially while married to a man like Randall Emerson. The result—she was no different than her immoral husband who had illicit affairs. She was now like him… guilty of more than drugging a horse.

She touched the entry again. "Called Karma."

She was certainly going to be late, but it didn't matter. That was Gigi's MO. Besides she was one of them now, like Randall, a criminal. Guilt slammed her, but she swept it away. She had no choice.

Gigi tucked the bag Carlos had given her deep inside her oversized satchel and hopped in her white Mercedes. He had given her a few months' supply but warned no more. She tossed the bag on her passenger seat, knowing the contents must be kept in a secret hiding place at all times. Gigi drove, her pink nails tapping to the music. Somehow she would be confident she would ride Kit T Kat like they were one, putting the others to shame.

When Gigi arrived in the barn, the music was blaring so atrociously loud that not one of them heard her calls. She could hear the three singing while organizing the tack room.

Gigi yanked the plug from the wall. Sparks flew, and the music went silent.

Their voices descended from overzealous vocals to mere humming off-tune as they scanned the aisleway. Gigi was planted in front of the empty stall in search of her mare.

"Gigi, you're back! We thought you..." Rachel exclaimed hopping out of the room. The dust had collected on her silver and blonde waves in feathery puffs like bunny tails.

"First, have you seen the board? The house, dusting, painting. Come on. I draw a line! But more importantly, where's Kit T Kat?" Gigi's hand clenched her hip as she stood in a delicate pink Carhartt she'd purchased two days earlier.

"No idea. We thought you hauled her home."

"Although I would like to, I am committed. Now where can I find her?"

The discussion was interrupted by a familiar bellow from a pasture afar. The cries resonated through the stable.

The four rushed to the end of the barn. Reaching the outside first, Gigi curdled a scream, octaves higher than any warbling Kit T Kat could manage.

Gigi struggled to speak, "Who turned my mare out? And with no blanket!"

Kit T Kat was almost unrecognizable as her rump muscles curled and nostrils flared with snorts like a steam engine. She raced the fence with the horse in the adjacent pasture.

The stallion in the round pen seemed to be taking pleasure in the excitement, as were the other steeds in the fields.

The mare was crusted head to hoof in grime, her mane twisted in knots and her tail wringing with joy.

"Sweet mother of God," was all Rachel or anyone could say.

"Gert was right," a voice interrupted their horror. "The mare needed to be a horse. Perfect weather, too. Otherwise, it would have been too cold for her, as her hair isn't overly thick because you blanket her all the time."

"Maggie? You... you... turned my horse out?" Gigi's violet eyes were afire.

Maggie's pixie of curls was coiling in multiple directions. "I did what I was told. When it comes to the horses, Gert's the boss. I am sure you remember this. Plus being late for the gate is not good. Need I remind you?" Maggie pointed her finger at Gigi.

"*Grrrr.*" Gigi stamped her feet. Her hands fisted by her side. "Well, someone is going to clean her up!"

The tip of Maggie's ears blushed. "That's not the way this works. This is a team effort. You are like the four musketeers." She cleared her throat. "Now, Gert asked that you all catch the horse together, except for Presley. Seems she's had a long enough day. Presley is to come in and review paperwork with Gert. After you all finish with the mare, you can come in for some lunch, or maybe supper, then she'll talk with you about the future."

"What about riding?" Gigi nipped. "That's why we're here."

"No saddling, today. There will be no lessons." The redness had swelled to Maggie's cheeks. "And remember, catch her then bathe her. Dry her then cover her in her winter blanket. Also please hang all your appropriate gear in the tack room with assigned names. Okay, go to it!" Maggie turned to leave, but after just one step she paused and spun back. "Oh, and ladies, the barn looks great."

Presley was standing at the kitchen window next to Maggie. They had a complete view of the struggles in Kit T Kat's pasture. The three were chasing Kit T Kat to no avail. The horse appeared to relish the cat and mouse game. When any one of them reached within an arm's length, Kit T Kat popped, reared, or pivoted on a quick turn and sprinted off again. Gigi removed her pink coat before tumbling several times. Her white sweatshirt got covered with a matching film of mud and dirt.

"Will that woman never learn to stop wearing white?" Maggie stood bewildered.

The mare flattened and galloped another thundering pass to the top of the pasture.

Presley finally sat down to wait for Gert. The kitchen seemed brighter than before, even cleaner. "I hope she learns that as quick as she learns to work like a team member."

The three entered the farmhouse in a clamor. They were dressed in sweat, dirt and suds. Their coats were off, and they stripped down to their long johns.

Rachel moaned. "Mother Mary, that horse needs a white pill! Do they even have them for horses?"

"You could say they do, but they're illegal," Maggie informed. "None of that here."

The remark hit Gigi with a shockwave, and she feared the others saw her cheeks flush. She heaved a chair to sit, scratching the floor, then plopped her head down on the table releasing a muffled, "This is nonsense."

"Are you having a heat flash?" Rachel asked. "Because you look terrible."

Gigi's clothes were soaked from bathing the horses, as the ancient hose had spewed water from multiple holes and tears. A concentrated fragrance of the horse-whitening shampoo, Simply Silver, seemed to linger in every orifice.

"That horse has been sheltered. When was the last time she was allowed to gallop through the fields without any restraints or rider?" Maggie asked.

"Kit T Kat is a top-notch show horse." Gigi remained facing the table, her voice muffled.

Gertrude strode into the kitchen. "Even the best show horses need play time! I make the rules here." She paused as if to assess the situation then sat. She was not wearing the metal apparatus.

Instead, one blue-checked flannel plaid arm was stitched shut at the elbow.

Maggie set a plate of homemade chicken salad sandwiches in the center of the table as Gert continued speaking. "Presley helped me devise a schedule for the year."

"We're going to compete in the Silver Spur?" Gigi perked up. "So, you do believe in us!"

"Hardly." Gertrude's response fell like a dead leaf to the ground. "Listen, ladies. I'm not gonna lie to you."

She raised her left hand to shield her face. "Maggie, dim the light, please. It hurts my eyes sometimes. Maybe light the candelabra instead."

Maggie obeyed with a *tsk.* She set an ornate fixture with four candles next to the half-emptied tray of sandwiches. With a match to each wick, the room glowed. Maggie then disappeared from the kitchen.

Gigi wasn't sure which eye to look at as she met Gertrude's stare. She zeroed in on the blue one, which sparked with life, then shifted to the brown which seemed to be pointblank targeting her.

"The Silver Spur is a serious competition," Gert said, "and although there is a novice division, it's never been won by a team over age fifty. The versatility show accepts any discipline and breed, but not a band of unskilled equestrians like yourselves. You couldn't do it thirty years ago, so I'm not so sure how you think you can compete now, let alone become champions."

"We have determination..." Wheezy confirmed, "...and we have you, Ms. Steele."

"Louisa Mae, in case you haven't noticed, I am handicapped. I also have not trained seriously in quite some time, and I no longer am..."

Presley cleared her throat. "We understand, but we're committed."

Gertrude Steele sighed, transforming her face into a deranged expression like a mad scientist. Her eyebrows convened as one, her eyes tightened, her forehead reduced in size and her jaw tensed. "There will be prep, grueling hours upon hours... I need commitment from everyone as an entire team. If anyone wants out, do it now."

The room was silent.

"The competition has many divisions. The team enters five, and one may be the trainer. I understand you believe you have English, Western, Halter or Showmanship, and Games. But I will determine the final entries."

Gigi jerked forward. "That's not how it works. I am English, one hundred percent!"

Gertrude sliced her with the brown eye and resumed.

"Mondays and Wednesdays are your riding days. This first month, you will find yourselves exhausted. Tuesdays and Thursdays are my days with the horses. Chores will be posted daily. For now, Presley will organize the show charts, points, etcetera. But we will need an extra hand—someone good with figures, organized, who doesn't miss a number. Even a half-point makes a difference. This riding will be laborious, especially at your ages, competing against twenty and thirty-year-olds who have stamina, strength and can stay up all night."

"I stay up all night now," Rachel chimed.

"It's your age," Gigi whispered.

"You're practically the same age as me..."

Again, Gertrude discounted the remarks. "Teamwork is key. This bickering must stop. First show is April..."

The words brought raucous cries of objections. "Wait, did you say April? That's just a few weeks away."

"How will we even be ready?"

"Oh, mother Mary." Rachel panted in short bursts. "I can't do that!"

Gertrude slapped her hand on the table. "I need to see the level of your skill."

"Well, I can tell you mine." Gigi sat back with confidence.

"Wrong. This is going to be your worst nightmare. Don't you even think this will be a piece of cake. When I commit to something, I intend on winning. Might as well know where we stand. We're entering a small walk-trot show to determine if the Silver Spur is even possible. I warn you, this will start as chaos. They're going to laugh at you, and talk about me, but this will fool them. If we succeed, and improve over the following months, we may just have a chance. We can ambush the others by having a team ready to win!"

"What kind of plan is that?" Gigi popped to her feet. "Look, you're the trainer, but I can't be sore all the time. I don't saddle my own horse or warm her up. That's your job."

"Ms. Titless, sit down."

The name hit her like a bomb. No one had called her that in decades. She wanted to correct the woman, but the words were shellshocked in her throat.

Rachel slid a sandwich her way, while Presley rested a hand on her forearm to bring Gigi back to the seat.

"Again, if you haven't noticed, I have one arm and a limp. You will each saddle and exercise your own horse. You will be riding so much you'll have blisters and boils on your asses. Chaffed knees and muscles. You're about to throb with pain, but if you survive the summer, I promise you'll forget about life's problems—hot flashes, bad husbands, empty nest, guilt... even your own mortality. You'll be living again. Fall in love with horses again. The passion that's nagged at all of you since you were born."

Gigi tried to mask her astonishment. *How does she know about my cheating husband?*

"Where's Maggie? I think Gert's going nuts." Rachel scanned the room.

"I told you, she's *a nutball,"* Gigi grunted behind her hand in Rachel's direction. "Thank God she doesn't have that claw on, or we'd be goners."

The candles flickered, and as Gertrude Steele rose, her shadow from behind had risen, seemingly elevated above them as if a Holy Roller pastor in a horror flick at midnight just before living dead rise from the grave.

All four focused, silent, waiting for lightning to strike from heaven.

"See you Wednesday," Gert said. "And don't be *late*."

The girls had been completely unaware Gertrude was observing their interactions and activities. She had studied them completing the blackboard tasks, cleaning their tack and the horses. She was watching from a monitor in the pantry. Gert had cameras installed when she thought there was an intruder on the property. Instead, it had been a young black bear who thought he would slumber there for a time.

Maggie appeared for a fresh cup of coffee, her straight back and elevated chin communicating the cold shoulder. Gert was cognizant that Maggie still wasn't dropping her guard.

Maggie flicked the light on. "Why do you try to use scare tactics? Like you're some crazed lunatic. These are grown women."

"Who are acting like children. At least two of them. They either want this dream or they don't need to waste my time."

"Why? You've been wasting your own time, and maybe it's you that will come alive. Now, what exactly is the plan?"

"They will have no choice but to get in shape... not simply from riding, but the chores and the bonding will happen between them and their horses, or else they will have no team."

"That isn't exactly what I meant. You, Gert, have not competed or seriously ridden for some time. And you're no spring chicken. How are you going to hop right on a horse of that caliber?"

"The white mare?"

"Yes, Gert. The mare. She's a lot of horse. I do worry."

"Well, if all goes as planned, these ladies will quit after the first show."

"Gert! I expect you to fulfill your promise to Brad and Presley's father. Forget about Randall Emerson. I wouldn't be surprised if he was out for his own benefit. So, let's pretend these ladies do surprise you and have what it takes. In the event they don't quit... the white horse is still a problem."

Gert rose, clearly stiff. She hobbled to dim the light again. The candles flickered, wax streaming down the sides.

"Let's get one thing straight. A horse is never the problem... the human is. I know someone who can help. He owes me quite a favor."

She pointed to an equine journal on the counter. The front cover pictured a Brazilian horse whisperer.

Wyndham Glick
returns to America
after year hiatus

"He's right over the border in Maryland working with racehorses who balk at the starting gate. Says he's searching for a respite spot for them."

Both Gert and Maggie examined the front page. The man's broad smile, dark skin, chestnut eyes, and the silvery dusting in his ebony waves sparked with life. "There he is, leading the horse quietly to the gate. Wyndham Glick. My friend… and he's in America. That is my plan."

Then Gertrude laughed as if howling at the night in the glow of the room.

Part Three

The Ride

Chapter 24

When Wyndham Glick's trailer drove into Steele's facility it wasn't simply the horses parading with vigor because another visitor had arrived. Gertrude's heart hadn't pounded like this in a decade. She had ceremoniously showered, washed her hair, even shaved.

She stood alone, studying her appearance in a full-length mirror wrapped only in a bath towel. Gertrude fermented on where she had been the last ten years—a depressed recluse, dismembered by a community that once respected her.

Her body bore the scars of an arduous life. But at present, she appeared rekindled, almost vivacious like in the early days when Tut was a star. This revival wasn't because she had an attraction to Glick in a sexual way, not at all. Instead, his method of kindness and honest commitment had been an inspiration. He was one of a handful of people who could knead her hardened heart until pliable.

Gert touched the picture from long ago that rested on the sideboard in the foyer. In retrospect, it was a memorable moment. Wyndham's gallant arm wrapped around her shoulder, his formidable forearm draped over her chest as both wore potent smiles of joy. Gert never thought she would see him in person again. Yet, as the memories flooded, a dam broke. Today she watched him leap from his truck as if he'd never left.

Gertrude paced her steps, trying to contain the bubble bursting inside as she walked to meet Wyndham.

He was just the opposite, leaping three porch steps to bear hug her.

She could hardly contain herself. He didn't examine her, or shy away upon seeing her. Nor did Wyndham question the elephant in the room, her missing limb. He squeezed her like he had the day Tut won the versatility championship.

"Such a gift that you reached out. I've thought of you so often. You helped me so many years ago. I will never forget your kindness. A time when the others snubbed my heritage. You had faith. I am forever grateful." The Brazilian's words occasionally resonated as if he was a seductive foreigner serenading her for a drink. "My horses most certainly need a rest."

They conversed for hours until Gert believed her missing limb needed to surface. She raised her wounded arm and laid the empty portion of her plaid shirt sleeve on the table. She paused, expecting an antiphon of empathy, sympathy, or at least an observation regarding her life of limitations.

Nothing. Finally, she stirred the pot.

"I guess you're wondering about my handicap?" Gertrude raised her partial arm, the barren sleeve waving like a white flag of surrender.

"Handicap?" Wyndham acted nonplussed. "Your only handicap is here." He tapped his index finger to his head. "If you believe in your ability, then your students—both human and horse—will believe."

"Wyndham?" Gert's face daubed with shock. "My area of expertise was Working Cow. How could I ever compete? My balance affects my horse."

"Then center yourself." His unyielding tone accepted no defeat. "Wouldn't that be a lesson for your students?"

I have no more students. But that wasn't true. At present, she did have four students.

But not for long though, she predicted.

Yet Gert wanted to believe Wyndham's words were loaded with fundamental advice... She wanted to confess to him about the accident—the injection over a decade earlier that had caused the road to this unfortunate event. However, the looming possibility of losing his friendship forced her to maintain a stiff upper lip. Instead, she concentrated on her new mission, even if it would be a short-lived glory ride. Defeat, sorrow, always lurking around the corner. She swept the concern under her saddle, because the next weeks, Tuesdays and Thursdays would be comprised of what she missed—horses. With Wyndham Glick by her side.

Maggie tracked their progress in the ring from the kitchen window. Her heart caught whenever Gert shifted off-balance, either mounted or dismounted. She walked, jogged, trotted, and cantered rails in L shapes, crossed in foot-high jumps, or spread out in split rows. The girls wouldn't suspect Gert's body was as blistered and bruised as theirs, because she was a master at veiling both physical and mental agony.

Maggie had to ready a warm bath at night, something she had not prepared in years. She rubbed on the Bio Freeze, placed heat compresses overtop and administered ibuprofen. All worth it, to savor the renewed luster, the brightness in Gert's blue eye and the gleam in her brown one.

Maggie had another secret. She had discovered some incriminating items in Gigi's possession. The discovery had been an accident after Gigi tossed her sack on a bale of hay while raging to find her mare. Kit T Kat had been turned out without a sheet. When Gigi tossed the bag, the contents plummeted across the aisleway. While the girls were busy catching the spitfire of a mare, Maggie retrieved the injections clearly meant for a horse. There would be none of that here, and for that Maggie would make sure.

The next six weeks were a repetitive seven-day schedule, a circadian rhythm: girls, Wyndham, girls, Wyndham, girls, finally two days off, which on a horse farm were never off.

Gert spread the girls' times, so the barn and housework was completed throughout the day. Separating the team did not fortify camaraderie between them, but Gert was trying to avoid bonding anyhow. She had no intention of making Silver Spur a reality. She was finished being a laughingstock in the community that once respected her.

Gert posted her rules on the board. First, they could not visit on Tuesday or Thursday. The early shift rotated: one was in lesson while the other worked on chores. The second shift took over until the barn lights were turned off. Gert staggered them to keep them apart. By their limping strides and moans, muscles had awakened after years of inactivity. They had no inkling that Gert secretly shared their aches, as well as the one in her heart.

Gert managed to ensure their dislike for Gigi continued. If she could never get restitution from Randall Emerson himself, she could at least deliver vengeance on his spoiled wife.

This had been Gert's true intent from the beginning of this entire shitty scheme—keep the team at odds, inevitably quitting, Gigi the buffoon instead of Gert and Emerson embarrassed with no trophy.

But on Tuesdays and Thursdays, while training with Wyndham, she observed him with Kit T Kat. Her conscience knew she was making a mistake.

Gert didn't inform Wyndham about the upcoming horse show. She had hoped it was to be the team of four's demise. The last thing she wanted was for him to insist on helping. So she didn't post information about it until he was gone on the Thursday prior.

Gigi had been throwing tantrums as to why she could not ride her Kit T Kat at lessons.

"Neither you nor she are ready yet. Cleo is a good mount for you to build strength." Gert had answered firmly. But Friday Gert said, "Gigi, you can ride Kit T Kat in the first show," and Gigi jumped, clapping her hands.

Gert was completely aware Gigi would make a fool of herself. The horse was far too much for Gigi to handle at her present skill level. And that was Gert's plan. In fact, it was her plan that all of them fail.

Rachel on Hannibal, even though sturdy, would be too overwhelmed with nerves. Again, the cumbersome tingle of guilt burdened Gert as the girls—including Gigi—were overwhelmingly excited. Gigi surprisingly cleaned Kit T Kat herself with the bluing shampoo then snapped the mare tightly in a beautiful brand new fuchsia sheet.

"Wow, Gigi," the three pined.

Gigi smirked. "Yes, at least one pair of this team will make a statement. When I take off the sheet, the spectators will be awestruck by her sparkling whiteness."

Presley was most prepared. The positive, caring woman had been through quite a lot. But Gert suppressed her opinion by reminding herself she too had struggled.

Then there was Wheezy. That woman had singlehandedly proved she could drive a rig, manage a company of mostly ill-mannered men, and unload horses. Unfortunately, she too was not ready for the arena lights. This scalded Gert's heart. Wheezy had thanked Gert and meant it. Unfortunately, Gert would think of Wheezy as a sacrificial lamb, like Joan of Arc right before she was burned at the stake. So she blocked the thoughts. Gert simply had one trophy in mind: Emerson.

At 5:00 AM on the morning of the show, Presley, Wheezy, Rachel and Gigi were relieved when Gert mentioned she would not ride with them to the event. They unanimously expelled exaggerated "Ahhhs and nooooos," as if saddened.

"No worries, ladies," said Gert. "I'll remain hidden at the upper end of the ring sitting in my truck. It would be a mistake to let people know I've returned to training. If they notice the one-armed trainer, well... that would take the focus off your performance. I want the judges to concentrate on you and not my handicap."

Gert recalled Wyndham's inspiring remarks. She hesitated then lied, "I want you to have your best chance. I'll be analyzing exactly what we need to work on."

In Wheezy's truck, Rachel rejoiced. "My lucky day! I'm a wreck and I don't need Gertrude Steele sitting near me." The other three agreed, as they entered the cab. But their luck ended when they drove out the lane.

The weather, as pleasurable as it had been on the previous day when Gigi bathed Kit T Kat, was now icy. The late April air dipped to a record low. A late nor'easter had blasted across the state during the night. The obscure grey clouds reminded Rachel of the first day they had driven to Gertrude Steele's. Her nerves mounted. As they pulled in and unloaded, the crisp air mixed with a drizzle that pelted them like needles.

"This isn't g-good," Rachel stammered.

"We have no choice but to do this, Rachel. We'll saddle outside, tied at the trailer." Presley led Cleo down the ramp first. "You can do it."

"Their cold backs will make them higher than kites," she mumbled.

Rachel tripped leading Hannibal off the trailer. She dropped her hat in the mud and her pants were squishing her to death. Then she noticed her blouse was buttoned crooked. That's when she met Hannibal's soothing teddy bear eyes.

"Oh please, take care of me, boy." Rachel stroked his already moist mane.

Rachel had squeezed into an outfit that morning from the trunk in her room. She had laid on her bed to zip the outdated high-waisted Rocky jeans. *Why not? The high waist is back in style.* When the zipper closed tighter than expected, her belly bulged. She didn't want to rush out and buy new clothes even though she had lost some weight in the past few weeks of riding. What if she decided to quit? But now she was sorry she hadn't.

At present, she was steaming hot from the uncomfortable fit, barely able to swing her leg over Hannibal.

Rachel eyed the ring where others were already exercising their horses. Simultaneously, she wished the show would cancel due to weather. She wasn't ready. She was too old for this. *Horse showing at fifty? Am I crazy?* Rachel swiveled back in the saddle carefully as her jeans brush-burned her waist with every movement.

Presley was tightening the cinch on Cleo. She looked focused, even while being pelted with raindrops that felt more like sleet.

"Are you coming?" Rachel whimpered, her belly cramping in waves. With Presley by her side for support, Rachel thought she could do it.

The hollow stomping of the last horse off the trailer commanded their attention. Gigi appeared with her mare blanketed in fuchsia, prancing like a queen. Both raised their heads as Kit T Kat snorted a trumpeting scream that echoed across the show grounds. Gigi tried to tether the mare to the trailer hook, and Kit T Kat pawed at the ground in anticipation.

Presley was now mounted and to Rachel's relief called, "Let's go."

They reached the entrance to the ring when a shriek rattled their nerves. *Gigi.*

Like other spectators, they rubbernecked in the direction of the uproar. Gigi had removed the pink sheet and stood like a wax figure in a horror museum, the massive sheet bunched and cradled in the petite woman's arms.

The sheet had left an imprint on the mare like a brand new hot pink t-shirt left accidentally in a Clorox-filled washer of whites. Kit T Kat was hued in a fluorescent pink residue, Gigi in cheeks of red.

"Rachel, Rachel!" Gigi cried. "You're a hairdresser. What do I do?"

Rachel was stunned. The horse was glowing. A group of girls in their twenties in the next trailer snickered.

"Did you cover her with that sheet while she was still wet? The sheet must've been new, and the color wasn't set! Didn't you learn this same lesson thirty years ago?" Rachel shifted in the saddle, conscious how her pants rubbed. Served Gigi right. *At least one pair of this team will make a statement.*

Presley intervened. "Gigi, it's not only too cold to bathe her, but it's too late to remove the stain."

Kit T Kat's behavior was amplifying to anxiety. It seemed the entire showground was rampant with whispers and giggles. The mare was a giant pink flamingo-colored horse.

Gigi slapped her sides. "What can I do?"

"Ride, woman." Wheezy brushed past in a nonchalant manner. She had come from the tented stand selling tack and possessed a new pair of silver spurs in her hands. "I always wanted a pair of these western spurs." Wheezy jiggled them in the air, cherishing her treasure. "I'll be like Wyndham Glick."

"We should have just taken yoga," Rachel moaned. "I can hardly swing my leg over a horse today. I'm so sore."

Without warning, a palomino pony skirted between Cleo and Hannibal in a dash to enter the ring. There was barely enough room for the tiny tank to barrel past, scraping the saddle and side of Hannibal.

"Hey ladies, my daughter's a serious contender and needs in the practice ring. Mind taking the socialization elsewhere?" The mother rolled her eyes, and directed her nine-year-old to continue against the rail in warm-up.

The pair were perfectly attired in a matching blanket and glittery pigtail ribbons. Their nose and chin were cemented to the sky, shoulders square and the girl's skinny legs tapped resolutely at the pony but couldn't make contact as they were too short. The saddle shined with water protectant as drizzle beaded and dissipated off without streaks. The pony's bridle was trimmed in decorative silver with a matching engraved tag denoting her name, *Annie's Promise.*

Hannibal stretched his neck in response as they forged by. His ears pinned flat, he grunted but remained stationary.

"Oh sweet Mary, a pony! That's all I need. Hannibal hates them."

"Rachel, keep his attention on you. You'll be okay," Presley coached.

Rachel's practice went surprisingly well. By the time the actual Walk-Trot Novice class was called, she trusted that Hannibal would listen to her.

"Stay centered and don't think about the pony," Presley advised.

It worked for the first two times around the ring. The fuzzy little pony and the adorable nine-year-old were trotting at a pass, the pony's tail swishing, the girl's pigtails bobbing.

Hannibal dodged at them in a sharp jolt, ambushing the pair. Rachel unintentionally freed his reins, allowing him to soar forward as the pony bounced past with arrogance.

Hannibal was possessed, flapping his jaws in gator style, seizing a chunk from the pony's rump.

Rachel collapsed forward, landing on his broad neck helplessly like a cement column. It was her jeans that kept her stable like a pillar, like the Johnny West dolls she'd played with as a child, their legs unable to bend, hips pinched together.

Finally, she nabbed a left rein and veered the overgrown horse toward the fence.

No longer in view of the pony, Hannibal stood quietly as if nothing had happened, his mouth crunching on wet and bloody fur poking out the rotating corners in triumph.

Annie and Promise were screaming, and blood seeped from a section of the pony's torn hide. The mother rushed like a fullback into the ring, hysterical, spectators leaning into one another in revulsion.

The judge motioned to the show secretary to halt the class.

Rachel teared at the disqualification announcement that resounded over the loudspeaker. Her half-century-old shoulders slumped, rain spilling from the brim of her cowgirl hat covered in plastic.

As she exited the ring, Wheezy was waiting at the gate with Cleo, ready to lead her into the ring for the Halter class.

"It's alright, Rachel. It's the first show."

Rachel walked Hannibal to stand next to Presley on the outside of the ring. She would stay to cheer on her friend even though she felt like crawling in the trailer and bawling her eyes out.

When Wheezy's number was called, she simply had to lead Cleo in a jog approximately twenty feet to the ring steward, square Cleo off, and then pivot the mare on her back haunches and return to the start at a faster trot.

Wheezy was dressed in black jeans and the hydrangea scarf for good luck. A mint Wrangler shirt matched the mint leaves of the scarf.

She jogged Cleo in a precisely executed straight line to the steward then squared her off instantly as Cleo was a pro. They continued to turn to trot home. It was perhaps the jingle that alerted Rachel's friend.

"She's wearing spurs?" Presley acted astonished.

"Yes, they're nice. Wheezy just bought—" Rachel leaned down from atop Hannibal.

"You can't run in spurs!" Presley whispered in an unusually elevated voice. It was too late.

Wheezy should have known better. Gertrude had informed her decades earlier never to wear spurs in a showmanship nor halter class. Too risky.

Wheezy had been trying on the western spurs at Clyde's Western World tack sale table. The rain had stopped, and she felt so confident in her attire that she forgot to remove them.

When she turned Cleo on her back end, it was angelic. Wheezy reveled in delight that the pattern was meticulous. And she proceeded to guide Cleo into a proud peppy trot home.

All was well right up until Cleo's hoof pinned the back rowel of one spur into the mud. Instantly, Wheezy was immobile, her spine snapped back.

Then Cleo released her weight, reaching for the next stride, which catapulted Wheezy's body into the cold spring slush, face first with a splat.

CHAPTER 25

The show was a complete disaster. Rachel rejoiced that she was not the sole team member to be DQed. She shared the limelight with both Wheezy and Gigi. Gigi had entered her English division mounted on the four-legged pink flamingo. She had no choice. Practically every human and non-human halted what they were doing to witness the class. As luck would have it, the local news station was present to interview 4-H students on their first show of the season.

The weather didn't deter the interview by the left side of the outer edge of the ring. In fact, after the entries were asked to trot by the ring steward, Kit T Kat with her already heightened adrenaline, immediately skipped the request initiated by Gigi. The mare broke into a canter on her own accord. The camera man was forced to focus on the class as the 4-Hers had lost interest in the anchor's questions and had relocated, clinging to the rail to ogle the excitement. His lens couldn't catch a clear image on the fuchsia blur that passed him several times at record speed.

After Gigi lost both stirrups, the mare zigged and zagged across the center ring, veering off pattern. Reason enough for disqualification. The mare jetting in between other horses caused them to buck or rear out of control, dismounting riders like flies. The runaway disrupted every equestrian on the premises. The cries and gasps from the crowd only fueled the unrest until the class had to be halted. The show steward and judge were finally able to corral the hot pink steed with the help of a few wranglers.

By the time the four loaded their horses, they were barely speaking. Especially Gigi and Rachel who took a last visit to the porta-potty. Gigi at that point was huffing from embarrassment and the audacity that she had to use a porta-potty instead of the trailer bathroom.

"The trailer is all locked up, Gigi, so go use the potty before this rig pulls out." Wheezy whipped her hydrangea scarf off and popped into Venus with a mutter of disgust. "It's good enough for the rest of us." The engine revved, leaving Gigi no choice yet again.

The porta-potties were located in a direct path to the secretary stand. Once inside, the slats in the top portion of the unit allowed Rachel to hear a familiar mother from the show stand complaining that she wanted to sue for the missing rump of her daughter's horse.

The secretary defended in exhaustion, "Look, this has been a day. You show here at your own risk. Read the signs."

The TV crew had gathered their equipment and trudged past. "Well, that English class will make our year-end bloopers segment for sure... the over-the-hill wife of Randall Emerson on a pink flamingo!"

But when Rachel heard the ranting voices of four younger women pass after collecting ribbons from their winnings, she wished to lock herself in the odorous unit until dark.

She pictured the group of fresh faced, wrinkle free, flat-bellied, twenty somethings... the same ones parked next to their trailer. Their fashionable show clothes still neatly pressed, still spotless, even in this weather with styling high ponytails, a precisely smoothed tease bump and magazine figures. Rachel had first noticed them at the secretary booth signing up that morning.

"Did you see the bunch of old ladies? Crack me up," one started.

"The group with that lady's picture plastered on the back of the trailer?" another remarked.

"You couldn't miss them. The plump one smells like moth balls. She must have drug out her old show clothes because she was busting out of them."

Rachel cringed as she tried to yank up her Rockies in the confined space without falling back in the abyss of filth.

"And that giant pink horse, what a joke."

"How about the Black lady?" the woman hesitated in laughter... "falling... when the horse stepped on her spur."

"Not half as funny as the princess pony. I heard he needs four stitches on his rump." The women were catching air between elevated giggles.

"Did the bald lady expect sympathy to help win herself a blue ribbon?" an assured voice declared. "That first place was all mine."

The last statement boiled inside Rachel. It didn't matter what they said about her, but Wheezy and Presley? She wrenched her body to button the jeans. She'd give them a piece of her mind. Didn't they realize what she and her friends had been through?

One of the girls continued, "I heard they plan on entering the Silver Spur."

"Really, come on. Plus, we have a shitload of money behind us. And the best horses. What do they have?"

"Wrinkles."

Rachel fought to connect the jeans, but the more she clenched, sucking in the awful stench to hold her stomach in, the hotter she grew. Then she lost her balance. She stumbled out the plastic door, hitting the next person in line, a small 4-Her and... another mother.

"Really! Aren't you the same person whose horse bit Promise?"

Rachel regained her composure, realizing her button was still two inches apart. "Oh, for Blessed St. Mary, shove it!" Rachel barked, overwhelmed by a blistering hot flash. She scanned the area for the twenty-year-olds who were staggering, laughing hysterically. They never noticed Rachel's stumbling entry back into the fresh air.

Rachel struggled with her pants. As she slipped away, Gigi exited the neighboring potty, pinching her tiny nose in repulsion. *She had to hear the conversations taking place.* Neither spoke as they returned to the trailer. And thank goodness, neither Presley nor Wheezy heard. But Rachel couldn't forget the plump accusation or the smell of her mothballed jeans. The wet weather must have caused the odor to maximize.

A staff member in fluorescent orange was directing the exit. He motioned Wheezy to stop and lower her window. In his hand was a small business card.

"I remember you girls, showing 25 or so years ago. The secretary reminded me. Those were the days! And that trainer, Gertrude Steele, parked at the end of the ring. She's with you, right?"

No one in the truck responded. He forced the hand with the card further in the window.

"Maybe you all need a new trainer? Just saying... I heard she's crippled."

Wheezy sighed, instantly rolling up the window, almost crushing his arm. "Jerk."

"Look, Steele's already long gone," Rachel added.

"What exactly are we paying for?" Gigi noted.

The ride home was silent. Presley fingered her second-place ribbon in the front seat.

"I guess we ought to quit," Rachel softly remarked as they pulled in the lane at Steele's.

"Stupid dream." Gigi nabbed her satchel and unlatched her door. "Well ladies, it's been nice."

Her door was barely ajar when Presley whipped off her ballcap then spiked it to the backseat between the two. Even Wheezy sat straighter. "No, ladies. It is not over. You made a commitment."

Rachel jumped. Gigi's violet eyes popped.

Presley had delivered an order. Her index finger shook as fast as her lips moved.

Her voice rose like a preacher from the pulpit. "There is no quitting. You both will see this through. I am tired of your bickering. My father, my husband Brad, my boys, all had faith in me. I will not let them down nor listen to Tilly's goddamn bitching. You understand?"

Presley's demeanor was out of character. The two bobbed their heads like a pair of puppets as they inched to exit the truck.

"She's losing it," Rachel slurred.

"Who is Tilly, anyway?" Gigi whispered.

"Move it." Presley caught them off guard and they scattered. Like ants on fire.

Gert was concealed in the kitchen at the window, watching the truck return under the barn lights. Hiding, like she had been at the show where the truck had idled. She'd lied to the show secretary by declaring she needed both heat and windshield wipers to watch. She had never moved until that final burst of havoc by Gigi and Kit T Kat. She had seen enough; her plan was working. Now she witnessed them fighting like hyenas on a fresh kill. Even positive, Presley appeared angry.

Gert felt the pinch of guilt again that she had driven a woman who almost died to that point of fury. But it could not be prevented. This was about her own revenge.

Maggie had snuck in quietly. "Why?"

Gert shuddered. "Why, what?"

"You're trying to get them to quit. Make 'em or break 'em? Your motto, right."

Gert released a puff of air as if she conquered the globe. "Look at them. They are broken."

"You are as cold as ice. I thought maybe Wyndham's presence had transformed you. He would be appalled."

Maggie had hit a nerve. Gert spiked with anger. "You keep this between us."

"Just say your plan fails, Gert? What's your next step? To keep sabotaging their desire to ride until they finally quit? You owe them."

"My plan won't fail. I have too much riding on it. But I have a backup."

Maggie tilted her head in an inquisitive concern.

"Two words... Poker run."

Maggie slivered her eyes with angst. "When will you let it go, Gert, and start living?"

Gert shrugged.

"I won't tell Wyndham... under one condition."

Gert snapped to face her, the shimmering glow of the woodstove flickering the evil in her blue eye and igniting her brown.

"I won't tell Glick, as long as you promise that if the poker ride plan is a bust, you'll give in. Take them to the Silver Spur in style, and for gosh sakes, take them to Clyde's Western World for new show clothes. That Rachel smells like moth balls."

The cell phone vibrated on the table interrupting their dispute. Presley's name flashed across the top. Maggie reached for it in a slow deliberate manner as both anticipated the conversation to come.

After answering, Maggie held the phone tight against her bosom. She was grinning, her cheeks bulging, her wrinkles lifted. "She wants to know when you want them to report back. In case you left the show early, she said, and didn't see the events, they have a lot to work on." Maggie cleared her throat. "I guess you need to prepare them for that poker run?" Her latter statement was almost inaudible.

"We shall see." Gert snatched the phone.

When Gert hung up, she was not without culpability. She knew that early spring trail rides were not for the faint at heart. There would be horses and riders busting to break out from the winter confinement. No manners, no rules, just yahoos.

"It's called a poker run," Presley explained. "A ten-mile trek through the state park. At five selected locations, your team picks a card from an administrator. Once over the finish line, your team presents your hand. The best hand wins, combined with time."

"Kind of like a paper chase," Rachel added.

"Or a foxhunt. You and Kit T Kat are pros at foxhunts, right?" Wheezy added.

Sure, Gigi wanted to respond, but she couldn't. They were trying to convince her not to be uneasy. What they didn't realize, she was scared to death. She had lost the bag that Carlos had given… the injections. To top matters off, she was not feeling well. Most likely her nerves.

"Yahoos ride on trail rides… and poker rides," she grumbled.

"And there aren't yahoos on foxhunts? I heard the headmaster once drank himself so silly at the Sun Tree Hunt Club. Galloped the course until he fell off, landing on top of the hounds. Injured two and broke his own leg."

"You know what they say. If a horse is afraid of dogs, foxhunt. A horse who doesn't want to run, foxhunt. A horse that wants to run, foxhunt. Well, I say trail ride. We load up at 6:00 AM tomorrow." Presley made it clear she wasn't accepting any objections. "I am sure there will be some wild people, but we will go slow and stay away from them."

Gigi was still complaining in the morning as they headed to the state park. "I don't see how this will make us better. We'll just hate each other more."

Presley smiled internally. Gigi had showed up, on time. That was what counted. Presley was finished being the positive one, the glue that silently held everything together. She had a rough year of acceptance, now she wanted to live.

Days were growing longer, and this was a warm spring day. Presley raised her face toward the rising sun as they unloaded. She breathed in the budding trees, the fresh green grass, and could hear in the distance the babbling creek. A picturesque day. A gift of friends and a new horse for her to ride. Presley jittered with an awakened excitement.

"Presley, thank you for lending me Cleo." Wheezy had gleamed with appreciation.

"She will be excellent! I suggest a pair of mini-English spurs because she could be a little lazy." Presley held out her hand.

"Well, I'll take lazy because I have a bad taste for spurs right now." They chuckled. Presley was also looking forward to a leisurely trail ride.

"Hey, I brought snacks." Rachel pointed to a bag she tacked on to the back of Hannibal's saddle. "Peanut butter and jelly in mini potato rolls."

"Of course you did," Gigi snapped. "And nerve pills, too, I bet."

"Already took one, if you must know. And I have rosary beads in the bag!" Rachel steered Hannibal away.

Presley read the anxiety on Gigi's face as she tacked the already full-of-herself Kit T Kat. "Listen, we'll go at your pace."

"I will be fine," Gigi bit as she mounted. The mare pranced, refusing to stand.

Presley curled her lips. She had offered assistance, but the rejection was enough. She walked over to a silver gelding. He was sixteen hands, big and bold like Kit T Kat. She had noticed him in the field on the first day. Steele Magnum was his registered name, Magnum to Presley. He was young, willing and a challenge. Gert had entrusted her to ride him, and for that she was grateful.

They had arrived ahead of the trailers that were presently roaring in and signing up. They could start ahead of the commotion in hopes of a quiet ride. Most of the course would encompass the woods surrounding a large reservoir, but at the very beginning half-mile they bounced along a clearing, following the path edging the woods.

Everything was picture perfect. Presley had placed Cleo in the front to tailor the pace. Hannibal quietly followed second. She put Kit T Kat third to press her slower, and Magnum would bring up the rear. By the feel of the moment, it would be an ideal trail ride until they entered the woods.

The locomotive thundering from behind perked up four sets of furry ears. The earth quaked from a herd of horses galloping the clearing to reach the trees. The other oodles of entries were in a race to the first card selection point. The rumble intensified and when combined with the *yippee, whoops* and hollers of reckless riders with no accountability, there was one description—yahoos.

Surprisingly, even Cleo jigged in anticipation of the encroaching stampede. Presley was relieved Wheezy had refused the spurs.

"Wheezy, think of her as a big semi," Presley hollered up the line. "You got this!"

Kit T Kat now forged like a bull, surging forward. As the first group of yahoos crimped them on both sides, she reared to follow, unfortunately Gigi clenched the reins too tight. Kit T Kat swished into an acrobatic ballerina buck.

Gigi released a squeal. "What should I do?"

"Should have taken a nerve pill!" Rachel's voice quivered with Hannibal's bobbing jog.

Presley checked her legs and reins, first aiming to rein in Magnum. As bands of others careened around the four, climbing the rocks and ducking, the girls were imprisoned by stampeding runaways.

"Alright. You want to get through this? It's called teamwork." Presley darted alongside of Gigi. "Move your fingers. Loosen up. Work them like this. Make Kit T Kat use that little brain of hers. The same with your legs. Center of your seat now."

Gigi was frozen with panic.

"Trust me, Gigi. We'll encircle you, box you in. Kit T Kat will have no choice but to stay under you… If you stay calm."

Presley had Hannibal lead with Cleo on the left and her on the right. "We will stay right with you."

A ride that should have taken three hours lasted most of the day. Hannibal dove at passing ponies, Cleo confronted an angry goose protecting a nest of honking babies, Kit T Kat's adrenaline spiked, and Magnum spent a good forty-five minutes insisting he was avoiding the creek to reach the other side.

Rachel learned to keep Hannibal's thoughts on her. Wheezy had the time of her life dodging that goose. And for once, Gigi didn't care she was splashed in dirt.

Best of all, Presley hadn't dwelled on her illness or baldness even once.

At the final checkpoint, a man handed them a wild card. "Good luck with your poker hand, ladies. Looks like you have some mighty fine horses there. They aren't acting like idiots, like some others. You might not have the best qualifying time, but you're clearly expert horsemen. Patience wins the prize. And you are all still in the saddle, not on the ground, to finish the course. Like I said… looks like you all are quite experienced."

"Oh, I was born in the saddle." Wheezy shifted her nearly numb rear.

When they untacked later, Kit T Kat refused water. The mare was so angry she had not been permitted to yahoo.

Rachel's peanut butter sandwiches were smashed to smithereens. Wheezy's silver hairs were splintering and boing-ing all over her head. And Presley could only smile, her voice hoarse and her tush as sore as the others.

No one said a word upon entering the cab of Venus... until Wheezy started to giggle. "Born in the saddle!"

Then even Venus appeared to rumble with amusement, as did the others the entire journey back to Holly Hill.

Chapter 26

Dear Diary.

A transformation occurred on the poker ride today, especially for me. We didn't win—our poker hand stunk except for a pair of 2s. First, I actually rode Kit T Kat without any help from Carlos or "modifications" (and you know what I mean). Kit T Kat may have been a little annoyed because she refused her treat at the end, even a slurp of water. But I did it! That mare rumbled under me. Of course, I had no choice but to accept Presley's guidance. What a day! Rachel even offered to help scrub the rest of the pink which is still lingering on Kit T Kat. And we laughed together! I tried not to, in my usual snot-ass manner. Why am I like this? I didn't want them to know that my smart remarks are nothing more than my own fear and ignorance. Why can't I be vulnerable? Transparent?

No one was dwelling on life problems or cheating husbands. Just horses. We were riding, together, as a team. I can't wait to tell my friend Carlos.

Gigi stopped writing. Her sore muscles were cramping from her cross-legged position on the floor, plus she heard voices from the porch. *Good!* This could be her opportunity to sneak out and visit Carlos.

She tiptoed downstairs, bypassing Randall's library. She peered in. The room was shadowy, the corners dark. Only the small desk light was on. But by the slight reflection, Gigi could see the safe was ajar. Another opportunity!

Gigi crept inside, tightening her silky robe over a pink negligee. God forbid Randall should walk in and find her, or worse, desire her.

Gigi tapped the ornate door as softly as possible and proceeded across the room. As she passed the desk, a sudden burst of light flickered, followed by a vibration in rhythmic low groans. A vibrating phone. She practically peed herself at the shock, clutching her own heart palpitations. Her eyes darted the room. No one appeared.

Gigi examined the device. She placed it in her palm, barely touching as if it was on fire. *Not Randall's regular phone.* Then Camilla's emblem flashed! She was sending a message to... Asher. Yup, Gigi recognized the revolting face in the profile picture. How could someone be simultaneously debonair and revolting?

Ash, are you there?

Gigi scaled a previous message. She touched the screen and momentarily regarded her nails, the pink paint half-chipped. So not Gigi. She shrugged and smiled, thinking of the poker run.

Daddy's plan is working. Ditz-ball Gigi is making a fool of herself. She will be busy for a time. Out of his hair. Frankly, I would like our little princess out of the picture all together. Ideas? Deem her demented, have her committed or imprisoned?

Gigi heard footsteps closing in from the hall. She sprang up and down several times, veering left then right like a fish out of water. *What to do? What to do!*

Then she remembered Presley's chant on the trail ride. *"You got this!"*

Gigi ripped open the sash of her nightie, dropped the phone on the desk, then perched her tiny body on the edge. She crossed her legs in a tantalizing pose. Not a minute too late.

Luckily the phone stopped buzzing before the light switch flipped on. Asher Devine was planted in the doorway, a demonic glare of apprehension on his face, which thawed to a slobbering smirk.

"Gigi. What the hell are you doing here?"

Gigi raised her bosom. "This is my house, and well... frankly, I was expecting you."

Asher etched his nose higher, prided by her words. He waltzed closer carrying a leatherbound record book which she had seen before. He tucked the book under his arm then slipped a USB drive into his pocket. "A lonely woman? Waiting for me? I know." He held up his hand. "Randall is going to throw you away like trash. And you realize that someone needs to save your tiny ass."

How dare he!

Gigi had an overwhelming thirst to retrieve the book, or at least the USB clip.

Asher brushed her, squeezed her taut thigh above her knee, then he beelined to the safe. She winked, although her eyelid tried to refuse. She followed as if interested in him. He secured the book on the top safe shelf at shoulder height and placed the clip atop it. Asher touched the edge of the door to close it.

Good thing he's short!

Gigi pressed in, spooning against him, wrapping her arms slightly above his belt. The gesture forced him to spin, facing her. Gigi swallowed her disgust and walked her hands up to his neck.

"Asher?" Gigi whispered. Her height forced his stare to fall on her smooth and glittery decolletage.

He blinked.

She unbuttoned his shirt to press her two endowed gifts against him. Then she stretched her arms inside his elbows.

His lips molded against her neck and climbed to her chin. Immediately, Gigi laid her head into his—not only in avoidance, but for the leverage to maneuver behind his back. She stretched her hands into the safe. They spidered across the ledger until her nail hooked the USB clip, securing it in her palm.

Trapped, she had to free herself. There was only one thing a girl in trouble could do. Gigi caged his man-ness with her other hand, causing his body to lurch forward in distress. This gave her the opportunity to shove the safe door and force Asher against it. His face was smothered in her chest but her body was at least free of his hands.

"Ouch!" he winced. "You play dirty."

Gigi had escaped. Asher attempted to hook her again, but he was recovering from his aching groin.

"Hey." His ego was wounded, by the rile on his face.

Gigi panicked. Luckily, at that moment, a voice resonated from the phone on the desk. "*Call from Camilla.*"

"I have to take this," Asher snipped. "You wait. Or better yet, be ready in your bedroom."

Gigi didn't answer. She couldn't. Her mouth was filled with the putrid taste of him.

That text conversation had alarmed her. She had to retaliate.

In a scurry, Gigi gathered her necessary belongings—mainly her diaries, fluffy slippers and makeup. Nothing else was left for her here. She already had everything vital where she would be headed.

One more stop. *Carlos.*

This would be the last time she saw him. Gigi was positive.

But the moment he opened his door, neither could control temptation. For a second time, the two melded in an interlude before he slipped her a brown paper bag.

"Only one injection, Gigi," he whispered in his seductive manner. "Use this wisely. Only as a last resort. You don't want to be caught." Then he bestowed a final kiss that stole her breath. And her heart.

"Alright, ladies. Time to get serious." Wheezy began to read the blackboard with her hands gripping her hips. "The schedule." Wheezy pointed to the board. "*I have completed all the paperwork for the Silver Spur... all you have to do is qualify.*"

The four were screaming in delight.

"*Take today off. You earned my trust. Two requests: We need a point recorder—a numbers expert. Someone meticulous. The championship could be won by a tenth of a point. Secondly, go shopping for attire at Clyde's Western World. He has both English and Western. He is expecting you. I cannot take the smell of mothballs.*"

Wheezy knew who smelled. But most of all, she knew who to call—an expert in numbers.

Stan.

Gigi made the trailer her home. Besides, it technically was hers. Her face was plastered on the back. She had slipped a plea to Maggie using some exaggerated version about a threat on her life. No one was to know she was a tenant of the trailer, especially when they hauled it to shows. She'd vowed to pick up after herself and maintain the trailer—cleaning the shower, and the potty. She'd be alone, in the dark. Hard work for someone adjusted to maids and stablehands. But she had to do it.

In turn, she had to promise Maggie to hide her Mercedes. And on Tuesdays and Thursdays, she had to hide herself as well. Because Gert, on those days, had a guest.

Surprisingly, Gigi couldn't have been more content, except that it was difficult to fit all her clothes in such a miniscule closet. She could be closer to Kit T Kat—plus the solitude allowed her more writing time, stirring a passion in her soul. Gigi never felt talented enough but maybe she could write an article on her summer return to riding.

Most of all, every Tuesday and Thursday, she was hypnotized by Wyndham Glick.

The horse whisperer had no clue she ogled him while he rode, or while he taught Gert from the center of the ring. When he gently held the hose toward his lips for a sip of water, Gigi nearly hyperventilated like Rachel. The drips moistened his small, blocked area of wavy chest hairs while dampening the front of his half-open shirt. She had to throw herself across the trailer bed, moaning for Carlos, whom she missed dearly.

The next two months, June and July, were nothing short of adventure—riding through breakfast, lunch, and dinner. Stable and housework in the pre-AM and post-PM hours. Practice in rain, practice in heat, practice when sore, and then more practice and more aches. They showed several times, with both bad and bonding experiences. Wrong numbers, wrong tack changes and wrong patterns. They trail rode through creeks and galloped from bees. They rode against the rail, in patterns, working the dreaded gate, bridge weaving serpentines.

There were manure-filled wheelbarrows and cobweb dismantling, baths and trimming muzzles and ear hairs—which Kit T Kat tried to elevate so no one could touch hers—and mane plaiting.

Then came barrel racing, turn on haunches, flying lead changes, posting trots, right leads and left leads, and terminology tests that Maggie gave them at the end of each week. Gert insisted they pass with straight As or she dished out extra chores.

Show weekends went from 4:00 AM Saturday until dark, only to wake up on Sunday and repeat. When their heads hit the pillow at night, their dreams filled with English bits, Western cantles, and ground ties—but nothing of life's worries.

Yet something was transforming between them.

Stan was thrilled. He had been terminated by his new boss, Asher Devine, even against Frank's objection. Stan never missed a show and his placement calculations would satisfy Albert Einstein himself. Steele's team was on course to qualify for the Novice Silver Spur championship.

At the same time, Wheezy spent extra hours combing papers and files from F.G. Transport. Finding nothing. Stan informed her the Feds were breathing down Frank's neck, threatening charges. Darren continued with the belief that truth would prevail.

Wheezy noticed another issue, too. The white Mercedes was MIA, yet Gigi was always first at Gertrude's. Plus, she never left with them. She always argued that some task took precedence over her leaving… extra tack, or cleaning and mucking stalls. *Gigi?*

The night that Wheezy stayed late to investigate, she scaled the back barn wall in her own covert mission. Oddly, Maggie had asked Wheezy to park the trailer farther around the back weeks ago. Tonight, she discovered why. Indeed, an orange electric cord tracked to an outlet and fuse box at the back of the barn. A light shimmered from the upper bunk window where a mattress rested over the hookup into the truck. Someone was living inside.

Wheezy shut the breaker off.

Wheezy recognized the high-pitched shrill when the woman started rummaging in the dark. She listened to the fumbling as Gigi climbed out of the top bed area, into the main living area. When her head bumped a cabinet searching for a flashlight, Wheezy couldn't help but snicker.

"What the heck," Gigi complained.

To Wheezy's amazement, Gigi not only bravely stumbled out of the trailer, fiddling to switch the flashlight on to guide her to the breaker box, but she knew what to do.

Her shuffling gave Wheezy enough time to sneak into the trailer and rest at the table on an undersized thin cushion chair and wait.

When Gigi returned, wrapped in her silky robe, she screamed as loud as Annie's Promise when Hannibal had torn flesh.

"Gigi, Gigi," Wheezy attempted to calm her.

The petite woman was holding the metal flashlight in the air as a weapon.

"Gigi, it's me. Wheezy."

Gigi's mouth suspended as if howling at the moon, the flashlight extended in the air. "What are you doing here?"

Gigi sealed her lips and shook her head.

Wheezy snatched the flashlight. "Put this down before you kill somebody."

Gigi let Wheezy remove the device from her hand. "That was the idea. But you know you have this way of making people do stuff with your eyes," Gigi scoffed. "So what are you doing here?"

Wheezy smiled then swung her around by her tiny hips. "Look, girl." She placed Gigi on the seat. "What are *you* doing here? I knew there was way too much of you in this trailer." Wheezy gestured her arms around the room of jewelry, makeup area, and clothes. "It looks like you're living here."

Gigi didn't answer.

"You are living here?"

"I can't go home," Gigi confessed. "They're trying to kill me."

"Who's trying to kill you?"

"Everyone... Asher, Camilla, Randall... everyone." Gigi rubbed her face in her hands.

Wheezy steepled her index fingers and placed them over her lips. *Gigi is losing it.* "Maybe you ought to get some of those little white pills like Rachel. You're getting a little paranoid or..."

"No! I am not." Gigi jetted forward. "Something is wrong at the estate." Gigi's violet eyes sparked. She seemed to be holding something back. She rushed to the small kitchen sink and gagged.

"What's wrong with you?"

"Look, please. I'll let you in on a secret."

For the first time, Wheezy saw in those violet eyes someone who was lonely, spoiled and had no one else.

For a second it was as if Gigi was going to reveal something very vulnerable. Then she blurted, "Wyndham Glick. He's here."

Now she's hallucinating. Wheezy tried to mask her shock.

"I'm telling the truth. On Tuesdays and Thursdays. He's Gert's secret. You wonder why Kit T Kat is better? It's because he rides her."

"The hot Brazilian horse whisperer?"

Gigi nodded.

"We have to tell the others. It's only fair. We're going to have a Monday night sleepover! Here in this trailer. Besides, this will prepare us for the Silver Spur. We'll be here on Tuesday morning."

Afterward, Wheezy called Presley and Rachel to schedule the outing.

Rachel had only one thing to say. *"Quite honestly, I will bring the pills."*

Chapter 27

The firepit in front of the trailer flickered as the four nestled around wearing the vintage t-shirts signed decades earlier by Wyndham Glick—even though Gigi was *busting* out of hers. The August Monday had been a scorcher. They rode early, letting their four amigos dip in the water hole in the lower meadow on Gert's farm.

Presley had not been bareback in shorts since childhood, unless in a dream, and Magnum's initial avoidance of water made it seem impossible. But today, he'd paraded into the water hole with her on his bare back like a soldier entering battle. His threads of silver mane clenched in her hand shimmered in the late morning sun.

The cool water drops had splashed on their bare legs. Then they turned them out to "be horses" while the four of them cleaned the stable and completed chores in the afternoon.

Hannibal and the other horses were now bathed and chewing on a round bale, savoring the moonlight in the field below.

The campfire and sleepover made it seem like they were teenagers on a scouting adventure.

Rachel passed the bag of marshmallows to Wheezy. "I wish I had chocolate for s'mores." She'd lost plenty of weight and could use a dose of sugar. She jiggled her shorts. "Remember my too-tight pants back in the porta potty episode?"

They all laughed.

"You'll have plenty of sugar in this champagne." Presley handed her a bottle. "We have four!"

"This is a dry run for the Silver Spur. After we qualify—and we will qualify—we must be prepared to stay at the arena for the entire competition. The four of us in there." Wheezy pointed overhead to the trailer... the one where the picture of Gigi glowed in the light, her violet eyes piercing them.

"You look like a goddess with those tough-colored eyes!" Rachel twirled her marshmallow on a stick as the logs spewed a loud crack. "Not to mention your figure."

"There is only one goddess," Gigi humbly remarked. "That's Venus, Wheezy's truck."

Presley continued to marinate on the three. How they all had changed, grown. Gigi now seemed unpretentious compared to the woman they'd first reencountered months ago. Rachel complimented her instead of bickering and popping nerve pills. And Wheezy, their strength, was riding Cleo and ready to advance. Each had new friendships to support them.

"Tomorrow morning, the truth will be visible, whether the horse whisperer Wyndham Glick is simply a figment of Gigi's imagination." Rachel removed her flaming marshmallow from the stick.

"The global sensation, here on Gert Steele's Farm?" Wheezy spoke with a voice as if calling for the Ouija ghosts at a séance while holding a bottle of cheap champagne.

"Yes." Gigi snatched the bottle to pop the cork. "It's true."

"I still think you are losing it," Wheezy ribbed.

But Gigi didn't take offense.

Presley handed her a plastic wine glass after she inserted the stem.

"You'll see." Gigi passed the bubbly-filled glasses around the fire to the others.

"I never felt this good," Rachel commented.

Looking around the fire at her friends in canvas folding chairs, Presley silently agreed. They were slimmer, tanned from riding in the outdoors, and seemingly happier. Seemingly younger, too. Even with her barely nubs for hair, Presley might soon have a silver pixie.

"I've been slaving away in the beauty salon for thirty years," Rachel continued. "Finally I'm living."

"Now, you just need a man," Gigi remarked flatly. "When was the last time you had sex?"

Rachel gasped. "Sex? How dare you!" Her face liquefied to an emptiness.

As if magic, a man was skipping toward them in the dark under the barn's outside lights. He was waving a box of graham crackers and chocolate.

Wheezy placed a hand over her brows as if it helped her see. "Stan?"

"And we have s'mores!" Presley announced.

"You can't leave me out. I am part of this team now." Stan took in a breath and clutched his chest. "Nothing like a campfire. I'll take a marshmallow! And I wouldn't miss seeing the hot, one and only Glick! Besides, you need me. You're just one-tenth away from qualifying this weekend. We need to cinch the championship. I can forge numbers if needed."

Wheezy shot him a despairing look.

"*Kidding*." Stan took a glass of champagne from Gigi. "Now what's this I hear about sex, Rachel?"

"Since... H-Heath passed," Rachel stammered, embarrassed. The fire reflected from tears that ponded in her eyes.

Stan fanned himself. "You're kidding right? That's..." He was counting with his fingers.

"Stan, we're okay with the numbers right now. I think we can figure it out. It's been a long, long..." Wheezy paused, "...*long* time."

"Girl, that is going to change."

"You don't understand. I couldn't, and I can't. Heath and I had a fight. He raced out. That's when he had the car accident."

Gigi handed Rachel a tissue.

"I had a candlelight dinner ready to apologize when the police showed up. Heath never made it back. It was my fault. I made him drive fast and crash. I don't deserve to love. But I have Jemma. I did what I thought I had to. I raised that girl, solely focused on what I had done."

"Rachel..." Presley touched her arm. "That's like saying I didn't deserve to ride Cleo because my father died without me fulfilling his dream. I've lived with that guilt for years."

"I hid in my life for years. Praying the rosary, I begged for forgiveness. I prayed they would never take Jemma."

"They who?" Wheezy quirked.

"I don't know. Heath… *them*. They are up there." Rachel pointed up. "Mad at me."

Wheezy slid a melted marshmallow between some chocolate and graham crackers. The white cream dripped over the edges. "I dreamt of being a horsey showgirl all my life. I never thought a Black girl from the city was worthy." Wheezy licked the cream. "Now I understand that I didn't want to marry Darren until I proved to myself that I could reach my goal. A small piece of me is stuck on the jerk I chose all those decades ago. I've lived with my own humiliation. I allowed him to hit me and tell me I was insignificant."

"But you got out," Presley reassured.

"I did, then I focused solely on developing a formidable career to prove to my kids and everyone that I was significant. I drowned out my passion. But my love of horses always resurfaced, every time I looked at our picture."

Presley and Wheezy made eye contact, as usual sharing a moment of ESP. Presley had noticed Gigi was quiet, not sipping any alcohol or getting tipsy like the rest of them. Instead Gigi was fiddling with Rachel's phone.

"Gigi, what about you and Randall?"

Gigi ignored the question. "Now I'm putting Wyndham's number in your phone."

"Give me that." Rachel seized her cell. "Are you crazy? Where the hell did you get his number?"

"I told you, he comes here twice a week."

The second bottle's cork popped and champagne made the rounds. By the fourth they were giggling like twenty-year-olds.

A soft voice interrupted. "I understand feeling not good enough. And I know those dark spirits." Gigi's statement stood alone above the crackling embers that drifted toward the starry night sky.

Stan cleared his throat to break the silence.

This was the first time Presley had more than one glass of wine in well over a year. "Wellll..." her hazy brain stumbled. "Let them old spirits out, ladies! Up to the stars."

"Yeah. To the stars!" Wheezy raised her glass. "Time for compliments. Presley, you look amazing on Magnum. Rachel, you're stunning on Hannibal, and you..." Wheezy pointed to Gigi. "On Kit T Kat, you're our queen. Hallelujah."

The others rose. "Here, here."

Presley noticed Gigi pour water into her plastic wine glass.

"A toast." Following Presley's lead, they raised their glasses together like the day they had joined glasses months ago in the cab of Venus.

"To us! When I lost my hair, it felt worse than the illness. Everyone knew I was sick. They'd lie and say I looked *awesome*. I hated that word. I was wrinkled and bald." She hesitated to retain her balance. "I am still wrinkled and bald but transformed, stronger inside, like I can face anything because I have you." She raised her plastic vessel higher and wobbled.

Wheezy braced her.

Presley smiled while simultaneously releasing a hiccup. She apologized with a giggle. "To our friendship, and the loves of our lives... the ones who make us look and feel better than we are... our horses."

Stan was thrilled. The next morning, more than the weather was sizzling.

After relocating Gigi's abundance of belongings, none of them had enough sleep. The blank stares on their faces were not only from the late-night hangover they sustained but also from shock. Before them stood Wyndham Glick, perhaps approaching sixty, but looking not a day over Robert Redford with no shirt in *The Electric Horseman*.

"That is one sexy man!" Stan murmured an *mmm-mmm* from the side of the arena.

All five of them ogled under dark shades. They were gawking, stationary with their horses in tow. Except for Gigi who was pressed next to Rachel. "Told you! In the flesh."

Wyndham was touching Kit T Kat's forehead, standing in front of her on the ground while schooling Gert on balance.

"I think he's whispering to Kit T Kat right now."

They leaned into each other, mesmerized by his aura.

"He can whisper in my ear," Gigi moaned. "Better yet, in Rachel's."

Wyndham must've heard them because he grinned. His dreamy eyes checked in their direction, and he tipped his hat. "Come on, ladies. Join us. Who's brave enough to trust?" He invited them in that innocent yet sensual twang, wavy locks spewing around his head. His muscles were defined—brawny arms, shoulders rimmed firm in a cream-colored shirt with the warmest smile indenting the dimples in his cheeks. His wrinkles were in all the right places, like the hairs peeking out from his chest.

"She will," Gigi broadcasted. "Rachel's scared to death to run the barrels, but she has to do it for the championship!" She shoved Rachel, who unsuspectingly stepped forward. Then Gigi slapped Hannibal's rump, trotting him forward alongside. "Go on, Rachel. You are elected."

Rachel tried to object, but Wyndham was waving, drawing her in like a cobra to its master. When he cupped his hand to give her a leg up, she could not refuse. She was tongue-tied and under his spell—first, because he was damn gorgeous, and second, because his hand was pressed against her thigh.

"Close your eyes," he said, "and follow your heart."

In a daze, Rachel hadn't heard a word when his mouth moved. "What?" she faltered.

The horse whisperer's hand moved an inch on her thigh. "Close your eyes," he repeated.

Rachel was glued to that hand, hypnotized by its size. Then she obeyed and closed her eyes.

No man had touched her thigh in over twenty years. Well, maybe the old man who sat next to her in church. When he tried to pass the collection basket, he'd always managed to touch her thigh, until she decided to change pews.

Rachel pressed her eyelids tight. Her life shuffled like a deck of cards before a poker game. The salon, Roxie, church, Mother Mary, Jemma, Heath, lost love, death and forgiveness.

"Let it go. Feel Hannibal. He will hold you. He will take care of you. All of you."

He knew! Wyndham knew! He'd read her mind, her past. How?

"Now drop your reins."

Rachel's eyes flipped like a dislocated shade on a window.

"Please, close your eyes. Feel him breathe, the beat of his heart. You are with the horse. He has you."

Rachel softly edged her eyes closed again. She wasn't sure why, but his hand was welcoming, and she didn't want him to know she was scared.

"Trust."

Wyndham's hand slipped away. He repeated his words as she could hear him drifting farther from her and Hannibal.

"Now, come to me," he called from a distance. "Listen to my voice and let Hannibal come to me."

Rachel shook her head slightly. "I can't." Her voice was a whisper.

"Hannibal can. Trust him. Let him take your fear."

Rachel's mind clouded with one mantra as if she was repeating a Hail Mary. *Hannibal...* his inviting aroma, his velvety fur and toned muscles. She squeezed his barreled girth and shuddered on the first step. Then she sat straight, controlled her pelvis in a cue, asking him to follow Glick's voice until they stopped.

Rachel felt the fingers touch her calf this time but she didn't open her eyes. She was too consumed, tasting the salt from tears streaming down her cheeks.

The others cheered. "With no reins, girl!"

At the end of the day, Wyndham circled them around. "You can call me anytime for help. I'll be present at the Silver Spur."

"Here," Gigi said, handing him a slip of paper. "Give Rachel a call, then she can share your number with the rest of us." Everyone looked at Gigi confused.

"But you..." Rachel attempted to remind Gigi.

Too late. Wyndham was already dialing.

Rachel's phone barked in a robotic alert, *"Big Sexy Glick."* Rachel's jaw dropped.

"Seems you already have the number," he smiled.

Her phone repeated his name, *"Big Sexy Glick,"* while Rachel fumbled to shut it off.

His dimple popped. "Call me anytime." Wyndham tipped his hat with a wink directed at Rachel.

She eyed Gigi. "What did you do? Did you do that last night at the fire?"

The two bantered in friendship as the horse whisperer walked away.

"You need a little, you know... Rachel, it has been way too long."

The qualifying show was finally upon them. Gertrude had chosen their divisions. She couldn't believe they actually had made it. People were even acknowledging her... instead of her prosthetic. Showing her respect. And the girls... they'd earned it. She had coached them into being a team.

Cleo and Wheezy, in Halter and a Walk/Trot class, would certainly make a point. Magnum and Presley were expected to win the Working Trail, as no other rider could touch her precise patterns. And Rachel... well, after several lessons with Wyndham this past month, she could walk or trot the barrel pattern with ease. Only Gigi was still an issue. Hopefully Kit T Kat would be on her best behavior today. But a nervous rider could spell disaster.

Gigi stood alone in the stall next to Kit T Kat. She rolled the needle in the palm of her hand. She had no choice, for two reasons. In her condition, she had to stay safe. She wanted a baby more than anything in the world and the doctor informed her at her age it was risky. Second, for the team.

Gigi wiped the surface of the mare's neck clean and held the needle in place. Kit T Kat's eye rolled back at her. That immense brown eye.

Gigi hesitated. "I can't be the embarrassment. I can't be the loser. You are more horse than I am woman, girl. I'm sorry."

Gigi had no choice. She knew if caught, Randall could get her out of it. She could say it was Gert. People already thought that was Gert's M.O., even though Gigi knew the truth about everything. Gert would have to take the fall.

"Damn, Kit. Don't look at me like that. This is for the team."

Gigi raised the needle.

"It will only sting a little."

Stan read the standings from the paper held in his hands. "It's not official yet, but you are in second place behind those mean girls in their twenties." He was actually tearing. "Tissues!"

The four girls huddled with interlocked arms, chanting "The Silver Cowgirls." Even though Gigi placed fourth, Gert had planned well. She'd placed the girls and herself along the rail and coached Gigi through the course.

They were still celebrating when a sober voice interrupted them.

"Oh no, the drug tester…" Stan pointed to a burly woman followed by a crew and the posse of four twenty-year-olds. "She's headed our way."

"We have nothing to worry about. Nothing." Wheezy brushed it off, grinning at the standings.

Then a small man became visible trailing behind them. A smoking gun, shot full of self-assurance.

Asher Devine washed Wheezy's smile away.

Chapter 28

"I saw her! That one. That older woman had a needle in the Tobiano's stall this morning." One of the twenty-year-olds with a perfect ponytail and double set of eyelashes aimed an accusing finger at Gigi who was leading Kit T Kat. Gigi stopped and turned only herself.

"The test can't be right." Another twenty-something—bleached blonde, taut skin, slim figure—stamped her feet as her posse hollered revolts in agreement.

"Negative." The woman clenched test results in one hand and a clipboard in the other, her lab coat buckling between the snaps above an apple-shaped middle. A stitched emblem on her chest pocket bore the initials D.A.

"I saw her! That one," another girl holding a Scripto marker pointed to Gigi. "She was the one with a needle in the stall this morning. I know it."

"Look, I'm a certified drug tester. See these initials—D.A., Drug Authority. Don't mess with me; it will only get you DQed. And as of now, you girls are headed to the Silver Spur as well. So what's your problem? Seeing a needle doesn't mean she used it." The woman was stiff except for her flaring oversized nostrils.

"And so are we..." Wheezy stalled. "Yes!"

Gert had closed her eyes as if in prayer. The crowds began to disperse.

"Not drugged," the woman pronounced. "Clean as a whistle."

Stan's hand gripped his hip. He bounced in a display of triumph and pointed at the four younger girls, shooing them away. "Game on!"

Asher Devine had been standing behind Gert, practically breathing down her neck, waiting to handcuff her. He reeked of disappointment. "You won't get away with it," he threatened.

"Asher," Gigi called, ebbing into Kit T Kat a step as if for support. "Gert didn't do anything."

"She has a past," he railed. "She hasn't gone clean."

Gigi muttered, "Asher, are those young ladies the team that Randall is supporting?"

He refused to reply but his expression verified the answer.

"I saw the text," Gigi informed with an air of confidence.

"Really? Well, I have a witness to the needle injection."

Kit T Kat appeared agitated at Asher's presence. She stomped a back hoof hard in his direction.

Gigi paid no attention. "I also know that Gert didn't drug any animals decades ago. Not with the kind of drugs that were found in that horse's system. It was Randall. He wanted to destroy Gert, because he couldn't tolerate being in the reserve under a woman trainer. I have it all documented in my diary."

Asher laughed. "Then we're even. It's my word against yours. A pen and paper are worthless." He grunted. "Just hearsay by a *nutball*. You know, you might look good, but you are dumb as a stone."

Kit T Kat pinned her ears flat with a brisk head shake as if stung by a bee.

Gigi felt Wheezy near her side as the flawlessly coiffed man spun to walk away.

"One more thing, Asher." Gigi grabbed Wheezy's hand and flattened her palm.

Wheezy's face scrunched with confusion. "What are you doing, girl?"

"I'll tell you something else, Asher. See this USB drive?"

Asher rotated, his eyes staring a hole in her palm. "You stole that!"

"No, Asher. It was in *my* safe in *my* home."

"Randall will destroy you." Asher stepped toward her with a fervor in his eyes.

"Not before Wheezy destroys you." Gigi closed Wheezy's palm over the flash drive. "This has all the proof she needs to take to Frank... and the authorities."

Asher lunged, his hand raised, clearly with intent to hit Gigi. "You bitch."

But another hand blocked him about to swat Asher to the ground. Instead, the Tobiano mare flicked her hock like a whip, making direct contact with Asher's calf, flogging him to the ground.

Still nearby, instantly the D.A. and show staff converged on the situation.

Asher stumbled to stand, slicking the sides of his hair while hopping on one leg. "You ladies better watch your back. That beast, too!"

"Maybe it's you and Randall who need to be on the lookout. The Feds might get wind of this. Nothing better happen to any of us... or the horses."

The staff corralled Asher toward the exit gate as Kit T Kat appeared to relish her victory.

When the two women were alone, Wheezy said a heartfelt, "Thank you." Then Wheezy looked into Gigi's eyes. "And thank you for not following through this morning."

"No," Gigi replied. "Thank you for protecting me. I should've given that drive to you the minute I retrieved it." Then she added, "I thought you said you never hit anyone."

"No one ever tried to hurt my friend before."

Wheezy wrapped an arm around her and handed the USB drive to Stan who had raced to join them and was tearing up again.

That night, Gigi was called to a meeting with Presley, Rachel and Wheezy at the trailer.

"We have to show you something," Presley timidly revealed to Gigi.

"Prepare yourself," Wheezy added.

They led Gigi to the back of the trailer to face her immortalized image on the steel door—her plump breasts, uniformly figured hips, stunning eyes, ski-sloped nose and a newly scribbled handlebar mustache above her perky lips in thick black Scripto marker.

Gigi hesitated. Her lips pressed flat.

"This wasn't us, Gigi," Rachel quivered. "Swear on the Holy Mother. We don't know who the culprits were, but I have a few ideas."

Then to their amazement, Gigi liberated a long restrained, high-pitched, unforgettable laugh that lingered on like a hot shower you want to savor five more minutes before shutting it off.

"It will never come off unless you paint the trailer, you know," Wheezy tried to dent Gigi's joy.

"I don't care. I like it." Gigi just laughed and laughed, ignoring the fact it might cause wrinkles. "Wheezy, you were the only person I had for a friend, even though I drove you that year. You taught me humility and perseverance. And now you will switch horses with me."

"What? Ride Kit T Kat? Are you kidding?"

"No, I am not. And yes, you can. Because I can't."

"You just did, today."

"I came in fourth. I was too timid, too worried about falling off."

Wheezy shook her head. "Wyndham will work with you."

"No, it's not safe."

"What are you talking about?" Rachel questioned.

"I knew it," Presley whispered in discovery. "You're pregnant!"

Gigi endorsed the revelation with a twinkle in her violet eyes. "Wheezy, I want this baby."

Rachel started clapping. "What will Randall do? Are you scared of his backlash?"

"This baby isn't Randall's."

The three gasped, eyes as wide as lemurs.

"As I explained, about my short fall and contemplating the meds I demanded from Carlos, which thankfully I did not use after having second thoughts. I wasn't merely picking up an injection," Gigi confessed.

"Carlos." Presley confirmed, taking her hand. "We understand. Wheezy will ride Kit T Kat."

"What? No," Wheezy objected, her voice exploding with panic.

"The doctor says I'm high risk, especially at forty-eight."

"Absolutely not!" Wheezy retorted. "I'm not riding Kit T Kat."

"Boy, the country club is going to talk," Rachel said with a smile.

"I know," Gigi acknowledged.

"I said no!" Wheezy repeated.

"That will be one heck of a scandal," Rachel commiserated.

"I'm not afraid. I have amazing friends to support me." Gigi shrugged. "I also wrote an article telling our story. I queried it to *Houndstooth Magazine*. They showed definite interest about my article on older women showing at the Silver Spur and Randall Emerson's indiscretions for decades in the equine and trucking industries. If we win, maybe they'll publish it."

Wheezy was still objecting as they wrapped Gigi between them and headed inside the trailer.

The October Silver Spur competition arrived faster than any of them could have imagined.

Frank Galzone called the morning of the show. Stan had shared the evidence that Asher and Randall were trying to destroy him. Galzone wanted Wheezy back as CEO and Stan as her executive assistant.

"You know, Stan," Wheezy said. "I have some loose ends in my life. I need a gap year—like the kids take. I want to ride horses, marry Darren, and then start my own trucking company... if you'd care to join me."

Stan bear-hugged Wheezy before she mounted Kit T Kat.

"That's if I live through this," she added.

The girls and Gert were lined around the ring.

"Wheezy, there is nothing you can't do," Gert coached her. "Now fix that hydrangea scarf and go kick ass."

Wheezy didn't remember entering the arena mounted on Kit T Kat. The horse surprisingly relaxed, her head willingly bent at the pole waiting for each command. They were both oblivious that the stands were filled not only with her fiancé, Darren, and her beloved children, but also devoted friends like Gator and Semi Sam. Wheezy never heard Sam holler, "Put your big girl panties on, Wheezy!" either as she trotted past him on the rail to the first fence. The only sensation she recalled was the mare giving as she carried her over the novice jump and continued in perfect cadence as they veered to the second.

Gigi didn't mess up once on Cleo, who carried her through the Walk/Trot like she was caring for two. And she was. What Gigi didn't realize was at that exact moment, Frank Galzone was infuriated with the news that Wheezy was not returning to be CEO of his trucking firm. He had failed the most dedicated and unsurpassed employee he had ever hired. He immediately called the Feds. Frank would personally see the collapse of Randall's warped empire. He wanted the authorities to meet him at the Silver Spur competition armed and ready for Randall's arrest.

"Instead of holding any trophy, I want him handcuffed to the rail!" Frank crusaded.

Presley buried the thought of her upcoming doctor visit somewhere in the deep abyss of her mind. She would concentrate completely on the ride. She and Magnum both had a natural affinity to the Trail course and he proved an expert contender, perking his ears at every obstacle. Their working gate was impeccable, including the L-shaped back through and the flying lead changes. If the pair were in the Olympics, his performance would rate a perfect 10. To her surprise, Tilly was cheering Presley on from section B. She had reserved an entire busload of seats in that area for the retirement facility residents.

"Tilly, I thought this was Casino weekend?"

"Are you kidding?" she answered coyly as she passed the olives for martinis to the others flanked in several rows with plastic glasses. "We wouldn't miss this for the world. We're all so proud of you, honey, for living. Besides, that Wyndham Glick… he's hot as hell. I want to take riding lessons on Cleo this winter."

"Tilly, you're eighty-three," Presley reminded, then realized her error from the scouring expression on her mother's face.

"What does that mean?" Tilly declared. "Who do you think took care of the old girl, Cleo, as we waited for you to come home? Sure wasn't the neighbor boy." Tilly hugged Presley with all her might while Brad and all three boys were beaming with admiration.

The team of Silver Cowgirls were standing at the gate waiting for Rachel as she approached on Hannibal. It was the final class—the gaming class, the Barrel Race.

Gert was next to Maggie when a young girl and her mother approached.

"Ms. Steele." The mother wanted to introduce the two but appeared to ramble instead. "This is my daughter. My daughter… she was born with one arm… as you see, and she'd been dreaming of… well… riding. As parents, we taught her it was too dangerous, but… then she heard about you. She's been nagging us ever since… Could you tell her how difficult…" The woman stopped. "Well, anyway. This is Eva."

Gert touched the girl's shoulder. "What discipline?"

"English Hunter. Jump. I would like to jump," Eva answered.

Her mom prevailed from behind and shrugged, as if expecting Gert to explain how difficult, how dangerous and perhaps impossible that would be.

"Well, little lady," Gert began. "That is a piece of cake. We'll have you balanced and jumping three feet in no time. Maybe start by barrel racing. That will give you a good seat. When do you want your first lesson?"

Maggie clapped her hands. "Gert, I called your daughter, Sheila. She's coming for dinner this weekend. We certainly have a lot to celebrate."

Hannibal and Rachel were moving to the gate. Her number was called when Stan dashed to them puffing and heaving. "We're all but tied… with the mean girls! Rachel, if you run, we could win! But walk or trot won't cut it. You have to run."

"Are you kidding? I can't gallop." Rachel peered down at Presley, Gigi, Wheezy, Gert and Stan from atop Hannibal. Hannibal was stately and quite the gentleman in his turquoise blanket, bell boots and bridle that matched Rachel's shirt.

The girls ogled her with puppy dog eyes.

"Do it for Wyndham," Gigi pleaded. "Remember, trust Hannibal."

"Don't look at me like that. I said I can't gallop."

Gert motioned the girls and Stan away with an arch of her arms. "Just do your best," she advised. The announcer called Rachel's number for a second time. "We don't want her dead, ladies. You made it here, and you competed in the Silver Spur. All of you. And me, I'm chasing cows on my Palomino next week. Just have a good ride, Rachel."

Rachel was astounded at Gert's remarks. She was the sinister motivator, the gladiator with a vengeance, the witch with a voodoo doll. Had Gert changed too? She was now the woman living with a disability, encouraging, caring and conquering life. Guilt fluttered inside Rachel. Then she searched the audience for her daughter, the love of her life. Jemma was fisting the air in a display of encouragement. Beside her was Roxie and several patrons from her salon

"Ladies, it's okay," Presley chanted. "We competed for the Silver Spur. *The Silver Cowgirls.* How can we ever top that, even if we come in second?"

"Oh, we are going riding on the beach next trip, like you dreamed! I have been researching getaway riding adventures!" Wheezy said then turned and winked at Rachel. "Here, take my lucky scarf. Don't give up. My grandmother, she'll be riding on your shoulders. Oh and if we win, you can drive the trailer. I reserved some time for Wyndham to teach you!"

Rachel turned up the corner of her lip with a twitch. "Nice thought. But I can't do that either."

Wheezy pointed to the rail at the second barrel. Behind the rail stood Wyndham. He raised his hat in an acknowledging tip, winked and mouthed, "Good luck!"

"He's already agreed."

"What? Are you..." Rachel tightened the scarf and squirmed in the saddle. Hannibal seemed as confident as usual and headed through the gate.

Hannibal and Rachel prepared to walk their courtesy circle for the judges before trotting past the timer to the first barrel.

Simultaneously, Wheezy caught a glimpse of the pony, Annie's Promise, a mere ten feet from them. The stout pony leisurely wandered in the aisleway. *Untied?* Her owner was on the other side of the arena with friends enjoying ice cream. Annie's Promise miraculously must have become untethered. Wheezy exchanged a premonition with Presley.

"You're thinking what I'm thinking, aren't you?" Presley divulged.

Wheezy nodded. "Gigi, what do you think about borrowing a pony?"

"Oh my, Annie's Promise is loose! We must catch him and find the owner," Gigi exclaimed in an exaggerated tone.

"You know..." Presley began. "Rachel can't drive a trailer. You could be asking for trouble."

Wheezy smiled. "Never say never. And Wyndham can handle her."

Gigi gathered Annie's Promise unnoticed, while Presley coached Rachel to make a second circle for good luck and to calm her nerves.

Rachel and Hannibal maintained an extended trot to the first barrel then managed to kick into a rhythmic lope in route to the second.

Stan was yelling, "Add more speed!" as he watched the clock, bouncing up and down as if it helped.

Wheezy inched open the gate, as all spectators were fixated on Rachel and Hannibal. She positioned Annie's Promise in direct line of the third barrel. The only audience member who noticed was Randall Emerson, but his heralds of disqualification were not heard as he was distracted by his hands being hooked in cuffs. He could only stomp like a bruting child as he was read his rights and dragged by the Feds out of the arena.

Wheezy explained the plan to Gigi. "Hannibal will round the barrel and see one thing—this pony. You 360 that pony and go right back out the gate. I'll shut it before they cross the finish!"

Sure enough, when Hannibal caught a glimpse of Annie's Promise, chewing contently on an apple treat from Gigi's hand, he flattened his ears, flapped his jaws and beelined for home in a full-fledged gallop... the same gallop that made him a national barrel racing champion.

The little girl, Eva, was standing next to Presley. "Oh my, she has grey hair! This is going to be an *awesome* ride."

"No, honey," Presley assured her. "This barrel pattern is going to be nothing short of *spectacular*. Get your camera out. These Silver Cowgirls will need a new picture."

Rachel's cowgirl hat hit the dirt as they headed home, her silver streaks shimmering in the arena lights. Hannibal's hooves digged deep, his haunches low as he extended with every stride. His nostrils flared and he made the sound of a runaway locomotive headed for the next stop. Home.

The crowd roared to a standing ovation, masking Rachel's scream. The woman repeated a two-word mantra in her quest for the finish line. Not a Hail Mary, but a rejuvenating Hallelujah, Amen!

Sneak Peek

The Silver Cowgirls Ride Again

Chapter 1

When Presley walked out of the doctor's office at Peach Tree Women's Medical Center, she never expected an entourage of comradery to be waiting for her. Three cherished equestrian friends, Rachel, Wheezy and Gigi, were arced in front of the doorway with open arms as a nurse led Presley into the reception area. The women, clearly energized, had assembled for a good reason. Their hands held flowers, signage, and an array of glittering paraphernalia. The four had not been together since the Silver Spur championship in October, and with the holidays fast approaching, none of them seemed to have the time to connect. Finally they were together again.

Presley noticed Wheezy first. She was dressed in a lemon-colored sweater and a floral scarf that spilled with happiness. She was the tallest of the others, same in height as Presley, and holding a store-bought bouquet of Firecracker Sunflowers which brightened the entire room from its dismal grey. Presley had rarely seen Wheezy's dark hair fall loose from the tight ponytail normally tied at her nape. At present, her hair was corkscrews of ebony and silver curls bouncing as cheerfully as her smile. Even the faces of anxiety-stricken patients who were awaiting anticipated diagnoses were flushed with color. However, Wheezy's shimmer, Presley knew, radiated from her ring finger. The woman's hand gripping the posies twinkled under the incandescent lights from the new engagement diamond that Darren had recently slipped on her finger.

Rachel, on the other end of the threesome, was clutching a bulging-at-the-sides-two-foot-high gift bag, decorated with a horse's head on the front and sequin words imprinted, *You did it!* The bag was overflowing with trinkets and tissue. Her blue shirt had a quarter-sized spot, no doubt morning coffee and perhaps a glazed donut smear next to the breast button. Presley smiled thinking, *That's our Rachel.*

"Wheezy, flowers? They are lovely!" Presley declared. "Rachel? What is all this commotion?"

"Presents for you, this woman of steel who champions everything in her life!" Rachel tooted. "Our idol. The glue that holds us together."

Presley blushed and covered her eyes as if blinded from the sunflowers. What she thought inside was an objection of *Not really*. Yes, she had survived her twelve months of waiting for the results of experimental treatments the year before, and their friendship held her up like a canopy. But it was Brad, her husband, who needed her attention now.

Presley dropped her hand and appeared immobilized by their surprise appearance, hiding the truth under a colossal smile. She had waited the entire year for this doctor appointment; the diagnosis should be the most joyful moment in her life next to the birth of her three boys, now grown and dispersed throughout the globe. Yet, all Presley desired was to find her husband Brad. She wanted to discuss so many challenges facing them. Her own stalled life with no direction, her empty nest, yet his more than ever demanding career. Was he ever going to slow down as he'd promised, or should she dust off her archaic nurse's license and enroll in advanced classes? And then there were her concerns regarding Cleo, her aged mare, her heart horse, and the growing concern about her health. But the elephant that stood between them, the one neither had addressed, was that their relationship—the power couple everyone admired, Brad and Presley—felt, frankly, *off*.

Rachel stepped forward. She had trimmed down after devoting nine months to riding and showing with them. Her silver streaks with white-blonde highlights accentuated her bob, a mess of the new modern waves everyone adorned lately, a perfect style that seemed to swivel right on the edge of her shoulders as she raised the bag with excitement.

"Trinkets and treats. Wait until you see the restaurant gift card we picked to celebrate. Delicious!"

"Always about the food for Rachel." A petite woman sandwiched between the two added a *tsk*. The woman was a mini brunette Barbie, even with the bulge in her mid-section. The bump appeared like a small yoga ball, dead center, rounding out under her crisp pure white shirt. The starched collar stood at attention around her taut neck even at almost fifty. Tight black satin pencil pants were impeccably creased in a perfect line. Spiked stilettos made her seem as though she just walked out of a *Cosmopolitan* magazine photo shoot. Next to Rachel, Gigi was glowing for a different reason than Wheezy, although her expression reflected annoyance at the moment.

"Gigi," Presley acknowledged in a soft tone. "Look at you! You are elegant as always and radiating, too."

"Ha, I am radiating alright, all over this room like a middle-aged hippo," Gigi protested. "What was I thinking, pregnant at my age?"

Gigi was swinging a florescent green posterboard by her side. She raised it along with a snarky smirk as if to hide her protruding middle. It read a Scripto marker message, *'You did it, Cowgirl.'*

Presley noticed a string tied to the woman's other wrist and trailed it to the ceiling. A massive horse balloon tapped the tiles above. Presley sighed, "That is one gigantic chestnut equine!"

"A Clydesdale, like me," Gigi grumbled.

"Blessed be, what? That little baby bump? You look incredible. My figure never looked so good even after I lost weight." Rachel elbowed Gigi with a snip. "And everyone can't be like you. Mother Mary, forgive us if a crumb of cake touches your lips."

"You guys... you shouldn't have." Presley ignored the two bickering as a swell of emotion ponded in her eyes.

"You deserve a medal for what you have been through." Wheezy focused on Presley. "And holding our team together."

"No thanks to me," Rachel mumbled. "You are amazing."

Without any indication, others in the room tuned to their lively conversation. The nurse initiated applause as she tilted her head with an *ahhh* in support. Another person's clap echoed in unison, then another, until the entire room was under a cloud of thundering applause. Unexpectedly, patients and family rose in a standing ovation for Presley.

Presley wanted to brush off the attention, to tell them, *There really is no reason to applaud.* So many others deserved it more, with life challenges more difficult than hers. She scanned the waiting area. Searching. *Where is he?* Trying not to act concerned, Presley maintained a cheery countenance as best she could.

The three friends encircled Presley as if at a church camp about to sing Kumbaya. Then Rachel began rummaging through the gift bag in her usual shushly manner, while tissue and ribbon floated to the floor until she pulled out a new ballcap that read, *I am a survivor.* After a quiet study of Presley, something in her demeanor shifted. Rachel shoved the cap on top of the gifts again.

"We have reservations to take you to lunch in celebration, even though we know you would rather go for a joy ride in the saddle," Wheezy informed. "But you know our trainer, Gertrude Steele. She has laid the rules down. 'The horses are on winter break for a few months after an exhausting year.' We can plan out that beach ride you have been dreaming of."

"Yes, it was exhausting, for us too," Presley added, "but the most exhilarating year I had in a long time."

"You got that right, girlfriend," Wheezy agreed. The two made eye contact with a wink.

"Wheezy, you look so happy!" Presley commended. "It is the wedding plans, right?"

"Well, not quite. Been a little preoccupied for that. Wait until I tell you about my new business venture!" Wheezy's dark eyes sparked wider.

"Gosh! Who is calling us over-the-hill grandmas?" They shared a laugh, shaking their heads in agreement, except for Rachel,

Presley noticed even though tears were hazing her vision. Something was off with her.

"Oh no, don't cry! I will be next. In this hormonal state, I tear up at the sight of a pony." Gigi elevated her hand to fan her face. The horse balloon's body trotted on the ceiling.

They huddled momentarily like a ball team in prayer prior to entering the field.

"Lunch?" Presley whispered. "I will need that hat! Look at me." Her hair had grown out about an inch. She didn't mind her golden red naturally infiltrated by the new sharp streaks of white. What was most discouraging was her crowning glory of once perfect curls now wound like a Tibetan Lamb's wool against her scalp since the treatments. "These curls, are hardly long enough for me to stretch into a stylish haircut." She patted her head, but the curls refused to flatten.

"What are you talking about? Exactly why I put the cap away. You're rocking it!" Rachel stepped closer and fluffed them with a free hand. The bag scrunched between them. "Come see me in the salon. I can help you."

The protruding baby bump moved closer, pressing the poster to the bag. "You look beautiful!" Then Gigi grimaced as if someone suddenly jabbed her with a pin.

"Oh my gosh, Gigi. You need a pink balloon tied to the wrist, instead."

Gigi crinkled her ski sloped nose. "I am inflated enough! What the heck was I thinking? Look at my figure going to pot. This body was hard work," she moaned, arching her back. "Dang little one, must be at kick-boxing class since morning."

"Well, she is just getting ready to head out into the world," Rachel commented.

"I am not ready yet. She has another month."

"Yes, and today we have a *party*." Rachel shimmied her body and snapped her fingers while exaggerating the final word.

Presley smiled. What dear friends, but if they only knew. She sheltered them from what she was truly feeling.

KEEP YOUR HORSE SADDLED FOR

The SILVER COWGIRLS *Ride Again*

Acknowledgments

Please understand that this novel is a complete work of fiction. No artificial intelligence was utilized. Although the year in my early twenties was indeed one of the of the most memorable in my life, this story is fictional and the characters, setting, and events are my own invention.

The dream of returning to that show year lived decades ago, inspired this novel. I hope my story empowers the acceptance of each others' diversities, to face aging and never stop diving into life's adventures. Bringing a dream to fruition or at least the journey to try, creates joy and fulfillment in a world that is complicated. Tomorrow is a brand, new day to follow your heart and trust the Lord. Now on to the thank yous!

With heartfelt thanks to my daughter J.J. and my husband Scott who have been inspirations and tolerated my constant working and dreaming.

Demi Stevens for her roadmap and belief in me.

Best-selling author Debbie Herbert for taking the time to mentor me during her busy career at the onset of my writing journey.

My dear friends Rhonda Rodriguez and Teresa Shaub who pushed me on the journey from the beginning, and to Darlene Smith, grammar guru-in-chief and a woman made of courage.

An enormous thank you to Stacy Bankert for her creative and artistic abilities. Her talents are highly recommended for design and marketing.

My treasured equestrian friends at Evergreen Farms, Terry and Peg Helder, who shared their lifelong talents and expertise, in addition to many a meal over the Lazy Susan on their kitchen table.

To my dear friends Carol, Carla and Connie. If we could only go back knowing what we know now. Thank you. And Jeff who believed every woman can drive a truck and trailer.

To Helen Gildein who is no doubt a woman made of steel and dreams. Thank you for the inspiration to never stop following your heart!

My family, salon friends, and equestrian lovers who continue to cheer me on, including JoAnne and Eileen, and all my beta readers.

To Liz Shorb for the equestrian knowledge and her enduring support.

And thanks to renowned horseman Guy McLean, his wife Emily, and his magnificent team for the words of inspiration to follow your dream.

Books by Alicia Stephens Martin

The Spurred Trilogy

The Silver Cowgirls

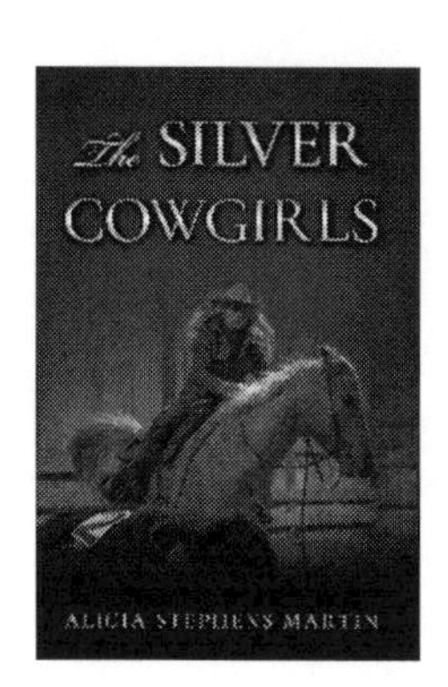

Leave a Review

Loved *The Silver Cowgirls?* Please consider leaving a review on Amazon, GoodReads, or other book recommendation sites! This is one of the best ways you can help other readers find my books, so I can continue to write more stories you want to read.

Discover more articles and fiction by Alicia, and be the first to learn about new releases by subscribing to the blog:

aliciastephensmartin.wordpress.com

About the Author

Alicia Stephens Martin had three passions in early life—writing, horses and hair. She became a Cosmetologist and mastered the craft as a successful stylist, salon owner and teacher. But her other passions tormented her. After losing a husband at age 46. She returned to college, as a solo mom, and obtained a bachelor's degree in creative writing. Her daughter became a champion equestrian and Alicia drove the horse trailer and wrote.

Alicia's short fiction and non-fiction stories have been published in *Salon Ovation* magazine and PBA Progress, and the non-fiction piece, "Healing in a Pocket," won the Bob Hoffman writing award. Her articles have also been published in *PA Equestrian, East Coast Equestrian*, and *From Whispers to Roars*.

In addition to an interactive children's workbook called *Let's Go to the Hairstylist*, Alicia has published a romantic mystery trilogy, the Spurred series, and a rom/com, *Private Mom*, all set in central PA with equestrian themes. *Silver Cowgirls* is her latest novel, in the hopes of inspiring others to follow their heart, no matter their age or diversity!

She lives in south central Pennsylvania on a farmette with her husband and an Old English Bulldog, Scarlett.

Connect with the Author

Alicia.StephensMartin

ASMartin_Author

Made in the USA
Middletown, DE
19 October 2024

62405756R00182